Born in Lancashire and educated in Yorkshire, Alexandra Connor has had a rich variety of careers, including photographic model, cinema manager and PA to a world famous heart surgeon, but it is as a novelist that she has found her real forte. As well as writing over twenty acclaimed sagas she has also written thrillers and non-fiction art books. When she isn't busy writing, Alexandra is a highly accomplished painter, and presents programmes on television and BBC radio. She is also a Fellow of the Royal Society of Arts.

THE LYDGATE WIDOW

Adele Ford would always remember her father's many stories about the enigmatic Lydgate Widow. But at eight years old, Adele and her sister are orphaned. Julia ensures their security by marrying; years later, Adele, intrigued by the antiques business, finds work in a Failsworth shop. But then her reputation is threatened by a wrongful accusation of theft, Julia's husband deserts her, and Adele is betrayed by her own suitor . . . She weathers these hardships with the help and support of her mentor, the local dealer Turner Gades. But when she marries Col Vincent, his violence soon renders the marriage unsafe for her and their son Paul, and they flee . . . Then a startling revelation sheds new light on the haunting memory of the Lydgate Widow — and the man who has loved Adele for decades.

ALEXANDRA CONNOR

◆

THE LYDGATE WIDOW

Complete and Unabridged

CHARNWOOD
Leicester

First published in Great Britain in 2006 by
Headline Book Publishing
a division of
Hodder Headline, London

First Charnwood Edition
published 2007
by arrangement with
Headline Book Publishing
a division of
Hodder Headline, London

British Library CIP Data

Connor, Alexandra
    The Lydgate widow.—Large print ed.—
    Charnwood library series
    1. Single mothers—England—Lydgate—Fiction
    2. Mothers and sons—Fiction
    3. Lydgate (England)—Social conditions—Fiction
    4. Large type books
    I. Title
    823.9′14 [F]

    ISBN 978–1–84617–610–4

Published by
F. A. Thorpe (Publishing)
Anstey, Leicestershire

Set by Words & Graphics Ltd.
Anstey, Leicestershire
Printed and bound in Great Britain by
T. J. International Ltd., Padstow, Cornwall

This book is printed on acid-free paper

For my father: missing you.

Acknowledgments must go to Elizabeth Bottomley at the Morecombe Tourist Office, and again to Nicola Plant, for the invaluable legal advice.

PROLOGUE

The Lydgate Widow ... No one could really remember the details of her life. Where she had come from, what she had done. She had just become a vague, if enduring, myth: a rural sop to the hard cases in the industrial towns. If she was mentioned at all in Salford or Little Lever she would have been given short shrift. Who would have been interested in a woman with money who had ended up alone in an impressive house? A widow. So what? The streets were full of widows.

But to Adele Ford, the story had a fascination. Perhaps it was the way it had been told to her; by a father who embellished the tale every time he related it so that, in time, the Lydgate Widow became a tragedy of Greek proportions. In one version her husband had killed himself; in another she had lost him in wartime; in a later, more accomplished telling she had become a lunatic recluse, losing her mind but keeping the strange house up on Lydgate Hill.

'Look,' her father said one evening as they walked past Lydgate church. For the hundredth time — or so it seemed to Adele. 'You can see her.'

'Who?'

'The Lydgate Widow.'

'You said she was dead.'

Her father sighed, disappointed by her lack of

1

imagination. 'Adele, she *can't* die. Don't you remember the story? She's locked to the house for ever. There, look, can't you see her? She's there, outlined against the horizon.' He dropped his voice. 'She's alone. Always alone. Looking for her husband.'

'I can't see anything,' Adele had replied honestly.

Exasperated, he had raised his eyebrows. 'Nonsense! You're just not trying hard enough — '

'I *am trying*!'

'No you're not,' he had replied, his own imagination big enough for both of them. 'I can see her so clearly. Look, Adele, look at the house.' Obediently, her gaze moved back to the old building. Its arched windows, stone turrets and exotic, almost Moorish architecture always fascinated her. 'Now, open your eyes, Adele. Look at the end of the garden. Look at the Lydgate Widow.'

She stared ahead, longing to see what her father saw.

But seeing nothing.

PART ONE

1

It was suffocating, dark, crawling with spiders. Shaking, Adele huddled to the back of the under-stairs cupboard in the blackness, footsteps sounding overhead, her pants damp from where she had wet herself. Biting down hard on her bottom lip, she began to rock, the raised voices overhead reverberating in the cupboard.

'*You cow! You bloody cow!*'

Then she heard a thump, a dull, waxen thud of fist on flesh . . . Her teeth bit down harder on her lip, drawing blood. Think about something else, she willed herself. Think about something else . . . The blackamoor, she liked that. And the painting of the Chinaman her father had paid too much for at auction. The heavy feet echoed terrifyingly overhead. Oh God, Adele screamed inwardly as they descended the steps. Oh God . . . She huddled back against the wall, scrunching her six-year-old body into a tidy, hidden parcel of flesh.

'Wait here,' her mother had told her only moments before. 'Keep quiet.'

She couldn't be more quiet.

But it wasn't quiet outside. On the other side of the cupboard door she could hear a muffled scream, followed by her father's voice.

'*You drive me crazy! You make me crazy!*' Then, suddenly, his voice petered off into silence.

What was happening?

'Victor,' Adele heard her mother say quietly, soothingly, 'it's OK, it's OK. We can sort it out.' She wasn't frightened any more, Adele could tell that. She was back in control. 'Darling, come on, come on,' she coaxed him, comforting the man she adored. The man who adored her. 'Victor, go upstairs and lie down.'

There was a long pause. Adele screwed her eyelids even tighter. This was worse than the screaming. This pause, extending too long and too eerily. What was happening? Would the cupboard door be snatched open suddenly to drag her out? God . . . she thought helplessly. God . . .

Then she heard her father's voice again. Not violent any more. Tender, muffled.

'Jesus, Lulu, Jesus . . . '

She could imagine his face pressed against her mother's shoulder.

'I never meant . . . '

'I know, Victor,' her mother said gently, 'I know . . . You're overwrought, darling. Go upstairs, get some rest.'

'I didn't mean to hit you . . . '

'Sssh, it's forgotten. I love you, Victor.'

'I love you too,' he replied desperately.

'We love each other. Always and always,' Lulu went on, her tone almost hypnotic. She was curbing his violence with tenderness. 'You and I, always together. The two of us . . . Now, darling, go and lie down for a while. Rest a little. And forget what's happened.'

Crouched inside the cupboard, Adele was still

6

shaking and utterly confused. How could everything change so suddenly? From being terrified, her mother was now calm. From being violent, her father was now mild. How could it happen? *How could anything change so quickly?* A moment later Adele heard her father's footsteps going upstairs. Ascending the steps over her head as she cringed in the cupboard below.

Then followed the closing of the bedroom door. A moment passed. Another. Then finally the latch of the under-stairs cupboard lifted. Automatically Adele cowered further back.

'It's all right, sweetheart . . . Your daddy was just ill, that's all.' Leaning inwards, her mother reached out to her, her figure silhouetted against the light of the hall. 'Come with me, little one, come on.' She took Adele's hand and pulled her out into the daylight. Terrified, Adele studied her mother's face; swollen, liver-coloured on one side.

'*Mum!*'

'It was nothing, sweetheart,' she said reassuringly. 'Nothing to worry about. Your daddy wasn't feeling well. But he's fine now. He loves me very much, Adele. He loves us all. But sometimes he gets all worked up.' She stroked her daughter's cheek. 'You'll understand, when you're older. Love does strange things to people. They hurt the ones they can't be without . . . Don't be scared, Adele, please. Nothing's changed. Nothing at all.'

Which was when Adele realised that adults — even the ones you loved the most — could lie to you.

2

1916

The war had emptied the streets of men. Only the old were left behind — and Victor Ford. An accident in childhood had kept him home, off the battlefields, out of the bloody reports from overseas. On 4 May 1916 a tighter conscription law had been put into place, to Lulu's horror. Apparently there hadn't been enough volunteers and the Government had been forced to call married men to fight. She was further alarmed when — a little while later — men previously rejected on medical grounds were being re-examined.

But July came, then went, and Victor was still home. The medical report had cleared him. Which, by rights, was fair. After all, he had had an ankle deformity since childhood and wore an iron brace. The fact that the vain Victor had managed to hide his handicap so well had worked for him in the past, but not now. Now it seemed that he was getting away with something, and irritated by people's assumption that he was draft dodging, he hoisted the bottom of his left trouser leg at the slightest provocation.

'Look!' he'd say to the dealers, or the market traders. 'That's why I'm here. I can't fight with an iron on my leg.'

Not that he really wanted to fight. Not when the images of the Somme and the photographs

8

of injured soldiers were splattered regularly across the front pages. He listened to the reports on the radio and seemed to hear daily about some family's loss. A complicated man, Victor was torn between guilt and relief and tried to assuage his conscience the only way he knew how — by making many and various gestures of help to the bereaved.

People who had been suspicious of the flamboyant Victor Ford now saw him in a different light. He would — unexpectedly — come calling at some stranger's house and give them something. Some object he had got at auction or off the markets. *For your son . . . your father . . .* he would say, hurrying off, knowing that they could sell it on. It was odd behaviour, typical of his extravagant nature, and it made an unexpected hero out of him.

Street angel; house devil. Wasn't that how the saying went? And at first it was never more true of anyone than Victor Ford. But as time passed his public concern took precedence over his private rages, Lulu encouraging his generosity, shoring up his self-esteem. Before long, The Coppice had a saint in the making. Only Lulu realised how he struggled to control his temper. Weeks would pass quietly, and then some random word or action would spark an inferno of violence.

She loved him because she knew how hard he tried to keep himself in check. He idolised her because she loved him enough to forget.

★　★　★

It was later that summer, in August, when Adele and her sister Julia were taken out for the day to Alexandra Park, Oldham. Hardly a long way from home on The Coppice, but — as Lulu said — it was a change of scenery. What she didn't tell her daughters was that it was a private daydream. One she shared only with Victor. In the rambling park, with its steamy summer borders and clipped lawns, its stone steps, its teahouse, bandstand and lake, Victor and Lulu were at home. Or *felt* as though they were. Their childish pretensions to grandeur allowed them to share the unspoken fantasy — that one day *they* could have a grand home and garden. That Victor would make that dizzy sale which would propel them from The Coppice into untold riches.

And yet, to many people, living on The Coppice was no mean achievement. A road of neat semi-detached houses with back gardens and plenty of trees. The sooty smug of Oldham was within walking distance, the turgid poverty of Salford not that far away. But The Coppice was respectable, with nice neighbours and net curtains. And residents who didn't go out in curling rags, spit in the street, or steal. It was the kind of road that the slums looked up to, and the well-to-do on Park Road could mildly patronise.

Sighing, Adele glanced over at her parents. Two years had passed since she had witnessed that terrible fight, and it was as though it had never happened. The Ford family behaved exactly the way they had always done. Loving and affectionate. In fact, as Adele watched her parents, Victor kissed his wife on the cheek and tickled his elder daughter, senior to eight-year-old Adele by ten years. It was all perfect. Or so it seemed to everyone, except her. Nothing had been the same since that night, and although Adele loved her parents as much as she had always done, she remained baffled by their marriage.

Julia was immune to any ructions within the family. If she knew about the violence, she had never mentioned it to Adele. She either lived in ignorance or colluded with their parents; either way, she didn't confide. After all, her sister was too much of a baby, whilst she was grown up, already eighteen.

Watching her sister as she reached for a book, Adele leaned back against a tree. It was warm, the sun high and hot, the tree branches swaying in time to the breeze and the marching tune from the bandstand in the distance. For a moment it seemed possible to forget the war, to imagine the world as it had been before the outbreak of hostilities. But the sight of a uniform reminded Adele of reality; a soldier sitting with his girl on a park bench, snatching a few hours before he would go off to fight again.

Feeling sleepy, she tipped her sunhat over her eyes, her parents' voices low and intimate, an unintelligible murmur.

★ ★ ★

'We could do anything, even move away from here,' Victor was saying quietly, so that their

11

daughters wouldn't overhear, 'Lulu, we could do *anything*.'

Her name wasn't really Lulu, she was called something else entirely, but for years he had referred to her by that name and now she had no other. Snuggling against her husband, she turned her face upwards.

'We have a home here,' she replied, not unreasonably. 'Why move? Think about it, Victor, there's a war on, we can't up sticks now.'

But the thought stimulated her; kept away the threat of impending boredom. She loved Victor Ford for many reasons — one of them his reckless streak. His terror of monotony, which coincided so perfectly with her own. Real life was dull and both of them dreaded melancholia. They thought alike, felt alike, were so much a part of one another that separation would have meant the death of both.

'Just think about it,' Victor murmured, laying his head on her lap.

For years they had lived on the meagre inheritance from Victor's father. Along the way Victor had indulged his love of antiques and curiosities, making a modest fortune sometimes; making a fool of himself at others. Lulu's work as a part-time cook helped, even though her ability was never up to her ambition. But when Victor's parents died and they inherited a tidy sum, the Fords took their biggest gamble to date and bought the house on The Coppice. The trouble was *keeping* it.

'Lulu? What are you thinking?'

She hushed him, her thoughts running back

12

over their life together.

Being careful had never been their style. Their recklessness *should* have been followed by ruin, as night follows day; but they had been lucky. And luck had always come just when it was most needed. If they ran out of funds, Victor made a sale. If they lost money on one purchase, he would recover it — twice over — on another. The sums had never been huge, but it had been the excitement that counted. The certainty that there was no certainty. The luminous pull of the risk.

Flanked by a teacher on one side and a bank manager on the other, the house on The Coppice had told everyone the Fords had arrived. But fitting *in* was another matter. Lulu hadn't been interested in the other wives' chats and visits to the Mothers' Union, and Victor had had no time for pubs or church. Instead, on many a Sunday morning, the neighbourhood had been treated to the sight of Victor unpacking boxes from the back of his car. His *car*, the first in the area. The one he only ran when he could get a ration of petrol. Which wasn't often.

As so many said, 'Typical! It's all show with the Fords.'

But they were jealous. Everyone stopping to stare at the little car — as they stared at its occupants. Victor, polished and attractive, Lulu in her best clothes, glamorous on a shoestring. No one knew her clothes were cast-offs from the wealthy Jewish women in Southport and Lytham St Annes; no one needed to know that her exquisite boots were stuffed with paper at the

13

toes to make them fit. It was the impact of their appearance that mattered, not how it had been achieved.

But now times were even tougher. It was wartime, after all, and people had more important things to think about than bric-a-brac. Which was not to say that there weren't private sales still to be made. Widows who had fallen on hard times, families selling off possessions to keep a roof over their heads. They were more than eager to sell to Victor Ford, and he was always generous with his payments. It was a hard way to make a living, but Victor — for all his lofty ambitions — was a grafter.

Lulu stirred suddenly, Victor's head heavy on her lap. 'If we did move, where would we go? The girls are settled in school here, we shouldn't really move now. I mean, it's wartime . . . '

'The war can't go on much longer!' Victor replied brusquely. 'The soldiers will come back and then where will we be? We should move *now*, whilst we can. Go down south, maybe. We could settle anywhere, and the girls would like a change.'

He knew it was selfish to uproot his daughters and leave The Coppice, but lately his forays had led him further and further afield in order to find anything worth having. Burnley, Leeds, Halifax.

'We could buy a shop. No one else would want to buy a shop in wartime.'

'You said the war was going to be over soon . . . '

He tensed. 'What's the matter? You don't like my idea?'

14

Lulu winced. The idea was intoxicating, and frightening. But more frightening was crossing her husband when he had that edge to his voice. Smiling, she stroked his forehead. If she was careful she could coax the temper out of him. Draw the violence out as effectively as lancing a boil. After all, Victor had a right to be exasperated, frustrated at not hitting the big time. He was just as smart as the top Manchester dealers, but he had never got the big break, the major sale.

The reason was obvious to everyone but Lulu and Victor. There was no point hoping to sell a silver candelabra in Oldham. Or a stuffed deer head in Bolton. If she had reasoned with him they could have made a better business. But Lulu didn't want to reason. She was absorbed by her husband, sexually fascinated by him, too much a part of him to think for herself. She loved Victor, as Victor loved her — both of them stuck in a gluey web of fantasy and hope.

'You're right, darling, we could do anything. You know how much I believe in you.'

'We have to get a break soon,' he said, rapidly soothed.

'It could happen any day now.'

'Any day.'

'You just carry on, darling,' she mollified him.

'We'll show them,' he said, taking her hand and kissing the palm. 'We'll show everyone what we can do.'

'Of course we will. You'll see, Victor, we'll get what we deserve in the end. We'll make it. We'll surprise everyone.'

3

'You mind what you're doing!' Mrs Redfern called out, running down the path on her stocky bow legs, one hard fist waving at Adele. 'If I catch you ruining my garden again . . . ' She made it to the gate and stopped. 'It *was* you that spoiled my apple tree, wasn't it?'

'I never.'

'You did!' Mrs Redfern snapped back, her eyes bulbous behind her glasses, a faint moustache on her top lip. All those bridge parties, Lulu used to say, you'd think she'd look in the mirror now and again. 'You were swinging on a branch.'

'Only the one that comes over our side,' Adele replied, remembering what her father had said. 'Dad told me it didn't matter if it was on our side.'

Mrs Redfern flushed. 'I don't care what your father might or might not have said. It's what *I* say that goes.'

Stunned, Adele moved off, Mrs Redfern calling after her. But she wouldn't stop. The woman was a bitch — hadn't Julia said that? Head down, Adele turned the corner and began to trail a stick along the railings of another garden, ruffling the azaleas behind. The rainwater fell from their petals and mottled the stonework underneath. Everyone was against her. Mrs Redfern; her teacher, Miss Egan — and now she had detention. *Again.*

Slowly Adele walked back into the playground of St Luke's. The girls at school had been teasing her, mocking her father.

'Everyone knows he sells on the market, even though he pretends to be a dealer . . . '

'My mother said he was a knocker . . . '

'Isn't fighting in the war, though, is he? Pretending he has a bad leg, dragging that leg iron around when everyone knows it's a fake . . . '

That last insult had been too much for Adele. Without hesitation, she had struck out at her tormentor and sent the girl falling backwards into the watching group. Ten minutes and a cut lip later, Adele had found herself in trouble. All booked up for detention. And why? Because a girl from The Coppice shouldn't act like a slum child.

'They were saying things about my father — '

Miss Egan cut her off short. She had — like everyone else — heard the rumours. The Fords were little more than a laughing stock, for all their airs and graces. But Adele was different, a mature eight year old with a good head on her shoulders. Which was more than could be said for her sister . . . Miss Egan considered the attractive, rather vacuous Julia. A determination to marry was her only ambition in life. Or so everyone thought. But was there something else under the marshmallow coating, as Miss Egan suspected? Some sliver of well-disguised steel?

'Adele, you have to listen to me,' Miss Egan went on. 'Fighting is not the way to sort out your

17

problems. It's unladylike, common. Only rough children fight.'

An old memory rattled inside Adele. She wanted to say, 'You're wrong. All sorts of people fight.' But she held her tongue. You didn't talk about family. Or family secrets.

'You have to use your wits in life, not your fists. Use your intelligence, Adele, if you want to get on. You want to be someone, don't you?'

'I don't know who someone is,' Adele replied truthfully. 'My father always talks about *being someone*, but he never seems to become him.'

Miss Egan blinked, wrong-footed. 'What I meant was that you want to make something of your life.'

'My father says that too. All the time,' Adele answered. 'He said it last Saturday when he brought home a piano. Said it would bring a fortune and we could all make something of our lives.'

Miss Egan regarded Adele thoughtfully. She was an attractive girl, with large dark grey eyes that seemed to bore into you and read your thoughts.

'Adele,' she continued patiently, 'what do you want to do with *your* life?'

'My sister wants to get married.'

'But what about *you*? I know you're only eight, but you're a sensible child, so I think I can talk to you about such matters. What would you like to do?'

Adele gave the question some thought. No one had ever asked her before.

'I like things.'

'What kind of things?'

'Paintings, furniture. You know, objects, books. Stuff like that.' She warmed to her theme, encouraged by her unexpected audience. 'We've got a bearskin rug at home.'

Miss Egan's only brush with a bearskin rug had been in her nude baby photograph.

'It's not really a career, though, is it?'

'It's my father's career.'

There it was again, the level, unfazed gaze. Smiling, Miss Egan let the matter go. Adele Ford was very young, after all, no good forcing a child to grow up before their time.

Something else was forcing Adele to grow up fast. Something that had nothing to do with Miss Egan, or careers.

★   ★   ★

Julia sat by the window, buffing her nails and watching her mother bring in the washing from the back yard. It would be nice to have a garden, but you couldn't have everything and they did have a lawn at the front. Which was bigger than Mr Redfern's next door, and wider than the bank manager's on the other side.

Julia noticed such things; it was automatic for her to measure out people's lives in terms of their possessions. You could measure out a good job in inches, a nice house in feet, and a marriage in yards. Which was why she wasn't too bothered about the job she had just begun in Mrs Short's Florists. Mrs Short might be stocky, and sometimes too lazy to move, but she was

19

Mrs Short, and in Julia's eyes that was all important.

'Good Lord,' Lulu said, walking in and tossing the laundry on to the kitchen table. 'It's so hot out there.'

'You should wear a hat.'

'Not to get in the washing!' her mother remonstrated, quickly pulling down the cuff of her blouse.

But Julia had already seen it: the bruise. Just as she had seen the others over the years, and chosen to ignore them. If there was something her mother wanted her to know, she would tell her. If not, why poke your nose where it wasn't wanted or start imagining things? Her mother and father were happy, everyone knew that.

'Your father and I . . . ' Lulu paused, bending down to pick up a towel she had dropped, 'are going to an auction tonight. It's so exciting. Daddy's seen a particular lot he wants.' She waited for a response, then hurried on. 'A washstand. French, your father thinks. And done up, it could bring a pretty profit.'

'A washstand?' Julia intoned softly. 'What do we need a washstand for?'

'Your father is going to do it up and sell it.'

'Like the one in the shed?'

'That was different,' Lulu replied curtly.

'It's a washstand.'

'But this one is French.'

'And it needs doing up. Like the other one.' Julia stopped buffing her nails and shrugged. 'He'll never repair it, Mum. You know that.'

'Of course he will!' Lulu responded half-heartedly. 'Your father has a good eye for a bargain.'

'Don't let him bid too much, Mum.'

'He knows what he's doing.'

Looking away, Julia decided that further intervention would be pointless. The outcome was easy to predict. Her father *would* bid too high, carried away by the auction, not the lot. Her parents would come home giddy with excitement, going on and on about their wonderful buy. The French washstand would be sighed over and admired — and at the end of three days would be relegated to the garden shed.

'We'll be home late, love,' Lulu went on, making for the stairs. 'Sort Adele out for me, will you? See she gets a good tea and goes to bed early.'

Nodding, Julia glanced at the clock. Five fifteen. Adele would be home from school any time now and her parents would be gone by seven. If she was lucky she could get her sister to bed and then meet up with John at the corner around nine. She smiled to herself. John Courtland, twenty-two years to her eighteen, blond, tall — and if a little thin, that could soon be remedied by good cooking. As for his character, well, it was perfect for the ideal husband. It wasn't that he was a complete fool; he was just pliable, eager to please. And dangerously uncertain of his own judgement. Julia frowned. She would have to watch that trait in him; make sure that *she*

21

made all the important decisions. Make certain no one else got any influence over him. Mollified, she smiled to herself. John might not be a world beater, but he would do for her — and she found him very attractive. Mr John Courtland, soldier, but previously working as a clerk at the County Bank, Union Road, Oldham. A white-collar worker once. And would be again when he got home after the war.

Oh, he would do very nicely, Julia thought, snuggling up to her secret. They might only have been going out for a couple of months, but she was going to marry John Courtland. She thought then of her sister, Adele, catching them the other night when John had come home on leave. They had only been talking, but after a couple of minutes Julia had noticed a faint rustling behind the hedge. Once. And again. Then suddenly she had felt something cold and slimy slip down her collar.

'God!' she had shrieked, spinning round just in time to see Adele laughing and running away.

Of course John had been charming and concerned, but all chance of romance was curtailed as Julia had wriggled frantically to get the worm out of her blouse. He had gallantly offered to help. Red-faced, Julia had declined. The worm had then made its way — slowly and inexorably — down her camisole. Finally, panicked, she had dived behind the next-door hedge in the darkness, pulling off her top and shaking the worm into the bush.

Flushed by the memory, Julia decided that it

was time she left The Coppice, the washstands — and her damn sister. Her future was clear. When the war was over, she was going to marry John and escape.

It was just a matter of time.

4

Bored, Adele gazed out of the window, then brightened as she saw a cat staring balefully at her from the garden wall opposite.

'Hey, puss, puss,' Adele called to it.

The cat blinked.

'Hey, puss, puss.'

Irritated, the cat turned its back on her and jumped down off the wall.

'Well, honestly!' Adele snorted, flopping back on to her bed.

The summer night was warm, the clouds unmoving, the air still as a millpond. She knew when she heard the latch lift that Julia was sneaking out to see her soldier boyfriend. Adele smiled to herself. That worm had been an inspiration — and who could Julia tell? Not their parents, that was for sure. Their father would be enraged, and his temper wasn't something anyone wanted to provoke. No chancer boy-friends for Julia; no soldier lads come back with big medals and big heads to carry off one of his precious daughters. Oh no, in time Victor himself would decide which suitors were right for his girls — although Adele had the sneaking suspicion that no one would ever come up to scratch. To hear their father tell it, the Ford sisters were the most intelligent, beautiful and desirable girls in the north-west.

Shame no one else saw them that way, Adele

thought, rolling on to her side. The net curtain fluttered in a sudden unexpected breeze, then fell still again, limp as a glove. She imagined her parents at the auction and then driving home with something in the back, something daft they'd bought. Something destined for the shed. She could visualise her mother holding on to her hat as they drove through the summer night, her father, dashing and confident, flushed with importance. *They were bidders at an auction.* And for a while they would ride along in that euphoria. Buoyed up by a mirage; the old car shaking their bones fitfully as they took the road back home.

He would be telling her mother stories, Adele thought, thinking about that peculiar, intense connection between her parents. Thinking that one day they might turn the old car around and head *away* from The Coppice and on to only God knew where. She could picture them, their heads together, silhouetted against the moon as they drove into a distance which didn't involve her. Or her sister. *Somewhere only they could go.*

A sudden palpitating unease made Adele nervous. Swinging her legs over the side of the bed, she stood up and walked to the window, then peered into the shadows below. She could see nothing, but after a moment there was a faint flicker of a light. John Courtland was smoking a cigarette on the corner, waiting for her sister to come out to him.

Smiling, Adele decided that if she was smart she could use her sister's romance to her advantage. Get Julia to do the washing up and make the beds — with the threat of telling her parents about John. She leaned out of the window, the August night sweet . . . Or she could play another trick on Julia, something *really* funny.

And then she heard it, the sound of someone hurrying up The Coppice. Unknown feet, determined feet, moving very fast. Purposeful . . . Transfixed, Adele listened to the footsteps coming closer along the street, along the row of neat houses, along the trimmed hedges and netted windows. Past the Redferns — and then the feet stopped. Outside their front door.

Moving downstairs, Adele could see her sister in the doorway, Julia shaking her head and then stepping back into the hat rack. So clumsy, so unlike her. Then John Courtland appeared in the hall, cigarette still in his hand, his expression bewildered, overwhelmed. And then she saw the owner of the feet, the man — the police officer — and he was talking.

' . . . They were going too fast . . . Rounded a bend too sharp . . . I think your father lost control of the car . . . So sorry, Miss Ford, I'm so sorry. Is there someone I can contact?'

Step by step, Adele slowly made her way downstairs, Julia finally turning to her. 'Go back to bed, love . . . '

'What's happened?'

'Adele, go back to bed. It's all right, it's all right.'

But she wasn't fooled. How could she be? Even if she hadn't heard what the policeman had said, she would have known. After all, hadn't she already seen her parents go driving off, silhouetted against the moon? The old car turned away from home?

Hadn't she seen it? Hadn't she already known?

It wasn't until years later that Adele discovered *how* her parents had been found. They hadn't died instantly, but had held on for a little while, grievously injured. It was supposed that her father had struggled to get out of the wreckage to raise the alarm. But Adele could never decide whether he had left her mother to get help, or to save himself.

I remember how much my sister cried that night.

I heard her, in the room next door, and later felt her lie down on the bed next to me. My own shock was too intense to let me cry; there was nothing in me but a feeling of isolation, of fear for the future, of disbelief that people so recently living could be so suddenly dead. I worried, too, about where they had taken our parents — and then thought of all the stories I had heard about people putting their dead relatives on display in the front room.

I prayed so hard that they wouldn't make us do that.

'Adele? Are you awake?' my sister whispered, taking my hand. Her own was cold, her fingers wrapping tightly around mine. 'Adele?'

I should have comforted her, but I couldn't. I was just a child and my parents were dead and only my sister — just her, just Julia — was left. And it wasn't enough.

'Adele?'

I wanted to turn over and hit her, slap her viciously across the face, pummel her until she bled. But then I realised she wasn't to blame. Julia hadn't killed our parents; hadn't propelled me out of my eight-year-old life into this limbo. It wasn't her fault.

So I squeezed her hand. And a moment later I

rested my head on her shoulder and we both gazed up at the ceiling together. For the remainder of that first night we lay there; on my parents' bed, holding hands and staring into nothingness.

We held hands too when we visited our parents' bodies in the chapel of rest, and later at the funeral. We held hands whilst the clergyman preached and people offered condolences. We held hands when mourners talked about our parents and how special they were. How unusual, how full of life.

They weren't full of life any more. I knew that. They were dead. There was just my sister and me left. And I was holding on to her as tightly as she was holding on to me. We withstood it all together. Our hands clasped so tightly that our flesh burned. It seemed that if either of us let go we would break apart.

Separate we were nothing. Together we would survive.

5

Miss Egan had been right. The flicker of steel she had suspected in Julia Ford came to light with the death of her parents. Suddenly the rather indolent eighteen year old changed into a woman with very firm ideas. No, she told everyone, they had no other relatives. But what did it matter, she would look after her sister. She was grown up, after all.

On the night of the funeral, Mrs Lockhart from next door called round. She stood awkwardly in her black suit and hat, an overlarge handbag clutched in front of her like a shield.

'We've been talking. I mean, me and Mr Lockhart.' She paused, adding unnecessarily, 'He's the assistant bank manager at the Midland, as you know . . . '

Julia smiled inwardly. John Courtland would be an assistant bank manager one day. *Bank manager*, in fact.

'Yes, Mrs Lockhart?'

'We think that you need some guidance. Some sound advice.'

Julia didn't like the idea. It felt too much like interference and she wasn't going to have any of that. However much she might have loved her parents, and be grieving for them, Julia was a realist. Oh, she had let them think she had been fooled, but she had known for years that the marriage had been complicated. But what was she supposed to do about it? Interfere? No, that wasn't Julia's style. Besides, the violence had been intermittent, quickly outweighed by her father's tenderness. She might see bruises, but how could they mean anything when her mother would sit by the fire letting Victor rub her feet? Or giggle when he brushed her hair, the sparks flying off the bristles, her father picking up the tresses and burying his face in them? They were in love. Any fool could see that. And if that love came with something peculiar and dark, Julia didn't want to know.

So having inherited both secretiveness and passion from her parents, she had already begun to plan her future. Although initially daunted, she decided that looking after Adele would be easy, and might well prove to be a short cut to her longed-for destination as Mrs John Courtland. How impressed John would be when he realised she was now an heiress. How surprised when he saw her running the house alone. And caring for her sister too.

In one deft stroke it would demonstrate that here was the perfect wife and mother. *His* perfect wife.

And no one, Julia thought, was going to ruin it for her.

'Mrs Lockhart, you're very kind, but we can manage.'

'But money — '

'We're fine,' Julia replied, wondering just what the solicitor was going to tell her the following day.

'But, my dear,' Mrs Lockhart continued, 'you

can't live here alone.'

'Many women are already married at my age,' Julia replied reasonably. 'I'm not a child. I can look after Adele perfectly well alone.' She walked to the door, smiling and holding it open.

Realising that she had been dismissed, Mrs Lockhart smiled awkwardly and then reluctantly left.

'What a nerve,' she told everyone later. 'That cocky girl needs to be taken down a peg or two. Being a responsible adult isn't as easy as she thinks it's going to be . . . '

★ ★ ★

At his Oldham office, Mr Bernard Hoggard looked at the papers in front of him and shook his head. What a turn-up, what a turn-up . . . Sighing, he leaned back in his chair and scratched his thick ginger hair — wincing as the liberal slick of oil made his hand instantly sticky. He could put a whole bottle on his head and minutes later his hair would spring back to life like Lazarus. Women never liked a man with ginger hair, he thought ruefully, even a relatively comfortably off middle-aged solicitor. It was a curse, he decided; red hair meant romantic death. In fact, if all the bachelors in the world were lined up in a row, Bernard reckoned most of them would have ginger hair. It made an outcast out of you, that was what it did. Made you a flaming outcast.

Glancing back at the papers, he read through them again. It had been a tragedy, Mr and Mrs

Ford being killed so young. But that was the way life went; you never knew when it was your turn. The war was proving that daily. God knew how many young men had died on the Somme — the Government kept changing the numbers — but it was thousands. A generation, gone in hours.

Sighing, he looked back to his papers.

'Two hundred pounds annually,' Bernard said out loud.

Now that wasn't a fortune, but it wasn't too shabby either. Enough to keep the house on The Coppice and to support two young ladies. Especially as Julia Ford was already bringing in a wage . . . Preoccupied, Bernard remembered the Fords' erratic lifestyle. Their second-hand clothes which no one was supposed to know about, and the ridiculous antiques Victor had bought at auction. Strange man, but good-looking. After all, even a man with a leg iron was better than a redhead . . .

Bernard sighed again. Victor Ford must have wasted a small fortune, thrown money away, to end up short with such an income. A prudent man could have lived well on two hundred pounds, but not Victor Ford, too busy showing off. Too busy with bearskins and washstands to save for the future. Too busy thinking his judgement was unquestionable. Oh, it was all right spoiling your family with fripperies, but that was no substitute for financial security.

'Mr Hoggard,' his secretary said suddenly, interrupting his thoughts, 'Miss Ford is here to see you.'

He blinked, nodding. 'Yes, yes, send her in.'

33

Hurriedly he tried to calm down his frizz of hair, then wiped his oily hands on his handkerchief, smiling as the door opened.

'Miss Ford, how nice to see you,' he began. 'May I say how sorry I am for your loss. Such a pity, so difficult.' He could feel his hair creeping up again and plastered it down firmly with his hand. 'It must have been such a shock for you, and for your little sister too.'

Julia nodded. 'We miss our parents so much.'

'Of course.'

'Nothing's like it was . . . ' She paused, unexpectedly distracted by the sight of Mr Hoggard's hair taking on a life of its own.

Hoggard picked the moment Julia looked away to pummel his hair into defeat. 'I know this may sound hard to believe now, Miss Ford,' he said. 'But despite the terrible circumstances of your parents' death, I think life might turn out to be relatively pleasant for you in time.'

She was banking on it.

6

There were so many ways to be an outcast, Adele thought. For a couple of years she had had to contend with teasing from her fellow pupils about her father, but now she was being singled out for quite another reason. Pity. And that was harder to bear. She kicked at the dirt in the playground. It had only been a couple of months since her parents had died, and yet it seemed like a century. Fighting tears, she looked down. Try as she might, she couldn't remember the colour of her mother's eyes, and she didn't want to ask Julia. It would be such a shameful thing to admit — as though she didn't care. Adele could see her mother's face, but when she tried to remember her eyes, there was nothing. The thought was crushing, forcing the breath out of her.

Miss Egan was watching from the staff room window.

'You can't get through to Adele Ford. I've tried, but it's no good.'

'Give her time,' a male teacher replied, glancing over Miss Egan's shoulder as he walked past. 'Kids take death hard. And she's not the only one, there's many lost their fathers lately.'

'But to lose *both* of your parents at the same time . . . '

'She's got a sister, though.'

'True,' Miss Egan replied thoughtfully. 'But that's not enough. Adele's too young to lose her mother.'

Still staring out of the window, she wondered if she should try to approach the girl again, then noticed someone walking towards Adele. A girl who was tall for her age, and out of place with her dark, exotic features. Interested, Miss Egan leaned forward to watch. Now *that* might be the answer, she thought. Two outcasts could form a strong bond.

★　★　★

Unaware that she was being watched, Rebecca Altman approached Adele, then leaned against the wall beside her. She didn't speak, just looked around. It wasn't difficult to see how upset Adele was; after all, her parents' deaths had been gossip for weeks. Adele's face was masked by her hair, but Becky could hear the faint, muffled sobbing.

'It gets better.' Adele stopped crying, but didn't lift her head as Becky continued. 'My parents are abroad, I haven't seen them for years. I live with my grandmother . . . I know it's not the same, but I miss them . . . I can't imagine what it's like to lose your parents. I mean for ever.'

'It hurts.'

'Sorry?'

Slowly Adele lifted her head, her expression defiant and helpless at the same time. 'I said it hurts. I miss them.'

Wiping her nose hurriedly, she studied the girl beside her, her curiosity piqued. Wasn't this the Jewish pupil? The one everyone talked about? Avidly she studied the girl's dark eyes, black hair and olive skin, and found her fascinating.

'I'm Becky Altman.'

'I'm Adele Ford.'

Becky smiled. 'I know.' Leaning back against the wall, the two girls — so dissimilar in appearance — stared out at the playground together.

'I can't remember the colour of her eyes . . . ' Adele said at last, ashamed and yet relieved to have shared the confidence. 'I can't remember what my mum's eyes were like . . . '

Becky nodded, as though she understood and wasn't going to pretend that words would help.

'He hit her.'

'*What?*'

Adele bit down on her lip hard. Why had she said that? *Why?* To break their trust? To punish her parents for leaving her? To hurt them as she was hurting? Her face was scarlet with embarrassment. 'I shouldn't have said that!'

'It's OK,' Becky reassured her.

'But I shouldn't have said it . . . '

'It's OK,' Becky repeated quietly, lapsing into silence.

Instinctively Adele realised that her confidence was not going to be broken, and that somehow this relative stranger understood perfectly.

A friendship was born which would last a lifetime.

Dear Julia,

I got your letter and I'm so sorry to hear how hard things are for you. If you need help, you could always ask my mother. Be sure she would be only too glad to give you a hand with anything.

Everything is difficult everywhere. This terrible war is ruining everything. I've lost so many friends. And every day I hear about men getting killed, some just lads. You wouldn't believe the conditions out here, Julia. But I shouldn't complain, you have your own worries.

I will write again. Take care of yourself.

Yours,

John

Coming in from work, Julia read the letter twice, then tossed it on to the kitchen table. The concern was genuine enough, but why was he asking her how she would cope? *Who will you turn to?* Hadn't she hoped she could turn to *him*? As for asking his mother for help, she didn't need anyone! She was doing just fine, she wasn't a child. Was that what he thought of her, that she was a child?

It was so stupid, couldn't he see what was under his nose? She was coping with a house and looking after her sister now. She was capable, a fully grown-up woman . . . Upset, Julia glanced around the kitchen. There had been no outpouring of affection from John Courtland in his letter, no *I'll look after you now*. No reassurance. He didn't think of her as she thought of him, obviously. She had been stupid, wrong.

Her disappointment was numbing. It was bad enough to lose her parents, and now this distant condolence. Julia picked up the letter again. She knew that John was fond of her, attracted to her. But that wasn't enough, was it?

Letting the letter drop from her hands, Julia glanced around. The silence upset her most. That terrible blankness when Adele had gone to school; that absence of life. Why was it so quiet? Julia stared at her handiwork, the perfect, immaculate kitchen. There were no dirty dishes in the sink, no ashes left in the grate. No daily paper discarded over the chair.

Suddenly, almost as though she could see her mother standing in front of her, Julia looked up. There had always been noise in the house before. Sounds from the shed outside, her father moving things, packing things, taking objects from the car boot to the shed and then back again. And inside her mother would be cooking or sewing, altering the second-hand clothes to fit.

She missed them, Julia realised helplessly. There was no point trying to pretend; she *ached* for them. Her daydreams about John had been a way to ease the pain of loss, but they hadn't been based in reality. Not really. Just hope — and that was never enough.

Slowly Julia rose to her feet. There was no avoiding it, life had to be lived. Day after day, until the time stretched out and put some distance between her parents' death and the present. Until she didn't mind the silence so much, or long, helplessly, for the quick slam of the door.

Suddenly she rallied, impatiently shaking off her depression. She wasn't going to give up! The hell she was! John Courtland was hers. She knew it, and he would have to be made to realise it. Flushing, Julia reached hurriedly for some paper, then paused, pen in hand. She would convince him, using all her subtle skills of persuasion. After all, this was John Courtland. An attractive man, but not strong-willed. Easily led, easily persuaded. She would woo him by letter, build up his self-esteem gradually. Make him need her, long for her, because she would be his security. She would become everything a soldier needed when he was far away from home, and afraid.

Julia stared at the paper, and then began — confidently — to write.

7

The third Christmas of the war began, the stalemate in the trenches making for a melancholic season. At Verdun alone, 700,000 men had been lost. The Somme had finally claimed 650,000 Allied soldiers and 500,000 Germans. Bitterly disputed front lines moved a couple of bloody, desperate miles. No more. News from the death fields came knocking on many doors. Miss Egan's cousin had been killed on 9 December, and on the 12th news came that all three sons from the Lucas family had been slaughtered.

'You could spend Christmas with us,' Adele said, taking her seat on the tram and turning to Becky. It was bitterly cold, everyone complaining about the shortage of fuel. The war wouldn't be the only thing to claim lives that winter.

'We don't celebrate Christmas,' Becky replied, dropping her voice.

'Oh,' Adele replied simply, wrapping her scarf around her neck and shivering. 'You could come and have tea with us anyway.'

'I'm OK with my grandmother. I couldn't leave her alone.'

Nodding, Adele sat back in the tram seat. It was snowing, the Oldham streets treacherous underfoot, a few shop windows displaying Christmas decorations. But no lights after dark. Food was in short supply too, luxuries unheard of. But somehow Julia had managed to find a goose:

'We're having goose for Christmas. You can tell all those horrible girls at school about that. See how smug they are then . . . '

She might only be a kid, but Adele knew how much that meant.

'She's had another letter from France,' Adele told Becky, pulling a face. 'From her boyfriend, John.'

'What's he look like?'

'Like . . . ' She paused, letting someone pass between them. 'Like no one really. Just a fella.'

'You promise not to tell anyone?' Becky said, dropping her voice still lower.

'Promise.'

'*I*'ve got a boyfriend.'

This wasn't welcome news. 'You never!'

'I have,' Becky insisted, her dark eyes fixed on Adele. 'Howard King.'

'He's a gypsy!'

'No he isn't!' Becky retorted hotly, then lowered her voice again. 'He's asked me to go to the pictures with him.'

'He'll kiss you.'

'No he won't!' Becky replied, horrified.

Adele pushed her advantage. 'Oh yes he will. Boys do that. I saw John kissing Julia.'

Uncomfortable, Becky blustered, 'That's different! They're grown up.'

'It's not a bit different,' Adele continued, impressively knowledgeable. 'That's what boyfriends do — they kiss you. And then you get pregnant.'

42

'What!'

'Think what your grandmother would say about *that*. You'd get all fat, have to leave school, and then have the baby. And people would point at you and say, 'There goes that Rebecca Altman, having a baby at her age.' ' Adele was warming up, Becky staring at her thunderstruck. 'The shock would kill your grandmother, and think of the shame. If she *did* live, your nan couldn't hold her head up in the town any more. And as for you, your life would be over, just because you let your boyfriend kiss you.'

'You're talking rubbish!' Becky replied, but she sounded unsure.

'No. I'm not.' Wanting to add some extra weight to her story, Adele went on, 'Remember, I've got an older sister and Julia tells me *everything*. I heard that if you had a boyfriend at our age and he gave you a baby, the baby would be a monster.' Becky was rendered silent. Adele nodded sagely. 'Oh yes, a baby born with . . . ' she was momentarily stumped, but recovered quickly, 'the head of a rat.'

At that moment the tram came to a sudden stop and Becky jerked forward in her seat. Righting herself, she glanced out of the window into the falling snow. *A rat baby*. God, that was terrible . . .

'And how could you let anyone know?' Adele said, her voice hushed. 'You couldn't push it out in a pram.'

'No, but you could charge a penny a time to see it at the fairground!' a man behind them said, laughing as he stood up. 'My God, I've

43

heard some stories in my time, but that one takes the bloody biscuit.'

Infuriated, Adele ignored him. Becky looked at her questioningly as the man got off the bus. Finally Adele turned back to her friend, all righteous indignation.

'Well, what does he know? He's a man.'

★ ★ ★

Tipping his head over to one side, John Courtland listened. It was just after dawn on a bitingly cold winter morning in France. Around him he could see soldiers sleeping, others smoking in silence. Snow had fallen but melted, the freezing water adding to the trench's filth and slime. He listened again carefully. *There it was*, the sound of a blackbird.

His eyes closed, and the bird stopped singing. For a long moment he kept the notes in his head, then felt them fade away. Reluctantly he opened his eyes. The blue light of the cold morning danced along the horizon, only the barbed wire between him and freedom. Because he was as trapped as the enemy. All the soldiers knew that; there had been too little ground captured at Peronne to count as a victory. They had spent months fighting over a patch of dead earth where nothing grew. Bones and blood for compost. No one was free here. Certainly not the soldiers, whichever side they were on. The only freedom John had seen for months had been that one solitary blackbird. And now it too had gone.

Sighing, John reached into his jacket pocket and took out Julia's letters. He couldn't believe how much they meant to him; couldn't believe how much a person could change. His old life had been so simple, so organised. He would be a clerk, be promoted, end up assistant bank manager one day, if he was lucky. And somewhere along that civilised line he would meet a girl, marry her, and have a family. But there had been no rush for that. Not then. Not when life was safe, not when you knew what you'd be doing from one week to the next. Not when one pretty girl might so easily be supplanted by another.

But in the trenches, where the smell of sweat and shit and vomit clawed at your senses, there was no time, and yet too much time. Time to wait, to fight, but no time to live. To hold a girl's hand, to worry about buying a new jacket . . . John found his hand clenching the letters fiercely and winced, hurrying to smooth out the papers. He had always liked Julia; what man wouldn't? She was pretty, lighthearted, good company. And if he had decided, with a little help from his friends, that he didn't want their romance to be too serious, that was reasonable. Then.

But time and fear had changed his mind . . . John paused. He knew he found it difficult to make decisions. Knew he was indecisive, that sometimes he relied too much on other people's advice — *but he was sure about this*. Sure enough to keep quiet and not risk anyone changing his mind . . . He thought of Julia

45

tenderly, clinging to the memory of her. She was his link to sanity, the old life. She was the one and only continuity left. In his letters to her John had confided more and more as time had gone on. He admitted to her what he would never have admitted to another living soul: how afraid he was. And she had written back, encouraging, soothing, talking about when he came home as though it was certain he would. As though it was only a matter of time.

So over the months, and the dance of the letters, a light romance had turned into love. How had he *not* seen her qualities before? John wondered. After all, Julia had experienced a lot in her short life. She knew about grief: hadn't she lost her parents and been a surrogate mother to Adele? That took guts. Running a house alone when all the men were at war. And not a word of complaint, no moaning, no wondering how she would cope. Oh yes, John thought admiringly, Julia Ford was extraordinary.

His widowed mother had thought the same, reminding him often that Julia had inherited the house on The Coppice and — some said — a tidy little allowance. A pretty young woman with means was a catch. His mother's approval had nudged John's affection along. When he had first heard about the tragedy, he had seen it quite differently. Julia would be desperate, needing someone to lean on, a woman with responsibilities and a kid sister in tow. Too much for a young man to take on when all he wanted was a light romance. Too much. *Then.*

But now it looked so different. Now John

thought about what his mother had said and reread Julia's letters avidly. Then he remembered the kitchen at the house on The Coppice, thought of Victor Ford's collection of bric-a-brac, the washstands in the shed, and the garden, untended and neglected outside the mourning house. He thought of Julia and how she laid the table, *playing house*. Playing life . . . And he wanted to be a part of it. Wanted to sit in that chair by the kitchen range, have letters addressed to the house on The Coppice and a pretty wife taking his hand in the dark.

He had almost made up his mind — but not quite. And although he had resisted turning to anyone for advice, John still couldn't make the final step alone. It had been the blackbird which had decided him. He had come out into the trench that morning as dawn broke and asked for a sign, something that would tell him he was making the right decision. Then the bird had sung — and he had known. And so a scruffy little blackbird in a far-off foreign field had decided the fate of two human beings in a smoggy northern town.

Suddenly John realised that there was no reason to wait any longer. *Why* wait? Why waste a moment of God knew how many he had left?

Balancing a piece of paper on his knee, he began to write:

My dearest Julia,
    That is how I think of you now, as my dearest Julia. I cannot wait to see you again. No chance of leave over Christmas, but then

you know that already. Maybe New Year? Maybe the spring?

Keep writing your letters, sweetheart, they do so cheer me up. You've no idea how good it is to read about home. I think your ideas for the front room are wonderful, and new curtains would be nice when you've got some cash. I wonder if I can help you put them up? And do the decorating for you? I could smarten the house up really well if you'd let me — even paint that washstand of your father's.

Julia, I want us to be together after the war. I want to take care of you. I want to marry you, because

He paused, then pressed on quickly.

I love you so much. You don't know how much. I've realised you're the girl for me and hope you think I'm the man for you. Say yes, sweetheart, and I'll make you happy for life. Say yes and you'll never want for anything ever again. We could have a good life, a really good life. After the war, when I get home.

Write and say yes, please say yes.

With all my love,

Your John

Smiling, he reread the letter, folded it and then tucked it into his pocket. When the mail was collected it would be on its way to England and The Coppice. And his girl, waiting there.

Adele could feel the pins and needles in her legs, but didn't move. Didn't dare. There wasn't a lot that fazed her, but this old woman did. Watching Mrs Frida Altman carefully, Adele stole a glance at Becky. But her friend was preoccupied, pouring the tea for her grandmother.

'Adele!'

Jumping, she looked at the old woman in the high-backed chair. The old woman with thick purple veins on the backs of her hands and a strange, accented voice. Rebecca's grandmother, with whom she lived, in a poky, overfurnished house in Park Street, Oldham.

'Yes, Mrs Altman?'

'Do you take tea?'

Adele nodded, then added, 'Lovely.'

'Thank you.'

'What?'

'You say *thank you* when someone has offered you something,' Mrs Altman went on, sitting upright, her slate-grey hair arranged loosely on top of her head. A lot of hair for an old lady, Adele thought. 'And you say *pardon*, not *what.*'

'Wh . . . pardon?'

'It is very plain that you have no mother around,' the old lady went on, rearranging her long skirt over laced ankle boots. 'Your manners have lapsed. But then you're only very young and can be improved.' She paused, taking her cup of tea from Becky. 'Thank you, my dear.'

Relieved that the attention was now off her,

49

Adele sneaked a glance around the room. Her eyes immediately lighted on a small picture, painted on gold, with a silver frame. Her parents had had no truck with religion, but Adele was sure this was religious.

'It's an icon.'

'Pardon?' Adele replied, the old woman smiling approvingly.

'I collect religious artefacts. Of course, although we are not Orthodox, my own religion is Jewish. You do know that, don't you, Adele?'

She nodded. 'Becky told me.'

'And do you find us both strange?'

'No. Only you.'

Laughing, the old woman put down her teacup. 'You really are a most unusual child. My granddaughter tells me that you like beautiful objects. I had a friend once who loved antiques. This is a long time ago, when we were young, in Vienna. She settled in England long before I did. In fact, she and her husband lived in Lydgate and my friend was widowed there. In a very strange-looking house — '

'That house!' Adele said, interrupting, then apologising. 'Sorry — it's just that I know that house. The one on the hill?'

Mrs Altman raised her eyebrows, her accented voice curious. 'Yes, the one a little way from St Anne's church.'

'My father used to take me there, oh, loads of times! He said the widow never died,' the old lady's eyes opened wider, 'and that she still haunts the house. Looking for her husband. He used to be able to see her, you know. I mean, not her husband, *my father*. Dad could see the Lydgate Widow walking around at night, searching.'

Really, talking to Adele Ford was like being run over, Frida Altman thought, secretly entertained.

'What was her name?' Adele asked.

'Ninette Hoffman.'

'*Ninette Hoffman,*' Adele repeated reverentially. 'What a lovely name. What did she look like?'

'She was very beautiful.'

Adele was in a world of her own. 'I love that house . . . '

'It's quite absurd, in a way. Neither one thing or another. At first I think it was supposed to be Gothic and then someone else altered it so it became Moorish. Almost heathen, in places. As for the entrance hall, it's huge, with a giant mosaic floor. Fascinating, but weird.'

'If it was mine I would *love* it,' Adele went on, enraptured. 'I would rebuild the high stone wall around it — to keep the people I loved in and the rest of the world out.'

'What about the ghost?' Mrs Altman teased her.

'Oh, there's no ghost! Dad said there was, swore he could see her himself, but I don't believe it. Anyway, I think Ninette Hoffman was happy there. I think she'd like to see her house used again.'

Rebecca's grandmother laughed quietly. 'You talk about your father a lot.'

The first sign of reserve came over Adele. The

51

old woman noticed it but continued. 'You two were very close?'

'Yes,' Adele replied stiffly, glancing over to Rebecca, who held her gaze. The look was obvious. No, *I've never broken your confidence.*

'And your parents had a happy marriage?' Frida Altman went on.

'Very.'

'What did he do for a living?'

Adele visibly relaxed. 'My father was a dealer. Well, he used to buy and sell stuff. And Mum helped him. They used to go to markets and sometimes auctions. Before the war, so Julia said. I don't remember that far back. But there's loads of lovely things at home. Some odd things too — '

'Enough!' Mrs Altman said, putting up her hands. 'Speak more slowly. You rush on so.' Impatiently she flicked her hand at Adele, who was flushing. 'Now, *slowly*, tell me more.'

'He bought washstands.'

'Indeed.'

'And paintings.'

'Good.'

'And skins.'

'*Skins?*'

'Fur, animals. We had a bearskin rug that a woman bought for her husband — he's a photographer in Manchester. And then Dad went off and bought this *whole* bear at a sale,' she mimicked the bear with her arms raised up, 'and when he came home Mum said that he was crazy and had to shift it into the shed. But Dad said that ... ' Adele petered off, then began again more slowly. 'He said that someone would pay good money for a bear.'

'Did they?'

'Did they what?'

'Did someone pay good money for the bear?'

Adele shook her head, her plaits flapping madly for an instant. 'Oh no! It's up in the loft.'

Amused, Mrs Altman regarded Adele thoughtfully. She was certainly a very sparky nine year old, with enormous confidence. A bit precocious, in fact. So unlike Rebecca, who kept everything to herself.

'I have some jewellery you might like to see . . .'

Becky's head shot up. '*Jewellery?* You've not shown me your jewellery for a long time, Oomi.'

The old woman smiled at the affectionate Yiddish name for grandmother.

'You never asked me to. But now I can show you both.'

Slowly she got to her feet. She approved of Rebecca's choice of friend. Adele Ford might well bring her granddaughter out of herself a little. Which she needed. It wasn't good for a young girl to spend most of her time with an old woman. Carefully she mounted the stairs, as always irritated by the pokiness of her surroundings. To lose so much, to be reduced to so little . . . Then she thought of Adele Ford. The girl reminded her of herself a long time ago. Same spirit, same energy . . . Frida paused on the stairs, taking her time. A little dip into the past would do her good. She would show the girls her jewellery; even talk about the old days, the times of plenty, of fun, of men, of flirtations, of dramas.

There was only one subject she would have to avoid. The one she always avoided. Her son and daughter-in-law; Rebecca's parents. She would skirt them as a ship skirts an iceberg, or a cart avoids a pothole in the road.

There were memories. And then there were *memories*.

8

'*GOD!*'

Adele heard the screamed word and ran, hurtling down the stairs two at a time. Julia was standing in the kitchen, her face flushed, a letter gripped in her hands. 'Oh my God! *I did it! I did it!*'

'What's the matter?' Adele asked, astonished when Julia hugged her tightly.

'This, my little sister, is my marriage proposal!' Julia beamed, glowing with triumph, as she shoved the letter under Adele's nose.

Mischievously Adele reached for it, but Julia held it high over her head, waving it like a flag.

'No! You can't even touch it! I might have it framed! I might have the words embroidered on a cushion.' She laughed, then paused, her voice electric. 'John wants me to be his wife.'

'You don't say,' Adele mocked her.

'Huh! Wait until you get a proposal, then we'll see how casual you are about yours!' Julia replied, pretending to be put out. 'He says he loves me. That he'll make me happy . . . '

'And you believe him?'

'You really are *evil*,' Julia replied, laughing and hugging Adele again. 'I do love him, you know. I mean *really* love him . . . We'll be so snug here, John and me, and you. All of us together. You do like him, don't you?'

'I hardly know him.'

'But you will,' Julia replied, smiling. 'You will.'

Flopping on to the old sofa, she patted the seat beside her. Immediately Adele sat down and began to read John's proposal letter.

'It's very romantic . . . And he can spell.'

'I'll be Mrs John Courtland,' Julia mused, kicking up her legs and shrieking with pleasure. 'That old bat Redfern next door will have to call me *Mrs* Courtland.'

Adele pulled a wry face. 'She'll enjoy that.'

Suddenly Julia became serious, jerking upright. 'Oh my God! I have to write back *now!*' she said hurriedly. 'You'll run down and post the letter for me, won't you, sweetheart, on your way to school? If I write it now it'll catch the first post. It'll be off at dinner time.' She raced to the table, snatched up some paper and began to scribble frantically.

'You've only just had the proposal!' Adele teased her. 'He's not going to change his mind.'

Oh, but Julia wasn't too sure about that. John's outpourings were obviously sincere. He was clearly desperately in love. But he was still John — easily swayed by other people. Her pen moving rapidly across the paper, Julia accepted his proposal, piling kisses and promises on the postscript. Then, sealing the missive, she passed it over to Adele. This was the last hurdle. As soon as the letter was in the postbox, it would be on its way. Once John had the reply, it would be official, their future settled. Then he would come home. And then they would be married.

And *then* Julia could relax.

* ★ ★

Frida was watching her granddaughter carefully. How striking Rebecca was; how sure to attract male attention. Just as *she* had done. Just as her mother had done ... Frida glanced away, pretending to read. The past had to be faced sooner or later. It could be avoided — but for only so long. Rebecca was no fool, and she was growing up. She had a *right* to know ... But how could Frida tell her? she wondered, biting her lip. *How?*

Time was passing. At first the lie had been to protect Rebecca, but as time had gone on the deception was becoming harder to maintain. And Frida was getting older. What if she died before Rebecca learned the truth? Frida sighed to herself. She had to confide in her granddaughter. Had to face what she dreaded so much. The next time Rebecca made enquiries, Frida would tell her. It was not a task she looked forward to.

★ ★ ★

Nine months later came the travesty of Flanders. British soldiers were clogged down in the mud; casualties drowned where they had fallen. The poor weather and double the average rainfall had made a sodden hell out of the fighting fields. And still the war ground on.

Having accepted John's proposal by letter, Julia lived for the day when peace would be declared. It was 1917 — surely the war couldn't

57

go on any longer? Times were hard; she was still working at the florist, but business was slow, apart from the wreaths which were ordered almost daily. And when she returned home — before Adele got back from school — there were always the chores to see to.

When the roof sprung a leak for the second time, there was no workman around to fix it. It was, like so many, a job Julia would have to do herself. Clambering up into the attic, she jumped at the sight of the old stuffed bear and then struggled over piles of old boxes and crates towards the far gable. There was a hole big enough to put her fist through, the September wind blowing in cold. But her parents' death, and the war, had taught Julia to be tough. So she hammered a piece of board over the hole in the roof and then looked around for another piece, fixing that one over the first. Stepping back, she admired her handiwork. Well, it would keep out the worst of a northern winter. She wondered then how many other women were fixing their homes themselves, doing jobs that the men would usually have done. Hard jobs, manual jobs, which made women's hands coarse, their skin pitted.

Back downstairs, Julia flopped on to the old sofa in the kitchen, dropping the hammer at her feet. It was true that the Ford girls had inherited a yearly income, but it wasn't much when you had to pay for everything out of two hundred pounds. Heating, lighting, clothing, food. Adele was still growing, she had to have new clothes, and the flaming boiler had cost nearly forty pounds to replace. God, thought Julia despondently, even with her wage money that month had been even tighter after she had paid out for Adele's new skirt and her own nightdress. But what could you do? She had patched and darned everything until there was more darning than garment. Thinking back, she remembered her mother sewing, but that had been different; the house had had a warm feeling then, the fire banked high, sounds and movements keeping it alive. Not like now; now the only time it came to life was when Adele was home.

Julia tried to get up, but flopped back exhausted into her seat. How easy life had been before the war, before their parents' death. How cocky she had been to think she could take over the running of the house so easily. It wasn't easy at all. Especially when she had a job to go to as well, and little support. Adele helped, but the burden fell mostly on Julia's shoulders. What she wouldn't give for the war to end, for John to come home, for them to marry. To have her own man. To be able to lean on someone again.

* * *

When Julia woke several hours later, she was confused, stiff with cold, her neck aching. Wincing, she got to her feet and banked up the meagre fire, turning on the gas light. The kitchen looked gloomy, bleak — and there was no sign of Adele. Anxiously Julia walked to the bottom of the stairs and called up, but there was no reply, and no light burning. Where was her sister?

59

Panic set in quickly. She shouldn't have fallen asleep, what was she thinking? Adele should have been home long before now . . . Julia glanced at the clock — quarter to ten! God, where was she? She was only a child, only nine years old. Julia should have been looking out for her; anything could have happened.

Wrenching open the front door, Julia looked out. The street was dark, empty. Her imagination ran riot. Hadn't there been tales of decent women being assaulted at night? Of children disappearing? No, it was just talk, she told herself, just foolish talk . . . People loved to tell scare stories; it was just rubbish, gossip.

But where was Adele? Where was her little sister? What if something had happened to her and Julia was left alone? Her heart hammered with fright as she moved to the street corner, pulling her shawl around her shoulders. The houses loomed around her like a brick forest, all closed off, no refuge anywhere. She hurried back to her house and stood on the doorstep, shaking. Perhaps if she went to talk to the Redferns or the Lockharts next door? Julia shook her head. No, they would be sure to tell Bernard Hoggard, and then where would she be? The solicitor would think she was incapable, neglectful; he might even take her sister away from her, send her off to some children's home. And all because Julia hadn't looked after her well enough. Hadn't cared enough . . .

At that moment Adele walked through the front gate.

'Where the hell have you been!' Julia snapped,

dragging her sister in through the front door and locking it after them. 'Look at the time!'

'I was — '

'*I don't care!*' Julia cut her off. 'It's wartime, you idiot. You could have been killed.'

'Why would I be killed? I'm not on the front line,' Adele retorted smartly, wriggling out of her sister's grasp.

'So where were you?'

'I was busy.'

'WHAT!'

Adele hopped from foot to foot. 'I was walking.'

'At nearly ten at night?'

'I forgot the time, Julia . . . Aw, come on, I'm OK. Everything's OK.'

Julia's face was ashen. Fear of the war, the long wait for John . . . the pressure was suddenly too much for her. Everything was OK, was it? Maybe. After all, the war was coming to an end — or so everyone said. But she had heard that before. It seemed to her that the war would *never* end, that the men would *never* come back. That John would stay over in France and all her hopes would moulder over there with him. In fact, the more people talked about the end of hostilities the more Julia worried. Bad things always happened when you least expected them.

'You have to let me know where you are at all times!' she said coldly, turning to the kettle and putting it on to boil. 'I worry about you. And I don't like being here on my own at night. The place is creepy.'

Adele shrugged, glancing over to the fire. 'It's cold, too.'

'There's no coal left in the scuttle!' Julia snapped back. 'Go and get some from the shed; I'm not going out there when it's dark.'

Not wanting to push her luck any more that night, Adele went out into the back yard, hardly able to see where she was going. Hauling the scuttle over to the smaller of the two sheds, she shovelled as much coal as she could into it and then half carried, half dragged it back into the kitchen.

Julia stood, arms folded, watching her. 'Where were you anyway? And don't say walking.'

'I went to the market.'

'The market!'

'Tommyfields.'

'That's across town, Adele! And it closed over an hour ago.'

'I couldn't get a tram. I walked home.'

'*Walked!*' Julia repeated heatedly. God, when would her sister ever learn? Didn't she have *any* sense of danger? 'What were you doing at the market anyway?'

'I was looking . . . '

'For what?'

'Mum and Dad used to go there.'

'Well they don't any more,' Julia replied, throwing some coal on to the fire and keeping her face averted.

'I know they don't go any more,' Adele said, very quietly. 'I just wanted to go there myself. See what there was to buy.'

'WE HAVE NO MONEY!' Julia shouted. 'Are

you stupid or what? We need every penny we can lay our hands on just to keep ourselves going.'

'I was trying to *make* money!' Adele snapped back, close to tears. 'I was trying to make some money.'

'With what?' Julia demanded, her hands on her hips. 'You're as crazy as our father was. What in God's name have *you* got to sell?'

'Nothing . . . '

'That's right, Adele, *nothing*.' Julia's voice fell. 'That just about sums it up. *Nothing*. The trip was a waste of time, wasn't it? Just a damn waste of time.'

Slowly Adele walked over to her sister. She was about to touch her arm and then thought better of it, slipping something into her apron pocket instead. Still irritated, Julia took a moment before reaching into the pocket. Her fingers closed over a small object. Surprised, she pulled it out and found herself looking at a rather ugly figurine of a pot pig.

'It's for you,' Adele said quietly.

'But you've no money,' Julia replied, choked.

'I took some bottles back to the shop for Mr Pelt.' Adele moved closer to her sister, looking at the pig in her hand. 'It's not much, I just thought you might like it . . . You know, pigs are supposed to be lucky . . . Well, like I said, it's not much . . . '

'It's *beautiful*,' Julia said, turning and hugging her sister tightly. 'In fact it's the most beautiful thing I've ever seen in my life.'

★ ★ ★

Stopping for the third time in a minute, John Courtland adjusted his soldier's cap. Then adjusted it again. Tipped it over one eye, then the other. Finally he picked up his duffle bag and turned into The Coppice. He was on leave for the first time in eighteen months. *For the first time since he had proposed to Julia, and she had accepted.* His excitement was suddenly shaken by his customary uncertainty. What if she was disappointed when she saw him? What if she had changed her mind? What if she had another man?

No, not Julia, he reassured himself. He stopped walking again. He hadn't told her he was coming home. Hadn't told anyone. It was to be a surprise. But what if the surprise was unwelcome, what if he walked up to the house and was seen off? What if . . .

Oh for God's sake, John told himself. Get a move on, you're about to see your girl.

Further along the road, a front door opened suddenly, an old man spotting the soldier outside and waving to him. Soldiers were heroes, everyone loved them. Wasn't that the truth? John didn't really care, as long as Julia Ford loved him. As long as when her door opened she was happy to see him. Not fake happy, not forced, but 'in love' happy. He would know in that instant if she was still his girl. If he was her man. If the blackbird hadn't been mocking him.

His heart in his mouth, John Courtland knocked on the door and waited. His pulse hammering, he stared at the door knocker and then heard footsteps running to answer. It seemed like hours before he heard the chain slide off the lock and watched the handle turn. And then the door opened.

Julia said nothing, just launched herself into his arms, her head resting against his neck, her voice so soft he had to strain to hear her.

'Welcome home,' she said simply. 'Welcome home, sweetheart.'

9

1918

The war ended on the 11th November on an overcast, wet morning, not unlike many other winter days.

Then, at eleven o'clock, as the Armistice took effect, church bells began to ring around the country. Within minutes, the streets were full of people cheering. From Manchester to London, the Union Jack was waved and fireworks exploded. Blackout curtains were pulled down, lights went on in shop windows and the pubs were left open until they ran out of beer.

And Big Ben — silent for four years — chimed the hours again.

I remember it so well. Even though I was only a child then.

Julia heard the news first and came rushing into the kitchen, snatching the Union Jack from over the mantelpiece and then grabbing my hand. We took the tram down into Oldham, into the main part of the town, the conductor ringing the bell like a fire alarm. When we reached Union Street you could hardly move for people. They were standing on the Town Hall steps, banked up like flocks of migrating birds, the clock ringing out, everyone shouting and cheering and Julia waving the flag above her head like a child.

They had given us the day off school and Becky came by the house later. She was as composed as ever, her dark eyes unfathomable. Julia fussed around her and sent back some cake for old Mrs Altman. When we were alone again, my sister sat me down on the sofa in the kitchen and told me that after she married John Courtland we were all going to live together and be very happy.

She was luminous when she said it. All her phantom prettiness had returned and she was Julia again. Julia before our parents' death and before the war. Julia as I remember her most clearly, glossy with hope, her future certain and safe.

The war was over; we had nothing left to fear.

10

'Hey, remember this?' Adele asked Becky as she passed Julia and John Courtland's wedding photographs over to her.

It had been a winter wedding, taking place on 2 February 1919 at the local register office, not the church. As Julia said, she had no father to give her away, and she wasn't religious. She *was*, however, determined to look good on her big day and had altered one of her mother's old dresses to fit, adding a stunning cloche hat and an extravagant bunch of flowers. As for Adele, she had been wearing a dress so fussy that at every opportunity she had hidden from sight. Despite her efforts, she had been caught for posterity on a photograph.

'That dress wasn't really you, was it?' Becky said tactfully.

'I felt like I'd fallen off a damn float.' Adele replied, turning over the page hurriedly. 'Julia looked good, though. Like the cat that got the cream. Even John looked handsome.'

He had. A little awkward, uncertain, but happy with his bride. How quickly people altered, Adele thought. In only a year her brother-in-law had changed from a hero soldier to a smug, self-satisfied bore. Far from suffering the fate of many soldiers home from fighting, he had immediately resumed his previous position at the bank, an increase in salary swelling his head impressively. So much for his supposed lack of self-esteem, Adele thought. Julia had done a fine job of giving him confidence. Perhaps too much . . .

Julia hadn't been slow in telling everyone about her husband's promotion either. John Courtland was going to be someone.

'Anyone could be someone if they'd had it laid out on a plate for them,' Mrs Redfern had said, unaware that Adele had overheard her talking to Mrs Pelt at the end of the road. 'I mean, that house isn't his, and he might contribute to living expenses, but it's Julia's money in the end. Not that John Courtland likes to remember that.'

Slamming the wedding album shut, Adele pushed the memory out of her mind and looked up at the trapdoor above her head.

'I want to know what's up there, Becky. Dad was always putting stuff aside. There could be a fortune in the attic.'

'You were told not to nose around.'

'I'm not nosing, I'm *looking*,' Adele shot back, climbing up the trapdoor ladder. 'I'll be quick.'

'I can hear footsteps!'

Startled, Adele jumped, banging her head on a roof beam. 'Damn!' she snapped, walking over to the hatch and looking down. 'Are they home?'

A moment later Becky reappeared under the trapdoor. 'No, you're OK, it was next door. Come on, Adele, I feel bad about this.'

'Why? I'm just having a look.'

'But Julia said . . . '

'Julia didn't say anything,' Adele corrected her. '*John* did. And what John says, Julia does. She thinks he's God just because he can mend a leak . . . I heard he was showing off at the bank like he was a big shot. And flirting. Honestly, Becky, I don't know what Julia sees in him.'

'She loves him.'

'I know that,' Adele agreed. 'That's what makes it worse . . . You stay on watch, I'm going for one last look.'

'Oh, must you!' Becky urged her, moving back to her lookout post at the window at the top of the stairs.

The Coppice was laid out before her like a prize waiting to be judged. All perfect compact little houses, with perfect front gardens and perfect painted doors. And a perfect couple walking up the road.

'*They're coming!*'

Hurriedly Adele scrambled out of the attic and banged the trapdoor shut, reaching the top of the stairs just as Julia walked in, John following.

'It's heavenly in the park.'

Adele rolled her eyes.

'John said we might all go to Southport for the day. Or Lytham St Annes.'

'I don't want to go . . . '

'I'm not forcing you!' John replied curtly, puffing out his chest. 'I don't need some kid dragging along after us.'

'John,' Julia coaxed him, 'you mustn't tease Adele like that.'

Giving John a murderous look, Adele left the house with Becky. When he was sure she was out of earshot, John turned back to his wife.

'She's always causing trouble. Don't you

remember what she was like when we were courting? That flaming worm, for one thing . . . '

'She's just high-spirited, darling.'

'She's spoilt.'

'If you say so,' Julia replied, about to sit down on John's lap.

But he had other ideas. He had borrowed some money off Julia to buy a car — even though they could hardly afford it — and now he wanted to show it off at the pub. There he would buy his boss, Mr Thornhill, a drink and then offer to drive him home. Letting him see that John Courtland was used to the good things in life.

John didn't realise it, but Julia was slowly turning her indecisive, easily led consort into a braggart. As he had done so often in the past, John believed what he was told. And as Julia was now the greatest influence over him, he accepted everything she said. She told him he was clever, ambitious and bound to go far in his profession. She also told him that he was an amazing lover and a witty conversationalist. And he believed her. A brighter man might have laughed off some of Julia's more far-fetched compliments, but John swallowed them whole, until he was plump with conceit.

'Look, love,' he said, getting up, 'I'm just popping out . . . '

'John, it's Saturday! I thought we could go out.'

'We've been out.'

'I mean tonight. We could go to the music hall.'

He flushed, looking away. So perhaps he shouldn't have taken Susan Fleetwood, one of the bank tellers, there, but it had been innocent. It had been her birthday and she was one of his colleagues. It was just good manners, really. But perhaps not something he wanted Julia to hear about. She was so possessive, she would be bound to get the wrong idea. Didn't she hang on his arm when they went out? Laugh at all his jokes? Tell everyone how well he was doing? Hadn't it been her who had told him he was attractive? And obviously it was true. John sighed. His wife would have to realise that other women would always be after him.

'John, are you listening to me?'

'What?'

'If you don't want to go to the music hall, we could go to the pictures, see that Charlie Chaplin film . . . '

'Julia,' he said, his tone tired, 'we can't spend every minute together. We can't live in each other's pockets.'

She was stunned, but kept her voice light. 'We've only been married for a year! You can't be tired of me already.'

'I'm not tired of you,' he replied, kissing her on the cheek as he eyed the door — and his escape. 'Silly girl, how could I be tired of my Julia? I just want to have a drink with someone important. You do understand, don't you?'

No, she didn't. But she let him go anyway.

When the door closed, Julia sat down again and pondered for a long time. Oh, she had what she wanted: John Courtland, her husband. But perhaps she had overdone the worshipping wife role . . . Kicking off her shoes, she stared into the fire. She loved John, liked having sex with him, and by flattering him she had certainly effected a change. But perhaps her encouragement — like castor oil — would be just as effective in small doses.

11

Unusually agitated, Becky came out on to the corridor just as her grandmother was walking up the stairs. Frida was in her nightclothes, her long hair in a plait over her shoulder, her form fragile, frightening so. Vulnerability had never been Frida Altman's style, but in a flannel nightdress and bedjacket she looked her age — and she looked frail. Her mind, however, was as alert as it had ever been.

'Whatever's the matter, Rebecca?'

'I . . . I . . .'

Surprised that her calm granddaughter was so unnerved, Frida took her arm and led her into her own bedroom. Sitting Becky down on the bed, she asked: 'Is there something you want to tell me?' Becky stayed mute. 'Something about growing up?'

Surprised, Becky gave her grandmother a sideways glance. What would an old lady know about such things?

'Are you menstruating? Losing blood from down below?'

Mortified, Becky nodded.

'That's nothing to worry about,' Frida went on calmly. 'We can sort that out. It happens to every girl. It happened to me — about two hundred years ago! You're growing up now, Rebecca, you'll change, mature. I know you always behave well, but you have to be very careful around boys.'

For another half an hour Frida Altman explained what was going to happen. Amazed, Becky listened, and finally she relaxed. There was no embarrassment about it, no shame; the old woman simply told her granddaughter the facts. After all, she had known that this day would come and had been prepared for it. In *her* youth mothers had seldom explained anything to their daughters — and ignorance, Frida knew, was dangerous.

When she had finished, she studied her granddaughter. 'Is there anything else you want to know, Rebecca?'

'Yes.'

Frida knew the risk she was taking, but took it anyway. 'What is it? You can ask me anything.'

Could she? Becky wondered. Could she *really*?

'It's about my parents — I want to know . . . Where are they? When will I see them again?'

This was the question Frida had dreaded, and now the moment was here. She had run the scenario over and over again in her mind, but had never decided on exactly what she would say. Instead she had been relieved that the months and years had passed and her granddaughter had referred less and less to her parents. Maybe her own reticence on the matter had prevented more enquiry. Rebecca was, after all, a sensitive child, reluctant to upset anyone.

But now she wasn't a child any longer, and she wanted an answer.

'They . . . ' It was proving so difficult. Frida

was old and hadn't expected her life to turn out this way, with so many problems at the end. 'They aren't coming back, my dear.'

'Why not?' Becky asked, her voice muted.

'Your father's dead.' Frida took her granddaughter's hands and held on to them tightly.

'*Dead?*' Becky echoed, her voice hardly audible. 'But my mother? What about my mother?'

'After your father died, she ran off with another man,' Frida said finally, hurrying on. Should she stop there? No, the truth had to be complete, not abridged. 'Don't be too hard on your mother . . . '

Rebecca's voice was wavering. 'Why didn't she come back for me?'

'She wanted to. But there was an appalling tragedy in her life. It broke up your parents' marriage and everything fell apart.'

'What happened?'

Frida met her granddaughter's gaze steadily. 'You had a brother.'

Rebecca flinched, hardly able to take in what she was hearing. Suddenly her father was dead, her mother estranged, and she had learned of a sibling she had not even known existed.

'I have a brother?'

'He died when he was a baby. It was before you were born, sweetheart,' Frida went on, fighting emotion. She had to be strong, calm. 'When you arrived, your mother loved you — never think she didn't — but she couldn't stop worrying, fretting about your brother's death. She had some kind of breakdown, started mistaking you for him. Started being afraid that you would die as well.'

'Why did my brother die?' Rebecca asked, her face ashen, drained of colour. '*Why did he die?*'

'He was ill.'

'What was wrong with him?'

Frida glanced down, then looked back to her granddaughter. Here was the moment, at last. The moment which would end Rebecca's childhood for ever. The moment when she would be propelled from ignorance into a terrible knowledge.

'Your brother had a heart problem. He only lived for a few months.'

Glancing away, Rebecca bit her lip. Frida waited. A minute passed. She ached, wondering what her granddaughter was thinking.

Finally Rebecca spoke again. 'Is there anything wrong with me?'

'No, no!' Frida reassured her. 'No, you're well. Perfectly well.'

'But my brother . . . ' Rebecca paused, intelligence in her eyes. Intelligence and then dread. 'Was his condition . . . Was it passed down? You know, did he inherit it?'

After a lengthy pause, Frida nodded, the words balling up in her throat. 'The doctors believed so. Your uncle died young, in his twenties.'

'Then . . . then if *I* had children, could they . . . '

'Could they have heart problems? Yes.' Frida clung to her granddaughter's hands. 'But then again, they might not.'

'But I wouldn't know that until they were born?'

God, Frida thought, she was old, life didn't matter so much to her. But to hear such news when you were a girl. When your life *was* family, children . . .

'No, you wouldn't know until they were born,' she agreed.

'They could die?'

'They might not. Listen to me, Rebecca, the doctors know more these days. They can do more . . . '

'*But they could die!*' Rebecca replied, horror-struck.

'And they could live long, perfectly healthy lives,' Frida replied, her tone gentle. 'Can you understand your mother a little, sweetheart? She was so desperate, she couldn't face the prospect of your loss.'

'But I was her daughter. I wasn't her *son*!'

'No, but she got so confused she couldn't see that,' Frida replied, holding tightly on to Rebecca's hands. 'She couldn't believe that she wouldn't lose you too. I know she meant to come back for you, when she was better.'

'Where is she?' Rebecca asked urgently. 'You said she was coming back for me! For years you told me she was coming back.'

'She told me to tell you that!' Frida retorted, her voice broken. 'And I thought it was the truth. I believed her. Then your father died and she took up with a new man. She wanted to forget.'

'*She wanted to forget me!*'

Helpless, Frida clung to her granddaughter.

'Rebecca, try and understand. She told me that she was going to come and get you and that you were going to be a family again. *I believed her* . . . Then she wrote me a letter . . . ' Frida paused, unable to interpret the expression on Rebecca's face. 'She said she had found someone else and that I was to take care of you.'

'Where is she!'

'There was no address on the letter,' Frida replied, her voice losing some of its strength. 'Maybe I should have told you — but how could I? You wanted to believe she was coming back. How *could* I tell you? The truth would have been too much for you. You were only a child, Rebecca. You were only little.'

'Maybe she didn't write the letter . . . Maybe it was a lie . . . ' Becky said, her voice trailing off.

But she knew only too well that her mother *had* written it. She had suspected for a long time that there was to be no glorious reunion. Suspected it when her grandmother had given her birthday presents and cards supposedly from her parents. But the handwriting had never been disguised enough and the gifts were too English to have come from abroad.

'Are you *so* unhappy living with me?' Frida asked sadly.

'No,' Becky replied, her hands gripping her grandmother's.

The old lady was shaking, racked with remorse. 'What can I do?'

'Nothing . . . There's nothing either of us can do.'

Getting to her feet, Rebecca walked out of her

grandmother's bedroom and into her own, sitting down heavily on the bed. In truth she could hardly remember her parents, only vague mental snapshots, memories. The lie she had been told — and had believed for so long — had served her well ... Turning to stare into the mirror on her dressing table, Rebecca studied her face. She was a forgotten child. A little girl shunted off abroad to live with her grandmother. The child of a dead father and a weak mother, the sister of a dead boy ... Slowly she traced the outline of her face. She didn't know if she was like her parents, because there were no photographs. She didn't know if she sounded like her mother, because there had been no contact by phone. She didn't know if she walked, acted or laughed like either of her parents, because they had vanished from her life entirely.

For a long time Rebecca stared at her face, then finally she moved, her course of action decided. It was good that her parents had disappeared so completely. All the better really. Certainly her grandmother would never mention them again, nor the scandal. No one would ever know the truth — and if Rebecca kept it hidden, *nobody* would see her as a cast-off, a girl no one wanted.

No one would know about her brother, and his death. About the health problem from which she might be exempt — but which she might well carry and pass on. Her eyes closed against the thought. One day she would meet a man she wanted to marry. And she would have to tell him. Would he still want her then? Knowing that their children could well be cursed?

Rebecca's eyes opened slowly. She could stay silent, keep her secret, trust to fate. But no, lies weren't the answer. Maybe the man she married would understand. Maybe he wouldn't want children. Maybe she would never marry, never risk any baby coming into the world. Maybe, maybe, maybe . . . The words rattled like stones in a tin can. If, if, if . . . The thought repeated itself. What if, what if, what if . . .

There were no answers. And on the night Rebecca Altman began puberty, she left her childhood behind in more ways than one.

12

Another year passed, and another. On many occasions Adele walked up to Lydgate House, standing outside and staring into the overgrown garden, remembering what Frida Altman had told her about Ninette Hoffman. She made up her own fantasies about the widow, embellishing the tale her father had begun. Then, one summer night, she stayed on very late, well after dusk, and imagined that she saw something. She even called out — hoping Ninette Hoffman might hear and answer her. But it was only a summer fox, making its way back to its den.

Alone, and in secret, she also began to visit the market stalls and fairs. At first she had been apprehensive, but she was soon accepted by the regulars.

'Yer round 'ere again, Adele?' an old man called out from his stall on Tommyfields market. 'Yer thinking of making a living out it, like yer dad?' He picked up a battered old skillet. 'Wot yer give me fer this? Hey, wot about it? I'll do yer a deal, Adele. Make me an offer and we'll do a deal.'

On the next stall, Mrs Hodges had spotted Adele and waved her over quickly.

'Come away, luv. Yer want nowt to do with that fella. I caught a cat pissing on his pots the other day and he sold 'em on without washing 'em.'

'Oi!' he shouted from the next stall. 'You talking about me?'

'Yer right there! And yer know wot about. *Dirty beggar,*' the woman replied, turning her back on him. She was wrapped up against the cold, a dark wool shawl around her head and mittens over her cold hands. 'I were hoping yer'd come, Adele,' she said, smiling. 'Yer couldn't keep an eye on the stall fer me, could yer?'

Willingly Adele agreed, watching the woman hurry off to the tea stand. Above Adele's head the overcast sky threatened rain; the noise and clatter of a hundred stalls reverberated with cries of:

'*Roll up, roll up! I'm not asking a shilling, even a sixpence — what yer offer me, Mother? . . . Name yer price . . . I can only refuse yer and no hard feelings . . .*'

Some of the men employed a different techniques, especially those selling soap or the pungent home-made perfume they swore came over from France.

'*Yer don't need anything, young lady. Yer a beauty and no mistake . . . I'll give yer this bottle cheap — just fer a smile . . .*'

The hours were long, many of the stallholders arriving early on cold mornings to catch the factory workers. Often they would stay on their stands until seven at night, ten or eleven on Fridays and Saturdays, eager to get rid of meat, fish and fruit. After all, there was no profit in leftovers.

The better stalls weren't on Tommyfields; the pricier items — linens, lace, glass, china, furniture and fabric — were sold at the covered market. But there was still a pecking order on Tommyfields: the more refined bric-a-brac and china stalls didn't pass the time of day with the rough traders with their orange boxes and potato sacks. Of course some of the men were wide boys; spivs who had profited from the war and were now selling on stolen goods. They didn't stand on the stalls themselves, but got runners to do it for them. And then there were the immigrants; the stallholders with their foreign accents and coloured glass. Elderly men who would tell anyone who wanted to listen about the old country, or how they had once been well off. In this motley sea of people there were a few soldiers, back from the war. Ones who couldn't find work and who took a market stall instead. Selling donkey stones, tin cans, milk churns, dented fenders which were long past their best. Cast-offs, in fact, that only the very poor would buy — and for a pittance.

Taking another glance at the darkening sky, Adele stood upright behind the stall, hoping that passers-by would think she owned it. After all, she was very nearly grown up — and hadn't her father been a well-known dealer round these parts?

'I want a yard of that blue ribbon, and be quick about it,' a customer snapped suddenly. Adele measured the ribbon and then folded it into a brown paper bag.

'That's tuppence.'

'It's bloody not! Tuppence! Yer off yer mind. I paid a penny only the other month. If the usual lady were here, she'd tell yer — '

'Yer a bloody liar, Betty Collins!' the owner of the stall snapped, re-emerging and taking the bag out of the woman's hand. 'It were tuppence then, and it's tuppence now. And if yer don't want it, they're plenty that do!'

Reluctantly the customer paid up, then walked off muttering. Mrs Hodges turned back to Adele. 'They'll all try and best yer. Yer mark my words. Yer 'ave to 'ave yer wits about yer, Adele. Yer father would have done better if 'e'd kept 'is wits about 'im a bit more.' She put up a mittened hand to stop Adele interrupting. 'Not that I've a bad word to say about yer dad. 'E were never a snob, never thought 'imself above us, even though he did buy and sell at auction when 'e were flush.' She nudged Adele in the ribs and winked. 'Not that 'e were as flush as often as 'e'd 'ave liked, hey?'

'No,' she agreed, 'not as often as he'd have liked.'

Lacking snobbery herself, Adele found it easy to mix with the market traders and just as easy to go to the auction houses. Victor Ford had only taken her to one auction, but she had never forgotten it. The rush, the thrill, the adrenaline buzzing in her veins . . .

Leaving Mrs Hodges back on her stall, Adele walked on, deep in thought. If Julia found out about her sister's forays to Tommyfields she would be outraged. How *could* she mix with those low types? Julia would ask. When she was the sister-in-law of a man soon to be an assistant bank manager? A man with a future. A man who lived on The Coppice. Albeit in his wife's house.

So Adele kept her secret and pretended that she was visiting Becky when she went on her jaunts, knowing her friend would always cover for her — even if Becky had her reservations.

'What if you bought something by accident at an auction?' she asked. 'What if you spent a hundred pounds by mistake?'

'I don't put my hand up,' Adele told her loftily. 'I don't bid. I know what I'm doing, Becky, stop worrying.'

But only the previous week she had nearly been caught out, at the Ram's Head public house, Uppermill. Sliding in at the back of the pub, Adele had hidden herself amongst the press of people and watched. Auctions in pubs were always interesting, more often than not held by bereaved relatives wanting to sell off goods without attracting the heftier commission of the town's auction houses. Beside her had been a fat women from Tommyfields, and an elegant man Adele had seen around the covered market. A well-dressed man, with a shock of prematurely greying hair.

The bidding had begun listlessly with a piano stool. Then a couple of watercolours had come out, Scottish scenes, hurriedly bought by a dealer Adele had seen around the markets, a shifty Welshman from Hanky Park.

Squeezed by the press of people both sides, Adele had been gradually pushed closer to the front, where the publican of the Ram's Head was watching with his arms folded. The auctioneer, Henry Shine — oiled with old malt — had been getting well into his flow, pointing to an old marble clock with a black surround and two morose angels on the top. As he indicated it, the clock had chimed mournfully, making everyone laugh.

'Who'll give me a tenner for this lovely clock? London maker, good condition . . . '

The clock chimed again melancholically.

'A tenner? Come on, I can't be giving it away.'

Everyone had looked at the clock; and everyone had decided that they didn't want it. Unperturbed, Henry Shine had gone on: 'Come on, someone make me an offer. We'll start at five pounds.'

At that precise moment, someone had nudged Adele accidentally from behind. She reacted by jerking her arm. Henry Shine's eyes fixed on her gratefully.

'We have a new young lady bidder . . . '

Adele had looked round, flushed, and then blathered, 'Oh, me? No, I wasn't bidding . . . '

'Any advance on five pounds?'

Five pounds! Adele hadn't got five shillings.

'I . . . I . . . '

'Now, lass,' Henry had warned her, 'don't go bidding against yourself! That'll never do, will it?'

As she had panicked, everyone else had laughed, and Adele had prayed that someone would put in another bid for the hideous clock. By this time her face had become flame red — her embarrassment obvious to everyone but Henry Shine.

'Going once . . . '

Oh God.

'Going twice . . . '

'Five pounds and two shillings,' a voice had said suddenly. Adele had caught her breath with relief and turned round.

For a moment she hadn't known who had spoken, and then she saw the greying man nod his head in her direction. Relieved, she had smiled, and at the end of the auction hurried out after him.

But by the time she got into the street he had gone. Taking the ghastly clock — and her undying gratitude — with him.

13

Taking an amused glance at the hideous marble clock, Turner Gades checked the mechanism inside. One good thing about it — it was reliable. He then carefully checked every other clock in his shop, adjusting them where it was necessary, before locking the front door and pulling down the steel shutters. Having inherited the business from his father, Turner intended to run it exactly as it had been run for the last hundred and twenty years. It was a promise he had made himself during the war. If I get back I want everything to be the same. The peace, the serenity of the shop. If I get back I want to move into that building, live there and die there.

He *had* got back, and he *had* moved into the flat above the traditional antique shop in Rochdale, in the centre of the town, near the Town Hall and the formal gardens. And he had taken on his late father's life, living a quiet existence. Because that was all he wanted. Turner had seen war, death, suffering. He had seen ambition, petty spite and heroism. He had seen enough of man — in his three years in France — to last him a lifetime.

He wanted a quiet life . . . Trouble was, the women of Rochdale and its surrounds could recognise a good thing when they saw it. And

89

when Turner returned from the war he was seen as a real catch. Although his face was youthful, his prematurely grey hair gave him an air of experience, of prosperity. A well-off businessman *and* a war hero. Hadn't all the women heard about his exploits? Well, not from the man himself — Turner Gades wasn't one for bragging — but the rumours. Rumours of how he had returned to the battlefield for a friend. Why, wasn't that how he had turned grey so young? The shock?

And many a girl wanted to soothe that shock. To take Turner Gades in her arms and hustle him up the aisle before anyone else did. Invitations from Rochdale doctors, vicars, dentists and solicitors came regularly. Each professional man had only one thing in common — a daughter of marriageable age. A daughter who needed a husband. A well-to-do husband. After all, Turner Gades wasn't a shopkeeper, he was an antique dealer. A *proper antique dealer*. A man who had been abroad for his goods, and often went to London. Sotheby's, even. This wasn't some crummy little shop, this was Gades — and everyone knew the name. A byword for quality, for elegance. Working-class men who had made sudden money in the cotton mills and pits had often turned to Turner's father for advice. The old widower had been a fastidious, cool man, but an aesthete. You could learn taste from Julian Gades, everyone knew that. You could give him money and he would make your home into the definition of sure-handed style.

As with the father, so with the son. No one could remember Mrs Gades, and there were no other Gades offspring, but luckily Turner had inherited his father's talent. Not Julian's coldness, but certainly some reserve. Turner wasn't a misanthrope, he just wanted to distance himself. In clocks, paintings, pieces of furniture, he found stillness. Whereas Victor Ford had lived for the thrill of the auction, Turner lived for the calm accumulation of goods, building an elegant barrier between himself and the world.

Smiling again as he spotted the black clock, Turner thought of the girl who had been so clearly out of her depth at the Ram's Head. But plucky, he thought. Courageous enough to go to the pub alone and watch the auction. He had done the same once — though with his father, not alone. He wondered then if he would have had the same nerve at her age. The same interest which had defied convention. She was, after all, a girl in her teens visiting a pub — albeit for an auction. He thought of how she had flushed with a kind of angry embarrassment and how the auctioneer, Henry Shine, had been too plastered to notice. And then he remembered how she had smiled so gratefully when he had put in his bid. Turner had known then that she would follow him out after the auction and want to thank him, and that was why he had hurried away. He liked to help — but from a distance.

Then he decided, in a sudden, whimsical moment, that he would never sell the clock.

That, hideous as it was, the black timepiece would stay on its shelf behind the counter at Gades. It would be a regular feature in his now regular life. It would be an example of everything stable and constant.

Chiming his days in. And chiming them out again.

14

It was at the end of the following summer that Becky dropped her bombshell. She and Adele had gone out for the day, bicycling up to Hawkshead Pike and then getting off their bikes and sitting down on the warm grass. It was there that Becky told her. Her parents weren't coming home that year. Or any year . . .

'My father's dead and my mother went off with another man.'

'What?' Adele said, stunned. 'Are you joking?'

'No,' Becky replied, her voice detached. 'I've known since last year. But I didn't want anyone else to know . . . Not even you.'

'Oh . . . '

'I'm sorry,' Becky said, gazing out over the horizon.

She had grown accustomed to her secret. It had become part of her, hardly noticed any more. But she *had* run her grandmother's words over and over in her head. Considering the complications, the effect on her future. Being reserved by nature, Rebecca had kept such thoughts to herself and Frida hadn't brought up the topic again. Instead the knowledge had shimmied between them, shared but unwelcome. And unacknowledged. Until something happened which knocked even such devastating news into second place.

'That's not all . . . '

Adele kept her voice even. 'Want to tell me?'

'I had a brother. He died. He had heart problems . . . ' Becky paused. She wanted to go on, to share the worry of his condition, and how it might affect her own future. But she couldn't. Somehow she couldn't admit — even to Adele — that she might never be a mother. Or worse, might be the mother of a sick child.

'God,' Adele said sympathetically. 'How old was your brother when he died?'

Hesitating, Becky picked at the long late summer grass. 'I don't want to talk about it any more.'

'OK.'

'I *can't* talk about it . . . '

'It's OK, Becky, I understand. I'm just sorry.'

'Anyway, I've got other things on my mind.'

Curious, Adele studied her friend, instinctively knowing she hadn't got the full story. Then she remembered how much Becky kept to herself. How secretive she was. How she hated anyone meddling in her private life. Adele liked to show her feelings, but Rebecca spent her life covering hers. There was no point asking for more information now. Adele would be told in time. One day, when Becky decided. But not a moment before. It was the only condition of their friendship.

Immobile and silent, Becky stared ahead. Adele wondered how to break the gloom.

'I've got a boyfriend.'

Becky turned, smiling. 'Oh yeah? Who is he?'

High up on Hawkshead Pike, they could see virtually the whole county. On one side was

Lydgate, Oldham below in the valley, the cotton mills stretching their smoky necks upwards to the sun. And far away, the heather-bearded Saddleworth Moor.

Taking a picnic out of her bike's saddlebag, Adele offered a sandwich to her friend.

Becky accepted, then asked, 'What's he like?'

'He works on the market . . . '

'Adele!'

'Oh, for God's sake, you were once smitten with that King boy.'

'Who was going to give me a rat baby,' Becky reminded her poignantly. 'Anyway, that was just kids' talk. We're fifteen now. Grown up.'

'You wouldn't think so, the way Julia talks to me. She still thinks I'm a kid. And when I said that no one was wearing those thick black stockings any more, she went mad! Crazy! Called for John and all. God, what a racket! And what does he know about girls? Doesn't even have a flaming sister. On and on he goes: '*Only fast girls talk about clothes. You're just a kid.*' I mean, didn't Coco Chanel say only this February that sweaters can be chic?'

'So who is he?' Becky asked patiently, returning to their previous theme and curious to know about Adele's boyfriend.

'Tim Malkin.'

'*Tim Malkin!*'

'Is there an echo up here or something?' Adele asked, miffed. 'He's very good looking.'

'He's old! He must be fifty.'

'Thirty, actually.'

'Thirty!'

'Yeah, and he's getting a wheelchair next week,' Adele replied smartly, lying down on the grass and beginning to eat a sandwich. 'Tim's got muscles, and he knows about things.'

'I bet.'

'I don't mean that! I mean he knows about furniture.'

Becky took another sandwich and lay down beside Adele. 'Has he asked you out?'

'Nah . . . ' Sighing, Adele admitted the truth. 'He's not my boyfriend *really*.' Her disappointment was obvious. 'He doesn't even know I exist. More's the pity.'

'You're only fifteen . . . '

Adele sniffed. 'In the olden days girls married at twelve. Don't you remember what Miss Egan told us about the royals, how they had to marry so young?'

'Tim Malkin is no prince,' Becky replied, taking another sandwich. 'These are good.'

'Julia made them. Being kind — and hoping that by making a picnic I might keep out of the way when John got home!' Adele laughed loudly. 'She relies on him so much. It seems incredible that she used to mend the roof when the war was on. She won't even dirty her hands now. And she's talking about John being a bank manager one day and how they'll have to decorate the house again before they can invite people round.'

'They've decorated already!'

'That was three years ago,' Adele replied, 'and now *Good Housekeeping* states that the sitting room should be papered in florals.'

'Go on!'

'True! And blue is the colour of the season.' Adele laughed, then noticed that Becky was silent. Concerned, she glanced over to her friend. 'You OK?'

Becky didn't reply, just held the sandwich limply in one hand and stared ahead.

'Becky? What is it? Is it about your parents?'

She winced. 'No.'

'Then what?'

'My grandmother would have liked me to go to finishing school in Switzerland. Only we don't have the money any more — so I'll have to get a job instead.'

Adele stared at her, aghast. 'Not yet?'

'Plenty of other girls work at fourteen, never mind fifteen,' Becky replied, composed, although in reality she was mortified. All her worries about her future had suddenly dwindled faced with the reality of her immediate gloomy present. 'There's a job going at the Ash — '

'That's a mill!'

'I never knew you were a snob.'

'I'm not!' Adele snapped. 'But you're better than that. Working as a mill girl, it's not good enough for you.'

'We're short of money. I need to work to pay the rent. My grandmother had some savings, but they're almost gone now. And she's not that well. We had the doctor out last week.' She hurried on. 'It won't be so bad, and it might not be for long.'

Becky paused, sitting up and glancing down at the ominous blackened mill chimneys. Her face was calm, but there was a vein throbbing in her neck. Adele watched her anxiously. How could Rebecca Altman work with the mill girls? she thought uneasily. How could such an exotic, singular person ever hope to fit in?

'What about getting some shop work instead? I mean, I know Julia's only part time, but she could ask at the florist for you.'

'I've already asked them. I've gone round everywhere. It seems that only the mills are still hiring.'

'Look,' Adele said quietly, 'I could lend you — '

'*No you couldn't!* I don't want charity. It's OK, really it is,' Becky said hurriedly, always loathing pity — even from Adele. 'After all, how hard can it be?'

★ ★ ★

Miss Egan put on her glasses and scowled out of the window into the playground. She scowled a lot now. Her one and only love had been killed in the war and no other man had ever caught her eye. Or so she said. In fact, due to the massive number of fatalities in the war, there was a shortage of men — and Miss Egan had never been a beauty. So, forced into living a solitary life she had never anticipated, age continued to do her a disservice. She had not mellowed, but grown more acid by the year, her tongue as sharp as a barber's blade. But her interest in her pupils was still acute, and having attained the lofty height of deputy headmistress, she was watching Adele Ford avidly.

There was something special about the girl, she thought, sneezing loudly and then blowing her nose equally loudly into her handkerchief. If only she would take some advice. After all, Adele's ambitions couldn't be the same as her sister's, could they? Not another Ford girl seeing marriage as the be-all and end-all of life? Studying Adele's curvaceous form and luxuriant hair, Miss Egan wondered suddenly if marriage might not be such a bad idea after all. Otherwise the exuberant Miss Ford might find herself another hobby. And Miss Egan didn't mean macramé.

'Adele! Adele Ford!' she shouted, rapping loudly on the window.

When Adele looked up, Miss Egan beckoned for her to come over. They met at the top of the outside steps, Adele hurriedly refastening one of her plaits.

'I want a word with you.'

'I haven't done anything,' Adele replied, on the defensive immediately.

Sighing, Miss Egan opened a door off the staff room and gestured for Adele to follow her in. 'What are you going to do?'

'About what?'

'With your life!' Miss Egan snapped. 'What are you going to do with your life?'

Adele shifted her feet. If the truth be known, she was hating school without Becky, and was uncertain of what to do next. If she left, she would have to take a job. Certainly not mill work, Julia would *never* hear of that. Maybe a job in a shop . . . But Adele didn't care for that idea either. There was only one thing that she had any real interest in. And she couldn't make a career out of that.

Or could she?

'Actually, I have got an idea.'

'Oh,' Miss Egan said, relieved. 'What is it?'

'I want to be a dealer.'

'In what?'

'Antiques! You know, bric-a-brac.'

If Adele had said 'arms dealer' Miss Egan wouldn't have been any more shaken.

'That's not a career for a woman!'

'There are loads of women working on Tommyfields, or in the covered market — '

'*Tommyfields!* On the market? You want to work on the *market?*' Miss Egan managed to make the word sound like *sewer.* 'What good is an education if you end up on the market next to coarse men selling cheap teapots and chamber pots!'

'I like it there!' Adele replied hotly. 'You can learn things, and people are nice to me.'

'You could be a nurse.'

'I don't want to be a nurse!'

'Or a teacher.'

'I don't want to be a teacher either.'

'What about a hairdresser?'

'*Hairdresser!*' Adele repeated, horrified. 'What would I want to do that for?'

'Times have changed, women want different things now. In my day we were more sensible, but now . . . ' Reluctantly Miss Egan pulled her thoughts back to the present. 'Well, anyway, since the war ended, women want to change their lives. There's a lot of money to be made from hairdressing and such things.'

'I want to be a dealer.'

'Don't be ridiculous! That would take years to do properly. Unless, of course, you want to follow — ' Miss Egan skidded to a halt, both of them fully aware of what she had been about to say: *Unless you want to follow in your father's footsteps.*

'I'm going to do it,' Adele replied, her tone freezing. 'I'm going to work part time somewhere whilst I learn the business properly. You'll see, one day I'll work in — or even *own* — one of those big antique shops in Manchester or Liverpool.'

Her patience gone, Miss Egan snapped, 'It's ridiculous!'

'To you, maybe. But not to me,' Adele replied, her voice composed. 'I know what I'm doing.'

'Well,' Miss Egan snorted, 'I wish I had a pound for every time some idiot girl's said that.'

15

Mr Norman Buckley was five foot eight. He told everyone he was five foot eleven but that was only if the other person was standing in a trench. Having built up a considerable fortune in sanitary ware, he was the owner of a fine house on the outskirts of Rochdale, a loving wife and an impressively plain daughter. With heavy bushy eyebrows jutting over ink-black eyes, coarse black hair and a powerful frame, Norman Buckley was not a man to be messed about. And so he told everyone, several times a day. He wasn't to be messed about by his tailor, his wife, or his daughter. If anyone tried it they had better watch out. He was a dragon when he was roused.

'*A dragon!*' he bellowed, slamming his clenched fist down on the dining table, his plate and knife and fork all jumping an inch into the air. 'I have told you not once . . . '

'Eat your dinner, dear,' Beryl replied, her soft Edinburgh accent soothing as she turned back to her lamb.

' . . . but over and over again. *I will not be messed about.*'

'It's getting cold, Norman. Eat up, come on.' She smiled, twinkling at him. 'You do go on so, love. So bad for you, so very bad.'

'I — '

'I thought a game of bridge would be pleasant

tomorrow evening. I could invite the Hendersons, the Butterworths, oh, and that nice man Turner Gades.'

Norman was suddenly soothed. He had an adored — but unmarried — daughter to get off his hands. And Gades was a bachelor . . . His pale blue eyes studied his plump, pretty wife.

'Turner Gades?'

'Yes, dear. Such a pleasant man.'

'He's old.'

'Not even forty, darling.'

'He's grey.'

'Only at the temples, dear.'

'He's a shopkeeper.'

'He's an *antique* dealer.'

'Stuck up for Rochdale.'

'You know as well as I do that there's a great deal of money around there. Big houses.'

'Not as big as ours.'

'No, dear, but a lot of people rely on Gades.' She paused, laid down her knife and fork. 'You remember the canteen of cutlery . . . '

'I was messed around with that!'

She smiled impishly. 'That was *Julian* Gades, dear. Not *Turner.*'

'What kind of a name is Turner anyway?'

'Apparently a very lucky one. I mean, he came home safe from the war — a hero too. And he has a very lucrative business . . . '

Norman snorted, but he was being won over. 'I don't want my daughter living over the shop!'

'My dear,' Beryl said, laying her plump hand over her husband's. 'We have to get Mr Gades interested first, before we think of our daughter's living accommodation.'

'And this Turner Gades plays bridge?'

Beryl smiled patiently. 'I feel at this juncture that is the least of our problems, Norman.'

★ ★ ★

At the same time that Mr Norman Buckley was trying to activate his daughter's nuptials, John Courtland was regretting his own. Chewing on the end of a well-sharpened pencil, he leaned back in his chair at the bank in Union Road. It was lunchtime and he was staying behind deliberately. After all, the boss would notice his hard work, and coupled with his intelligence, he might just be on his way to a promotion. And not before time. Hadn't Susan Fleetwood said the same thing only the other day?

John spun round on his chair, glancing over the top of the glass stall into the area beyond. He had done his stint as a teller, enjoyed it even, but his longing was for the back rooms, where there was no glass. No means by which he could be observed. *The back rooms*, where the assistant deputy managers were, next to the deputy managers, and then, in the corner office, the manager. Still chewing the pencil, John slicked back his fine blond hair, sighing. It would take him a while to get to the corner office, with the view over Union Road, but he might just make it to assistant deputy manager soon, if he played his cards right.

Besides, Mr Thornhill liked him. *Mrs* Thornhill liked him too — and that was important. What was also important was that the Thornhills were friends of the Lockharts — neighbours of John's on The Coppice. It was all so insular, so neat, so tied up. If John was clever, he could map out his whole life, tracking the Thornhills and the Lockharts like a social stalker. There was only one problem — *Julia*. Tapping the pencil against his teeth, John whistled, thinking of something else Susan had said. About how a man on the up should marry a woman with contacts . . .

Suddenly unnerved, John found himself panicking. Maybe he had come a cropper with Julia. Maybe even Mr Thornhill thought so . . . Oh, she was undeniably pretty, and very attentive. But she hadn't been so attentive *lately*, not quite so impressed by him. And him up for promotion . . . Didn't she understand that he had to feel good about himself all the time? Didn't she know that he needed constant support? That he had to impress his superiors?

Apparently not. Julia didn't think that having a drink with Mr Thornhill was important, and she couldn't understand why she had to be particularly nice to Mrs Lockhart.

'What are you talking about, sweetheart?' she had asked him only the previous night. 'I don't even *like* Mrs Lockhart.'

'You should like her for me.'

'*She* doesn't have anything to do with your career, John,' Julia had replied, her tone soothing. 'Anyway, she's a nasty piece of work, always has been. She hated my father.'

'With good reason.'

Julia had tensed. 'What did you say?'

'Well, he *was* an oddball, love,' John had replied, remembering something he had overheard Mr Thornhill say. 'And Adele's turning out the same way.'

Actually, his sister-in-law needed a kick up the arse, John thought bitterly. She'd become a real irritation. Oh, he'd heard the gossip about her going to the markets and even an auction at the Ram's Head! A pub, *a girl* going into a pub . . . He would have to be very careful, he told himself. If he wanted to rise in the banking ranks he would have to make his wife fit in. And that meant her sister too . . . His attention was suddenly caught by a young woman coming back from lunch. Peering over the top of the glass partition, he noted Susan Fleetwood's slim legs and thick dark hair. This was the teller he had taken to the music hall once. The teller who liked him. A good-looking girl, whose late father had been head clerk. *The sort of girl John should have married.*

What a life he would have had then. Just the two of them, no ready-made family, no shadow of eccentric relatives always threatening to trip him up. No headstrong sister-in-law. Just a well-connected young woman who knew her place. Not like Julia, who relied on him for everything now. Oh no, Susan Fleetwood was one of the new breed of young women, independent, cool, and from a good family.

As though she realised she was being watched, Susan turned, then walked over to the partition. Leaning her slim arms on the top, she smiled.

106

'Hello, John. Working hard as usual?'

'It pays — if you want to get to the top.'

She smiled again, amused by his misplaced pomposity. 'My father said that Mr Thornhill thinks very highly of you.'

John was transfixed. 'He did? He said that?'

'Oh yes . . . ' she replied mischievously. John Courtland was good looking, but impressionable. Easy to string along. 'I think people have big ideas for you.'

With that, she walked back to her teller's position. She had no idea what Mr Thornhill really thought, or if he had even spoken to her father about John Courtland. All she knew for sure was that John was the only man in the bank worth a second glance. So what if he was married? *She* didn't want to marry him — just be with him, have some fun. Glancing over her shoulder, Susan smiled coolly and then turned away.

Mesmerised, John watched her, sexually excited. God, why had he got himself tied up so young? One woman for the rest of his life. What kind of sentence was that? It was all the fault of the bloody war, he thought angrily, flopping back into his seat. It had distorted everything, made him behave out of character. Made him do things he would live to regret.

Like marrying the wrong woman.

16

It was bitterly cold that November morning. At five thirty the knocker-up had gone around the streets, tapping on the bedroom windows to waken the workers, the gas lamps still on, smearing a smoky blue light into the foggy terraces. Getting out of bed quietly, Becky looked in on her grandmother — who was still sleeping — and then tiptoed downstairs. Her stomach was empty, but eating was difficult, the bread sticking to her throat, her mouth dry. There was no point being upset, it was just the way life went. Something that had to be done. Closing her eyes against the image, Becky thought of the mill she had visited the previous day. The noise had been overwhelming, the clatter of the looms, the shouting of the women and the clanking of what seemed to be a thousand clogs striking the bare floor.

As she had looked around, the women had regarded her curiously. It was obvious to everyone that she wasn't the usual mill girl. Not in looks, or manner. Uneasily Becky had found herself staring at the end of one loom where there had been a basket laid underneath with a very small baby inside. The foreman explained. Women too poor to take time off brought their new offspring with them. There had even been kids born in the mill . . . Stunned, Becky had kept looking round. There were old women, sly-featured women, women who stared her out, and a few younger ones who nodded a greeting. But all in all, the image of that yawning vault — hammering to the thundering sound of the striking looms, the cotton dust falling like hell's snow — had been terrifying.

Shivering, Becky's thoughts came back to the present — and what she had to do. Drawing on her coat, she left the house and pulled the door closed behind her. She knew how hard it was for her grandmother. How Frida had sold everything she could to avoid Becky having to take menial work. But there was no more money, and there were no more choices.

Walking to the street corner, Becky stopped and listened. For a moment there was silence, then in the distance she caught the sound of women's voices and laughter. Longingly, she thought back, remembering the promise of a future that had never come.

And then — her face blank — she walked on.

★ ★ ★

'Oh, for God's sake!' John exploded, his hand slamming down on the kitchen table. Flinching, Julia stepped back.

'But I don't want Adele to leave school so young. She's not sixteen yet. She should stay on . . . '

'She's nearly sixteen. And why make her stay on? She doesn't want to,' John replied, calming himself and taking a seat by the fire in the kitchen. Pulling down his white cuffs, he let the beer take effect and placate him. 'Julia, your sister knows her own mind.'

'My parents wouldn't have wanted her to leave school.'

'Your parents are dead.'

'I know that, John,' she replied, feeling a cool draught of anxiety.

They were growing apart, Julia thought. She had seen the signs for a long while, but ignored them. After all, marriage was hard, everyone knew that. Everyone said there were good times and bad. Wasn't that what her own mother had told her? She would ride it out with John. They were just going through a bad patch. Nothing to worry about. He still loved her, still made love to her. Often, in fact. And she tried not to bother him about anything — especially now, when he was up for a promotion before Christmas . . . Julia could tell that the waiting was playing on his nerves; he was edgy to a fault.

It was just that she had *had* to ask for his help in this. And who did a woman go to for help but her husband? After all, Julia couldn't confide in Adele. Could hardly ask her younger sister for help when it concerned her. Maybe, Julia thought, if she had been living with her husband alone, a newly married couple without family — even a sister — maybe then it would have been easier. She winced. What was she talking about? She loved her sister. Hadn't it been Adele and her, long before she had married John?

Regarding her husband thoughtfully, Julia remembered what Adele had said only a little while ago.

'John doesn't know how lucky he is. He came here, to a readymade home he could never have earned himself. He should be nicer to you . . . '

But that was what you did for your husband. Shared everything with him. That was what you did — wasn't it? Julia paused, irritated and suddenly allowing herself to recognise John's ungratefulness. She had only asked for help! Surely she had given him enough in return?

'Darling,' he murmured suddenly.

'What?'

'Oh, come on, don't be cross with me,' he cooed. Julia relaxed and slipped on to his knee, all criticism put on hold. 'Don't let's fight about this. If Adele wants to leave school, let her.'

'But she wouldn't have a career . . . '

'*You* haven't got a career.'

'But I'm married,' Julia replied, burying her head against her husband's neck.

He knew that, only too well.

'Not all women want to get married these days,' he went on, glancing at the clock hurriedly.

He would be late, but Susan would wait for him. His guilt was fading fast. After all, the way Julia was nagging him — what man could put up with that? She had *forced* him into another woman's arms.

'Adele's after a job in that little antique shop in Failsworth. She's determined to get it, even though I told her Saul Hill was a swine of a man. Anyway, she insists that she can learn the trade that way. You know, do what our parents did.'

'There you are!' John replied, eager to be gone. 'She's got it all worked out. I tell you,

111

she'll do things her own way, be independent. Some women want to have their own lives.'

'Maybe they do. But I wouldn't have any life without you,' Julia replied soothingly. 'I wouldn't *want* to have a life without you.'

★ ★ ★

The fog was choking, the hooter sounding out into nothingness as the mill gates swung open. As one, the mill workers moved forwards, some talking, all heads down against the bite of the November night. Even though the gas lamps were lit, there was hardly any visibility. Becky pushed forward with the crowd, a man ringing his bicycle bell angrily as she stepped off the kerb. Fighting tears, she turned for home. The famous camaraderie of the mill girls had not been extended to her; instead they had mocked her accent and her clothes, one woman throwing a bobbin into the workings of Becky's loom so that the runner jammed, the infernal clanking of the juddering machine bringing the foreman running.

He had been furious, bellowing about how Becky had to shape up or get out. He couldn't have shirkers, he said. And then he'd set up the loom again and Becky had threaded the cotton, the white dust settling in the coal blackness of her eyelashes and hair. Beside her a woman with pale eyes and thin, marked arms stared at her viciously.

By the time Becky had been working for three hours, her hands were cut from the cotton, her thumbs bleeding. Exhausted from not having slept the previous night, her head thumped from the noise of the looms and the gabble of the women.

'Over here! Over here!' was the constant cry, followed by the clatter of bobbins thrown into a trolley pushed by a lad of no more than ten. He too had the same resigned look, the fine white dust making a pale spectre of his face.

I shall go mad here, Becky had thought, longing for home. Glancing upwards, she looked deep into the vault of the ceiling, the white cotton dust falling down on her, the skylights black already in the late November afternoon. She suddenly longed for her grandmother. The cruel truth of her past shimmered in front of her. Her parents were gone. Her mother was never coming for her. The mill was her home now, and it wasn't going to be for a week, or a month, but maybe for a long, long time.

Without glancing back at the mill gates, Becky moved on into the fog. Several times she heard bicycle bells ringing, men coughing, or a woman shrilly whistling a music hall tune. Her grandmother — the whole extent of her family — was helpless now. The only person Becky had left was relying on her . . . Suddenly light-headed, Becky stopped. She felt abandoned, as though the world had dismissed her. As though, after being discarded as a child, she was now being discarded as a human being.

'Hey!'

Turning, Becky peered into the fog. A figure was hurrying towards her.

'*Adele?*'

Adele nodded, linking arms with her friend. 'I thought,' she said simply, 'you might like some company.'

17

It all happened very quickly. Suddenly it was as though some malicious force had grabbed the house on The Coppice and rattled it, making everything shatter. Within weeks the even tenor of life had disintegrated into violent chaos. And it had all begun with Adele's first job.

She had been warned that Saul Hill was a bitter, difficult man. His large, bald head was as shiny as a doorknob; his watery gaze slid from customer to stock and back again, as though at any minute someone could pocket a sideboard. Widowed since his thirties, he hated company and had run the shop alone until ill health had forced him to employ someone. Adele had been determined that that someone would be *her*. Saul Hill thought otherwise. She insisted. He resisted. She persisted. He relented ... He didn't like her, but she was cheap — and keen. Not that he was impressed by her enthusiasm. Saul Hill wasn't impressed by anyone. He didn't like to waste money, time or breath.

The previous day Adele had arrived early to find him sitting behind his counter, winding a clock.

'Morning, Mr Hill.'

His limpid gaze moved to her and then back to the clock. Nonplussed, Adele continued, 'What shall I do?'

'Serve.'

'Customers?'

He gazed at her as though she was retarded.

'Nah, monkeys,' he replied nastily, moving towards the back door, his silhouette grotesque. 'Oi, you!'

Jumping, Adele turned. 'Yes, Mr Hill?'

'I've got my eye on you! I'm going out until closing time, but I've got my eye on you. You can't be too careful with people. They take your things, take anything they fancy.'

She flushed. 'Not me!'

'Nah,' he said dismissively, looking her up and not, 'maybe not. Or then again, maybe so.'

Edgy, Adele moved behind the counter, listening as the old man walked out into the big back yard. The shop clock read ten minutes past nine. The whole day and God knew how many others, stretched out before her.

'Why go to work for *him*?' Julia had asked her sister repeatedly. 'He's a vile old man.'

'There are no other jobs going in antiques.'

'*Bric-a-brac*,' Julia replied, smiling and nudging her sister. 'Hardly antiques in Failsworth. You should have looked around a bit longer.'

'I wanted to start work. You know, get on with it. And besides, Mr Hill said I could have the odd afternoon off to go to sales and auctions. There's not many other jobs would let me do that. And I'm bringing in a wage.'

'Well, mind he doesn't make you do all his running and fetching,' Julia replied protectively. 'Saul Hill's never had an employee before. Make sure he treats you right.'

A sudden shadow at the window brought

Adele's attention back to the present. It was Saul Hill peering in at her before moving off down the street. Relieved, Adele watched him go. In her dark dress and neat black stockings, her hair tied back from her face, she was the perfect shop assistant and trainee dealer.

Half an hour passed. Adele, bored with sitting at the counter, looked out at the Failsworth street outside. No one seemed to even pause to look into Mr Hill's window. And it was easy to see why. Everything was clean, but it was cluttered, without any kind of order. Oak sideboards and a couple of china chamber pots nestled uneasily against an old painting of a vicar. Deep in thought, Adele's gaze moved from the window to the street. If she rearranged the objects, people would be more likely to look in. And besides, why not keep herself busy? She was doing nothing else, and it was pointless just sitting around. Mr Hill would be pleased, surely?

For the next two hours Adele rearranged the window. A couple of housewives stopped and looked in, intrigued by the slim young woman tugging and straining to move a Victorian commode. But after a moment they passed on, bound for the butchers. Adele wasn't bothered. By the end of the day she would have people *flocking* to look in. Taking off her cardigan, she blew back her hair from her eyes and began to push the sideboard. It was hard work, but worth it. The window was already looking better. You could finally see what stock there was.

Exhaling, Adele leaned against the sideboard and then went into the back to eat her lunch.

She had been told that she could take three quarters of an hour, but after fifteen minutes she was back at work in the window. Months accumulation of dust made her sneeze as she tidied, polished and rearranged. By the time the daylight was fading at four that afternoon, Adele had transformed Saul Hill's window.

Satisfied, she wiped her hands and moved out into the street. The first snow was falling as she pulled on her coat, a man stopping to glance in at the window.

'How much is that fire iron?'

'Oh, hold on, sir,' Adele said, thrilled. 'I'll go and look for you.'

The man followed her into the shop, looking round. 'Old Hill dead, then, is he?'

'No!' Adele replied, shocked. 'It's my first day here and I was just tidying up.'

''E won't like that,' the man replied, paying for the fire iron and looking around disapprovingly. 'Man of 'abit is Saul Hill. 'E won't take kindly to some woman showing 'im where 'e's been going wrong.'

Flushing, Adele hurried to explain. 'I was just trying to help . . . '

'Nah, 'e won't like a chit of girl showing 'im what's what.'

By this time uneasy, Adele was beginning to wonder if she had time to put everything back where it had been before. It was her first day, after all; maybe she *had* got carried away. Maybe she should have minded her own business.

'*What the hell!*'

Both Adele and the customer turned at the

same moment to see Saul Hill walking in from the back. His bulbous gaze moved around the shop slowly, his lips tight as a closed zip. Then, from somewhere deep in his chest, a low rumble started.

'Mr Hill — ' Adele began, but she was cut off immediately.

'How dare you!' Saul Hill erupted, his tucked-in head jerking from side to side. *'How dare you!'*

'I was just trying to help,' Adele replied, mortified and embarrassed. Out of the corner of her eye she could see the customer watching, obviously relishing her discomfort. 'I thought — '

'*No thinking!*' Mr Hill roared. 'You're paid to keep shop.' He walked around, pacing his petty Failsworth kingdom. 'Where's the brass scuttle? You taken it?' He moved towards Adele, peering into her face. 'I know why you moved it all around — *covering up!* That's what you were doing. Covering up for your theft!'

'I haven't taken anything!' Adele said, stepping back, horrified. 'How dare you!'

'How dare I?' he snapped. *'I'm not the thief.'*

'Neither am I!' Adele hurled back, her voice wavering. It was all so unfair. She had just been trying to help, to keep busy. And the old sod was accusing her of being a thief — and in front of a customer. 'You can't talk to me like that!'

Saul Hill paused, his eyes narrowing. 'Turn out your pockets.'

'*What!*'

'Turn them out!'

'No!' Adele replied, close to tears. 'I haven't done anything wrong.'

'I'll get the police.'

She was badly frightened now. '*The police*! But I haven't done anything!' she said anxiously, hurriedly turning out her pockets and emptying her handbag on to the counter.

How dare he? she thought, her face scarlet. How dare he! The incident would be all over Failsworth in a matter of hours, the customer relishing his ringside view. Humiliated and upset, she watched the old man rifle through her things, then she snatched up her bag, her temper rising.

'How dare you call me a thief!'

'Maybe I was a bit hasty. You — '

'Can keep your job!' she snapped, walking to the door and slamming it closed behind her.

* * *

Busy, Rebecca turned away from the loom. Her beauty was becoming more obvious by the day, but she never played on it, never encouraged male interest. She didn't have to; many of the men at the Ash mill had already noticed and tried their luck, but her answer was always the same. No, thank you. Her attitude won her some friends, the women less threatened by her as it became clear that she wasn't a tramp. But others envied her too much to accept her, and still kept their distance.

A good worker, she made decent money and undertook extra shift work. But when she had caught a cold that winter, it had turned into bronchitis and soon she had been laid off. Suddenly the pressure of her situation had intensified. If she didn't work, she didn't get paid. She *had* to get back to the mill . . . But wishing and doing were two different things, and hard as she tried, Rebecca hadn't been able to hurry her recovery. Before long she had been off for three weeks and her meagre savings had been all but used up.

Then late one night, hearing a knock on the door, Frida had let in a young, ruddy-faced man, holding his cap in his hands.

'Mrs Altman?'

She had nodded,

'I'm Billy Kerr. Foreman at the Ash mill.'

At that moment Rebecca had made her way downstairs. She was drawn and pale, the illness obviously having taken its toll.

Ignoring Frida's curious gaze, Rebecca had shown the foreman into the front room. 'I'm coming back to work tomorrow.'

'Yer job's in the balance,' he had said, his tone suddenly sympathetic. 'I don't want to lose yer, Becky. Yer a good worker.' His hand had gone out to rest lightly on hers. 'I've covered fer yer best as I could, but the boss will have a word to say if I cover fer yer any longer.'

'You won't need to,' Rebecca had replied, withdrawing her hand. She had known what he meant, and was rejecting it. Not because he wasn't trying to help her, but because she would rather have dropped dead at the loom than slept with the foreman to keep her job. 'I'll be back in the morning.'

Her thoughts returning to the present, Becky noticed a shadow fall over her work, but didn't turn. Billy Kerr was watching her. He always was. Always ready to help. And from the sounds of it, popular. Certainly well liked by the women, and fancied by a few. But that wasn't Rebecca's way. She knew it, and the women knew it. But some — the ungenerous — wondered how long she would hold out.

18

John's head was spinning, confusion making an ass out of him. What was going on? What on earth was going on? He'd been so sure of that promotion; hadn't everyone expected him to get it? Hadn't Susan Fleetwood intimated that it was in the bag for him? Gulping at the air, John leaned against the outside wall of the bank, fighting panic. Snow began to fall, but he didn't even notice it.

Instead he was reliving Mr Thornhill's earlier words. Mr Thornhill, the man who liked him, the man he had cultivated so carefully, taken out in his car. Bought drinks for in the pub.

'John, you're not promotion material.'

'But . . . '

'There are two other men further up the ladder than you. Older and, it has to be said, wiser.'

Bewildered, John's mouth fell open. He knew suddenly that he looked foolish, and his self-esteem folded like a circus tent.

'You said . . . '

'I never said anything, John. You got the idea into your head, but I didn't put it there.' Mr Thornhill paused, feeling sorry for the man. Honestly, John Courtland wasn't the kind of person you could give responsibility to. He was too easily led, too impressionable. 'Listen, if you stay with the bank for a while, you could perhaps

123

work your way up to chief teller.'

'Chief teller!' John had hollered, aghast. His confidence was smashed, his confusion complete. And now he was feeling something else: a fool. Bitterness made him strike out childishly. 'I'm more than a chief teller.'

'Not to us,' Mr Thornhill had replied sadly, leaving his office and walking out into the bank.

Beside himself, John had followed him. He had no one to advise him, and he overreacted.

'That was supposed to be my bloody job!' he had said, losing his temper and turning on Mr Thornhill.

'John, your time will come . . . '

'It's my time now!' he had replied, his face white with shock. 'You led me on.' Then he had pointed at Susan, who was watching him — as all the bank tellers were. 'And so did *you*.'

Stunned, she had turned away, but John had blustered on blindly. 'I thought you and I were going to be together.'

Her expression amused, she had turned back to him then. And he had wanted to hit her, to strike out. She had lied to him, egged him on, and now he was making a fool of himself. Everyone watching, laughing at him.

'You're a married man,' she had said simply, raising her eyebrows at Mr Thornhill as if to say, *Honestly, the man is crazy! What can a girl do?*

'You went out with me.'

'You're a colleague. We all go out with each other at the bank,' Susan had replied, cool in the face of his emotional barrage.

John could feel the suppressed amusement

around him. The nudges between the tellers. The full, grotesque mortification of his humiliation. Sweating, he turned from one face to another, then back to Susan.

'I thought you liked me.'

Hearing a snigger from behind him, John had spun round to face his tormentors — and it was then that he had caught the look on Mr Thornhill's face. It said — clearer than words — *You're a fool. A married man obsessed by a pretty teller. What inappropriate behaviour. We can't have that at the bank. Oh no, you're not one of us. And obviously never will be.*

'I think you should leave, John,' Mr Thornhill had said, his tone disapproving.

'She egged me on! *She egged me on!*' John replied, trying to recover some ground and yet knowing that he was alienating his boss further with every syllable. 'She's nothing more than a bitch — '

'Get out!' Mr Thornhill had snapped. There wasn't going to be a promotion for John Courtland. There wasn't even going to be a job. 'Get out and don't come back.'

Pushing himself away from the wall, John started walking. He was still in his shirtsleeves, carrying his hat, his coat over his arm, his suit mottled with snowflakes. His head fizzed with confusion. Everyone had lied to him! *Everyone had lied!* Thornhill, Susan Fleetwood — all of them. *And Julia too.* After all, hadn't she been the one who'd insisted he was going places? Hadn't she told everyone? Bragged about him? Said he was up for a promotion which was

125

already his? It was her fault, all her fault. Now he would have to face the world, which was going to laugh at him. And it was all because of her . . . Dragging his feet, John walked on, the snow falling more heavily. He was mortified. He had lost everything. His job, his status, his woman. Not that Susan Fleetwood had seen it that way. She had obviously thought it was just a fling, and judging from the expressions on some of the other bank tellers' faces, it wasn't the first time either. And he had been taken in! Thought there was a future for them! That he would be promoted — a big shot, with a stylish wife.

In reality he had Julia. The woman who irritated him, the woman who — indirectly — had made him into a fool. Limp with self-pity, John trudged on. He would have to go home, there was nowhere else to go. But he knew only too well that he was weak and wouldn't be able to face the mockery, the humiliation of his downfall . . . God, it had all gone so wrong! He'd been a soldier, a hero, once. He'd had a future. What had happened to him?

Julia had happened to him. It was all her fault.

★ ★ ★

Walking in through the back door, Adele paused, listening to the shouting from above. Oh God, she thought, hurrying in. Someone else had had a bad day . . . Moving into the kitchen, she put on the kettle. It would be better to stay out of it; hadn't she learned her lesson about interfering? The slam of a door overhead made her flinch, the sound of John's voice raised violently reawakening an old memory.

Putting down the cup she was holding, Adele moved to the bottom of the stairs. For an instant she glanced towards the understairs cupboard where she had hidden so many years before.

'*John!*' her sister was pleading in the bedroom above. 'Please, wait. Let's talk about it!'

'I don't want to talk.' He had been drinking. Not drunk, just fired up, chock-full of disappointment and bitterness. 'I want to get away from here. From you! From this bloody place!'

'John, don't. Calm down!'

'Get out of my way!' he snapped back, coming out and stopping at the head of the stairs, a suitcase in one hand, his coat in the other. 'Adele,' he said nastily. 'Looks like you and your sister are going to be alone again.'

Hurriedly he descended the stairs, pushing past his sister-in-law and making for the front door.

Surprised, Adele moved over to him. 'What's happened?'

'What's happened?' he repeated viciously. 'I've buggered up my life, that's what's happened! I married the wrong woman. I had the wrong job. I didn't get the promotion — and now it's coming up to Christmas and the one place on earth I don't want to be is *here*.'

Adele could see her sister at the top of the stairs, watching them.

'John,' she said quietly, 'don't leave Julia. Don't leave her, please. She loves you so much.'

He turned, white-gilled with disappointment and self-pity. 'Does she? Does she really?'

'You know she does,' Adele replied. 'Look, if you don't want me around, I can move out. Go and live somewhere else.'

'Oh, it's not you, Adele,' he retorted peevishly. 'It's you *and* your sister, *and* bloody Thornhill, *and* this tin-pot house. Which was never *my* bloody home.'

Slowly Julia came down the stairs towards her husband. John turned to look at her. 'You wrecked my life. You held me back!' he said viciously. 'I can't *breathe* with you around.'

Julia sat down heavily on the stairs, her head hanging.

'Don't talk to her like that!' Adele admonished him. 'She's never done anything to you except try to make you happy.'

'Well it didn't work,' John replied, his tone mean. 'And I'm getting out now, whilst I still can.'

Julia's head shot up. 'You can't.'

Slowly, he turned back to his wife. 'Really? Give me one reason to stay.'

'I'm pregnant.'

PART TWO

I wanted to say I was helpless
But that was only a word.
I wanted to say I was sorry
But that sounded absurd.
So both of us stayed silent
And nobody was heard.

Anon

The third night after John left, Julia lost the baby.

We kept the miscarriage a secret from everyone. Only John knew, and he wasn't telling. He would probably have said it was a lie anyway. Just a ploy to keep him at home. But Julia hadn't lied, and their child hadn't lived.

She cried for days and then stopped suddenly. For a week or so she would seem to be all right, then she would break down again. Of course it wasn't just losing a husband, but the manner in which she had lost him. Not in the war, when she could have mourned a hero, but in a sordid, pedestrian way. After he left, we heard rumours about his affair and someone told us all about the argument at the bank.

Our next-door neighbour, Mr Redfern, was very understanding, but his wife — who had always loathed our family — shunned us like lepers. Which we were to some. Social pariahs. There were some who were sympathetic, surprisingly so. Mrs Short at the florist, for one — empathy coming from the most unlikely place. But to others, Julia had failed as a woman. She had not managed to keep her husband. She had given him a ready-made home, status — and still lost him. How careless was that? How like our reckless, capricious parents? Oh yes, some said, blood will out.

So our roles were reversed. Julia, who had looked after me, was now my charge. I know how desperately she waited for the footsteps at the door, the letter which never came — just as I did. For months I hoped for John's return, but there was no word. And finally hope ran out.

Alone again, we needed as much money as we could raise. After a couple of weeks, Julia went back to work at the florist's, full time. As for me, I took the tram to Failsworth. The old sod Saul Hill was sitting at the counter. He hadn't changed the window dressing, and said nothing when I walked in. And so I stayed there. Until damaging and incredible circumstances forced me out.

But I'm jumping ahead in my story, and that won't do. So now we go back to the time after John left . . .

19

Having already taken over half an hour, Julia was still arranging the small bunch of flowers on the florist's counter. Trying not to show her impatience, Mrs Short hovered behind her employee, her body tightly corseted, pince-nez balanced on the bridge of her squat little nose.

'Just a bit more on that side, love.'

Julia pushed another piece of fern into the arrangement, her tone listless. 'I'm trying to do a good job.'

'And you are — just be a bit quicker about it,' Mrs Short retorted, tapping her maternally on the shoulder.

Oh dear, she thought, poor Julia had certainly changed since John Courtland upped and left. She wasn't the woman she had been. No happy, bubbling, giddy little ways, no more *my husband this, my husband that*. Obviously she had had no idea about his cheating. His running around with another woman behind her back. Mrs Short considered the matter, remembering the weak but attractive John Courtland. God knows he had fallen on his feet with Julia, but then maybe he had now found an even comfier billet? She stole a glance at her silent employee. It was strange that in the months since he had left no one had heard a word about him. There had been rumours, naturally. The towns and villages in the area thrived on juicy gossip. But no sightings of John Courtland — and no sniff of a reconciliation. He had left The Coppice and apparently never looked back. Decisive. For once.

Julia was all too aware of her employer hovering behind her, and for an instant she wanted to throw the bouquet on to the floor. *A wedding bouquet* ... She found her hands shaking. She had hoped that the pain and humiliation of her husband's desertion might have lifted a little. But it had intensified. She thought about John constantly, ran over in her mind their marriage, month by month, day by day, looking for the mistakes she had made. The reason she had driven him away. Forced him to turn to another woman. It had all been her fault. Wasn't that what everyone was saying?

Mrs Redfern next door had had a field day. In fact, only weeks after John had left, Julia had heard her talking to Mrs Lockhart in the street.

'Well, she must have been a poor wife. Couldn't keep house — or maybe that awful Adele drove him away.'

In an instant Julia had walked over to the gossips, her expression stony. 'My sister didn't drive my husband away! Neither did I. He was no good ... ' Her head went up defiantly. 'And anyway, if you must know, *I threw him out.*'

For one hovering instant Julia had watched the two women consider this piece of information, and then, to her relief, accept it. After all, it was one thing to be deserted, quite another to send your husband packing. The lie was the first good feeling Julia had had for weeks, and she clung to it like a cripple to a cross. From that moment onwards, the story was fixed in stone: Julia Courtland had thrown her husband out. He may have cheated on her and left home — but she had made him. She wasn't quite the victim she appeared.

Naturally Adele had backed her up. Anything to save Julia's face, to limit the humiliation. But in supporting her sister, she realised that the lie had quickly become reality in Julia's mind. Along with a growing hatred of John Courtland and all men. The Julia who had longed to be a wife now despised males, covering her despair with bitterness.

Anxiously, Adele watched her sister's metamorphosis. Even Julia's movements altered, until they were jerky with distress, her disappointment ageing her. Then one night Adele woke to hear Julia crying desperately, sobs that echoed in the silent house. Quickly she made her way into the bedroom and lay down on the bed next to her sister. An old memory came back — of the two of them after their parents' deaths.

'You'll find someone else,' Adele said gently.

'I don't care.'

'You do.'

'I don't want anyone else!' Julia snapped, her voice breaking. 'I loved John so much . . . All I wanted was to be a wife.'

Adele took her hand. 'You still will be. You're young . . . '

Angrily, Julia hissed back, '*I don't need John!* I don't need any man! I was so stupid. Thought it was so important to have a husband. God, what a fool I was! He had everything here — I adored him, he had a good home. Jesus! I hate him for this! *I hate him!*' Her terrifying anger abated suddenly, her voice failing. Slowly she turned her head towards her sister, her face ghostly in the half-light. 'You'll never leave me, will you? We've still got each other, haven't we? Just you and me, like before. Like always?'

Cautiously Adele nodded. 'It will get better, Julia. I promise, everything will work out — '

'Yes,' she agreed eagerly, soothed like a small child. 'If we stay together, it'll all be all right.'

★ ★ ★

Her hair newly permed, Pauline Buckley walked into Kendal Milne, on Deansgate, Manchester, with her mother. For the best part of an hour they browsed through the clothes department, trying to find something for Pauline to wear that Saturday. It was going to be — she said firmly — her last try.

'You can't give up so easily,' Beryl Buckley replied in her soft Scottish burr. 'A man like Turner Gades has to be wooed.'

'I thought it was the woman who had to be wooed.'

'Don't be petulant, sweetheart. The bigger the fish, the better the bait.'

Pauline considered her mother's words and then paused, looking at a cerise dress. Wincing, her mother guided her over to an elegant black evening outfit. After all, cerise was not kind to hips over a certain size.

'What about — '

'He doesn't know I'm alive,' Pauline said suddenly, her voice a weary drone. 'It's a waste of time.'

'Your father doesn't think so,' Beryl replied. 'And he's not a man to be messed about,' they both chorused.

'Quite,' Beryl said, smiling. 'Mr Turner Gades would make a lovely son-in-law.'

'I thought Father didn't like him.'

'He's changed his mind.'

'Or did *you* change it for him?'

Beryl smiled warmly. 'One of the benefits of being married, Pauline . . . You'll find out soon enough.'

Pauline sighed, unconvinced. 'What if he's already got a girlfriend?'

'I have it on good authority that Mr Gades has no one special in his life,' Beryl replied with certainty, steering her daughter towards the changing room. 'Now, put that dress on, darling, and let me look at you.'

After a minute, Pauline emerged. The delicate black silk dress looked like a rubbing rag on her. Motherly love couldn't blind Beryl to the fact that her daughter was more duck than swan.

'Perhaps if you — '

'I'll never look right in it!' Pauline snapped, hurrying back into the changing room, her mother in hot pursuit. In the cramped space, Beryl's hat got knocked over to one side — her daughter's left arm stuck fast in the dress sleeve as she tried to take it off.

'I can't get out of it!'

137

'Ssh!' Beryl replied shortly. 'Do you want everyone to hear? If you tear this dress, we'll be made to pay for it.'

'If I don't get out of it,' Pauline snorted, red-faced, through the arm hole, 'I'll have to be buried in it.'

Carefully Beryl tried to pull her daughter's plump arm free. 'We'll try a bigger size . . .'

'What if I never get out of this one?' Pauline whined. 'I saw Mrs Forster watching us, and she'll tell everyone how fat I am, that I got stuck in a dress . . .'

'The way you go on!' Beryl retorted, laughing. 'Breathe in!'

'Breathing in won't make my arm smaller.'

'Just breathe in!'

With one gigantic effort, Beryl pulled the dress off, the sleeve making a loud ripping sound as she did so. Horrified, they both paused, holding their breath as they heard footsteps outside the cubicle.

'Having trouble, madam?'

Pauline looked pleadingly at her mother. But Beryl swept open the curtain in one swift movement, smiling winningly at the assistant. 'We love it! A perfect fit. Charge it to my husband's account, will you?'

★ ★ ★

Back in Failsworth, Saul Hill was looking out through his window, hopping from foot to foot. His bulging eyes were fixed on the snowy street outside, his hands blue-veined as he rubbed them together briskly. Watching from behind the counter, Adele wondered what had prompted such excitement from the old man, but didn't ask him. The relationship between employee and employer was a strange one. They didn't like each other, or wish to spend any time in one another's company. Saul Hill was grateful that Adele was cheap and enthusiastic; Adele was glad that she could learn about the trade from her morose boss. Beyond that, they remained little more than strangers. Adele had never forgotten Hill's distrust of her, but as the months wore on she realised the old man suspected virtually everyone of deceit.

'Bugger damn near ruined me. Stole from me,' he would say, to no one in particular.

At other times he would meet a rough dealer from the market, whispering with him in the shop's back yard. He never realised that Adele could overhear their conversation through the back door — or that she had learned a lot that way. Like how devious Saul Hill could be, deliberately chipping the edge of a piece to lower its value. Not that he wanted to rook his customers when he sold it on — often he simply wanted to hoard it for himself.

In fact, the flat above the shop was *crammed* with furniture. So much so that Saul Hill was forced to sleep cramped in a corner of his own bedroom, surrounded by a collection of books, tallboys, stuffed animals and boxed china. He *did* sell on his goods, but only after he had owned them for a while. That was the whole point of the exercise for Saul Hill — the owning.

Long past human affection, he could have a love affair with a commode, a flirtation with a washstand, or an infatuation with a bookcase. For a time he would adore his chosen idol, until something replaced it in his favour.

Though banned from the upstairs rooms, Adele had once sneaked upstairs and taken a look around. The windows had been covered with blinds, the eerie shapes of the furniture looming up around her. Hurriedly she had returned downstairs when she heard the back door slam, thinking of the shed in the yard and the impressively large outbuilding that Saul Hill always kept locked. No one knew what was in *there*. No one had ever even tried to break in, the door padlocked, the windows covered by grilles, the roof rim trimmed with glass shards.

'Old man Hill could be murdering people in there,' a local wag said drily, 'and no one would be any the wiser.'

Whatever Saul Hill *did* keep in there, his paranoia had increased so much that before long more locks had been added to the shed and the shop. That was all right for a while, until Saul decided further measures were needed. His obsession with theft grew daily, as did his attempts to prevent break-ins. The arrival of two large geese from a farm over at Uppermill marked a new episode in the shop's history. The birds soon became notorious for their savagery — running hissing, wings outstretched at anyone who so much as hesitated by the back gate. To increase their alertness Saul kept them hungry, little realising that Adele supplemented their meagre rations with bread she bought on the way to work.

Not that she had much money to waste. The loss of John's wage had hit the Ford sisters hard, and Julia's earnings — even full time — were limited. The job at Saul Hill's was vital if they were to keep afloat — however rough going it was for Adele. The old man's only virtue was his lack of interest in her. Adele couldn't have stomached his prying into John's departure.

'Ahhh . . . ' Saul Hill said excitedly, hopping from foot to foot again and sliding over to the door. He was ecstatic, gabbling, 'We have company! Big company. Big names.' He turned, as though suddenly remembering Adele was there. 'Not a word now. You hear?'

'About what?'

'What you see. Not a word. You have big eyes that see too much.' He paused, looking waspish. 'I might have to let you go.'

'What!' Adele replied, shaken. She couldn't lose her job, not when she and Julia depended on the income so much.

'You cost money.'

Her voice was pleading. 'Mr Hill, I thought you were pleased with my work . . . I can take a cut in salary if I have to, but don't fire me.'

'I might,' he replied, looking her up and down, 'if I've mind to. Then again, I might ask the geese what they think.'

Not for the first time lately Adele realised her employer was talking nonsense. But she nodded and sat down behind the counter on the hard stool, watching as a tall figure entered the shop.

The man was prematurely grey. And familiar.

'Mr Gades! Mr Gades!' Saul Hill cried, for once enthusiastic to see a human being. 'Good to have you here. Good. So good.'

Curious, Adele studied the customer, the same man who had rescued her by buying the old clock at the Ram's Head.

'Mr Gades,' Saul went on, 'so good of you to come. Got a nice piece. For you. For your shop.'

Pausing, Turner Gades noticed Adele and then looked away again. For a moment she had been about to smile, but had then thought better of it. Obviously he didn't remember her.

'You said you had a fine Derby vase?' he asked Saul.

The old man nodded and hurried into the back. There was a flurry of noise as he opened the door, the geese flapping their wings and hissing.

'BE OFF, YOU BUGGERS!'

Smiling, Turner Gades glanced at Adele. 'It's still working.'

'What?'

'The clock.'

She grinned. 'I thought you didn't remember me.'

'I was just being discreet,' he replied, 'in case you didn't want Mr Hill to know about your extracurricular activities.' He put out his hand. 'Turner Gades.'

She responded, putting out her own, 'Adele Ford.'

Another bout of manic squawking came from the back. Turner laughed.

'Do the geese go for him every time?'

'Every time,' Adele replied. 'They hate him. And it takes him ages to get all those locks off the door of the warehouse.'

Amazed, Turner shook his head and looked round. 'Weird place. It's been here for years, you know. One of Failsworth's landmarks. In his prime, Mr Hill used to have some good pieces. Still does, now and again. My father bought a French sofa off him once, for his best customer, Mrs Ninette Hoffman.'

Adele raised her eyebrows. 'Not the Lydgate Widow?'

He frowned. 'Who?'

'My father used to talk about the woman who lived in the weird house by the church in Lydgate.' Eagerly, Adele warmed to her theme, her imagination inflamed. 'Can you imagine living in that lovely place? That's what I want one day. A beautiful house with a high stone wall around it. So I can keep the people I love in, and the rest of the world out.'

An old memory, long forgotten, stirred inside Turner.

'My father,' Adele went on, 'said the Lydgate Widow still haunts the house.'

'Your father has a vivid imagination.'

'He did,' Adele agreed quietly. 'He's dead now.'

Taken aback, Turner Gades said awkwardly, 'I'm sorry . . . '

Adele hurried on. 'You might have known him, seen him around. He was a dealer. Well, not really . . . Victor Ford.'

'*He* was your father?' Turner Gades asked, surprised. 'That explains a lot. I wondered why you were so interested in antiques — even though you don't know much about clocks.'

She laughed. 'I nearly got landed, didn't I?'

'You're just starting out, you'll learn. I made terrible mistakes at first,' he replied kindly, taking to her.

She was bright, he thought, confident and likeable, just as her father had been. But Victor Ford — for all his charm — had made little money, and Turner knew how hard it was to make a living in the trade, especially for a female. But then again, Adele was young and pretty; before long she would have a husband to look after her.

'Is that why you came to work here?'

Adele nodded.

'I imagine Mr Hill would be a hard employer.'

'Very,' she agreed. 'In fact, he's just threatened to fire me.'

'Really?'

'I don't think he meant it. But you never know. And I need the wage.' She paused, then pushed her luck. Times were difficult; it paid to be a bit forward. 'Perhaps, if you heard of some other job in the trade ... perhaps you could keep me in mind?'

'I will,' Turner replied quietly, both of them turning to see a flustered Saul Hill walking in clutching the Derby vase.

Coughing hoarsely, he laid the vase on the counter and flicked at it with his handkerchief. Then he glanced over to Adele. 'Tea for Mr

Gades. Use the best cups.'

'Oh, don't go to any trouble . . . '

'No trouble,' Saul replied, jerking his head towards the kitchen.

Sliding off the stool, Adele moved into the back. The kitchen was old fashioned, with a black iron range and a big china sink. Curiously she glanced round, looking for the best cups. She had never seen anything other than the two thick white Tommyfields mugs that were usually pressed into service. Gingerly she opened the cupboard door under the stairs. In amongst a stack of boxes was a perfect tea service. Delicate white and red porcelain cups rested in intricate saucers; a milk jug and sugar bowl nestled beside a matching teapot. Stunned, Adele took them out and made the tea, setting out a tray and then walking back into the shop.

Saul eyed her warily, his voice a whisper. 'I know how many cups there are. You mind, now. I know.'

Infuriated, Adele poured tea for Turner Gades and then the old man, not daring to take any for herself.

'That'll do,' Saul said when she'd finished. 'You can leave early. But mind you make the time up. Go on, be gone! I'm talking business.'

Humiliated, Adele just had time to catch Turner Gades' sympathetic expression before she picked up her coat and left. The afternoon was closing in, it would be dark soon, and bitterly cold with the latest downfall of snow. Before long the roads over the moors would be impassable. She thought of Christmas suddenly,

145

of her and Julia alone. And of the previous Christmas, her sister confiding in her excitedly.

Julia had been glistening with excitement, her voice eager as she passed on the news. 'John wants to have a baby.'

'He can't, he's a bloke.'

Laughing, Julia had punched her sister's arm playfully. 'You know what I mean! He wants me to have his child.'

'What d'you think?'

'Oh, I want it too!' she had replied, her eagerness heart-rending. 'I'd love to have a baby, Adele. Just think, we'd be a proper family then. Me and John and our child — and you as its aunt. You remember how it was when *we* were children here? The house was alive, full of noise. And we could push the baby out in the pram when John was at work, have it christened up at St Anne's Church . . . '

'I can tell you haven't thought about it much.' Adele had replied, teasing her sister.

Then a cautious look had come over Julia's face, her voice low.

'I think it would be good for John. You know how he can be so indecisive sometimes? Having a child would make him responsible, a father. He would be more settled if he had a family, less likely to get sidetracked . . . '

Adele pulled her scarf around her head, trying to shake off the poignant memory. Slowly she began to walk the first part of the way home. She didn't mind the long slog, it gave her time to think. Think about her sister, about how Julia wasn't coping. Wasn't functioning. About how sad it was to see her waiting for the post every morning, always telling Adele, 'He'll write, he'll come home. He'll be back . . . '

And then raging against him when there was no news. Hating him. Calling him names. Vicious with grief.

Had she loved John Courtland *so* much? Of course she had, Adele realised. And incredibly — at times — Julia would still suddenly insist that it had all been her fault. She had been a bad wife, a poor housekeeper. She hadn't given John what he had needed. Too right, Adele thought bitterly. What he'd needed was a kick in the pants.

Against her better judgement, Adele had tried to get in touch with John herself to try to effect a reconciliation. So what if she had to humble herself? It would be worth it to see Julia happy again. But her enquiries at the bank had been met with distaste. No one wanted to talk about, or find, John Courtland. He had behaved disgracefully. Even kindly Mr Thornhill said so, urging Adele to forget her brother-in-law.

'He wasn't a good sort, dear. Your sister is better off without him.'

Julia's head would have known he was right, but her heart wouldn't have accepted it. And so, long after her husband had gone, she still veered between longing for John Courtland and loathing him.

Adele paused, hailing a tram and watching it creep towards her. Climbing aboard, she paid her fare and sat down, still thinking about Julia. Perhaps she was worrying too much. Hadn't people told her that time would heal? That Julia would meet someone else? *But who?* Adele wondered anxiously. Who came to the house on The Coppice any more? Where did her sister go, apart from her work at the florist's?

Unmarried, Julia Ford had been confident and attractive to men. Deserted, Julia Courtland was reserved, suspicious, embarrassed. Desperate to be loved — and even more desperate never to get hurt again.

20

Head down, Rebecca hurried away from the Oldham park. What in God's name had possessed her? Was this her, *was this really her?* She had always prided herself on being in control, aloof, and now she was acting like a whore. And why? She paused, breathing heavily into the night air. Because she had seen her future and feared it. Because she had seen the servitude of the Ash mill stretching out into infinity and offering no escape. Because she had felt the growing anxiety of looking after her grandmother and the worry of her own past.

Banging her fists against the brick wall, Rebecca fought tears. Of course she loved Frida, but it wasn't enough. Her heart longed for something more. Something to make her feel *wanted*. Not the lost child, the abandoned daughter, but a woman desired, made to feel chosen. Put first . . . And so she had gone with Billy Kerr. He was the best-looking lad at the Ash mill, and Rebecca had instinctively known that the only way she could score any points in an unfair world was to use the one advantage she had — her beauty. And if the mill workers were already jealous of her, they would be in awe of her now. After all, Billy Kerr was the foreman, not some yob lad off the looms.

Taking a deep breath, Rebecca shook her

head. Who was she kidding? She hadn't gone with Billy Kerr out of ambition, or to settle old scores. She had gone with him for one reason and one reason only: he had made her feel special. He had kissed her and held her, and — for a little while — made her forget her lost hopes and anxieties. With him she had closed her eyes and willingly lost her virginity in the deserted park bandstand. How sordid, Rebecca thought; almost funny. The kind of incident people made jokes about.

And how ashamed her grandmother would be if she knew. Frida Altman, who had come from a good family with money, a beautiful home abroad, a background of culture, learning, pride. But now Frida Altman's granddaughter was working in a mill and having sex with the grimy-handed foreman . . . Biting her lip, Rebecca stared ahead. It wasn't Billy Kerr's fault. He was a pleasant man, kind even. In fact, his kindness was what had seduced her. That, and his looks. And the fact that he — who could have anyone — had *chosen her.*

But for what? Rebecca thought, leaning back against the wall. Not for love. Not for marriage. But for some quickie in the park. Some fling another mill girl might laugh off. A conquest, of sorts. But not to Rebecca Altman. Slowly she turned her footsteps towards home. Tomorrow she would go back to the mill and find out just how kind Billy Kerr really was. Whether he had bragged about his conquest or stayed silent.

Frida put down her newspaper and looked up

as Rebecca walked in. 'Adele called round earlier.'

'Sorry I missed her.'

'She's still letting her sister rely on her too much,' Frida Altman said incisively. 'How long has it been now since that awful man left?'

Taking off her coat, Becky moved over to the day bed, relieved that Frida's attention was occupied elsewhere. For the last four months her grandmother had been sleeping downstairs, the stairs too difficult for her to climb any more. Despite ill health and advanced arthritis, Frida's brain was as alert as it had always been. Her days were spent staring out of the window, her front room a repository for all the local news. But although her intelligence had remained intact, Frida's world had soured. The life she had wanted for her granddaughter had not materialised. To Frida's horror, the temporary job at the Ash had become permanent. Once, their family had been prosperous, admired, but within a few short decades war and death had driven them down the social scale. They were now of no account; two women alone, with no men to protect them, little money and all possessions long sold off.

Sighing, she turned back to Becky. 'So, how long *is* it since John Courtland left his wife?'

'Just over two years,' Becky replied, thinking of Julia.

Over the previous two years she had undergone a complete metamorphosis; fiercely jealous of her sister and angry when Adele went out or — God forbid — saw a boy. Every male

Adele had taken home had been ripped apart by Julia — *he's no good; he's got cold eyes; he's a bad lot, a liar* — whereas in reality the only thing wrong with them was that they were rivals for Adele's attention. Something Julia couldn't stomach.

'Adele should get out of that house.'

'And go *where?*' Becky replied wearily. 'They have to club together to keep the place running.'

'Is the house *that* important?' Frida replied. 'To Adele, I mean?'

Becky nodded. 'She loves the place. It was her parents' home.'

'But if they can't afford to keep it . . . '

'They can, if they're careful,' Becky retorted, thinking of Julia's frequent illnesses, her colds, her sprained ankles, her sore throats. Her numerous whining means of getting attention, of keeping her sister close. 'Thing is . . . '

'*Yes?*' Frida replied, sensing some news.

'Adele's met someone.'

'Good!'

'And I've told her not to tell her sister. If she does, Julia will put a stop to it.'

★ ★ ★

A month earlier the fair had come to Failsworth and Adele — always a lover of fairgrounds — had begged Julia to go with her. Finally, exasperated by her sister's excuses, Adele had gone alone. On the way she had called at Park Street to see if Becky wanted to go along with her, but had been told that her friend was at work. Strange, Adele had thought, she had been sure that Becky had told her she wasn't working that Saturday.

Arriving at the fairground, Adele nodded to a number of people she knew. Now this was more like it! she thought happily, walking around the stalls and pausing beside the candy floss.

'By 'eck! Adele! Yer here.'

She smiled, seeing Mrs Hodges. 'I thought you were on the market.'

'Not when there's a fair in town. My family have been making candy floss for years.' She whipped up a frothy confection and passed it over to Adele. 'Free.'

'Free!'

'If you mind the stall for a while.'

Adele nodded willingly. 'Sure. Take as long as you like,' she said, moving behind the machine and watching as Mrs Hodges showed her how to work it.

'Got it?'

'Got it,' Adele agreed, watching as the woman walked off.

A moment later she was serving two small lads and then a woman with a pram in tow. From her vantage point Adele could see most of the comings and goings on the field, and her attention was suddenly drawn to the raffle. Leaning back, she could just see the stallholder pocketing half of the stubs he had taken off the tickets he had sold. Cheat, Adele thought angrily. That would halve the winnings in one go — and double his takings.

'Can I have some candy floss?'

She glanced at the young man looking at her. He was cleanshaven, with a mass of thick blond hair and flirtatious blue eyes.

'Small or large?' Adele asked lightly.

'Large. I'm a big fella.'

'You'll soon be a fat fella if you eat too much of this,' she replied, her tone light.

He smiled, liking the look of her. 'I've not seen yer before.'

'I'm just minding the stall for Mrs Hodges.'

'Seen her before. Wish I hadn't.'

'She's OK,' Adele replied, smiling as the woman concerned moved back to the stall.

'Thanks, luv. Yer go off and have some fun now.' She glanced over to the young man. 'And mind this one, Samuel Ayres. I'm still recovering from that fleecing yer gave me last winter.'

'It were a fair price!'

'Fer a bloody millionaire,' Mrs Hodges replied, winking at Adele. 'Go on, off with yer.'

Moving away, Adele hoped that Samuel Ayres would drop into step with her. Which he did, offering her a bite of his candy floss. She paused, shaking her head, suddenly embarrassed by the attention of this confident young man.

'I've already had enough of that stuff,' she said, then quickly pointed towards a far stall. 'Look, a shooting gallery.'

'I were going to buy a raffle ticket.'

'Oh, you don't want to do that!' Adele told him hurriedly. 'It's fixed.'

'It's a fairground! *Everything's* bloody fixed!'

Sam laughed, guiding her over to the shooting range.

The stall owner was a nervous, heavy-smoking man with a kennel cough. Taking a good look at Adele, he passed a gun to Sam. 'Yer's got three gos. If yer hit a duck and it gets knocked off the row, yer get a prize.'

Nodding, Sam took aim and smacked the duck full in the side. It shook. It shivered. But it didn't fall.

'Bad luck,' the stallholder said insincerely.

'Bad luck, my arse!' Sam retorted. 'I hit that bugger full on, it should have been knocked off.'

'Yer can't have hit it as hard as yer thought.'

'If I hit it any harder, I would have brought down Manchester Town Hall!' Sam went on, standing his ground. 'I want the prize.'

'Dream on.'

Infuriated, Sam climbed over the front of the stall and grabbed a stuffed pink rabbit. The stallholder clambered after him.

'Yer can't take that!'

'I won it!'

'The 'ell yer did!'

'It's mine!' Sam shouted, both men ducking as a sudden shot sounded to the left of them.

Having hit the farthest duck full on, Adele glanced over to the stallholder with an expression of triumph. With a grunt of irritation, the man walked over to the rocking duck and knocked it over. Hooting with delight, Sam tossed the pink rabbit to Adele, jumped over the stall and grabbed her hand. Then he pulled her away, both of them laughing as they ran between the lurid fairground stalls. Exhilarated, Adele grinned at everyone. She was lit up with excitement, feeling Sam Ayres' hand in hers, admiring the way he had stood up to the stallholder. She was out of breath with running and excitement and intoxication. In fact, she was feeling the first throes of falling in love.

21

Of course it wasn't an object Beryl wanted, but if her daughter's happiness rested on the purchase of a Derby vase, so be it. Smiling, Beryl put her head on one side, regarding Turner Gades thoughtfully. He had a good appetite, she thought admiringly, wondering if his appetites went further than food. After all, he might not be twenty any more, but he looked fit enough . . . Beryl had always been open-minded. She could think or talk about sex as easily as the latest news.

Smiling to herself, Beryl studied Turner Gades and then let her gaze move to her daughter. Really, Pauline was such a sweetheart, but a bit of a clot. She sat slumped miserably in her seat, staring fixedly at her dinner plate. The girl would never learn! Beryl thought sympathetically, knowing that Turner was as interested in her daughter as she was in fly-fishing.

But that was no reason to give up. Many a marriage had been based on convenience or property.

'My daughter is very interested in antiques,' Beryl said, her tone light. 'All kinds of bits and pieces she knows about. Really quite knowledge-able.'

Smiling politely, Turner glanced over to Pauline. 'You like collecting?'

'Huh?' Pauline said, her face blank.

157

'Tell Mr Gades about your paintings,' her mother prompted her, wedging her heel into the arch of Pauline's left foot.

'Oh, yes!' she said, wincing and trying to remember what she had been taught. 'I like English painters.'

Turner nodded, trying to help her along. 'Dobson?'

'No, English.'

He pressed on manfully. 'I mean, do you like the artist Dobson?' Her face was blank. Turner shifted in his seat. 'Gainsborough? Reynolds?'

'Yeah.'

'You like them?'

Pauline nodded, her face reddening. It was ghastly, she thought to herself. The handsome Mr Gades had no interest in her, and her mother was an idiot to think she could win him round. Mortified, Pauline tried to make further conversation.

'I like tables too . . .'

Beryl made a low strangled noise in her throat.

'Really?' Turner replied, trying not to look surprised. Obviously the poor girl had been tutored to pretend that she was interested in his line of business. It was excruciating — for both of them.

' . . . and chairs . . .'

It was too much, even for Beryl.

'We do so love the vase,' she lied, interrupting. 'And we have just the place for it.'

'In the bin,' Norman said, from down the other end of the table.

'Such a wit,' Beryl replied lightly, turning back

to her guest. 'You said we could pick it up soon?'

Turner nodded. 'Mr Hill is undertaking the restoration — '

'*It's broken?*' Norman's voice rose. 'Look, I'm not a man to be messed about! I don't want any broken vases in my house.'

'*Dad,*' Pauline wailed pitifully. Beryl intervened again.

'Darling Norman, this is a fine antique vase. Anything of such an age needs some restoration to the gilding.'

'I didn't know Saul Hill could restore things.'

'Very well actually,' Turner replied, trying to keep the atmosphere light.

Having refused a number of invitations from the Buckleys, he had been finally coerced into acceptance — and was now regretting it bitterly. This wasn't the first time he had been forced into a blind date. Dear God, he thought, just how many single daughters *were* there in the north-west? He wasn't interested in settling down — couldn't people accept that? One day he would find the woman meant for him, but that was the point, *he would find her.* She wouldn't be found for him.

And yet as he thought it, he felt real pity for Pauline Buckley. She was approaching her mid twenties, miserable, awkward, her dress too tight and too contrived. All dolled up like a dressed crab set before a hopefully ravenous guest.

'A vase is a vase. What's so special about this one?' Norman went on, well into his third glass of port, Pauline mute beside him.

'This is French — '

'We always beat the French in wartime!' Norman snapped, offering the port to Turner. 'Cowardly bastards, every one of them. And all that garlic. No civilisation worth its salt eats garlic.'

This was a conversational dead end.

'About the vase,' Beryl continued finally, 'when will Mr Hill have finished the restoration?'

'In about a week,' Turner replied. 'I'll call in and check how he's doing.'

'How kind,' Beryl replied, turning to Pauline. 'Isn't that kind of Mr Gades?'

'I don't think it's kind at all!' she hissed, red-faced. 'He's just pretending to be nice and he's obviously bored and doesn't want to be here. If you hadn't bought that stupid vase he would never even have come!'

And with that, she got up and ran out of the room, sobbing.

Blinking slowly, Beryl coughed; Norman emptied his glass. The fire crackled in the grate and the wind blew outside. Turner stared ahead, as mute as a log.

'Well,' Norman said at last, 'I take it you two won't be getting engaged.'

⋆　⋆　⋆

Standing on the landing above the mill workers, Billy Kerr studied Becky thoughtfully. He could sense that she knew he was watching her, but he knew that she wouldn't look up. She never invited attention; played it down in fact. If he was honest, he was mystified by her. He had wanted her, of course, but had never thought for one moment she would have sex with him. When she did, he was thrilled, ready to brag, ready to show off that *he* had been the one to bed the best-looking girl in the mill.

But something stopped him. He could tell she hadn't slept around, could tell that their lovemaking meant something much deeper to Rebecca. Was it because she was Jewish? Different from the local girls? Or was it because she was fascinating in her aloofness? Her dignity? He felt baffled by the thought. But for all his wanting to announce his conquest, Billy couldn't. He wouldn't make her into a tart, a piece of gossip. He didn't understand why, but it would have been like sticking a knife between her shoulder blades.

In that instant a bird flew into one of the skylights above, the loud cracking making Becky glance upwards. Above her head she saw it land, and flinched. The bird had broken its neck on impact and was lying, wings spread out, its inanimate face against the glass, its eyes unseeing, gone from the world.

★   ★   ★

At the top of Hawkshead Pike, Samuel Ayres looked out over the countryside. He could see the Ash mill and the smoking chimneys of Oldham below, the moors in the distance, and could sense the turn of the season in the cold air. Even at three o'clock the December afternoon was closing in fast. And it couldn't close in fast

161

enough for him. Smiling, Sam turned and began the long walk down towards Oldham and The Coppice. He was — if he was honest — more than a little smitten with Adele Ford. She was so pretty — and yet feisty at the same time. No walkover. Hadn't she told him from day one that she was a respectable girl? And he hadn't doubted it. Funnily enough, it hadn't put him off either. It was no secret that Samuel Ayres had an eye for the girls, but this one was different.

After their meeting at the fairground he had started to visit Saul Hill's shop in Failsworth — until the old man got suspicious and accused him of casing the place.

'Your eyes are everywhere!' he hissed. 'I know my stock. Know a thief when I see one.'

Beaten, Sam owned up. 'I been coming to see your employee, Miss Ford.'

'Really?' Saul replied meanly. 'Well, I pay her wage, I pay for her to work. Not romance. You want her to keep her job?'

'Course I do.'

'Then sod off!'

Sam smiled to himself again, thinking of how she had agreed to meet him later in Tommy-fields. Not that it was his usual stamping ground, he was more of a Burnley man himself. But you went where the work was, and the stall on Tommyfields had done well for him. Apparently the local people liked his ornamental brass, especially his horse trimmings. He'd done all right that day, and later, when Adele paused by his stall, he was delighted to play along.

'How much are these?' she had asked, picking

up a pair of plain brass candlesticks.

'Not much.'

'How much is 'not much'?'

'Two shillings.'

She had blown out her cheeks and put the candlesticks down. 'You'll be a millionaire before you're thirty.'

Seeing that she was about to walk off, Sam had dropped the price.

'One shilling and sixpence.'

Pausing, Adele had turned and looked back at him, still playing a game. 'You cold?'

He had nodded. 'Freezing.'

'If you're cold, get a stall in the covered market.'

'Expensive there.'

'With your prices you could soon afford it,' Adele had replied. Sam had shaken his head and laughed.

Of course it had taken him weeks — and the cost of a regular stall at Tommyfields — to get Adele to agree to go out with him. She was only young — eighteen she told him — but smarter than her years. A walk had proved to be pleasant for both of them, then a trip to the pictures had followed. But that had been awkward. Obviously Adele wasn't used to dating and had been ill at ease. With some perception, Sam had suggested that they go to an auction for their next date.

He would never forget Adele that day, standing up on her tip-toes at the back of the pub, determined to bid for an unwieldy monks' bench. She had seen it earlier and been convinced it was worth money, counting her cash twice to see how much she had. Her enthusiasm had been so endearing, her anxiety when the pub filled up almost painful.

'It's Henry Shine,' she had whispered to Sam, motioning to the auctioneer. 'Worse for wear again.'

And then she had spotted someone else she knew and nodded across the pub. Following her gaze, Sam had seen an elegant man with greying hair — and relaxed. Thank God, he was too old to be a rival . . . By the time the monks' bench had come up for bidding, Adele had been flushed with excitement. Raising her hand, she put in the first low bid, then another, then a third when she had been challenged. Sam had known how much money she had — and knew how quickly her funds were dissolving as the bidding fever rose.

Finally there was no hope left. Dejected, Adele had turned to him and shrugged.

'Never mind,' Sam had consoled her. 'You can't get everything you want.'

'No,' she had agreed, 'but you can try.'

And that was when he had fallen in love with her.

Smiling, Sam kept walking, thinking about his girl. Because she was his girl now. Pretty Miss Ford. Lovely Adele, smart as a whip. But hellbent on bettering herself. How many times had he heard about her father? The legendary — so Adele would have it — Victor Ford? Asking around, Sam had found out the real story. Victor had been a poor dealer, but a character, with great charm. All the older dealers remembered him — and his death.

Was that why Adele was so protective of her home? Sam wondered. He had taken her to meet his parents, but there had been no return invitation to The Coppice. She made excuses instead. Her sister wasn't strong; she couldn't cope with company very well, was still trying to recover from the failure of her marriage two years earlier. *Two years earlier*, Sam had thought, astonished. That was a hell of a long time to spend recovering.

He jumped suddenly, as someone put their hands over his eyes. Turning, he picked up Adele and swung her round.

'Hey, careful!' she teased him. 'My hat will fall off.'

'I'll buy you a new one.'

She pulled a face. 'You don't like this one?'

'I think it's adorable, like you,' Sam replied, putting her down and linking arms with her. 'I thought we could go to the flicks . . . '

'I can't tonight.'

'Why not?'

'I have to get home, Julia's not well.'

Sam was beginning to notice how often Julia wasn't well.

'OK, we don't have to go out. I'll come home with you. I'd like to meet your sister.'

Adele stopped in her tracks. 'Julia's not up to that.'

'Is she an invalid?'

'Don't be silly!'

'You treat her like one,' Sam replied firmly. 'She's a grown woman, she can be left on her

165

own for an evening.'

Stung, Adele stared him full in the face. She liked Sam Ayres, liked him a lot. In fact, he was her first real boyfriend. But that didn't mean he could criticise her sister. Julia came first, Julia needed her. He had to understand that.

'She's not well . . . '

He sighed, running his hands through his wiry blond hair. 'She's got you on a string.'

'How dare you!' Adele snapped, walking off. She was quietly besotted with Sam Ayres, but she wasn't going to show it. Neither was she going to let him walk all over her. Or her family.

Immediately Sam regretted his candour and ran after her. 'Adele, stop! Stop!'

But she wasn't stopping for anyone, simply picked up her stride. Sam had to almost run to keep up with her.

'Hey! Come on! Stop!'

She turned suddenly, Sam skidding to a halt in front of her.

'My sister needs me. You have no idea what our life has been like. A real struggle. There were just the two of us left when our parents died, and we needed each other. We stuck together and we got through. Julia looked after me then — and now I'm looking after her.'

He paused, picking his words carefully. 'I'm sorry, I didn't understand. It's just that she's older than you, and it's been a long time since her marriage broke up . . . She seems to lean on you a lot, Adele.'

He was right, of course, and Adele knew it. But she would never admit it to anyone. She had hoped that over time Julia's dependency might have lessened, but it never had. In fact, her sister seemed to want the world to revolve around the house on The Coppice and the two of them. The two Ford girls. Together forever . . . it was for this reason that Adele hadn't taken Sam home. Other lads had been introduced to Julia, and it hadn't bothered Adele when her sister had criticised them. But it was different with Samuel Ayres. Adele liked him, knew only too well that she was falling in love with him.

And there was no way she was going to let Julia threaten this relationship. For a moment she felt trapped between the two of them; then she made her decision.

'What time is it?'

Sam looked at his watch. 'Five thirty.'

'We could go to the early showing of the film, couldn't we?' Adele asked him, smiling. 'And I'd still be home before it got late.'

22

You couldn't trust anyone, Julia thought, her face burning with rage. Hadn't she seen her sister walking into the cinema with a man? Her little sister, creeping around with some curly-haired lad. And doing God knows what else with him . . . Didn't Julia know about men? Hadn't she tried to steer her little sister right when she had brought those other lads home? But now Adele was betraying her trust, lying to her. *Adele*, who had promised that they would never be apart. That they would always trust and tell each other everything.

Enraged, Julia flung down her bag and tore off her coat, throwing some coal on to the dying fire in the kitchen. How long had Adele known this man? *Was it serious?* Turning, Julia made for the stairs and then entered her sister's bedroom. Adele was young, she knew nothing about men, she could be hurt, *seduced*. After all, she was just a baby. Her little sister . . .

But perhaps not so little any more. Until that moment, Julia had never thought of Adele having a life of her own. Nothing beyond The Coppice and the Failsworth shop. She was only eighteen, for God's sake! Stopping dead, Julia reran the word in her head. *Eighteen* . . . Adele was, in fact, not that much younger than Julia herself had been when she married John Courtland. The thought made her panic. Adele wasn't going anywhere, Adele was going to stay with her. She had promised . . . Opening her sister's wardrobe, Julia searched through Adele's clothes. Then she grubbed amongst the boxes at the bottom. But there was nothing to find.

Determined, Julia walked over to the bed. Slowly she felt under the mattress. Nothing there. Then she slid her hand under Adele's pillow, her fingers fastening on a photograph. Slowly she drew it out. It was a picture of the blond man she had seen with her sister that night . . . Julia felt her heart pumping and remembered something. How Adele had asked her if she had considered divorcing John. Making a new life. A fresh start.

'After all, you could meet someone any day and you would want to be free.'

Julia had stared at her in amazement. 'I don't want to meet anyone! I'm happy as we are.'

But obviously Adele *wasn't*. Her sister wanted something more from life and was trying to push Julia towards some new man just so she needn't feel any guilt over her own love affair. Perhaps Adele was even thinking of getting married, leaving her sister . . . Julia took a deep breath. She would put a stop to this. It was the right thing to do, even if Adele might not see it that way at first. Julia knew about men, and now she would look after her sister as she had always done. Adele had to be protected.

After all, it was for her own good.

★ ★ ★

169

Adele waved as she saw Becky coming out of the Ash mill gates. Her friend seemed pleased to see her, but appeared remote, her thoughts patently preoccupied.

'I've not seen you for days,' Adele said lightly. 'You OK?'

'Busy.'

'We could go out at the weekend.'

'Maybe,' Becky replied distantly.

'What's the matter?'

Becky stopped walking, urging Adele towards a bus stop. Sitting down, she fiddled with her gloves. The winter evening was catching up with them, the dark forcing on the lamps.

'I'm in trouble.'

At once, Adele took her hand. 'What is it, Becky? Are you ill? Is it Frida?'

'No . . . I've been such a fool.' And then she started crying. Not loudly, just letting the tears pour down her face.

Horrified, Adele leaned towards her. 'God, Becky, tell me what's up. I can help, just tell me.'

'I'm too ashamed.'

'You can tell me *anything*, you know that.'

Becky turned her head away. 'Not this. If I tell you this, you'll hate me.'

'Like hell,' Adele said simply. 'What's the matter?'

'I'm pregnant.'

The shock made Adele take a deep breath. She had always known that Rebecca was secretive, kept her feelings close to her chest, but this? Becky pregnant? *Becky?*

'I didn't know you had a boyfriend . . . Well,

170

not anyone serious . . . ' Adele paused, then hurried on. 'Are you sure?'

Becky nodded, waxy with shock. 'What do I do? God, what do I do?'

Ever practical, Adele set aside her astonishment and thought quickly. 'Listen, remember Mrs Hodges? She works the markets, Tommyfields . . . She's been known . . . well, she's seen to a few girls. You know, when they've been in trouble . . . So I've heard, anyway.' She paused, out of her depth. 'I can have a word with her . . . unless you want to keep the baby . . . '

'How can I keep it!' Becky replied, uncharacteristically sharp. 'I can't have it! I never thought I'd get pregnant. I thought you couldn't the first time. Isn't that the old wives' tale?' She turned to Adele, searching her face for any sign of criticism or judgement. 'It was only once, I promise. Only once — and I thought it couldn't happen the first time.'

Adele held on to her friend's hands. 'Who's the father?'

'Billy Kerr. He's the foreman at the mill.'

'D'you like him?'

Becky laughed drily. 'Does that matter? He's a nice man, kind . . . It was such a stupid thing to do, but I just wanted to be with someone. A man . . . I should have thought about it, Adele, but I just rushed in. And now I'm having a baby and I'm going to have to get rid of it. Poor little mite would probably have died anyway.'

'*What?*' Adele asked, shaken. 'Why would it die?'

'You know that my brother died when he was

a baby . . . ' Becky kept her head bowed. 'The doctors think his condition could have been inherited. If so, I could carry the weakness. My children might die in infancy too . . . I've known for a while, Adele, but I couldn't tell you. Couldn't tell anyone.'

'God, Becky, why did you keep this to yourself? It would have been so much easier to bear if we'd shared it.' Adele stroked her friend's hair.

'I *couldn't* admit that I might never be a mother. Or that I might have a sick baby . . . I kept trying to work out how I would tell the man I wanted to marry. How I would explain about the illness. And now I've blown my chances of ever getting a good man. A decent man . . . ' She shook her head. 'Things have been so difficult lately. My life looked grim, I just wanted to forget it all for a while. I just wanted to be with a man. To feel loved . . . Can you understand that?'

'Course I can.'

'And you don't hate me for it?'

'No,' Adele said evenly, staring ahead. 'How far on are you?'

'I've missed my period for two months.'

'And no one else knows?'

Becky's head shot up. 'No!'

'What about Billy Kerr?'

'He doesn't know!'

'You should tell him.'

Becky stared at Adele for a long moment. 'Why?'

'Because he's the baby's father. He has a right to know.'

'And then what?' Becky asked. 'Think about it

— if he knows, he might offer to marry me. He might not — but he *might* want to do the right thing. And I would have to accept. Then my grandmother would find out . . . *I* might be able to live with the guilt, but she couldn't.' Her expression was pleading. 'I can't tell anyone, Adele! I have to get rid of the baby. God forgive me, but I *have* to.'

Pausing until a man had passed by them, Adele turned back to Becky, her voice low. She was just realising the full impact of the situation; on Becky and on herself.

'It's illegal. God knows what would happen if anyone found out. And more importantly, it's risky, Becky. Abortion is dangerous.'

Her voice was numb. 'I don't have a choice.'

'Maybe your grandmother would understand.'

'No, she wouldn't. You know that, and I know that.' Becky sat upright, wiping away her tears. 'I'm sorry, really sorry. I should never have got you involved in all of this. I can't ask you to help me, Adele. It's not fair.'

'Becky . . . '

'I'll sort it out for myself. I could ask one of the mill girls . . . '

Adele shook her head. 'No, you don't have to do that. You don't want anyone to know, remember? We can sort this out together, you and I. I'll go and see Mrs Hodges, have a talk.'

Gripping Adele's hands, Becky stared earnestly into her face. 'I trust you with my life.'

God, Adele thought helplessly, that just what you *are* doing. Trusting me with your — and your baby's — life.

23

Although she wouldn't know it for many years, Adele's conversation with Turner Gades had triggered an old memory in him. Suddenly the years had dropped away and he was returned to his childhood. Back to Lydgate House and all he remembered about being there. He had wanted to speak out, to tell Adele of his own connection to the place. But how could he say to a young woman he hardly knew, *The Lydgate Widow was my father's mistress. I know that house too. I have my own memories of it.*

Of course he couldn't. But now he was back, and so were the memories. Pulling his car up outside St Anne's church, Turner thought of what Adele had said about the Lydgate Widow. And then he thought of the woman herself, Ninette Hoffman. Ducking his head against the wind, he walked through the heavy wrought-iron gates which led to the empty house. As he did so, old memory images flashed back: of a stunning woman offering him some cinnamon cake, of a man in the background watching her. The three of them had been together in that vast drawing room on that blistering summer day. And he had stood watching them, the cake drying in his mouth, his father murmuring brokenly, and the woman — the beautiful woman — closing the door on them as they left.

Slowly Turner approached the house. The

place was well maintained, the roof newly repaired, the gardens empty but manicured. Obviously someone kept an eye on the property and kept it in good order. Yet no one had lived in Lydgate House for decades, the last occupant being Ninette Hoffman, *the Lydgate Widow* . . . Turner had forgotten the sobriquet until Adele Ford had reminded him. The Lydgate Widow, spectacularly handsome, fascinatingly foreign and uniquely mesmerising. He had never really understood the mechanics of the relationship between the three adults. Only that his widowed father had loved Ninette, and she — unusually for the times — had been Julian Gades' mistress whilst remaining on cordial terms with her husband.

But *had* they been on cordial terms? Turner wondered, walking around to the back of the house and trying to peer in through a gap in one of the boarded-up windows. A shaft of indifferent winter sunshine momentarily penetrated the gloom inside: a long, low scrubbed kitchen table coming into view, an empty black grate grimly foreboding against the far wall. He could remember that grate when it had been lit, a kettle set on top, the bell ringing in the kitchen from the drawing room beyond. And the cook hustling a maid out with a tray.

Turner blinked, and the image was gone with the sunshine. Looking upwards, he glanced at the first-floor windows, remembering how he had seen Ninette Hoffman standing there, watching him and his father arrive or leave. And then he remembered the last time he had seen her. Only then she was a widow, closing the shutters for ever.

Behind those shutters she had lived out the rest of her days. When she died, childless, her fortune was passed on to the charities she and her husband had supported. As for the house, she had insisted that it be boarded up. Not used, not sold, just left unoccupied for some indeterminate time that no one knew. The solicitors in charge sent builders to make sure that the maintenance work was carried out. But no one knew why. Or for whom.

Thinking back, Turner remembered the gossip at the time. Was there something in the house? Had Ninette Hoffman been hiding something? Was that why she had had it closed up? Or was there a relative who would later claim the place? Others said that Ninette Hoffman had loved the house so much, she couldn't bear the thought of anyone else living there — even after she was dead.

And then there was the rumour of which Adele Ford had reminded him only the other day. That Ninette Hoffman still walked Lydgate House. That her ghost passed through the corridors and past the boarded-up windows, searching for her husband. Was it true? Turner wondered, leaning against the outside wall and lighting a cigarette. The smoke fluttered in the winter air, curling upwards into the darkening afternoon. Was she *really* looking for her husband? And if she was, was it out of love? Or regret?

Turner sighed to himself, unusually morose.

Time had passed so quickly. Had it really been so many years since he had been that hesitant visiting child? Holding back, watching his smitten father talk to Ninette Hoffman on that blisteringly hot day? Had the dust motes floated past him so long ago? The cook hurrying the servant out of the kitchen? The gardener pausing to wipe his forehead? And Andreas Hoffman, still as a mill pond, watching his wife. *Had it really been so long ago?* Grinding out his cigarette, Turner walked back to his car. He was — he could hardly believe it — acutely lonely. Perhaps the time *had* come for him to find himself a wife, or the years would pass him by without his realising it, leaving him as bereft and abandoned as his father had looked that day, so long ago.

It was incredible, but for an instant Turner could again taste the sweetness of the cinnamon cake on his lips, and see the tall figure of a woman turning by the side of the house. A ghost woman he had forgotten for a while. Until a young, living woman had reminded him of her.

Surprised, Turner looked back to the house, but now it seemed changed. No longer deserted, but waiting. Holding its breath.

24

'*Don't lie to me!*'

Flustered, Adele shook off her sister's grip. 'What's the matter with you?'

'I want to know where you've been.'

'Out,' Adele replied, irritated and already unsettled by what Becky had told her. 'I have a right to live my own life.'

'And live it like a whore?'

Flushing, Adele turned on her sister. 'How dare you talk to me like that!'

'I saw you, with a man. Going to the pictures. You lied to me! You never said anything about him, kept it secret.'

Pulling off her coat, Adele walked into the kitchen. 'Calm down, I'll make us some tea.'

'I don't want to calm down!' Julia threw back. 'I want to know what you're playing at.'

'I'm playing at having a life of my own,' Adele retorted. 'It's allowed, you know.'

'But you kept this man a secret from me. Who is he?'

'A friend. You're acting stupid, Julia. Look at yourself, what's got into you?'

'*You!* You've gone behind my back.'

'Can you blame me!' Adele shouted, banging down the kettle. 'I knew you'd act up if I said I was seeing someone. You've never liked anyone I've brought home. You're always criticising them — and I'm sick of it.'

'You — '

'You don't own me!' Adele went on heatedly. 'I spend every night home with you. You won't even go shopping with me any more. Haven't you seen the new clothes, Julia? Short skirts, bobbed hairstyles, coats with fur collars — '

'Which we can't afford!' Julia retorted bitterly.

'That's not the point. We could *look*. It doesn't cost anything to look. Dream about what we could have, one day.' She paused, her tone softening. 'Don't give up on life, Julia, please.'

'I can't face people.'

'But people don't care about what happened, Julia. They've forgotten. We're young, we should be out enjoying ourselves. You have to get over John. You *have* to — or it'll ruin your life. I know he hurt you, but it was a long time ago.'

'This isn't about me!'

Infuriated, Adele's patience finally snapped. '*Of course it is!* Everything's about you, Julia. You, you, you. I have to do what *you* want, when you want. I have to listen to *you* and console *you* about your marriage — and frankly it's gone on too long and it's got out of control. John was a bad lot, but there are other men out there. Put it behind you, forget him. Think of the future. A new life. If you like, we could go out together. Think of it, the Ford sisters — we could have any men we wanted.' She smiled, winking. 'Come on, Julia, you're pretty, men used to love you, you had them all on a string.'

Julia listened in silence, then smiled oddly.

'I suppose your man friend told you to say all this? I imagine he advised you to tell your sister to pull herself together. Isn't that what everyone says?'

'Julia, *no one* is talking about you any more,' Adele said wearily. Turning away, she filled the kettle and put it on to boil.

'Hah! Don't you think I know that you all talk about me?'

'That's not true . . . '

But Julia wasn't listening. 'You think I want to make a fool of myself again?'

'Julia, no one wants — '

'You think I want people laughing at me again?'

Adele was getting infuriated. 'No one is laughing at you!'

'Or pitying me behind my back?'

'We don't need to pity you — you do enough of that yourself.'

Shocked, Julia took a breath. 'You've changed. You've only just started to see this man and you've changed completely. You would *never* have been so cruel to me before.' She moved over to her sister, taking her arm, her grip tight. 'Listen to me, Adele. Men bring trouble. And they'll turn us against each other if we let them. *We have to stick together.*'

Incredulous, Adele stared at her sister. 'I love you and I would do anything for you — but I won't ruin my own life because you let some man ruin yours!'

Incensed, Julia struck out. Adele was caught

off guard, and the slap rocked her. Almost knocked off her feet, her cheek burning, she stared at her sister in shock. Then she snatched up her coat, and, without another word, ran out into the darkness.

I tried so hard to see it her way.

I knew Julia had been crushed by John's departure, but I wanted to forget the past and move on. Yet I couldn't. It seemed that everyone was suddenly blocking me. There was the shock of Becky, the realisation of what would have to be done. And then my sister pinning me in. I wanted to enjoy Sam Ayres, my first love. I wanted to laugh with him, go out with him. Yes, I admit it, I was selfishly in love — and I wanted to relish it. Yet here were the two people I loved most in all the world undermining what I saw as my happiness.

That night — my face still smarting from where Julia had hit me — I walked for over an hour. I avoided Mrs Redfern with her scruffy Irish terrier and nodded to Mr Lockhart as he came home, I think a little in his cups. I remembered our parents, the washstands that still needed painting. And then I remembered how my sister and I had stuck together after their death.

Then I thought of the beautiful Becky, in such a dangerous situation, and how I had promised to help her. Me — of all people. What did I really know about life? About men? Relationships? Not much. But I knew enough to fight for what I wanted — and I wanted Sam Ayres. I wanted Julia to change too; to shake off her sickly bitterness. And I wanted Becky's baby to not be there at all. I wanted that the most. For there to be no baby. Because even though I knew that at two months it was only an embryo, it was still a living being. A little creature we were going to get rid of. A life that never stood a chance.

But as I turned my steps to home, I knew that what we want and what we get are two very different things.

25

Preening himself one last time, Sam walked up to the Ford house, his gift for Adele tucked under his arm for safety. He could see the welcoming lights and the small Christmas tree in the window. At last, he thought. At last he had been invited to Adele's home.

Hearing footsteps behind him, he spun round, smiling.

'I'm just coming to see you!' he said, kissing Adele on the cheek.

'Oh, you can't kiss me!' Adele teased him, trying to make her voice light.

'Not even a little kiss?' he asked, stealing another peck.

She took his arm, laughing, her hair covered with a patterned scarf, her bright red swing coat making a Christmas angel out of her. She was, Sam thought with admiration, adorable.

'Now, you know that my sister's been very poorly for a while with her nerves,' Adele went on, trying to sound relaxed. 'Don't mention her husband, or anything about her marriage.'

'Why would I?' Sam asked, baffled.

'I'm just trying to warn you, that's all.'

'So I won't go in there and say 'How d'you do? I hear your marriage was a right mess'?'

Punching him lightly on the arm, Adele pulled a face. 'You know what I mean. She's very edgy . . . '

'Edgy?'

'You know . . . '

'*Edgy?* You mean she might come at me with a carving knife?' Sam asked, feigning horror. Honestly, if it had been anyone but Adele he wouldn't have bothered. She was exhausting. Or he should say, *her sister* was exhausting. 'Julia *does* know we're going out together?'

'She does now, yes.'

Adele paused, thinking back to their argument. The bad feeling had intensified after Adele discovered that her bedroom had been searched. Repentant, Julia had tried to apologise, but for once Adele wasn't easily placated. She had even wondered if she might keep her distance from her sister at Christmas. After all, hadn't Sam's parents invited her for lunch with them? How easy it would be to punish Julia that way. But the temptation didn't last. It wasn't in Adele's nature to be spiteful, and besides, hadn't the two sisters spent every Christmas of their lives together?

So Adele forgave Julia, then decided that she was going to invite Sam to meet her. It was her way of saying *I don't hold any grudges, but this man is in my life and you have to accept it.* Indeed, Adele had decided that Sam's visit would be the adult thing to do. The grown-up way of showing Julia that she was going to live her own life, with whomsoever she chose — and that they could all get along together.

It had seemed so simple — but now they were walking through the front door Adele tightened up with nerves.

'Let me take your coat,' she said stiffly,

relieving Sam of his donkey jacket and scarf. 'D'you want to go into the front room?'

In fact he wanted to run, the atmosphere was so tense. Smiling awkwardly, Adele went off, leaving Sam to take a seat in front of the fire. The room was full of bric-a-brac. Sam studied a nearby fire iron and admired a parquetry table top. Victor Ford had had a good eye, Sam realised, stroking the side of his bergère chair. Everything was a bit worn, but good quality.

He was beginning to relax; at least they all shared an interest in collecting. Then the door opened and a disconsolate Adele walked in.

'She won't come down. She says she has a headache.'

Sighing, Sam slumped back in his seat, watching Adele chew the side of her fingernail. 'You want me to go?'

'No!' she said fiercely. 'We'll enjoy ourselves without her. She's just playing up, that's all.'

On edge, Adele sat down opposite Sam. She wanted to sit next to him, to cuddle up with him, but didn't feel comfortable enough. Instead she continued to chew the side of her nail and listen to the sounds of footsteps overhead.

'At least she still has the use of her legs.'

'What?'

Sam jerked his head upwards. 'Your sister — she's moving about.'

They both glanced up, then Adele took Sam's hand and squeezed it.

'I'm still glad you came . . . Don't worry about Julia, we can have dinner on our own.'

'Yeah, right,' Sam replied. The sound of

something heavy falling overhead making them both jump. Automatically he tightened his grip on Adele's hand. 'No, don't rush off to check on her. She's just doing it for effect; you know that as well as I do.'

Adele nodded, but her eyes strayed upwards. 'She could have fallen over.'

'She could have broken her neck, but I don't think we're going to be that lucky,' Sam replied drily.

Trying to break the mood, Adele slid next to him on his chair and laid her head on his shoulder. She could smell soap and the scent of cold air on his jacket, and finally she relaxed.

'Are you hungry?'

'Not any more,' Sam replied, hugging her as another heavy thud came from overhead. 'God, love, why d'you put up with her? She's impossible.'

'I suppose I keep hoping she'll go back to being the old Julia,' Adele admitted, upset and embarrassed. 'You're having a horrible time, aren't you?'

'I couldn't have a horrible time with you around,' he said gently, kissing her on the forehead. A flicker of affection suddenly passed between them, and Sam's lips moved over Adele's mouth and his arms wrapped tightly around her body.

At that precise moment, Julia walked in.

26

A blinding chill had come down. Adele shivered as she stood on the corner of Hardy Row, looking down the street. It was cold, bitterly cold, and she longed to go inside, but she couldn't. It wasn't just that she was chilled, she was also afraid. Her gaze kept travelling back to the back entrance of the house where Becky had met up with Mrs Hodges. Not that it was Mrs Hodges' house; it was somewhere she had borrowed temporarily.

Anxiously Adele looked round. The whole affair had been so secretive when she had approached Mrs Hodges on her stall at Tommyfields.

'I don't do it no more, luv,' the woman had said briskly, looking round. 'Have to tell yer, luv, yer weren't someone I reckoned would get herself in trouble.'

'I told you, it's not me.'

'Oh, aye?' the woman replied, folding her arms. 'Well, in a way that's a shame. I might have done it for someone I knew. Someone who could be discreet.'

Hating herself for lying, Adele said, 'She's my cousin. You'd do it for a relative of mine, surely?' She studied Mrs Hodges urgently. 'She's two months gone. She's desperate. Please. I can pay.'

'I'd want paying, luv. I mean, it's risky this, you know. Against the law. I could suffer fer this.

There's a couple of women round these parts been jailed.'

Adele knew that only too well, but she kept pushing her.

'Neither of us will breathe a word, I swear . . . How much money d'you want?'

'Ten pounds.'

'Ten pounds!' Adele replied, shaken. 'I haven't got it. No, wait . . . ' She paused, remembering. 'You like silver, don't you?'

Mrs Hodges' eyebrows shot up. 'Yer have to ask?'

'I could pay you with a couple of silver candlesticks,' Adele went on eagerly. 'I inherited them from my parents. My sister's hidden them up in the attic — said we could always pawn them if things got really bad. They'd be worth ten pounds to anyone.'

'I'd rather have the money.'

'I'd rather not have to ask, Mrs Hodges,' Adele replied coldly. 'I'd rather my cousin wasn't in this horrible situation.' She paused, and the woman's hand reached out and patted hers.

'Oh, come on, luv, we'll sort it out fer her. No one will be any the wiser.'

The strain was catching up with Adele. 'She will be all right, won't she? I mean, I've heard about botched jobs . . . '

'I've never botched mine,' Mrs Hodges replied, offended.

'I didn't mean that! It's just that if anything happened to her . . . '

'Look, she's young and only two months gone — it'll be easy.'

Easy? Adele wondered, her thoughts coming back to the present. Suddenly spotting a policeman, she winced, then turned away as though she was looking down the alley. God, that was a stupid thing to do, she thought immediately, how suspicious did *that* look? Behind her she could hear the footsteps approach, and her muscles tensed. The footsteps came closer, pausing at the end of the ginnel. God, Adele thought blindly. The police would put Mrs Hodges in jail, and God only knew what would happen to her and Becky . . .

'Miss?'

She kept her head turned, willing the officer to move on.

'Miss?'

Slowly Adele turned to face him, praying that Becky wouldn't come out at that moment, or Mrs Hodges call for her.

'Yes?'

'Aren't you Adele Ford?'

'Yes.' Her voice was hardly more than a whisper. Here she was, in the back streets of Salford, and this policeman knew her.

'Yer don't remember me, do yer?'

She shook her head, mute with shock.

'But I remember yer . . . '

The street started spinning around her. In the distance she could hear the sound of someone calling out the newspaper headlines, and a dog howling. Then she could feel the policeman's hand gripping her arm.

'Miss Ford? Miss Ford?'

Slowly she gathered her thoughts. Act normal,

she told herself, otherwise you'll really give the game away.

'Are you all right?'

She tried to smile. 'I'm just a bit light-headed. Haven't eaten since this morning.' She shrugged. 'I think I've got hungry and cold.'

He smiled. 'But why are yer here?'

'Someone said they would meet me. They had something to sell,' Adele blathered, praying that Mrs Hodges or Rebecca wouldn't suddenly come out and show her up for the liar she was. 'You know, I work at the bric-a-brac shop in Failsworth . . . '

The officer smiled. 'I know that, luv. I bought something there last summer. Yer served me. I reckon yer didn't recognise me wearing me 'elmet.'

She stared at him, then smiled weakly. 'Of course, of course I do.'

'I knew yer dad.'

'You did?'

He nodded, taking off his helmet and running his finger around the brim. Jesus, Adele thought, why wouldn't he go?

'Yer dad were very good to my mother. Helped her out once when we were on our uppers.' He paused, remembering. 'If it hadn't been for Victor Ford bringing in that food, we'd never have got through.'

Intrigued, Adele stared at him. 'My father brought you food?'

'He did. And for a few other people too. Not that he said much about it. Strange man, didn't like too much thanking. Thought the world of

191

yer two girls, though, and yer mother. We were all sad to 'ear he died. And yer poor mother too.'

Adele stared at the officer. This was a side of her father she hadn't known. Her heart shifted, admiration welling up inside her.

'I went into the business because of him, you know,' she said, then paused. There was a sound from behind her — and she suddenly remembered where she was.

'I should go!'

'I thought yer said they were meeting yer here,' the policeman said, putting his helmet back on.

'I might just walk down to the other end of the ginnel and have a look there,' she replied. 'The seller's an old man, he might have got lost.'

'Righto,' the policeman said, smiling at her and nodding. 'Yer take care of yerself, Miss Ford. No doubt I'll see yer again.'

He had only just rounded the bend of Gladstone Street when Mrs Hodges came out and hissed for Adele. Scurrying into the back parlour of the dingy house, she could see Becky sitting on a hard kitchen chair. Beside her the kitchen table was covered over with newspaper.

'I damn near keeled over when I saw yer talking to that copper,' Mrs Hodges said, helping Becky to her feet. 'Bloody hell, I thought my luck had run out good and proper.'

Adele stared into her friend's pale face. 'Is she OK?'

'She'll be fine. Get her home, will yer? Soon as yer can. And keep her warm.'

*   *   *

For years afterwards Adele would remember the journey back to Oldham by tram. Becky sat silent beside her, occasionally wincing and touching her stomach. When they reached Park Street, both girls were relieved to find that Frida had company, a next-door neighbour having stopped in for a chat.

Adele helped Becky into the kitchen, then followed her as she hurried out into the back yard, bent over in pain. Whilst Becky sat on the outside privy, Adele waited outside. She could hear faint moans, and dug her fingernails into the pointing between the brickwork, scratching at the grouting. At last there was silence. Tentatively she slid her hand around the door; Becky clasped it frantically.

Neither of them would ever forget that bitingly cold night when Becky lost her baby. Neither of them would ever be able to think of it without tears. The Oldham rain pattering on the corrugated-iron roof of the privy. The sound of voices from the pub on the corner. And the way Becky gripped Adele's hand through the half-open door.

27

Struggling to open the door of Saul Hill's shop with her gloved hand, Pauline Buckley hurried in from the cold. Once inside, she paused, looking round. Weird place, she thought, but some nice things in it. And it was very clean. That was something.

Suddenly, a voice made her jump. 'Hello, can I help you?'

Surprised to be faced with a young, pretty woman, Pauline hesitated. 'I came to see Mr Hill.'

'He's out at the moment,' Adele explained pleasantly. 'Maybe I can help?'

Instant dislike overwhelmed Pauline. Who was this good-looking girl, so composed, so pretty in an old-fashioned dress which should have made her look like a drab? Pauline could imagine herself in the outfit: the severe brown colour would turn her sallow skin dingy, the thick black stockings and plain shoes making her legs even more dumpy than usual. But not *this* girl; she wore the awful clothes like an empress.

'I need to talk to Mr Hill,' Pauline said imperiously. 'It's about a vase.'

Adele smiled. 'Oh, the Derby vase. Yes, he told me about it. He's been restoring it, hasn't he?'

'Has he?' Pauline asked, knowing full well he had, but being difficult. 'So, is it ready?'

Adele paused, looking puzzled. 'I thought Mr

Gades was coming to collect it?'

If she had drawn a gun on Pauline, the effect could not have been any more dramatic.

'Mr Turner Gades?'

'Yes,' Adele agreed. 'Such a nice man.'

'You know him?' Pauline asked, implying that Adele was too lowly to even mention his name.

By this time Adele had noticed the frost in the air and tried to effect a thaw.

'Mr Gades sometimes has dealings with Mr Hill. I imagine he bought the Derby vase for you — '

'My parents,' Pauline replied loftily. 'Of course, we usually buy things in Manchester, even London. Mr Turner Gades doesn't normally shop in places like these.'

Adele winced, trying to keep her patience. She might tolerate being treated like a servant by Saul Hill, but not by a plain woman not much older than herself.

'Mr Gades seemed perfectly comfortable here.'

She hadn't meant to imply anything, but Pauline took the words as some hint of intimacy. An intimacy that *she* had not inspired in the eligible Mr Gades. Her voice hardened.

'I want to talk to Mr Hill.'

At that moment he walked in from the back, taking off his hat. His round bald head caught the light, his forehead shiny as a tabletop. Harrumphing, he glanced at Adele and then at the customer.

'What's up?'

Pauline blinked. 'Your employee has been very rude to me.'

'*What!*' Adele replied, outraged.

'Very cheeky.'

Slowly Saul looked from Pauline to Adele. He didn't like women, and he didn't like arguments. Besides, he was feeling a bit strange, light-headed. And, as everyone knew, Saul Hill didn't drink, so there wasn't even a reason for it. He harrumphed again, in no mood for stupid females.

'Adele, go in the back.'

Annoyed, she looked at him, then caught the smug smile of triumph on Pauline Buckley's face.

'Go on! In the back!' he repeated, then turned to Pauline. 'What d'you want?'

'An apology from your assistant.'

'Hah!' he said simply, waving aside the words. If she had expected the old man to be on her side, she was going to be disappointed. Saul Hill was on no one's side but his own.

'I've no time for nonsense,' he said, coughing and then shaking his head like a dog with water in its ears. Pauline watched him, transfixed. The man was obviously crazy. 'What d'you want?'

'I . . . I . . . ' she hurried on. 'As I said, I came to collect the Derby vase.'

'I thought Turner Gades was coming for that.'

'No, I am!' Pauline replied.

The old man noticed her irritation. It was annoying when pretty women played up, but the plain ones should be *forced* to learn charm.

'Is it ready?'

'Not yet.'

'So when *will* it be ready?'

'In a day or so.'

'Can you tell me *which* day?' Pauline pressed him, her face waxy with temper.

'Tuesday.' Saul paused. 'Or Wednesday.'

'Fine,' Pauline replied, stung. 'I'll call by again on Wednesday.'

'Not *this* Wednesday,' Saul went on, enjoying himself enormously. '*Next* Wednesday.'

'But . . . '

He walked to the door and opened it for her. 'We'll see you then, all right?'

Thwarted, Pauline Buckley picked up what was left of her composure and left, almost slipping on a patch of ice on the pavement outside.

'Silly cow,' Saul mumbled, shaking his head again as Adele walked back into the shop.

She had heard the exchange from the back room, and knew that the old man's rudeness hadn't been on her account. As usual, he had just been playing games. She watched him silently as he walked over to the Derby vase on the worktop. It had been finished the night before — not that Pauline Buckley would ever know that. Curious, Adele studied the old man, his gait slightly more awkward than usual, his huge bald head balanced on his thin neck like a golf ball on a tee.

'Harrumph,' Saul Hill said, making a deep sound in his throat and then suddenly gripping the side of the chair next to him.

'Are you all right?' Adele asked, hurrying forward.

He seemed to take a moment to recognise her.

197

'Mr Hill, are you all right?'

His eyes were blank, eerily expressionless. And then he came to, snapping, 'Get back in the shop! I don't pay you to hang around doing nothing.'

★ ★ ★

The image came back into Julia's mind and pinched at her nerves. Her sister and Sam Ayres . . . *Kissing* . . . Her reaction had been mixed. Fury, envy — and then she had felt herself unexpectedly moved. Their embrace had been so tender, so gentle, so loving. Not just a flirtation. At least not on Adele's part. And it had reminded her of what *she* had experienced once. And lost. Of the affection she had found so easy to give and receive — and now longed for.

As though someone had thrown a floodlight on her heart, Julia could see what she had avoided for so long — and in that moment realised the mistake she had made. Galvanised, she looked in the mirror. Her sister had been right, she *had* neglected herself. And she wasn't that young any more. Twenty-eight, nearly twenty-nine. Approaching thirty . . . Critically, she studied her reflection — the pasty skin, the lank, underweight body — then she raised the hem of her skirt three inches. It was the new fashion. And she had the legs for it. Hadn't John always told her what good legs she had? Impatiently, Julia brushed aside the memory of her husband, and turned back to the fashion magazine. They hadn't the money for such luxuries, but Adele had found it discarded on the tram and pocketed it, bringing it home to share with her sister.

Such styles, Julia thought, eyeing the pages hungrily. She glanced back at the mirror. Too much for her though. Too daring . . . *and yet* . . . She raised her skirt again, looking at her calves. God, how the men had wanted her before. How she had attracted interest. Kept their interest. *Until John.* Until he had left her and taken all her confidence with him. He had made her feel worthless, ugly. He had crucified her — and she had let him. As Adele had said, Julia had allowed John Courtland to ruin her life. Some unfaithful, unloving, ungrateful pig of a man had turned her inside out, made her doubt herself. Made her plain . . .

Resolutely Julia took the magazine over to the mirror, comparing the model's face with her own. Perfectly made up, the magazine idol seemed unreachable, beyond emulation, the exquisite face and hair light years from Oldham reality. Despair overwhelmed Julia for an instant, then she rallied, some of her old steel returning. *John Courtland wasn't going to wreck her life.* She would show everyone that she was still worth having. That men could want her again, long for her, need her. He might have stripped all her esteem away, left her emotionally bloodless, but she was going to change all that.

Looking at the magazine again, Julia stared at the model. But this time, instead of seeing some unreachable image, she saw power. The same sensual power she had once wielded — and was going to wield again. Julia knew only too well that she had once possessed the siren's touch. She thought back to her sister kissing Sam Ayres, and her eyes closed, the image of their profiles imprinted indelibly.

And for a moment it wasn't Adele she saw, but herself.

28

The noise in the covered market was intense, the cold driving people inside, crowds milling around the stalls of bric-a-brac and oddments. So soon after Christmas the better stalls were struggling, but the outer, cheaper stalls were thriving. Nervously, Adele looked around her, then stared at the empty stall longingly. If only she had the money ... if only she could afford to rent it, she could make it work. She *knew* she could. Make some money. Not a fortune — but something decent. And then, before long, she could leave Saul Hill and set up on her own. After all, hadn't she bought and sold those old prints and made a profit at Tommyfields only the other week? But how many prints and profits would she *really* need to enable her to leave the Failsworth shop?

Thinking of the old man made her cringe. He was behaving even more oddly than usual, falling over in the yard, the geese pecking at him and hissing like steam trains. Alarmed, Adele had run out and helped the old man to his feet, but instead of thanking her he had told her to clear off.

'Get off! Don't you think I know what you're doing?' He had hobbled over to the padlocked storehouse. 'Want to know what I've got in here? No chance! No chance!'

'I don't care what's in there.'

He had waggled his finger at her, his bald head ghostly white in the cold morning light. 'I know better! I know greedy eyes and hands!'

Infuriated, she had walked off, slamming the door behind her as she re-entered the shop.

Still staring at the vacant stall, Adele realised the old man would never fire her. She was cheap and personable — and besides, who else would tolerate him? Anyway, working there *had* benefited her in some ways. She had learned about furniture and valuations. Not that Saul Hill had set out to teach her, she had just assimilated the information, overheard him talking to his customers. Or heard them discussing deals . . . Her eyes fixed on the stall, imagining how she would dress it, lay out the prints and maybe a few pieces of silver. Plate, of course. Oh, it might not be much to anyone else, but it was a step up from Tommyfields, and no mistake.

So intent was she that Adele didn't notice that someone was watching *her* . . . Only yards away, Sam was leaning against a friend's stall, smoking a roll-up. He could see her face, the excitement obvious — and felt dismayed by it. His affection for Adele went deep, but from the first something had warned him that this was not going to last. Adele Ford was ambitious, determined to succeed. It was obvious to him how much she wanted from life — just as it was obvious how little he did. A decent home, a few beers, a girl in his bed. Later, a wife and kids. Samuel Ayres was a sensible man and knew his place. He was an ordinary bloke — from a long line of ordinary blokes — set to have an ordinary life.

Not that being practical stopped the feelings in his heart . . . With sadness he kept watching Adele, trying to read her thoughts. Already she was dreaming of a stall in the covered market. And then what? Her own shop? Too ambitious for most, but not Adele Ford. Oh no, she might just be the one to pull it off. It never occurred to her that being female would be a hindrance. Instead, she would quote her father, talk about his life, the intimation obvious. If he could do it, *she* could.

And she was probably right. But how could Sam fit in with her ambitions? The house on The Coppice was too upmarket for him; Lyle Street was his stamping ground. Adele might laugh at people's snobbery, but he knew how much it mattered. And besides, even if she could cope with the differences in their backgrounds, could *he*? He hadn't her drive, her brains. And he didn't want to lead her on. She was too decent for that. Samuel Ayres might already have proved himself sexually, but he wasn't going to seduce Adele Ford.

Bloody hell, Sam thought to himself. He had never cared for anyone so deeply. Never considered anyone's feelings or welfare like this before. She was precious to him, important to him. He was in love with her.

And it was going nowhere.

* * *

Rapping on the window, Frida waved to Adele, watching as she crossed the street. Entering the cramped front room, Adele took off her coat and placed it over the rack in front of the fire. It was cold, and Frida was wrapped up in the downstairs bed, her skin deathly white. Obviously times were no easier. Becky might be toiling relentlessly at the Ash mill, but her wage only covered the bare essentials. Faded wallpaper peeled away in one corner of the room, and a winter draught blew in under the front door. Pushing a rag rug up against the gap, Adele smiled at Frida.

'It's freezing out there.'

'Did you get the tram?'

She nodded, looking round. 'Shall we have some tea?'

'I'd like that,' Frida replied, watching as Adele busied herself in the tiny kitchen beyond. 'Becky's going to be late again . . . I do wish she could meet someone nice. The right man would be the making of her.'

Wincing, Adele paused, then walked back into the front room with the tea, passing Frida a cup.

'So, what about *your* boyfriend, Adele?'

'He's nice . . . *very* nice.' She laughed.

'Well, make sure your sister doesn't interfere,' Frida replied shortly. 'I'm old, I can speak my mind. I don't want Julia putting your man off so she can keep you to herself.'

Adele nodded. 'I know . . . but she's not as possessive as she was. We had an argument and it cleared the air. She's getting better, honestly. Even started to go out shopping with me, instead of rushing to and from that florist's like a criminal. I can see some of the old Julia coming back, at last. And she's looking after her appearance, getting her confidence up . . . I think she might finally be getting over John. People don't realise how much she suffered.'

'Well, be that as it may,' Frida said evenly, 'times have been hard for both of you. You're overdue some luck, Adele . . . Is it serious with you and Samuel Ayres?'

Frida could see her hesitating.

'I thought it was just a flirtation, but not any more. I know, it's the first time that I've been in love! I know what you're going to say, 'Everyone feels the same', but . . . ' She looked up, her eyes brilliant, her voice low, confiding, fighting laughter. '*I love him!* Oh, Frida, you've no idea how much.'

29

Pauline Buckley could hardly believe her eyes. Ducking down the side of a shop on Travelli Street, Rochdale, she peered down the road at the couple deep in conversation. Of course she had heard the news — Turner Gades had a woman in his life. *But this woman!* Dear God, just wait until she told her parents. Just wait. They would have a thing or two to say. That he could reject her — Pauline Buckley — for a shop assistant! Enraged, Pauline stomped off, nearly knocking a pedestrian off the pavement as she did so, her face on fire, her chest as tight as a drum.

Only yards away, the objects of her fury were occupied, Adele's head tilted to one side as Turner Gades talked.

'Well, he wouldn't open the door to me either,' Turner was saying. 'I knocked and knocked, but nothing. You think he's ill?'

Adele shrugged, falling into step with Turner as they moved on. Her employer's behaviour was beginning to cause real concern.

'I don't know. I can't make sense of it. He was his usual self yesterday morning, and then in the afternoon he went strange. Like in a trance. He was looking at me as though I wasn't there. Perhaps . . . '

'Yes?'

'His brain's been affected by something?'

'You think Saul Hill's going senile?'

Adele shivered. 'I don't know. Maybe.'

'Has he finished the Derby vase restoration?'

Adele nodded. 'That's what I came to Rochdale to tell you. First thing this morning Mr Hill said I had to tell you it would be ready for collection tomorrow. That it wasn't finished yet.' She paused. 'But he finished it *days* ago. Then, when I was just about to leave, he asked me where I was going!'

'*What?*' Turner asked, pausing and looking at Adele, mystified.

'I know, it sounds weird, but that's what happened. So I went through it all again and he stormed off, telling me to stop wasting his time.'

'Perhaps he needs a doctor?'

'Well, I'm not suggesting it,' Adele said firmly. 'You can. But duck when you say it.'

He laughed, then changed the subject. 'There's an auction on this weekend. By private invitation, at the Brunswick Hotel in Southport.'

Adele blew out her cheeks. 'That's nice!'

'I'm going with a lady friend of mine. I wondered,' Turner paused, then went on quickly, 'would you like to come?'

'What!' Adele said, without thinking. 'Why would you ask *me* along?'

He smiled, impressed by her candour. 'Look, I know how much you enjoy this business. I know how much you want to learn. It would be a good opportunity to meet people in the trade, see some fine objects. If you want, you could come as our guest.'

Stunned, Adele stood silent. The Brunswick

Hotel, Southport. A private sale, with all the important dealers there . . . Her mouth fell open, then closed again. Despite being a man of some importance, Turner Gades was one of the most unaffected people Adele had ever met. Her brother-in-law had been puffed up with importance, but this man was genuine, willing to help.

The temptation to accept was immense; the invitation without strings. Hadn't Turner Gades invited her along with his lady friend? And yet Adele hesitated. What would she wear? How would she know what to say? Or how to behave? This wasn't the Ram's Head, this was upmarket.

Swallowing, she glanced at Turner, knowing he was waiting for an answer. 'I . . . I want to, but . . .'

He was ready to reassure her. 'It's nothing to be worried about. You would, as I say, be our guest. Come to the sale with us, Adele. Watch what goes on — that's how we all learn this business. By experience.'

★ ★ ★

Watching as Clemmie Brooks poured him a drink, Turner thought about their relationship, their companionship over the last eighteen months. It was effortless, the spontaneous friendship of two people with many interests in common. The fact that Clemmie — although widowed and older than Turner by seven years — was elegant and poised was a bonus. He also admired her for her intelligence and charm. But if he thought about her sexually — as a *woman*

— Turner found it more difficult.

Certainly Clemmie was attractive to him, but in a physical way . . . ? Or should he even be thinking about her like that? Maybe he should be simply grateful for her company and for the ease of their relationship.

'Penny for them.'

He blinked, looking at Clemmie as she passed him his drink. 'I was just day-dreaming . . . You know there's a sale coming up at the Brunswick in Southport?' She nodded. 'I've invited Adele Ford to come with us. Is that all right with you?'

Smiling, Clemmie took a seat next to him. 'Of course it is! I've heard so much about her, I'd like to meet her.'

'She's a nice kid,' Turner went on. 'I think she has the makings of a good dealer. With help.'

'Which you — of course — will give her.'

'I'd like to,' he admitted. 'She's got guts, working for that ghastly Saul Hill — and I happen to know she's on the lookout for another job.'

'Can't say I blame her,' Clemmie retorted. 'D'you know of anything going?'

'No, but I promised her I'd keep my ears open.'

'You like helping people, don't you?' Clemmie asked, putting her head on one side.

'So do you. You do all that charity work.'

'Hah!' she said dismissively. 'I'm just buying my way into heaven.'

'You got your wings a long time ago.'

They smiled at each other contentedly.

'My late husband used to say that there were

two types of people in the world — those who compete, and those who guide.'

'Which was he?'

'A competitor. Which I admired, but I admire you more,' she said simply, touching his arm 'You're the perfect guide. The ideal mentor, Turner. Patient, knowledgeable, generous. And if you say Adele has potential, she must have. You've always been a good judge of talent *and* character.'

Thoughtfully he looked at her as she turned away and reached for her drink. As ever, she was being perceptive. He *was* a good judge of character. But was he a good judge of *wives*? Would this lovely widow want him as a husband? And would he make her happy? Was friendship enough to base a marriage on? Still studying her, Turner decided that he would wait and see. If their closeness remained only a friendship, so be it. If it developed into something deeper, all the better. But its progress had to be natural and unforced.

30

Hovering around her unexpected guest, Julia
tried to make conversation, but it was hard
going. Repeatedly she glanced at the clock and
then back to her visitor. Sam sat rigid in his seat.
He had come round to see Adele, but for some
reason she wasn't home. Instead her sister had
opened the door . . .

'Oh, Mr Ayres!'

He had coughed. 'I came to see Adele.'

'She's gone to an auction in Southport
tonight.'

'Bugger!' Sam said, then checked himself.
'Sorry, I forgot.'

Frowning, Julia glanced out into the rain.
'Come in for a while. You can't walk back in this
weather.'

'But . . . '

'I don't bite,' Julia said, then smiled.

Uncomfortable, Sam smiled back, surprised as
Julia showed him into the front room and
poured him a sherry. She seemed different. In
fact, she was wearing make-up and was quite a
looker.

'Sorry if I'm keeping you.'

Julia raised her eyebrows, her old sexual skills
sliding into action. 'From what?'

'I don't know,' he admitted. 'I just don't want
to be a nuisance.'

He paused, smiling awkwardly. She smiled

back, equally awkward, but gaining in confidence. He's noticed, Julia thought with pleasure, spotted my make-up, and now he's thinking that I'm attractive. She smiled again, remembering how easy it was to draw a man in. Even a likely lad like this one. And Sam Ayres was a likely lad, a flirty, skirt-chasing kind of bloke.

'You work in antiques?'

'Bric-a-brac,' Sam replied, smiling broadly. 'Nothing fancy. I'm more into house clearances, you know the kind of thing. Not the upper-class stuff.'

Julia nodded. 'My father was in the trade.'

'Adele said.'

'He wasn't very successful. He had a good eye, but no business sense.' She paused, unused to talking to men, but finding it easier by the second. In fact she was getting slightly dizzy with excitement, the image of her sister and Sam kissing rearing up in front of her suddenly. For a moment she felt guilty, knowing that she was flirting with Adele's boyfriend. But the feeling was pushed aside by her longing for attention.

Nervously she fingered her wedding ring. Then she caught Sam watching her and began to bluster.

'I'm married. Rather, I was. My husband — I threw him out.' Pushing her hair back with her hands, Julia flushed, then decided to go for the spurned role. 'Actually, he left me.'

'Oh.'

'He was seeing another woman.'

'That must have hurt.'

She smiled, relieved. *He was sympathetic.* Not judgemental. She wasn't a failure in his eyes, just someone who had had a rough break. Relaxing further, Julia continued, 'It *did* hurt, but life goes on.'

'That's brave.'

'Not really . . . ' She paused, her eyes challenging him, her voice dropping slightly. 'I suppose you've been hurt, Mr Ayres.'

'Yeah,' he said slowly. 'Now and again.'

'You got over it?'

He was watching her, getting drawn in slowly and not fighting it. 'You have to.'

'Or find someone else to help you recover.'

A frisson passed between them. Julia was remembering how she used to feel in the past, and Sam was thinking that he should get out but couldn't, because Adele's sister was quite fascinating. And besides, it was only until the rain stopped. And they were just talking . . .

Realising Sam Ayres was interested — even though he was trying to fight it — Julia sat down and crossed her legs. Oh yes, she thought, carried away with her own power, he was noticing her. Taking in her smile, her eyes, her body. She wasn't invisible any more . . . In that instant, every sense was heightened in Julia as she slid eagerly out of her long emotional exile.

'*Love* — why do we do it?' she asked, sounding confident, a woman of the world.

Sam found himself on guard, but intrigued. Adele might have described her sister one way, but the reality was very different. He could see that Julia Ford had been damaged, but there was also a sensual side to her which was enticing. A sheen of sexual experience that married women usually had.

'We never learn, hey?'

Julia smiled. 'No ... Perhaps we're not supposed to. I mean, you can't hide away for ever, can you? I did, for a long time, but life goes on.' She was talking in forced clichés, but she didn't seem to be able to stop herself. It was her body talking, not her mind. 'I miss my husband.'

He knew *exactly* what she meant — and stood up.

'Well, I should be going. Tell Adele I called, will you?'

'You have to go so soon?' Julia asked, walking to the door with him.

He could smell her perfume and noticed the full outline of her upper lip. God, Sam thought, his excitement stirred, this isn't right. This is Adele's sister. Get out. Get out while you still can ...

'Bye for now, Mrs Courtland.'

She nodded. In full control. 'Until the next time, *Sam*.'

Hearing the door close behind him, Sam began to walk, fast. He was — the truth shamed him — attracted to Julia Ford. The feeling was simple lust. Nothing like the affection he felt for Adele. Stopping in his tracks, Sam lit a cigarette. He was confused and yet excited, his thoughts leapfrogging. He *couldn't* cheat on Adele. And yet hadn't he realised that there was no future with her? God, he thought — mortified that he was even trying to make a case for betrayal — what was he thinking? He was behaving like a shit, he had to pull himself together, walk away.

It was the decent thing to do.

31

Late for work, Adele ran for the tram and jumped on, scrambling for the last seat. She would get it in the neck, and it was deserved. And yet the auction the previous night had been so incredible, so worth the rollicking she would get from old man Hill . . . Her gaze moved out of the tram window, her thoughts beating a tattoo on the passing cobbles. The Brunswick Hotel, Southport . . . Turner Gades had picked her up from work the previous evening in his car. With him had been his lady friend, Clemmie Brooks. She was a mature woman, older than Turner. Very welcoming to a girl who was nervous and feeling out of place. Glancing over the back of the passenger seat, Clemmie had chatted easily to Adele about nothing significant, and if she noticed the poor clothes and worn shoes, she had said nothing.

Instead both she and Turner had made a point of including Adele, from the moment the three of them entered the Brunswick Hotel. God, Adele thought, remembering — those chandeliers, those silk wall coverings, those rows of little gold chairs. And the auctioneer — in evening dress. Adele had never seen anyone wearing evening dress. Amongst the excited hum of the buyers, Turner had showed Clemmie and Adele to their seats, nodding to several of his acquaintances. Nervously, Adele had fiddled with her bag and hair, her gaze moving over the paintings lined up on the walls, and the French furniture. She had never — in her life or in her dreams — seen anything so incredible. For an instant she had even caught her breath.

'The man over there,' Turner had said quietly to Adele, 'the big man with the white moustache, that's French Kettering. Called French because he's always dealt in French furniture.' He had glanced round. 'And the old man with the woman in the mink coat, he's Morris Devonshire — watch him, he'll bid for the Roberts watercolour.' He smiled at Adele, then explained, 'David Roberts was an important watercolour painter. Always fetches good prices at auction.'

She had nodded, making mental notes.

'Always watch what French Kettering buys. He has a good eye, probably the best in this area — a kind of intuition for what's going to be popular.'

Her head whirling with all the information, Adele continued to watch the auction proceed. There had been no boozy, sleazy Henry Shine, just the smartly dressed auctioneer with his polished gavel, standing on a raised dais like a glossy idol. God, she had thought suddenly, how her parents would have loved to have been there. She could imagine Victor and Lulu Ford, in all their finery, sitting on the delicate gilt chairs, revelling in the occasion.

'See,' Turner had said suddenly, breaking into her thoughts. 'Kettering's bidding for that French glass. Lalique, the catalogue says. Bound to be collectable.' His hand shot up, his bid taken, Kettering glancing across the room and nodding to Turner in acknowledgment. Three more bids were exchanged between them, Turner finally allowing Kettering to purchase the piece. 'Too expensive for me. I don't usually deal in glass.'

Adele had been gleaming with pride, dizzy with amazement. This important man — with his elegant companion — was trying to educate her. Not patronise, not show off his own knowledge, but share a mutual passion. *With her . . .* For the remainder of the evening, Adele had been in a dream world. For those few hours she had been in her element, a sleek young sprat in a busy shoal, protected by the biggest fish in the pond. And it was then, that evening, that Adele realised how desperately she wanted to succeed. Maybe Turner Gades was grooming her. Maybe he had her in mind for a new job. A position he had heard about. And after that, what? It was simple — in time Adele would have her own shop. She would be someone. A respected professional.

Under the chandelier, surrounded by expensive suits and dresses, Adele Ford had sat mesmerised. She had known it would end. In the morning she would have to go back to Saul Hill's, with the geese hissing outside and the old painting of the vicar leaning against the commode. It would be the same as always — and yet different. This time she would sit behind the counter and take all the old man's ravings in her stride, because finally Adele Ford knew where she was heading. She had seen it — albeit fleetingly — *she had seen her place in life*.

All that remained was finding the way to get to it.

Glancing at her watch again, Adele stopped thinking of the previous night and hurried into Saul Hill's shop. There were no early customers, but the till was open — and empty. Frowning, she looked round. Maybe her employer had already been to the bank? She had counted the takings herself the previous day and knew that the money had been left in the till overnight — so maybe Saul Hill had gone out first thing. Not that he usually did, that was a job for the afternoon. Surprised, Adele looked around. Of course he could have put the money somewhere else. Hidden it away. But why leave the till wide open?

Another thought hit her in that moment. *Saul Hill had been burgled . . .*

'Mr Hill?' Adele called out anxiously, walking towards the back room. The far door was open and it was very cold, snow falling heavily into the yard beyond. She had a sudden sense of dread.

'Mr Hill?' she repeated, walking through.

There was a scuffle of noise. Adele tensed and then watched Saul Hill come out of the storehouse, beating back the geese. Suddenly he stopped in his tracks, snow falling on his shirtsleeves, his eyes blank. And then, throwing back his bald head, he began to scream. Horrified, Adele ran out into the yard, the snow whirling maniacally around the two of them.

'Mr Hill, what is it? Are you all right?' She grabbed his shoulders, bony and ice cold. 'Mr Hill!'

Suddenly he stopped screaming and stared at her. For a long, penetrating moment he stood — perfectly still — in the blinding, whirling snow.

'Mr Hill?' Adele repeated gently. 'Come inside. It's cold. Come inside.'

He didn't move.

'Mr Hill, are you all right?' Adele asked again, frightened when the old man didn't respond.

Tentatively she shook his arm. There was no resistance. Then, very slowly, she led him across the yard back to the shop. Around their legs the geese flapped and then fell silent, following the strange snow-whitened couple. When they reached the back steps, the old man hesitated, as though trying to remember how to climb. He glanced at Adele blankly, then stepped up, his feet dragging.

Once inside, Adele sat her employer down and reached into the medicine cupboard for his brandy. Pouring a small tot, she turned round to give it to him — and flinched.

Saul Hill was standing on the chair, glowering down at her.

'Get away! I know you're trying to poison me!'

Scared, Adele put down the glass. 'No, that's not true.'

'*Liar!*' he said, jumping up and down on the well-stuffed seat. 'You want my money. My goods. Well, I've got the key.' He waved it in front of her, dangling it like a spider at the end of its thread. 'You want this?'

'No,' Adele replied simply, struggling to keep her voice even. He had gone mad, she thought, anxious for her own safety.

'You can't have it! You can't have it!' Saul said, his voice raised. And then suddenly he stopped shouting, climbed off the chair and sat down. Silent, staring ahead.

Her heart hammering, Adele could hear the clocks ticking beyond, the geese pecking at the stone flags of the yard and a tram passing outside, braking as it came to the bend. Never taking her eyes off the old man, she moved tentatively towards the door — but Saul Hill was there before her. His massive bald head was tilted over to one side, his eyes bright with malice.

'*Give it back!*'

'What?' she whispered.

'My money.'

'I don't have your money!'

'I want it,' he crooned, wiggling his head. 'You stole it!'

'Mr Hill,' Adele said, distressed, 'I haven't taken anything.'

'My till's empty. *Liar!*' he screamed, his eyes fixed on her, one hand raised, the fist clenched.

In that instant the tram sounded its horn outside, distracting the old man's attention. Taking her chance, Adele pushed him to one side and ran out. She ran so fast that before long she could hardly breathe, her feet slipping on the icy pavement. Gradually she slowed her steps. Saul Hill was crazy. He could have hurt her, killed her. Another thought followed. She had better tell someone The police? No, she would get home first, get back to The Coppice, to safety.

221

Seeing another tram approach, Adele hailed it and jumped on. Unnerved, she huddled against the window and tried to stop shaking. The tram shuffled and ground its slow way through the snow, Adele keeping her face averted, the image of Saul Hill replaying itself over and over again in her mind. He was insane, he had lost his mind . . . Be calm, she told herself, you're out of there now, you're safe.

Finally Adele reached her stop and got off, hurrying into The Coppice and home. Fiddling with the key in the lock, she pushed open the front door — and then paused. There were voices coming from the other room. Two voices, her sister's and someone else's she knew well. White-faced, Adele crept over to the door, laid her hand on the wooden panel and gently pushed.

They didn't see or hear her. But she saw *them* — her sister and Samuel Ayres, kissing, their figures silhouetted against the window and the chilling winter light.

32

Bewildered, Adele had backed out of the house. There was an unreal quality to the morning, a dream-like atmosphere which left her wondering if she had really seen her sister with her boyfriend. And old Saul Hill raving, about to attack her. Was she asleep? Idiotically, she pinched her arm, the sting making her wince. No, she was fully awake and it was all real. It was all real . . . The snow flurry had ended and a peevish little sun sliced through the soft underbelly of the clouds as she walked away.

Confusion made her head swim. She was walking away — to go where? She couldn't — wouldn't — go back to the shop, so where else? And there was Saul Hill to think about. She had to get help, call a doctor . . . Numbly, she walked out of The Coppice, back into the centre of Oldham. Around her, people were busy shopping, the mill hooter sounding in the distance, a boy shouting out the newspaper headlines.

Her feet moved automatically. So much so that it took her a while to realise how cold she was. Her sister and Sam. *Her sister and Sam* . . . Was it deliberate? She couldn't understand it. Couldn't work out the motive. Had Julia done it to get back at her? For what? Adele stopped walking, a huge chasm of grief opening up inside her. *Julia had betrayed her.*

But how could she? After what she had suffered with John, how could she go behind her own sister's back? Stealing her boyfriend? Adele shook her head, oblivious to the passers-by.

'Why?' she said softly to herself. 'Why?'

Forcing herself on, Adele kept moving. And how could *Sam* cheat on her? She realised then how much she had fallen in love with him, how much the hurt was chewing at her, ripping her insides. God, she thought desperately, *how could they?*

A car horn snapped Adele out of her reverie, a man driving past quickly. Brightly coloured cigarette billboards and OXTAIL posters glared down from the sides of buildings; the steps of the Town Hall came into view as Adele walked on. All around, the January snow smirked against the pavements, the drains dripping with slush. And overhead the sky darkened with the promise of another storm.

Finally, Adele came to her destination and knocked, walking in without waiting for an answer. Surprised, Frida Altman watched the young woman sit down at the foot of her day bed and begin to cry inconsolably.

★　★　★

Rushing out of Saul Hill's shop, the man almost knocked Pauline Buckley off her feet as he hurried past. Furious, Pauline stared after him, then walked into the shop. She was curious, rather hoping that the pretty assistant might be around and she could patronise her further

224

— but there was no sign of anyone. Ringing the brass bell on the counter, Pauline waited. Again she rang. No response. Sighing with irritation, she moved around the counter and then stopped. She could see at a glance that the till was open. And empty.

Her tongue clicked. 'Fancy . . . '

Nosiness pushed her on. It would be something to tell her mother later, that the ghastly old man had had a burglary. Another thought hit Pauline at once. Please God, the villain hadn't taken that damn Derby vase! She didn't dare return to Springhead without it.

'Hello?' Pauline called out tentatively, walking in a little further. 'Hello?' A sudden movement in the back made her jump. 'Hello, is there anyone there? It's Miss Buckley, I've come for the vase.'

Silence.

'The Derby vase . . . Mr Hill, is that you? Mr Hill! *Is there anyone in this shop!*'

Infuriated, she moved on into the back room, then screamed. On the floor, lying motionless and staring upwards, was Saul Hill. His eyes were fixed, his breathing hardly discernible, his body completely rigid.

Hurrying out, a startled Pauline made for the door. On her way she paused just long enough to grab the Derby vase from the top of the display cabinet by the door.

★　★　★

Bitterly ashamed, Sam Ayres inhaled on his roll-up. The noise of the market soothed him, his coat collar turned up against the cold. He would stay for as long as there was any trade — and that could mean nine or ten at night on a Friday. It was an old custom, keeping open late to cater for the factory workers coming off shift. Inhaling again, Sam hunkered into his coat, glad that the snow had stopped. On the side of his stall a paraffin lamp glowed, and a woman with two kids stopped to look at a chamber pot.

'How much?'

'Sixpence.'

'It's chipped!'

'I know,' Sam said wearily. 'That's why it's sixpence.'

He wasn't surprised that she moved on. His usual charm had deserted him for the present, his thoughts turning back to Julia Ford. God, why had he been such a fool? If only he had resisted the temptation. There were enough girls keen on him — why pick Julia Ford? Or maybe that was the point; there was an element of danger with her . . . Jesus, he should grow up! Sam thought angrily to himself, watching a pit worker stop and finger a latch.

'How much?'

'Threepence.'

'Right yer are,' the man said, digging into his back pocket and pulling out a coin. 'Fer my wife; she's wanted the lock on the back door fixing fer long enough.'

Nodding, Sam watched the man walk off. He would go home and mend the back door lock. His wife would be pleased, and then probably they — and their kids — would sit down for supper. Not a bad life . . . Moodily, Sam stubbed out his cigarette and then lit another, coughing. He would have to tell Adele. She would be angry, but he would *have* to come clean. But why? he thought suddenly. What you didn't know didn't harm you. And Julia was hardly likely to confess. He thought of her again, of her sensuality. She had come on to him and he hadn't fought her off. And yet after they had kissed passionately for a while, both of them had withdrawn. A mutual decision. Nothing much. Hardly worth worrying about.

But of course it was. It was a betrayal of Adele. And anyway, Sam had to admit that he was sexually stimulated by Julia. He would have to keep away, he knew that much. Certainly never go near Julia again, or God knows what would happen. He blew the smoke from between his lips thoughtfully. What a lame excuse he had used to get into the Ford house.

'Is Adele home?' he had asked, knowing damn well she wasn't.

And Julia had smiled. 'No, but come in anyway.'

'I just wanted to bring her this,' Sam had gone on, passing a scarf over to Julia. 'She left it on the bus.'

It was a scarf he could have given back to her any time, an article he had used just to get into the Ford house. A scam that Julia had understood and colluded with. Her face had been so expectant, her smile so welcoming; a sexual woman regaining her powers. And using them. Her mouth had been so hungry when he had kissed her. And then the awful pulling back, the expression in Julia's eyes which was more than shame. *Desire and shame.* A look which said she didn't want to betray her sister — but still wanted him.

'How much is that fireguard?'

Sam jumped, surprised out of his thoughts, and wrong-footed to see Adele facing him.

'Hello there,' he said, trying to sound normal. 'I wasn't expecting you.'

She ignored him. 'I asked how much the fireguard was?'

'One and six.'

'You're a crook, Mr Ayres,' she said, her voice expressionless.

She was wearing the same red coat that she had worn at Christmas time, and looked so pretty. But her eyes were only inches from tears. *She knows,* Sam thought desperately. *She knows. But how?*

'One and six is a lot for a fireguard.'

He tried a smile. 'Depends on the fireguard . . . ' His guilt made him flustered. 'I could always make a special price for you.'

'Oh yes, you always treat me right, Sam, don't you?'

Her stillness was spellbinding, Sam watching her as she fingered the smaller objects on his stall. He felt ashamed, embarrassed, sweating in the cold. And beside him the blue flame of the paraffin light hissed and fluttered in the cold night.

'Adele, what's up?'

'You know.'

'I do?' he asked brokenly.

228

She smiled, pale, distant. Almost intimidating. 'Tell me what happened, Sam.'

'I don't know what you mean!' he blustered.

'Just tell me the truth.'

And then Samuel Ayres made one of the biggest mistakes of his life, he lied. He lied to a young woman who had done nothing but love him. He lied to a kind person who had been his sweetheart. And his friend.

'I don't know what's got into you, Adele!' he said snappily, on the defensive. 'You're acting odd. Nothing's happened. Nothing's any different.'

Adele's expression never altered as with one quick, angry movement she tipped over the market stall. It fell with a resounding crash, people turning to watch as objects and bric-a-brac went flying. Startled, Sam jumped back, the upturned table clattering at his feet, the fireguard breaking in two as it hit the ground in front of him.

33

In the paper works, the noise was deafening, the smell of the hot size making the visitor retch. Impervious, Ernest Vincent kept walking along the gallery suspended high over the factory floor below. His voice was raised, one hand pointing downwards to the workers below.

'We can get out more paper than any other factory in Rochdale. Same goes for our place in Manchester,' he said proudly, turning to his visitor. He could see the queasy tint to the foreigner's face and motioned for him to follow him back to the office. Once inside, Ernest poured his visitor a brandy and then leaned back against his desk.

'You get used to the smell after a while.'

'I don't doubt it,' the Spaniard replied, taking another sip. 'You have a very impressive business.'

Ernest nodded, sitting down. He was approaching sixty, approaching overweight, and approaching alcoholism. But he was also very astute, very fair in his dealings and very well liked.

'I offered you a good deal. Better than you'd get in Madrid.'

The man nodded. 'You're right, and I accept your terms. You can expect to hear from my lawyers shortly.' Standing up, he made as if to leave. Ernest frowned.

'Don't rush off, you haven't met my son, Col,'

he said proudly. 'He's on his way over. Should be here any time.'

Col Vincent was, at that particular moment, reading the newspaper on the private toilet reserved for the Vincent family alone. With his legs crossed and propped up against the wall of the cubicle, Col knew that most people coming to look for him would be too embarrassed to persist. Languidly turning over the front page, he carried on reading about the racing driver Major Henry Segrave, who was training hard in Florida in preparation for his challenge to Malcolm Campbell's speed record. Col paused, wondering how it felt to drive so fast, and how much a car like Segrave's would cost.

A knock on the outer door made him look up, surprised by the interruption.

'Mr Vincent, so sorry to bother you, sir,' a hesitant voice explained, 'but your father is waiting for you.'

Resigned, Col stood up and flushed the toilet needlessly. Then, straightening his clothes, he moved out into the factory beyond.

There was something compelling about Col Vincent. Some quality that made people look at him. His bearing helped: he had the tall figure and standing of a military man, and wore his clothes with considerable style. Deep black hair, green eyes and a welcoming smile made him seem handsome, approachable. But in an instant Col's mood could change, his humour vanishing, the eyes hard and watchful.

His very capriciousness was catnip to some. Women liked the challenge of his shifting moods, and men reluctantly admired the air of danger around him. In reality, his term serving in the last war had been undistinguished, but no man had ever made a uniform work for him so well. His leaves of absence were punctuated with dates, assignations. He had even been engaged — for six weeks — to the daughter of a local politician. But it hadn't worked out. He wasn't a predator; that wasn't Col's way. Women simply gravitated towards him, and seduction was a simple, inevitable process. The miracle was that none of his ex-lovers despised him. They might miss him, regret losing him, but Col's charm left them soothed. And perhaps wondering if — sometime — they might have another chance with him.

Intelligent, but not gifted, Col was ideally suited to the family business. He had no inclinations elsewhere — and what was work apart from a way to make money? And why did he need to make money when the Vincents were well off and he was the only heir? It was true they weren't fabulously rich, but they were amongst the wealthiest of the families in the north-west. There had been fortunes to be made from cotton, timber and paper — and Ernest had capitalised on all three.

His son amused Ernest, made him laugh. Col's mood swings might be indulged by his father, but his mother, Mary Vincent, had limited patience, even though Col was her only surviving child. She had lost two other sons at birth and had spent Col's childhood waiting for the accident or illness which would take him away too. But Col had survived, his father's doting having a profound effect on his character. He had charm — and temperament. A lethal combination.

Climbing the steps to his father's office, Col extended his hand to the Spaniard. 'I hope we'll be doing business soon.'

The man nodded eagerly. 'Indeed we will. I have explained to your father that my lawyers will be in touch.'

'And charge for the privilege,' Col replied, smiling urbanely as he and his father saw their customer to the gates.

As they waved the man off, snow was falling, the temperature hovering around freezing. In the background, the steam from the mill chimneys slid up into the ivory heavens, the clatter of the paper presses echoing into the still afternoon.

'What d'you make of him?' Ernest asked, eyeing up his handsome son.

'Seems all right.'

'One of the richest men in Madrid.'

Col shrugged. 'I thought I'd get off home now.'

'I was going to talk about something important with you,' Ernest began hurriedly. 'We should discuss the business of expansion. Our rivals are opening up in Manchester, some as far as Leeds.'

'Why expand? We have more than enough to do already.'

Ernest sighed, turning to walk back to the office, his son following. 'Col, you and I think differently about the business. I want to expand, take on more, and so should you. You're a young man, with plenty of energy. You could be building your own future.'

'You've already built my future,' Col replied, smiling, amused. 'In fact you've repaired the roof, put in the windows *and* damp-proofed the cellar . . . '

Ernest laughed.

'I am to be the caretaker of your ambition. And that seems perfectly reasonable to me, Father.'

'You don't want to put your own stamp on the business?'

'It's not a prize heifer,' he pointed out, his tone light. 'No, Dad, I'm content. I couldn't possibly do it any better than you. Why should I demand changes to something that needs no changing? I admire you — and I'm quite content to trail behind you like an acolyte.'

Ernest gave his son a wry look.

'Oh come,' Col said, taking his father's arm. 'Don't look so serious. You just have to tell me what to do, and I'll do it. Now, I ask you, what father had a less demanding son?'

'You weren't so undemanding about that car.'

Col's dark eyebrows rose. 'You said the directors could all have a car.'

'Not a sports car.'

'You want me to look like a pauper?'

'No,' Ernest replied, smiling indulgently. 'But I don't want you to look like a gangster either. It would be bad for business.'

'Depends on the business,' Col replied drily.

And there it was, a smile of real amusement,

Col's defence against the world. Other men used a sharp tongue, a vicious weapon, a ruthless streak — Col Vincent used charm, a sweetness he could call on at will. A sweetness that was genuine but intermittent. And yet, despite all his other, darker moods, the charm lingered longest in people's minds. It might not be lasting, but it was mesmerically powerful.

34

Dear God, Julia thought, watching Adele throw down her bag in fury, what had she done? The answer was obvious: she had betrayed her sister, tried to seduce her boyfriend, thrown herself at a man she hardly knew! What had she been thinking? Julia blanched at the memory. But the feeling had been so intense, so overwhelming. She had been in control again, desired again . . . That was no excuse, though, she thought desperately; nothing was a good enough excuse for what she had done.

'Adele, listen to me, nothing happened . . . '

'*Shut up!*' her sister replied, walking past Julia into the front room. 'I saw you with him.'

'We were just carried away. We only kissed.'

'*Only kissed!*' Adele snapped. 'There's no *only* about it. Sam was my boyfriend.'

'Sam *is* your boyfriend,' Julia replied, desperate to try to make up the lost ground.

She had been racked with guilt about what she had done, but it had been a momentary aberration, a second's loss of control. She hadn't really known what she was doing — only that she had needed a man to want her again. Frustration had overwhelmed her suddenly, and coming out of her long drought she had guzzled down greedily the first opportunity she had had.

'Adele, listen to me . . . '

'You and me, always *you and me*. We'd be all

236

right if it was just the two of us, you said.' Adele paused, bitter. 'You hypocrite! You weren't trying to protect me, you were just wanting to get your hands on my boyfriend.'

'It's not like that!'

'What *is* it like?' Adele hurled back, flopping into a seat, tears close to the surface. 'You knew how much I liked Sam. I was in love with him. I suppose you think that's funny? I suppose you don't believe in love any more, Julia. Not after John . . . ' She bit her lip to stop the tears. 'I liked Sam so much.'

Julia's voice was pleading, desperate. 'You *still* like him.'

'Oh no!' Adele replied, her tone firm. 'How could I like a man who would cheat with my sister?'

'*We were just kissing!*'

'And then what? What about the next time?'

'There isn't going to be a next time!' Julia said brokenly, reaching out to her sister.

But Adele brushed her away, getting to her feet and walking over to the door. 'We've supported each other all our lives. We've stood up for each other, Julia. Protected each other. I know everything about you and you know everything about me. We were more than sisters. You were my whole family . . . I thought I could rely on you.'

'You can!' she cried brokenly.

'No,' Adele said, turning away. 'I can't rely on you now. I can't even trust you any more. And I needed you so much, Julia . . . '

'Adele, please . . . '

'Saul Hill went crazy,' Adele said, shuddering at the memory. 'I ran out of that shop as soon as I could. I thought to myself, if I can just get home, I'll be all right . . . '

Julia moved closer to her sister. 'What are you talking about?'

'But when I got home, instead of having my sister to turn to, she was kissing my boyfriend!'

Baffled, Julia pressed her to explain. 'I don't understand, Adele. What happened? In the shop?'

'Saul Hill is mad.'

'*What?*'

'He went mad,' Adele replied sharply. 'He was talking rubbish. Screaming. It was terrifying. I wanted to help him, but I couldn't even make him understand me. He was so far gone. And then he went off the deep end completely. He was going to hit me . . . '

'*Dear God . . .* '

Shaking her head, Adele struggled to compose her thoughts.

'When I arrived at work the till was open. Empty.' She was trying to piece together the events. 'Saul Hill was in the back yard. He was talking like a madman . . . and then he said I'd taken his money. He was beside himself. He was going to hit me . . . God knows what he would have done if I hadn't got out.' Adele shivered. 'Oh God, I have to tell someone. Get help. He could be ill, really ill. Or he could do something stupid . . . I think the old man's dangerous.'

There was a sudden knock at the front door.

Julia frowned. 'Ignore it. Whoever it is will go away.'

But they didn't. They knocked again.

Julia walked out into the hall. Adele could hear voices through the door.

'Mrs Courtland? I'd like a word with your sister, if I may.'

Surprised, Adele turned to watch Julia re-enter with a policeman in tow.

'Miss Ford?'

She nodded. 'Yes, what's the matter?'

'You are employed by Mr Saul Hill, of Saul Hill Antiques, Failsworth?'

Again Adele nodded. 'Yes, why?'

'Mr Hill has made a complaint against you, Miss Ford. He has charged you with theft — '

'Are you mad!' Julia blurted out. 'Adele's told me all about this. That old fool attacked her.'

'Really?' the policeman replied, his tone cool. 'He told us that your sister attacked *him*.'

35

February 1927

Valiantly trying to smooth down his head of wiry red hair, Bernard Hoggard applied a little more oil. Then he combed his hair again. He waited. It stayed put. Thank God, if he was lucky it might remain flat for all of an hour. Glancing at his notes, he thought about the Ford sisters. He remembered only too well the first time he had met Julia, but he had never encountered Adele. In all the years he had been solicitor to the Ford family, the younger daughter had never crossed his path. But that was about to change.

He had been expecting a visit from Julia for a long time. Naturally he had heard of her husband's desertion, and he had thought — not unreasonably — that in time there would be a reconciliation. Or a divorce. But apparently there had been no developments on the romantic front for Julia. And as for her sister, the news was of the most sensational kind. She had been accused of being a thief.

Dear God, what a thing to live down, Bernard thought. Even untrue, mud stuck like shit to a blanket. He coughed, glancing at his notes again and then looking up as the two Ford sisters were shown into his office. Julia was as good looking as Bernard remembered; a little older, perhaps a little less sure of herself, but still handsome. As for Adele . . . He scrutinised her thoughtfully.

More slender than her sister, her face intriguing, the eyes steady and grave.

'Mrs Courtland, Miss Ford,' Bernard said, showing them to the chairs opposite his desk. 'How nice to see you again.'

He could see at once that Adele was on edge. Not surprising. Bernard had heard the gossip over the last weeks. How Saul Hill had accused her of attacking him and stealing his money. Apparently Pauline Buckley had found him, and when he regained consciousness in hospital the old man had called in the police. From the first, he had been adamant in his story. Adele Ford had attacked him, knocked him to the ground and emptied the till, leaving him for dead.

An incredible story. After all, Adele Ford didn't look like a criminal, a woman with a vicious streak. She was little more than a girl. A friendly, harmless girl . . . Not that the envious Pauline Buckley saw it that way. Her bitter tongue incited the gossip fast. And so, from Springhead to Oldham, from Oldham to Rochdale, and from Rochdale to Failsworth the story travelled, gathering more mud than a farm cart's wheels.

But although some people relished the gossip, others leapt to Adele's defence. All her old friends on Tommyfields and at the covered market brushed aside the story. Mrs Hodges told everyone she knew that it was all a lie. As for Becky and Frida Altman, they wouldn't even consider it. Adele a thief? Never. But enough gossip was going the rounds to keep the doubts alive in some heads. And Adele, mortified by the accusation, found herself ill at ease and unusually on the defensive.

Still regarding her curiously, Bernard thought back. As soon as the police had visited The Coppice, Julia had contacted him, in semihysterics, blathering on about her sister and old man Hill. At first Bernard hadn't understood much, until he had spoken to the police. And then he had understood less . . . As the rumour keg started to smoulder, he had visited Saul Hill's doctor to assess the extent of the old man's injuries. Then, and only then, did it become apparent to everyone that Saul Hill was physically ill. And mentally delusional.

After his initial insistence that Adele was a thief, the story changed every time Saul Hill told it. Sometimes his neighbour had taken the money, sometimes his dead wife. Sometimes he described an Indian who had lurked around Failsworth for months, watching his shop. An Indian no one else had apparently noticed. The aneurysm which had ruptured in Saul Hill's brain — compounded by his encroaching senility — nibbled away at what was left of his reason. Before long he was, the doctor told Bernard Hoggard, totally deranged.

But try telling that to the gossips, Bernard thought. Try undoing the accusation which had been levelled at Adele Ford and which had been doing the rounds for weeks. It was going to be hard, very hard, he thought, glancing over to her. She returned his gaze levelly, as though she was trying to prove that she had nothing to hide. And never had.

'I suppose you're wondering why I called you in?'

Adele said nothing. Julia glanced quickly at her sister. She had seen a change in Adele. To be called a thief, even by a madman, was damning. And coming so soon after the incident with Samuel Ayres . . . Swallowing, Julia reached out for Adele's hand, but she pulled away, her face set.

'I have some interesting news for you,' Bernard began, noting the tense atmosphere between the two sisters. 'For you in particular, Adele.'

She glanced at him, her face unreadable. Get on with it then, she thought, let's hear it. Whatever it was, however bad, it couldn't match the past weeks. Hadn't her mother always told her that you found out who your friends were when you were in trouble? Lulu had been right about that. Samuel hadn't come near the house and Mrs Redfern — admittedly never a friend — had gossiped relentlessly. No doubt she hoped that soon the Ford sisters would be forced out of The Coppice.

But much as people liked to gossip, Adele was too popular to be made into a complete outcast. Some allies had emerged. Friends in unexpected places: Mr and Mrs Lockhart, and old Mr Thornhill, offering a sympathetic ear. And on the market she had been protected, defended constantly. But Adele had found that although Julia had backed her, somehow her sister's support didn't mean the same any more.

It had been late one evening — a week after

243

Saul Hill's accusation — that Adele had finally rallied, her old fight coming back suddenly. How *dare* anyone try to cow her? Who the hell was anyone to gossip about her? And, more pertinently, who of any importance would believe the accusation anyway? Galvanised, Adele had made a resolution: she wasn't going to be driven into a corner by what some madman said. She was innocent — and by God, she was going to prove it. She was also going to find another job. Hellfire, she had told herself, she was *worth* hiring! She was smart, willing to learn. In fact, she would start looking for work the following day.

An unexpected knocking from below had made her jump. Throwing open the window, Adele had looked out, trying to recognise the figure standing below.

'Adele?'

Her surprise had been obvious. 'Mr Gades?'

'I've been away on business and just heard what happened. I came as soon as I could.'

Adele had showed him into the front room and lit the fire, her hands shaking, flushed to the roots of her hair. This was the man who had treated her as an equal, been her mentor, and although innocent, she felt embarrassed, clumsy with unease.

'Of course it's all rubbish,' Turner said. 'Everyone realises that Saul Hill's lost his mind. Not that it wasn't very unpleasant for you, Adele. I can't imagine how hard it must have been. People love to gossip — especially about another person's reputation. Although how anyone could have taken his accusation seriously is beyond me. They found the money, you know.'

'No, I didn't know,' Adele had replied, surprised. 'No one told me that.'

'In that lock-up storeroom in the yard. Hidden in an old doll's pram, along with a whole pile of all sorts of bits and pieces. Just goes to show, doesn't it? Hill was paranoid about people stealing from him and it turned out that he was stealing from himself.' Turner had smiled wryly. 'Anyway, enough of him, what about you? Can I do anything to help?'

She had blurted it out without thinking. 'Well, actually, I need a job.'

'Oh.'

Flushing, Adele had turned away. God, how *could* she have been so blunt, so demanding? And with Turner Gades, of all people? How mortifying, she had thought. He was obviously embarrassed, with good reason. He had his reputation to think of and couldn't rescue her on demand. Besides, he had done more than enough for her already. For the first time in days, Adele had been relieved to see her sister walk in and break the tension.

'Miss Ford?'

Adele blinked, her thoughts drawn back to the present by Bernard Hoggard. 'Sorry, I was miles away.'

'As I said, there's been an interesting development,' Bernard went on. 'Obviously Mr Hill could no longer keep up the Failsworth shop, and so the lease has been taken over by someone else. Someone who is going to need a manager . . . if you are agreeable.'

'I don't understand,' Adele replied, bemused.

'Mr Turner Gades will pay the rent,' Bernard explained, 'if you agree to manage the shop.'

Bernard Hoggard appeared composed, but inwardly he was more than a little surprised. How incredible that Adele Ford should have such a protector! In fact, had Bernard been a cynical man, he might have suspected some emotional involvement. Were it not for the fact that Turner Gades was engaged to Clemmie Brooks . . . Bernard sighed, intolerant with human nature. One slip from grace — real or otherwise — and a person was marked out for life. As Adele Ford was now.

'What?'

'Mr Gades needs a manager for the shop,' Bernard replied. 'He's very impressed with you, young lady. So, are you interested?'

'Am I interested?' Adele repeated, grinning broadly. 'When do I start?'

36

In her lunch break, Becky called in at the Oldham library for some new books for Frida. 'Can you get me a biography?' her grandmother had asked. 'I love to read about people's lives.' Not for the first time, Becky wondered what Frida would have made of *her* life, if she had known the truth. Not that she would ever find out. Mrs Hodges wasn't going to tell anyone, and Adele could keep a secret to the grave. Only one thing puzzled Becky — why Mrs Hodges had never asked for a fee for the abortion. Adele had told her that she was repaying an old debt, but Becky wasn't convinced and had decided that one day — however long it took — she would repay Adele with interest.

As for Billy Kerr, he had never found out about the baby. And he had soon taken up with another girl, another mill conquest. Becky wasn't surprised; she hadn't wanted the affair to progress and had retreated back into her shell. Working hard and considering herself lucky that she had escaped a worse fate. But the memory of the abortion played on her mind. She had killed her baby. Oh, circumstances had forced her into it, but Becky never took any of her actions lightly.

'Sorry!' she said suddenly, walking into someone at the end of the aisle.

A thin, dark-haired man with glasses bent

down to pick up the two biographies Becky had dropped.

'My fault, I wasn't looking where I was going.' He glanced at the titles. 'Are you interested in Catherine of Russia?'

'It's for my grandmother,' Becky replied, smiling and moving on. Ten minutes later she bumped into him again, both of them laughing.

'I'm Isaac Jacobs,' he said, offering his hand.

'Rebecca Altman.'

They both noted the Jewish names. Quite a coincidence. But that was all, Becky decided. She couldn't get involved with any man. It was too painful, too difficult.

'Do you come here often?' He flushed to his roots, laughing, embarrassed. 'What a thing to say!'

Admiring his shyness, Becky found herself relaxing slightly. 'I get books for my grandmother every week. What about you? Are you a reader?'

'I work here,' Isaac replied. 'Since last week. I used to work in London, but I moved up here. A promotion, of sorts.' He flushed again, anxious that she wouldn't think he was bragging. 'I'm assistant librarian.'

'That's a good job,' she replied sincerely. 'A nice job.'

'What do you do?'

'I'm . . . ' She hesitated, then hurried on. 'I'm a mill girl. At the Ash mill.'

He was surprised, and showed it. 'You don't look or sound like a mill girl,' he said shyly.

Touched, Becky wanted to talk more to him, but she lost her nerve and, smiling, hurried away.

'You what?' Norman Buckley said, looking up at his adored daughter.

'You won't believe who I just saw together — Adele Ford and Turner Gades.'

'That bloody Gades man cost me a vase. For nothing! And I'm not a man to be messed about with.'

Smiling indulgently, Beryl looked at her daughter. 'It must have been innocent, darling. Mr Gades is engaged to Clemmie Brooks.'

'Whatever you say, I think Adele Ford tried to lead Turner Gades on but couldn't get her hooks into him. I mean, she's obviously capable of pretty much anything. Violence, stealing . . . '

'Saul Hill's story was proved to be rubbish.'

'Only because Turner Gades sorted it all out for Adele Ford,' Pauline replied, whining. 'Oh, think about it, Mother! When the old man was out of the way, he gave her Saul Hill's shop! There's got to be something behind it. No one just gives someone a shop for nothing.'

Norman glanced over to his daughter questioningly. 'If you want a shop so badly, Pauline, I'll buy you one.'

Enraged, his daughter flounced out of the room. Beryl turned to her husband.

'She doesn't want a shop,' she replied, her tone exasperated. 'She wants Turner Gades.'

'She doesn't even like him!'

'Oh, Norman,' Beryl said, her soft Edinburgh voice despairing. 'You can be such a fool at times.'

* ★ ★ ★

The weather had been overcast for many days, but that March morning dawned brilliantly, the sun making faces in at the windows, the street shimmering with an unexpectedly hard frost. Too nervous to eat breakfast, Adele changed her clothes twice and then rearranged her hair. She couldn't disappoint Turner Gades, couldn't fluff this chance. And she knew that everyone would be watching her. Talking about her, about her past. About her present. And about her connection with Turner Gades.

Her hands shaking, she pulled on her gloves, walking to the front door.

'You want me to come with you?' Julia asked anxiously.

For a moment it was *exactly* what Adele wanted. To have her sister with her . . . Torn, she hesitated on the doorstep. Why shouldn't she relent? Link arms with her sister and say: 'Yes, let's do it. Let's have an adventure. You come with me to Failsworth. We could run the shop together.' Not that long ago, Adele would have said those words. But not now.

'No thanks,' she said finally. 'I can manage.'

'That wasn't what I asked,' Julia replied, reaching out towards her sister. 'Let me help you, Adele. You'll need another pair of hands.'

'No,' she said sadly, making an excuse out of the weather. 'It's cold. You stay home, Julia. I'll be back later.'

At the bottom of The Coppice, Adele hailed a tram. Climbing on board, she took her seat and watched the streets pass. A mixture of apprehension and excitement filled her. *She was going to run a shop, an antique shop*. Dear God, what would her parents have said about that? What would her father had done to have his own place? Well, Adele corrected herself, maybe not her *own* place. But before long it might be. In time she would have splendid premises, and a splendid house. Like the Lydgate Widow. She was only nineteen, after all. Look how far she had come already. And look what it had cost her . . . A few minutes later, Adele got off the tram and walked towards the shop. Taking the old keys out of her coat pocket, she unlocked the door and then hesitated. An image of the sinister old man rose up before her suddenly. *Go on*, she willed herself, *go on, he's not there any more. Get on with it* . . . Walking in, she could smell dust and a faint odour of damp as she moved around. The flag was still there, the painting of the vicar still leaning boozily against the commode. Taking a deep breath, she sighed and continued into the back room.

At that moment a figure entered by the back door. Adele jumped.

'Sorry to frighten you,' Turner Gades said, walking in and smiling. 'I just wanted to be here to welcome you. Congratulations on your first day as manager.' He jerked his grey head towards the back yard. 'I've been feeding the geese.'

She relaxed, smiling. 'Did they go for you?'

'Not much,' he replied, glancing around and motioning for someone to come closer. 'I've brought a friend to meet you,' he went on,

251

pulling a face and winking. 'He's very rich and interested in antiques. In fact, for both our sakes I'm hoping he might become a good customer.'

Curious, Adele watched the stranger make his erratic progress through the geese. He was very tall and dark, genuinely amused as he dangled a bread crust at arm's length for the birds. For an instant he seemed almost surreal: the achingly bright sunshine shimmering around him, the gaggle of geese forming a froth of white foam at his feet.

Laughing, he smiled at Turner and then looked over to Adele, standing in the back doorway of the shop.

'Hello there,' he said cheerfully, making a pantomime bow. 'I'm Col Vincent. And you must be Adele Ford.'

Well, what can I tell you? I was fascinated from the very start. Was it a rebound response? A way of trying to obliterate the memory of Samuel Ayres? Possibly. But Col Vincent was no market trader. From the first moment it was obvious he was well bred, well fed, well read, well connected and well mannered. He was the living embodiment of the well-to-do. The kind of man my parents would have striven to know. The kind of man others try to impress. He was so far out of my reach that I could have caught the moon in the palm of my hand more easily.

And yet he was interested in me. I knew that much . . .

I was just nineteen, very pretty. My short life had been chock-full of incident and difficulty. In a few years I had seen more than most would ever see. I was older than my years, injured by events and yet desperately, grindingly ambitious. The gossip which had tagged me would — I realised — be no barrier to this man. Col Vincent had no need of respectability, or the mundane. He was already beginning to bore of life. I knew it, because he was — in that way — like my father.

Which was one of the reasons I should have run. Should have closed down my heart and put a barricade around my feelings. Should have listened to my instincts and bolted. But in the instant of our introduction I hesitated. Afterwards I tried to convince myself that it was manners. Col Vincent was a friend of Turner Gades, how could I be anything other than welcoming? But that was a lie.

One thing I know for certain is that Turner Gades would never knowingly have introduced me to anyone who would have done me harm. In the few years I had known him he had been a constant friend. Had always protected and nurtured me. Had welcomed me as an equal, when I was little more than a blundering tyro. His generosity and kindness had made so much that was unbearable, bearable.

And — like a fool — I believed that any friend of his would be the same.

PART THREE

The survival of the fittest.
Charles Darwin

Never underestimate the power of stupidity.
Anon.

37

Waving aside the dust, Turner coughed. Col Vincent was holding a handkerchief over his face. They were in the old storeroom, in the yard behind the Failsworth shop. The keys had been missing and finally Turner had broken the padlocks to get in. Shining his torch inside, a mess of objects had came under its beam. Crates, an old cart and a row of tin chests lining the walls. Pushing the geese back with his foot, Turner pulled the door shut behind them, and shone the torch around.

'I feel like Howard Carter.'

'You mean cursed?' Col shot back, laughing. 'What a dump!'

'What's that?' Turner asked, walking towards the back of the storeroom. 'My God, old Hill had a casket back here!'

'I told you, it's Tutankhamun's lost tomb,' Col went on. 'Any minute now we'll come across a mummy.'

'Like that one?' Turner asked, shining his torch over a swaddled shape.

'My God!' Col whispered, excited. 'You think the old man was killing people?'

'And embalming them out here? In the middle of Failsworth?'

'Maybe it's where he got all his good stuff.'

'From the Ancient Egyptians?'

Col pulled a face. 'From his *victims*.'

257

'Has anyone ever told you that you read far too many thrillers for a grown man?'

'But it happens all the time,' Col replied, tripping over a crate as he moved towards the swaddled shape. 'You read about it in the press. People are killed every day.' He paused, arriving at the figure and touching the wrappings. He sighed. 'It's just a bloody statue!'

'Shame,' Turner said drily. 'I was thinking we could open a waxworks.' Moving further in, he began to climb the steps to the upper level, Col hurrying after him.

'Why did we have to do this in the dark, anyway?'

'Because I wanted to sort it out when Adele wasn't around,' Turner replied, moving on. 'She has enough to do. And anyway, I didn't know what the crazy old fool might have in here.'

'How's Adele doing?'

'Good.'

'Really?'

Swinging the torch round to illuminate Col's face, Turner studied his friend. 'Yes, *really*. It's going to be hard going at first, but she's finding her feet.'

'Why?'

'Why what?'

'Why did you hire her as manager?'

'No, Col.'

Col frowned into the light, then pushed Turner's hand aside, the beam striking the ceiling.

'No what?'

'No, I'm not romantically interested in Adele. I never have been. Anyway, I'm marrying Clemmie.'

The mention of her name made Turner smile. Oh yes, he had been right to wait and see what happened, because slowly and easily a mutual friendship had turned into a deep love. Both of them found that life became less and less interesting when they were apart, and more and more natural when they were together. So much so that when he asked Clemmie to marry him, she said, smiling wryly: 'Seems like the perfect solution, doesn't it?'

Coughing again, Col broke into Turner's thoughts. 'I didn't ask if you were interested romantically in Adele.'

'No, but you were *thinking* it.'

'Am I *that* transparent, Turner?'

'Only to a friend.'

'If that's true,' Col went on, 'you've missed something.'

'That you're in love with Adele? No, I haven't missed that.'

Surprised, Col laughed, watching the beam of Turner's torch as it shone around a motley collection of furniture, most of it broken or riddled with woodworm. So his secret was out, was it? Well, he *was* in love with Adele and now he could finally admit it. Thinking of her, Col remembered the previous week when he had called into the shop and caught her struggling to lift a large gilt mirror. Hurrying over to help, his hands had brushed hers and he had felt a real jolt of attraction, intensified by the smell of her skin as they struggled side by side with the glass. The next day he had called in to see her. And the next. And by the fourth visit Adele was less surprised and seemed — or was he kidding himself? — to be *pleased* to see him. But not obviously. Not like all the other women who flirted and fawned over him. Oh no, Adele was her own woman, too ambitious and feisty to wear her heart on her sleeve. Which was the very reason she was different — and captivating.

'We'll have to burn the worst stuff.'

Col glanced over to Turner, pressing him on their previous topic of conversation. 'So, what d'you think? About me and Adele?'

'I think that if you hurt her I'll make you wish you had never been born.'

The words shook Col and it took him a moment to recover. 'What if I was serious about her?'

Again Turner shone the light into Col's face. Again Col guided its beam away. 'Are you serious about her?'

'I think I am.'

'Why, Col?' he asked, adding, 'No, don't answer that. I can answer it for you. She's different, she has a past. People gossip about Adele. She's unusual, she's out of the ordinary. She's pretty, clever, quick-witted. She's nothing like the other women you've known — and, most importantly, she's not in awe of you.'

'Christ,' Col remarked sullenly, 'you *do* know me, don't you?'

'Only as much as you want me to,' Turner answered soberly. 'I'm not that naïve.'

Moving on, he wedged the torch into an overhead beam so that it shone out over the mounds of decrepit rubbish Saul Hill had hoarded. Under a stack of old newspapers, a bathtub was filled with broken lamps, a garden urn stacked to the brim with firewood. Wall brackets, screens and shattered clocks leaned up against each other like exhausted refugees, a cracked plaster figurine glowing eerily out of the dimness.

'What was the point?' Col asked, looking round. 'All those locks and bolts on the door, to protect this load of junk? What for?'

'Because it was precious to him,' Turner replied. 'Because he could hide it all away, lock it up and look at it when he wanted. Because the hoarding was more important than the value.'

'Mad old sod.'

'Not that mad,' Turner replied sagely. 'At least he only chose objects to collect. Not people.'

*　*　*

Leaning against the back wall of the Failsworth shop, Kitty Gallager chewed the end of a piece of her hair. A tiny figure in a thin summer dress covered by a too-large wool coat, with Wellingtons on her feet, her alert, sharp-featured face was dominated by curious eyes and large, strong teeth.

'Bloody hell,' Kitty said thoughtfully to no one in particular. 'Bloody hell . . . '

Anything was better than the mill, she had decided, even cleaning.

261

Her head swivelled at the sound of approaching footsteps, and Adele came into view.

By contrast to her eccentric visitor, Adele was dressed sombrely, her hairstyle and clothing making her seem much older than her age. The previous week, on 6 September, she had turned twenty, but her manner and attitude put her a decade older. Which was exactly what she had intended. She didn't want to look like a kid, some girl. In order to hold her own at the shop and with the dealers, she had to seem more mature or they would wipe the floor with her.

Seeing her approach, Kitty walked up to her.

'Miss Ford?'

Adele nodded.

'I'm Kitty. I've come to clean.'

'Well, perhaps . . . '

'Oh, there's no perhaps,' Kitty went on blithely. 'I've no job, yer see, and I need a wage. And there's no one around 'ere who can clean like me. I don't mind toilets either. Yer know, I can clean up anything. M'dad — Pa Gallager — 'e said I can clean better than — '

Adele put up her hands. 'I'm seeing other people as well as you.'

'Yeah, but they'll not be right,' Kitty went on emphatically, dropping into step with Adele as she opened up the back of the shop. Stepping inside, Kitty whistled under her breath. 'Bloody hell . . . Yer've some right good stuff, yer have. Bet yer worry about thieving. I saw the geese, my brother said that geese are better than dogs any day.'

Warming to her, Adele showed Kitty around.

'I can't pay much . . . '

'Yeah, well, I can't clean much.' Laughing, she nudged Adele. 'Just a joke. It pays to have a laff.'

'How old are you?'

'Twenty,' Kitty replied, putting her head on one side. 'How old are yer?'

'Twenty.'

'Yer look older!'

'I want to. It's the impression I want to give.'

'I don't do impressions!' Kitty said, laughing again, then sobering up fast. 'Only kidding. Yer look dead smart.' She glanced round. 'So when do I start?'

'Miss . . . '

'*Kitty.*'

Adele nodded. 'Kitty, I . . . '

Moving towards Adele, Kitty dropped her voice. 'Look, I've taken a liking to this place, and I'm useful t'ave around. Not just fer cleaning neither. My family — well, m'pa, anyway, knows everyone. Yer follow my drift? Yer in any trouble, he can fix it. Yer need a bit of muscle, 'e can get it fer yer, no trouble.'

'Where d'you come from, Kitty?'

'Hanky Park,' she replied, raising her eyebrows. 'Yeah, I know, the slums. M'dad's famous — and not fer painting pictures.' She stopped dead. 'Sorry, I didn't think . . . '

'About what?'

'Yer know . . . yer had a bit of bother yerself a while back . . . '

So the news had travelled to Hanky Park, had it? God, Adele thought bitterly, how long would it take people to forget?

'Not that everyone didn't know Saul Hill were a crazy old bugger.' Kitty paused. 'I've a loud mouth, but I mean no harm. I just say what I think.'

Won over, Adele watched her. She liked Kitty Gallager. Liked her big mouth, her chat, her energy. Liked the look in her eye. And she was young. Adele wanted someone young around. Someone — dare she think it — who wouldn't judge her? It was hard to be always striving, trying not to do or say the wrong thing. Turner Gades was a fair employer and constant friend, but Adele was always aware that he knew her past and that she had to prove herself to him. In the six months she had managed the shop, she had driven herself relentlessly. She had kept the accounts perfectly, even fretting over any mistakes or deletions. As for the shop, nothing was out of place, the window changed weekly, the portrait of the vicar relegated to the back room. Trade at first had been reasonable, although Adele had enough sense to realise that most customers came to have a snoop or a gawk at the notorious Adele Ford. Funny how having a reputation could bring in business . . .

Embarrassed, Kitty hurried on. 'I'm not light-fingered! Don't hold with that. Never stole a thing in my life. Want to do it right, yer know? Yer can't say the same for my pa and my brothers — apart from Bert — but me, I'm straight as a dye.' She paused, suddenly serious as she saw Adele's expressionless face. 'Oh, I get it . . . Right yer are. I'm not yer type. Yeah, well, I'm a bit rough fer round 'ere. It's Failsworth, innit? I mean, not yer Monte Carlo, but a cut above Hanky Park.'

She moved to the door. Adele frowned. 'Where are you going?'

'Yer what?' Kitty said, turning back.

'Start tomorrow,' Adele told her, adding, 'Eight o'clock. And don't be late.'

38

Linking arms, Adele and Becky left the cinema. All evening Becky had been quiet, thoughtful, and Adele was curious to know why. Walking in step up Park Road, she asked suddenly, 'Have you met someone?'

Becky flinched. 'I . . . I . . . '

'You have!' Adele said, laughing. 'Oh, I'm so glad, so glad.'

Pausing, Becky stood under the lamplight, her dark hair shining, her face as exotically lovely as ever. But different, less sad.

'He's called Isaac Jacobs . . . He's Jewish, which is lucky. And he's very kind.'

'And you like him!' Adele cried, obviously relieved.

She had wondered for a long time when — or if — Becky would let down her emotional barriers. Careful not to push her friend, she had, however, tried to encourage Becky to think about a future. A husband, a family. But Becky would brush the matter away, with a slow look which always said the same thing: *You know my past. I can't* . . . Now, for once, she *wasn't* drawing back. She wasn't confident, Adele could see that only too clearly, but perhaps she was beginning to believe that there might be a future for her.

'Anyway,' Becky said hurriedly, 'what about Col?'

'I like him.'

'Is that all?'

'Oh, Becky, it's different,' Adele admitted, both of them walking on. 'I was in love with Sam, crazy about him. I don't feel that way about Col, but I admire him. How could I not? I know how much other women like him.' She pulled a face. 'God, *how* they like him! And I suppose I'm flattered that he likes me. But although he's funny and witty and fun, I don't feel that pinch to my heart that I always felt with Sam.' She shook her head. 'I want to fall in love, I really do! But you can't *make* yourself. I'm fond of Col, though, very fond.'

'I think I could love Isaac . . . ' Becky said quietly.

Surprised, Adele said nothing and kept walking, arm in arm with her friend.

'But I can't go on without telling him about what happened. It wouldn't be fair. Isaac is alone. He has no family, and he wants to settle down. He's even started hinting . . . '

'About marriage?'

Becky's head bowed. 'I know, it's madness! But he says he fell in love with me the moment he saw me. He says that he knew, that he'd waited thirty-four years to feel that way about anyone. And when he saw me, he knew we were meant to be together.' She stole a glance at Adele. 'What do I do?'

'What d'you want to do?'

She stopped walking. 'I want to marry him, Adele. I want to be safe. But I want to think about it for a while. I want to be sure that I'm not just doing it to escape the mill and get myself and my grandmother out of Park Street. Get us a better life.' She glanced down at her hands, always composed. 'But I have to be honest with him, I can't pretend I'm someone I'm not. Even if it's a risk.'

Adele asked quietly: 'Do you love this man?'

'Yes, I do.'

Becky paused. Did she? Did she really? Of course she did. She felt safe with Isaac, longed to see him at the gates of the Ash mill, waiting for her as she came off work. He had never made her feel her place, feel as though she should apologise for being a mill worker. From the day they had met, he had treated her like an empress. He wasn't good looking, but he was attractive in his way, a gentle man who bought presents for her. Not flashy gifts — he wasn't rich — but books of poems, flowers, ribbons. He would touch Becky's thick hair and then wind a red ribbon around its length, smiling at her, telling her she had the most beautiful hair in Lancashire.

Isaac's parents were dead, and he had no siblings. He had been alone a long time, without family, longing for a home. He had told Becky that only weeks after they had met, assuring her that he loved her, immediately, unconditionally — and that he wanted to settle down with her, have a family . . . Which was what every woman wanted to hear. Wasn't it? Of course it was. But Becky wasn't every woman, was she?

And sometimes there were other doubts:

Becky wondering whether the mill hooter and the responsibilities of her life were driving her into a hasty marriage. She had never fitted in; had been the butt of jokes and, later, ignored. Even her ill-judged fling with Billy Kerr had been hidden. An affair with the foreman would usually have involved the whole mill, but nothing had penetrated Rebecca's reserve.

Week in, week out, she had toiled at work she hated, taken home her pay and returned the following week. She had changed looms, changed bobbins, changed places under the vast mill ceiling. Cotton snow had fallen in the heat of summer and the hostile chill of winter. Every morning the knocker-up had shaken her out of her sleep, the factory hooter marking out her timetable. Only one person had stood by her, had been constant throughout the grinding, dreadful days. Adele.

Now, finally, Becky had an escape route. A way out. A means to get away from the piercing hooter and the clang of the closing iron gates. A way to restore herself, to be someone again. Mrs Isaac Jacobs. She would live in an ordinary little house, with ordinary possessions, and maybe some not-so-ordinary books. She would have a front door key and her grandmother around. Their lives would be ordinary, but not humiliating. And most of all, they would be a family. That status both she and Frida missed. That status Isaac longed for.

Yet if she told Isaac about her past, she would jeopardise all that. She would risk his leaving her. Lock herself into the mill for life . . . Her future hung on whether or not to confess. She knew it — and so did Adele. But this time Becky didn't ask her friend for advice.

This was a decision only one person could make.

39

Ernest Vincent leaned thoughtfully on the side of the raised gallery. Below him the workers scuttled around, the paper presses clanging, dust thrown up like summer pollen. His thoughts turned — as they had been doing more and more frequently — to his son's girlfriend. The first serious romance Col had ever had. It was no secret that there had been a number of women in his life, but no one had captivated him. Until now ... Drumming his fingers on the gallery rail, Ernest considered Adele Ford. He had been surprised to learn that she was only twenty, but when he had heard about her background, her attitude made sense.

This was no ordinary girl. No rich girl either. And yet she had caught the attention of an important mentor, Turner Gades. Who was no one's fool. Apparently, she was obsessed by antiques. Or so Turner had said. Adele Ford loved to buy and sell. Loved to deal. Had longed for an opportunity — which had come in the shape of Saul Hill's shop. Ernest frowned. At first he had thought that Turner was taking a risk on hiring an unproven young woman as his manager, but Adele had grabbed the chance like a greyhound would snatch a hare.

She had also snatched the attention of his son, by affecting no interest in Col whatsoever. Was that her being clever, or genuine? Ernest wondered. Was it guile which was ensnaring Col? His handsome, charming, easily bored heir? Hearing the blast of a car horn, Ernest leaned over the gallery to glance into the yard. His son had just driven in and was now helping a young woman out of his car. So this was Adele Ford . . . Ernest thought, hurrying downstairs.

She turned as she heard his footsteps on the iron steps, smiling, her hair pinned up on top of her head, her face flushed slightly with the winter cold. In her arms she was holding a car rug, her hands delicate and pale against the dark wool.

'Dad, this is Adele,' Col said happily, 'and Adele, this is my father.'

Ernest could see in that instant why she had inspired the protective instinct in Turner Gades. Adele didn't look fragile, or helpless. But there was a trace of vulnerability under her composure. A softness which was appealing and at the same time contradictory. After all, at first glance she appeared to be the epitome of modernity: her hair waved, her clothes demure but fashionable. One of the new breed of women who had first emerged after the war — and grown in stature ever since.

Young, confident, ambitious. And yet the perceptive Ernest could see in Adele Ford's eyes something entirely different. The lost child, the fatherless and motherless girl. The wronged innocent. With an achingly open heart.

★ ★ ★

'*Col Vincent!*' Pauline Buckley said, apoplectic. 'That Adele Ford's got Col Vincent now! What's she got that I haven't? She's no money, she's no class, no name. She's even got a reputation for stealing — '

'That was proved to be false.'

'Whose side are you on!' Pauline snapped, then slid her hefty rump on to the arm of her father's chair. 'You know that awful Turner Gades?'

'He cost me a vase, he did!' Ernest replied, stung. 'And I'm not a man to be messed about.'

'No one messes you about,' Pauline agreed hastily, 'but you remember him?'

'Well enough.'

'And you remember Col Vincent? Ernest Vincent's son?'

'Vaguely.'

'Well, that common Adele Ford has been stringing them both along.'

Norman was careful not to look impressed. 'Never!'

'She has, Daddy! And it's not right. Anyway, I've been very upset, but now I understand why it's been happening. Obviously men like independent women — '

'You're moving out?' he asked hopefully.

'Don't be silly! How could I leave you?' Pauline replied. 'Obviously men like women who have careers of their own. Women who are modern . . . So, will you buy me one, Daddy?'

He was floundering, out of his depth. 'You want me to buy you a man?'

'No!' Pauline said, laughing. 'A shop!'

273

'Don't yer say a word, yer hear?' Kitty said, glancing up at the huge Chinaman standing beside her. 'Yer hear me, let me do the talking, all right?'

He nodded, his shoulder-length black hair pulled back in a ponytail, his eyes alert as they waited in the back alley behind the Failsworth shop. Impressively oversized for a Chinaman, Dave Lin had an Oriental mother and a Liverpudlian father — from whom he had inherited his height and bulk. And his fists. He might have been a little slow, but Dave Lin had been the perfect rent collector. One look at him and everyone in Hanky Park had paid up. Until they had got to know his real nature. After that, any sob story a tenant told the Chinaman had resulted in an extra's week grace. And his sacking.

So now Dave Lin was standing, towering over the diminutive Kitty Gallager, in the alleyway. A man passed, noticed the Chinaman, and crossed over. Kitty smirked.

'Yer see, yer frighten everyone, Dave. They don't know yer round these parts, don't know yer a big old jelly.' She pushed him back against the wall hurriedly. 'Here she comes! Now, keep quiet, and let me do the talking.'

Walking into the shop, Adele turned the door sign to OPEN and took off her coat. Kitty Gallager hadn't lied; she could clean. Her skinniness was down to the fact that she never seemed to stop moving, or talking. She could tell a tale and dust, mop and scrub the front doorstep before it was over. As for gossip, she was invaluable.

'Morning!' Kitty said cheerfully as she spotted Adele. 'Yer look nice.'

'Thank you.'

'And right cold it is too, fer the time of year.'

Adele frowned. 'It's November.'

'Yeah, but . . . ' Kitty hesitated, buffing the counter to a shine. 'I've got someone to meet yer. Like. Yer know, yer said about getting a handyman to help out. Lifting things . . . '

Adele glanced round. 'You've brought someone for me to see?'

'Well,' Kitty replied, dropping her voice, 'don't be alarmed.'

'Why would I be?'

'He's big,' Kitty went on, looking round. 'Right big. But yer need that, don't yer? Yer need a man with big arms, not muscles like knots in cotton.'

'Where is he?' Adele asked cautiously.

'Round back.'

'Ask him in.'

Nodding, Kitty went to the door and bellowed. A moment later the Chinaman walked in. Trying hard not to show her surprise, Adele smiled a welcome. The man was huge, black-haired and very softly spoken. It was true that Turner had mentioned that they needed to hire a handyman — but *this* man?

'Say hello.'

Dave Lin duly said: 'Hello.'

'This is Miss Ford, she runs this place and

she's very important, so yer have to do what she says,' Kitty went on, a tiny figure next to his bulk. Her voice dropped although Dave could obviously still hear her. 'My pa's used him a few times.'

'*Your father?*' Adele replied, aghast.

'Aw, not fer funny stuff, just muscle. Dave's honest. Yer know, he'll be a good helper.'

Later that afternoon Adele told Turner that she had hired a handyman. She glossed over the facts about Pa Gallager and Hanky Park. He wouldn't understand, but she trusted Kitty implicitly. Although she did make a mental note to watch what she said in front of her cleaner, otherwise the shop might well be filled up with Kitty's Hanky Park cronies and lame ducks.

It was the kind of incident Adele would have shared with her sister a while back. But although they still lived together, their relationship had never fully recovered. They might talk more now, but Adele was still guarded. As for Julia, her guilt had not stopped her from trying to attract a man again. But her success was limited — unlike her sister's. Mortified to be hearing it second-hand, Julia had discovered the gossip by proxy. Her sister had a new suitor. Not a roughneck, not a factory worker, Julia thought enviously, but Col Vincent.

If Adele had set out for revenge, she had got it, in spades.

★   ★   ★

276

'You're not holding the cue right,' Col said, leaning over Adele and moving her hands expertly. His mouth was only inches from her ear, his body pressed for an instant against her back as he kissed her gently on the neck. She smiled, ducking out from under him.

'Tease!'

'Flirt!' she retorted. 'You're just trying to put me off my game.'

He moved over to her again, lifting her hair up and stroking the back of her neck. 'I adore you.'

She smiled winningly. 'You are altogether too confident with women.'

'It's a lie, I'm actually afraid of females,' he said, pretending to cower. 'It's all a front.'

'Well, it's very convincing,' Adele replied. This time Col put an arm around her shoulder. An old memory came back; of sitting next to Sam Ayres in the front room at The Coppice. Happy, in love, like a kid . . . Disturbed, Adele fought the memory. Wasn't it time to stop looking back? Wasn't it time to let the attractive Col closer?

She glanced over her shoulder flirtatiously. 'I thought we were playing billiards?'

'I'd never have taught you if I thought you'd end up so good,' Col replied, winking. 'Although I must say that bending over the table suits you.'

'I bet you say that to all the girls,' Adele quipped, taking a shot and potting a black ball.

Grinning, she straightened up and rechalked her cue. Her romance with Col had moved faster than expected, and had given her tremendous confidence. Sam's betrayal didn't hurt so much any more. After all, Adele had caught the attention of Col Vincent . . . And yet around Col she had her full faculties, immune to the sweet plague of infatuation.

It was amazing what a broken heart could do, Adele thought. By rights she should have been intimidated by Col's interest. He was experienced, charming to a fault. Out of her league. But he didn't make her clumsy, or nervous . . . She was flattered by his interest, but she was also in control. Why was that? The answer was simple. She had been in love with Sam Ayres; her first romance; her first sexual excitement. It hadn't been long-lasting — certainly not after Julia had ruined it — but it had been so sweet . . .

Sighing, Adele continued to chalk her cue. She was an idiot to be even still thinking of Sam. Here she was, in Col Vincent's house, playing billiards with the most exciting man in the area, and yet she was unimpressed. Suddenly she felt impatient with herself. It was time things changed. Col was a fascinating man who thought the world of her. What the hell was she doing wasting time dreaming about a nobody like Sam Ayres? It was time to kick-start her heart. Time to crush the memory of Sam Ayres once and for all. Time to cast someone else in the role of hero. Col Vincent, perfect hero material. The kind of man every woman wanted — but Adele could actually *get*.

Walking over to Col, she studied him. He was very attractive, his hair long at the front, his back broad. How had she not seen it before? How had she been with him and not noticed his masculinity? Suddenly wanting to touch him, she reached out and laid her hand gently on his arm.

'So, who's winning?' Ernest asked, walking in and breaking the moment.

Adele covered her irritation well. 'I'm letting him win.'

'He cheats, you know,' Ernest replied, smiling. 'You have to watch him.'

She had known from the first that Ernest Vincent liked her, and was relaxed with him. He had even asked her about the incident with Saul Hill and she had explained, glad to have the matter dealt with. But that was so like Ernest. Nothing hidden, everything exposed. Above board. Not at all like his son. Col didn't like confrontation; didn't like anything to be too straightforward.

'Incidentally, my wife is coming back at the weekend.'

Surprised, Adele turned to look at Ernest. So finally the elusive Mary Vincent was going to make an appearance.

'Her sister is well again and she's coming home.'

'That should put a damper on things,' Col muttered, potting a black.

'Ignore him,' Ernest told Adele. 'His mother doesn't indulge him as much as I do. I was wondering if you and I could have a chat.'

'Dad, we're playing billiards!'

'Continue on your own, Col,' Ernest told his son, smiling. 'It's probably the only way you'll win.'

Curious, Adele followed Ernest into the study,

taking the seat he offered. She felt suddenly uncomfortable, her old lack of confidence rearing its head. Pouring himself a brandy, Ernest offered one to Adele, but she refused, watching him anxiously as he sat down. His benign face was good humoured, his tone amused.

'You like the house?'

'Of course, who wouldn't?' Adele replied carefully.

Oakham Lodge was a comfortable villa, one of the impressive homes built by the cotton merchants in the old days. The furnishings might be old fashioned, but they were good quality, Col's interest in antiques obvious in every room.

'I don't care for it myself,' Ernest replied honestly. 'A bit too draughty, but there you go. It pays to look the part, show everyone you're doing well. And I *have* done well, Adele. Not made a vast fortune, but the Vincents are comfortable.' He paused, then reassured her, 'There's nothing to be worried about! I just wanted to get to know you a bit better. Seeing as how my son is in love with you.'

'I don't think so!' Adele said, laughing. 'We've only known each for six months.'

'Six months . . . Mary and I were engaged for seven years before we got married.' Ernest pulled a face. 'We thought we'd spend time getting to know each other, but I can't say we did. You only really know a person when you're married to them.'

'Mr Vincent . . . '

He waved aside her interruption good-naturedly. 'It's Ernest. And I know it all sounds a bit informal, a bit out of the ordinary, to talk like this, but I don't like surprises, Adele, I like things spelled out. Clear. That way no one gets muddled. Money hasn't changed my outlook on life. I came from an ordinary background and I don't rank myself as anything special now. So I don't expect my son to marry an heiress.' He smiled, amused. 'There are so many unwed girls around here, Pauline Buckley for one. Oh, I see that name struck a chord.'

'I've run into her a couple of times.'

'Difficult to miss her, I'd say!' Ernest went on, laughing. 'And all these women are out to nab themselves a husband.'

'I'm not after your son.'

'I know,' Ernest replied. 'Good thing too, because if you were we would be having a very different conversation.'

Shifting her position in the chair, Adele tried to marshal her thoughts. Was she being interviewed, or warned off?

'I like your son very much, but I'm not looking to get married to anyone. I'm only twenty, and there's so much I want to do with my life.'

'Modern woman, hey?'

'Yeah,' she nodded, 'a modern woman.'

'But my son loves you,' Ernest continued. 'Very much. If I've heard your name once, I've heard it a thousand times. I know your likes and dislikes, your taste in music — jazz, odd, but there you are. And I've seen the way Col is around you, how you stabilise him. How you

281

keep him amused, on the level. He can be very temperamental.'

'I don't see much of that.'

'Exactly!' Ernest replied quickly. 'You don't bring that capriciousness out in him. You only bring out the best in my son. So I have to take you very seriously, Adele. You aren't what I expected. You're very young, and, as you say, you're independent. Your background is unusual too — but why should that matter? You're good for Col, and that's what interests me.'

Flattered, Adele felt herself flushing and tried to interrupt. 'But — '

'Hear me out, please. You think it's just a romance, but there's more to it than that, Adele. I would never have spoken to you if I hadn't thought it was important. Usually I never interfere, but there's something you should know.' He paused, finishing his brandy, his tone compassionate. 'Six years ago, when Col was living in Italy, he was ill . . . He had a nervous breakdown.'

'I didn't know.'

'No, he never talks about it. Never even refers to it.' Ernest took another sip of his brandy. 'There's something else. My son had a marriage which failed.'

'He's married?'

'He *was*,' Ernest corrected her. 'Col was very young and the woman was unfaithful. She crucified him, tore him apart . . . We organised a divorce, it was all handled overseas, long ago. No one heard about it, and no one ever found out. Nor will they . . . So you see how I trust you?'

She nodded, almost overwhelmed to be drawn into the confidence of this important man. 'Col had a breakdown because of her?'

'Like I said, he was all but destroyed. She made a fool out him, lied to him. He couldn't believe anything she told him and yet she had him on the end of a leash. He was besotted. Finally she left — and the strain broke him. For a while. When he recovered, he came home. From then on he was as you see him now — amusing, fun, light-hearted. But he never fell in love again, until he met you.'

Stunned, Adele ran the words over in her mind. She was acutely aware of how much Ernest Vincent was trusting her, and suddenly saw Col in a new light. Compassion influenced her, making her judgement shaky.

'I don't know why you're telling me this.'

Pouring himself another drink, Ernest regained his seat. He was very serious when he spoke again.

'I don't want my son to have a relapse. He was sick — but now he's cured. *And I want him to stay cured.* The only way I can be certain of that is for him to be with the woman he loves. A woman I can trust to love him. Do you understand me, Adele? This conversation must never go beyond these walls. I am asking you to marry my son.'

'*What?*' Adele said breathlessly.

The words hummed in her ears. Ernest Vincent was asking her to marry his son . . . It was incredible. But tempting, very tempting. Adele glanced down. She had no father, and here was a kindly readymade father, an older man who was taking her into his confidence. And if she married Col — apart from being certain she could grow to love him — she would have a purpose in life. It was an intoxicating offer for a young woman who had no family apart from a sister, and no status in life. In a short time she had come from nothing, to this. If she accepted she was certain of security, financial stability and status. As the wife of Col Vincent she would be admired and envied. But more than that, she would be needed.

'I'm quite serious,' Ernest replied, setting down his brandy. 'I want you to marry Col.'

Adele stared at Ernest Vincent. She wondered momentarily if he was playing a cruel joke, but he obviously wasn't. His eyes were steady, calm, his expression composed. And although she was confused, there had been no automatic refusal on her part. What did that indicate? Adele wondered. That she was prepared to take on this role? Her heart began to thump steadily, her blood fizzing in her ears. Think carefully, she told herself, think very carefully before you answer.

A glass of brandy was suddenly placed in her hand. Ernest's voice was kind. 'You're not going to faint, are you?'

She shook her head. 'No . . . '

The brandy soothed her. Of course she cared about Col, how could she not? But he had also been ill. Wasn't that the very word his father had used? But then after that word came *recovered*. Col *had* been ill, but was cured.

'Adele, I *know* you care about my son . . . '

She looked over at Ernest, brutally honest. 'But I'm not in love with him. I *could* love him easily, I know — but is that enough?'

He was impressed by her candour.

'You're an exceptional woman, Adele. There's no one else I would trust with something so precious. I can recognise your qualities all too easily — just as Turner Gades does, and just as others will, in time. Don't misunderstand me, Adele, I can offer you a great deal, but I need you more than you need me. I can offer you my son; with him comes our name, our money, our standing. A comfortable life, with you free to pursue your own interests. I ask you to give up nothing. Just to take on Col, to love him and protect him. Make him happy and keep him well.'

She paused, her mouth dry. 'Col hasn't told me that he loves me.'

'Oh, but he has,' Ernest replied, 'in at least a dozen letters that he's ripped up. He's just waiting until the moment's right. Until he's sure he won't be refused.'

Adele glanced away, her feelings confused. 'You could be wrong . . . '

'No, I'm not, believe me. Everything I've said to you has been the truth. Would I lie about something so important? Would I gamble with my son's happiness?'

Slowly, Adele took a breath. She was flattered and suddenly felt safe. She had found her family, her niche. People who loved her, and wanted her. From now on, she knew exactly where she was going. And what she was doing with her life.

There was only one more question to ask. 'Does Col know about this conversation?'

'God, no!' he said, his tone sharper than she had ever heard it before. 'And he must never know about it. This is to be our secret, Adele, one you can never share with anyone. Not even with him.'

40

Mary Vincent returned to Oakham Lodge, shaking the rain off her umbrella and taking a moment to study the entrance. And check that the cleaner had kept her work up to standard. Nothing disturbed Mary so much as detail. Traumas she could take in her stride, mostly by ducking them, but the small minutiae of life were vitally important to her. Almost as important as avoiding scandal. All her adult life, Mary had abhorred gossip. And gossip about her own family she dreaded. Even feared. It had been drilled into her as a child that respectability and position were all-important. And she had questioned that only once.

Her own family had been wealthy and socially acceptable. Until some member of that family had married badly. Married a woman who caused a scandal. A foreigner, too . . . Mary thought back to the distant memories of the woman. So handsome, so compelling, so sad. Her situation had drawn pity from the young Mary as she heard the constant criticism . . . It was her own fault, family members had said; quick to bury the gossip and forget. But after Mary had expressed her view out loud — showing sympathy with her cousin's wife — she had felt the full force of the family's disapproval. They cowed her into their way of thinking, berated her into toeing the family line.

In the end — threatened and intimidated — Mary's small rebellion came to an end.

But all that was in the past, she thought, shrugging off the memory and opening the drawing-room door. At once Ernest jumped to his feet, kissing his wife on the cheek.

'Mary! Good to see you.'

'And you,' she replied evenly, glancing around. 'So, how are things?'

'Good, good.' He felt — as he always did — slightly overawed by his wife. Oh, Ernest had made money, but Mary came from a good family and carried the knowledge of her social superiority like a hidden dagger. Not seen, but there all the same. 'We've increased the business in Manchester and the profits at the Rochdale factory.' He watched his wife draw off her gloves. 'And as for our son. You have no idea how much he adores Adele — '

'You said in your letters,' Mary replied. 'I should like to meet her. After all, now that Daphne is recovered, I have some time on my hands.'

Amused, Ernest thought of his wife's sister. Daphne's health had become a vocation for Mary. Every six months Daphne would have a crisis and Mary would go to Berkshire to nurse her. The fact that Daphne had a husband and two children did not matter. It was always Mary she called on. And Mary who went . . . Ernest had met his sister-in-law only a few times — Daphne was wedded to the south — but he was eternally grateful to her. Grateful that her minor illnesses gave him respite from his wife.

Grateful that he could rely on Daphne's succour if he and his wife ever fell out.

Only twice in their marriage had he and Mary really argued. Once when they had lost their first son and both were finding it hard to come to terms with grief. And again when Ernest had teased Mary about her family's past, implying that they couldn't be perfect and that they had to have some hidden scandal. She had reacted violently, alarming him so much that he had never again touched on the subject. But it had stung Mary, and in retaliation she had upped and left for her sister's. On the first occasion she stayed for three weeks. On the second occasion — around the time of Col's breakdown — she stayed for two months. When she returned, no one said a word about her absence. She simply unpacked, laid her hairbrush and mirror on the dressing table and hung her clothes back in the wardrobe as though she had never been away.

Which was exactly what she was doing now.

'Adele is a wonderful young woman,' Ernest went on, sitting on the side of the bed, having followed his wife upstairs. 'You'll like her.'

'She sounds very pleasant,' Mary replied, sliding some undergarments into her chest of drawers.

'Very mature for her years, and she knows all about Col.'

Mary turned. 'She does?'

'Of course; they're going to get married. She had to know.'

'Shouldn't our son have told her?' Mary replied, raising her carefully pencilled eyebrows.

'He will, when the time's right.'

Mary was thinking that if she knew her son at all, Col would *never* tell his fiancée the whole story of his past. Ernest might believe in the power of love, but she doubted it. Closing the drawer, Mary did as she always did with anything distasteful: she shrugged off the old memories of her son's past and changed the subject.

'Will Col be home for dinner?'

'Oh yes,' Ernest replied, smiling as he heard the doorbell ring. 'And you're going to meet his fiancée sooner than you think.'

★   ★   ★

Adele's first memory of Mary Vincent was how tall she was, much taller than Ernest. It gave her an immediate air of superiority over her husband as she walked across to Adele and shook her hand. Her future mother-in-law's eyes were blue and calm, but there was something else about her which surprised Adele — a sense of pulsating sadness.

'How nice to meet you,' Mary said automatically, checking Adele over discreetly.

Good looking, nicely dressed, very respectable. The Fords might not have had money, but thank God it didn't show. And although she had been all but bored to death about Adele's intelligence, perception and strength of character, she hadn't heard a breath of scandal. Which was a change from Col's usual lovers. Dancers, actresses and God knew what else. Heiresses,

Mary decided pragmatically, weren't what they used to be.

So perhaps it would be better that Adele Ford came to the family with nothing. No dowry, but no airs and graces either ... Unexpectedly excited by the possibility of uncovering a friend in her future daughter-in-law, Mary found herself warming to Adele.

Col noticed his mother's scrutiny and — misreading it — butted in. 'Well, have I got myself someone fabulous or not?'

Mary raised her eyebrows. 'How on earth would I know that so soon?' she asked. Adele realised — with some surprise — that Mary was actually *teasing* her son. But no one else seemed to realise it. Obviously Col and Ernest were too in awe of Mary to think her capable of a sense of humour.

'But she's wonderful,' Col said defensively.

'I really can't make a decision yet,' Mary went on, unexpectedly taking Adele's arm and leading her into the dining room. 'We will have to get to know each other before I can really judge.'

The words were coolly delivered, but Adele felt — for an instant — a squeeze to her arm and realised with relief that she had made a valuable ally.

★ ★ ★

It was later that week, after Col and Adele had been out for a drive, that he suddenly became restless, preoccupied. Over the previous weeks Adele had opened her heart to him and found

291

that she hadn't lied to Ernest — it was easy to love Col. Once she had laid Sam Ayres to rest. Once she had realised what she had. So what, she told herself, if Col could be difficult? She hadn't experienced it, and for all she knew, she never would. Maybe all he needed was to feel safe and loved. Maybe then the moods and incipient boredom Ernest had warned her about would never return. Certainly she had seen nothing but devotion and kindness from Col, and was prepared to believe that his past problems were over.

'I meant to tell you something, Adele,' Col said quietly, staring ahead. 'It's about my past. I had a breakdown a while back.'

Sliding her arm through his, Adele's laid her head on his shoulder. She felt immediately protective. They were sitting in his car, parked up on Hawkshead Pike, looking down over the countryside and the mill town below. Adele's mind went back to the time she and Becky had visited the place, one hot summer day, the time Becky had told her about going to work in the Ash mill . . .

But that was all in the past. Col was her future now. And he was confiding in her, at last.

'What happened, darling?'

He paused, struggling for words. How much should he tell her? he wondered. Would it scare her off? God, he couldn't risk that, couldn't risk losing her. Without Adele, there would only be chaos. She had brought such stability to his life. Such calm. His moods — which had bedevilled him for years — were smoothed out when she was around. His capriciousness, so attractive to some — and yet so wearing to him — had now become merely enthusiasm for life, rather than the manic boredom he had suffered before. The ennui which crushed the joy out of every new experience. Col hadn't been bored with Adele once. She amused him, stood up to him, made gentle fun of him, and loved him with a completeness he had never encountered before.

At first he had thought he sensed some pity in her affection, but lately there had been no trace of that. Just a genuine, passionate love. After all, Adele didn't *kiss* him as though she pitied him. She didn't argue with him as though she was afraid of hurting his feelings either. In fact, she treated him as her equal, which fascinated him. She was the first woman in his life who had never been in awe of him.

But if he told her the whole truth, what was she going to think of him?

'I was ill a while ago . . . '

'You said that, sweetheart,' Adele replied gently. 'What was the matter?'

'I had a nervous breakdown.'

Adele waited, holding her breath. Finally Col was going to confide in her about his failed marriage, his illness. She had resisted the temptation to ask questions, just relied on the fact that he would tell her in time. She might not be in awe of her fiancé, but she was very young and — if she was honest — terrified of jeopardising the good fortune which had come her way. Besides, she had told herself, Col was older than her, and it was different for men.

They had pasts, women they had loved, things they had done which they would find hard to tell their wives about. Even past marriages. And divorces, that most scandalous of affairs. Knowing Mary, Adele understood why the family had kept it quiet, but she had longed for Col to confide in her.

Be patient, give it time. Hadn't Frida told her that, in one of their infrequent, but intimate talks? The old lady had given her the same advice she would have given her granddaughter — if Rebecca had ever asked. 'There are some things you can't ask a man — even your husband,' Frida had gone on. 'Besides, you know the story from his father. Be patient. Maybe later, when you're older and you've been married for a while, he'll tell you. But not at the start.'

But now Col *was* confiding, Adele thought, relieved. She would finally know about his past. There would be no secrets between them.

'What caused your breakdown, sweetheart?'

He paused, still staring ahead, his hand sliding over hers.

'I was . . . God, this is so difficult,' he said, still wondering how much to risk. After all, Adele knew nothing about his past. Perhaps he could tell her only as much — or as little — as he chose.

'Go on,' she urged him, 'go on.'

'I had a breakdown because . . . of circum-stances . . . '

'What kind of circumstances?' Adele asked carefully.

'Personal,' Col replied.

294

He was going to tell her about his wife. Or *was* he? Why did he need to? If he did, there would only be more questions, more revelations, the past thrown up. And for what? What purpose could be served by it? All it would do was drive a wedge between them. And that would be unbearable.

'Personal circumstances . . . '

Adele waited.

'I was travelling abroad . . . '

Go on, she willed him.

' . . . a long way from home. From everything I knew.'

All right, love, Adele thought, just tell me. Get it out in the open.

'There was an accident.'

Blinking, Adele wondered if she had heard incorrectly. *An accident?* Ernest hadn't mentioned any accident.

'Go on, Col.'

'I was driving and the car went out of control.' He paused, checking her reaction, then hurried on. 'I hit someone. They were all right, they were fine. But it had a terrible effect on my nerves.' He looked into her eyes. Could she see that he was lying? 'What is it? Are you shocked?'

She *was* shocked, and confused. This wasn't the story Ernest had told her. Where was the first wife? The adulterous woman who had broken Col's spirit? Where was the mention of the divorce? His father had never said anything about a car, or an accident.

'What else, Col?'

'Nothing else. That's enough, isn't it?' he

replied, his grip tightening on her hand. 'I got better, I've been fine ever since. I don't talk about it, though. No one knows in England, and they don't need to. I just wanted to put it behind me. A nervous breakdown isn't something to be proud of.' His tone faltered as he looked at her pleadingly.

A moment passed — and then she consoled him, held him, stroked his hair. She wanted to press him for answers, details, but couldn't. She was too anxious. Would she cause a mental relapse by stirring up old memories? She was mistaken, she told herself. Or maybe Ernest had got it wrong. But why would he tell her such a story? To force her hand? To get her to marry Col out of pity? But Col's version of events was far more likely to inspire pity in her. Unless he was lying . . .

'Is that all?'

His voice was wary. 'Should there be more?'

'No . . . no,' Adele answered hurriedly. 'I was just . . . No, darling, I wasn't expecting anything else.'

'You looked like you were.'

'I wasn't,' she hurried on. 'Why would I?'

He paused, anxious, his unease apparent.

Seeing his reaction, Adele quickly reassured him, determined not to let a wedge come between them. She had obviously misunderstood what Ernest had told her. She would sort it all out. In time. Like Frida said, she had to be patient . . . Anyway, maybe Col had lied to his father; perhaps he had made up some story to cover up the real truth. Whatever it was, he wouldn't lie to her. He had never lied before and Adele had no reason to think he was doing so now.

'A breakdown is nothing to be ashamed of, Col,' she said at last. 'You were ill, that was all. And anyway, you're fine now.'

'No one but my family and you knows,' he went on, relaxing. 'Not even Turner — and he's been a friend for years. But I *had* to tell you, Adele. After all, we're going to be married. And partners shouldn't have secrets, should they?'

No, they shouldn't, she thought, her eyes closing as Col kissed her. Partners shouldn't have secrets, lies, or half-truths. And partners shouldn't have two different versions of events which left one of them stranded in the middle, wondering what to believe.

41

Much to Ernest's amusement, the wedding was attended by a shambolic collection of guests. On Col's side, Turner and his elegant new wife Clemmie mingled with the groom's family, a number of Vincent relatives showing up, although Daphne was — naturally — too ill to attend. On the bride's side, Julia came to church with her new beau, bragging to everyone within earshot that he was an important businessman from Leeds.

'Henry's in cloth,' she told everyone she could. 'Silk and cotton. Isn't that right?'

Duly flattered, Henry smiled, prosperous in a good suit. 'Actually, I have warehouses in Manchester, Burnley and Leeds . . . '

Julia nodded eagerly, as though, if she encouraged him enough, he could materialise another in Liverpool.

'Henry deals with London regularly. Don't you, Henry?'

He nodded, pleased by Julia's interest and by the attention he was getting.

Other guests included the solicitor, Bernard Hoggard, Mr and Mrs Lockhart, and Frida Altman, in her wheelchair. Naturally Becky had been maid of honour, and since Adele had no father to give her away, that honour had fallen to Turner Gades. It was a duty he relished, smiling warmly at the bride and then at Col, his pleasure obvious. It was only when the vows had been said that there was a sudden crashing sound at the back of the church, everyone turning round to see a tiny woman berating a large Chinaman.

'I said watch out!' Kitty replied, mouthing 'sorry' to Adele as she hauled Dave Lin into his seat. 'Go on,' she then told the vicar, 'pretend we're not here.'

It became a standing joke for years afterwards when anyone made their presence felt: *Pretend we're not here.*

Soon after the reception began, Col and Adele slipped off to their honeymoon in the Lake District. They had rented a cottage beside Lake Ullswater, the bedroom window set low and looking out over the still indigo water. Falling on to the bed, they had stared for a moment at the cool silence of the lake, then Col had begun, slowly and tenderly, to undress his new wife.

Equally tenderly, Adele slid off her husband's jacket, shirt and trousers. Her hands shook, her back tingling as she felt Col's fingers running down the length of her spine. Finally they were both naked, lying on their sides, facing each other. Their gazes locked, Col resting his forehead against Adele's, their hands meeting, fingers intertwining. Slowly, in unison, they kissed, their legs wrapping around each other, their bodies rolling over on the bed. First Col was on top, then Adele, her hair falling over Col as she bent over him, their faces obscured by the thick fall of dark waves. Sighing, she felt him slide down under her, his mouth moving over her breasts and fixing on her left nipple.

Beyond the window, the dark lake shone under the April sky, the mountains arcing upwards to the dying light. Later, Col and Adele lay with their heads together, the day fading outside, their bodies sleek with sweat as they slept. Throughout that first night they made love repeatedly. There was no unease, no embarrassment, no words. Only the murmurings of love and passion, need and satisfaction.

Adele had not been in love with Col Vincent when she married him, but by the time the morning light rose on the lake she was committed to him as completely as he was to her.

42

Her heart hammering, Becky stared at her hands, trying to control her nerves. She was sitting by the back door of the library, Isaac having invited her to share his meagre lunch. Slowly she watched him as he passed her half of his sandwich. The sandwich he had made for himself that morning in his lodgings on Dover Street.

She had come to love Isaac for so many reasons. For his kindness, of course, both to her and to Frida, but also for the hundred little gestures which touched her heart. The way he smiled, the way he always made her walk away from the kerb — so he would get splashed, not her. The way he polished his glasses repeatedly when he was nervous. And the way he told her, over and over again, that he loved her.

Of course she should have been sure — but even after so long, she wasn't. Having said that, Becky was not prepared to continue the relationship any longer without confessing her past. It was only fair to be honest with a good man. Only what he deserved. Whatever it cost her.

'Isaac,' she began, 'I have something to tell you.'

He glanced over, smiling expectantly. 'Oh yes, what is it?'

'It's not something you're going to like. It's

not something I'm proud of, but . . . '

Immediately he took her hand. This was Rebecca, the woman he was going to marry. The woman he wanted. The only woman he wanted. There was nothing she could say or do that would change that.

'Go on, love.'

'A while ago, long before I met you, I was seeing someone else.'

He listened, the sandwich still in his other hand, his dark eyes steady. 'Yes?'

'I got pregnant with his child. He was the only man I ever went with, and I only went with him once. But I got pregnant.'

'Oh,' he said simply, dropping his sandwich. 'I . . . You never said . . . '

'I haven't told you a lot of things. I've wanted to — so often — but I couldn't. Forgive me for that, at least.' Becky hurried on. 'You know my father's dead and I never see my mother? There's something else . . . I had a brother, who died when he was a baby. He had a heart condition. And so did my uncle.'

Isaac frowned. 'What . . . what has this got to do with us?'

'The condition could have been passed down. They might have inherited a defect. *I* might have inherited a defect.'

'You're not ill!' he said, shattered.

And then she realised just how much he loved her. Despite being told such damning things, Isaac's immediate reaction was for her. For her welfare . . . Stricken, Becky wanted to throw her arms around him and cling on for dear life. But

302

she couldn't. She had to see this through. Wherever it took her.

'No, I'm healthy. But don't you see, I could pass the weakness down to any children I might have.' She paused, searching his face. 'Isaac, you want a family so much; what if I couldn't give you a healthy child?'

He was silent, his face turned away. Becky felt a clawing sensation of dread. Dear God, she had lost him! She had lost her beloved Isaac. Aching to reach out to him, she felt her throat tighten, her voice barely more than a whisper.

'Sorry, I was presuming too much,' she said, shattered by his silence. 'How stupid of me! I've confessed to carrying another man's child and here I am, still expecting you to want to marry me.'

He said nothing, just bent down and picked up the sandwich, dropping it into the paper bag and screwing it up. The gesture wasn't aggressive, just absent-minded, his expression unreadable.

'Say something, please, Isaac, say *something*. Talk to me.'

But he couldn't, and he remained mute, his mind hopscotching over her words . . . Becky wasn't a virgin. Could he live with that?

'Isaac, say something!' she pleaded, for once cut out of his thoughts, his kindness.

But he was too preoccupied to hear her. One man she had said, and only once. Could he forgive that? Could he?

'Please, Isaac, talk to me,' Becky said, her voice heartbroken. 'Talk to me now — or I'll go.

We'll stay friends, but I'll understand if you don't want me any more.'

Then, as she moved to rise, Isaac suddenly came out of his trance. Turning to her, he looked into her face. And then he knew that he had no choice. He would live with her past rather than lose her from his future. But as for the other matter — *the baby* . . . He shook his head, trying to compose his thoughts.

'What happened to the child?'

Becky took in a long breath. This was the worst part, the thing she regretted most. But she couldn't hold back now.

'I had an abortion . . . '

'God,' Isaac whispered, lapsing into silence again, the paper bag now screwed up into a tight ball in his hands.

'Adele was with me, she helped me. I couldn't have the baby, Isaac. I couldn't have done that to Frida, it might have killed her. She always wanted so much for me. I'm everything to her, how could I let her down?' She was pleading suddenly, desperately. 'Every day of my life I regret what I did. Every day I think about that baby.'

He was reeling from the news. Yet he knew that he couldn't let her walk away.

'I don't understand any of this, Becky. It's a lot to take in.'

'I know, I know,' she replied, defeated, her head bowed.

Seeing her dejection, he took her hand. 'The baby could have been ill,' he said quietly.

Surprised, Becky nodded. 'Yes, it could have

been. It might not have lived, might have died after a few months.'

'We'll never know.'

'No . . . ' she said simply. 'We'll never know.'

He was still holding her hand. But maybe that was just kindness, Becky thought, terrified of the rejection to come. Her man, her Isaac, was going to walk away. He had no choice really. And who could blame him? He was a lonely, loving, respectable Jewish man, who wanted a decent wife and family. And he had fallen in love with a woman who hadn't behaved decently, who couldn't even be certain of giving him a healthy child. What right had she to expect him *not* to walk away?

'I never knew about my parents,' Isaac said suddenly. 'Being brought up by a foster family meant I never knew if they were good people or evil. If they were happy or miserable. Healthy or sick.' He turned to look at Becky, 'Seems to me that some people go through life without the knowledge others take for granted.'

She stared at him, trying not to hope and yet longing for his next words.

'I don't care about the other man, Becky. I would like him not to have been a part of your life, but he was and I can't change that. If you hadn't told me, I wouldn't have known. But then again, that wouldn't have been you. You could have kept all these secrets and I'd never have been any the wiser. But you didn't — and being honest counts more with me than your past.' He rushed on before she could interrupt. 'If we had a child, it could have a weakness. God forbid, it could die. But there's something else we should consider, Becky. You know your past — but what about mine? What if *I* carried a weakness too? We wouldn't even know. We would just find out in time.' He lifted her hand to his lips for a moment, his gaze fixed on her face. 'You know too much about your past, and I know too little about mine.'

'Isaac . . . '

'Hear me out,' he said kindly. 'From this moment on, why don't we forget everything and start again? From *this* moment let's make *our* future, Becky. If trouble comes, we'll face it. If it doesn't, that's a bonus. But if you love me as much as I love you, that's going to be more than enough to get us through.'

43

April 1930

Trying on her outfit for the third time, Kitty Gallager looked in the mirror. Her reflection looked back, pleasing her. So the dress might be a bit roomy, but she was skinny, everything was loose on her. As for the shoes, well, they would take a bit of getting used to. But all in all she looked good, professional.

'What the 'ell are yer wearing?'

Kitty spun round, looking up at her boyfriend. 'I've got a job.'

'Oh aye, where?'

'The antique shop.'

Stan snorted. 'Yer clean there!'

'Not any more. I'm going to serve customers,' Kitty replied proudly. She could hardly say the words without grinning. It was like a dream come true. She wasn't a scrubber any more, she was going to be respectable. And it was all due to Adele having faith in her, encouraging her. Making her think she was more than Hanky Park riff-raff. Not that Stan would see it that way.

'That bloody Vincent woman's putting big ideas in yer head.'

'Well, there'd be plenty of room to put ideas in yers. God knows, there's nothing else in there.'

'Oi!' Stan replied, stung. 'I just like yer the way yer are, Kitty.'

'Sure yer do, I'm very likeable,' she teased

him, kissing him on the top of the head. 'But I'm going to get on, Stan, whatever yer think about it.'

'Yer've no education!'

'Maybe not, but I've a brain,' she said smartly, 'which puts me well ahead of yer fer a start.'

★ ★ ★

Isaac and Becky had been to see the latest Chaplin film. Afterwards Isaac dropped into the local pub for a drink, Becky walking on home to find Frida sitting by the fire in the dark. For one pulsating moment she thought her grandmother was ill, then she saw Frida move.

'What are you doing?' Becky asked, turning on the gas. The blue light hissed and popped into life. 'You gave me such a scare.'

'I was thinking . . . ' Frida said simply, her accented voice low. 'About the past. You do a lot of that when you get older. Day-dream about the way things used to be. People you used to know. And you remember things, put odd little details together — like you never have before.'

Curious, Becky looked at her grandmother. She was as slim as ever, older naturally, but still alive in the eyes.

'I should trim your hair.'

'For that ball I'm going to on Saturday?' Frida replied mischievously, her mind going back to her previous train of thought. 'I was remembering Ninette Hoffman.'

'You haven't mentioned her for ages,' Becky replied, surprised. 'Adele used to talk about her all the time, didn't she? She was fascinated by the Lydgate Widow.'

'Ninette *was* fascinating,' Frida replied. 'She was very extraordinary, you know. Very passionate. There were always rumours about her. She was the mistress of Julian Gades, you know. Turner's father.'

Becky took a breath. 'You never told me that before!'

'I only remembered it a little while ago, when you and Isaac were out. It just came back to me for some reason.'

'I could never cheat on Isaac,' Becky said firmly.

'No doubt Ninette thought that once,' Frida replied. 'I know she was very much in love with her husband when they married.'

'So what happened?'

'*Life* happened,' Frida replied, smiling wickedly. 'The same thing that happens to all of us. Funny, though, how I keep thinking of Ninette Hoffman. She couldn't have children, and that was a great blow to her. It was a real shame, because children liked Ninette.'

Curious, Becky sat down on the day bed next to her grandmother. 'Did you ever go to see her at Lydgate House?'

Frida sighed. 'Oh yes, quite often. I remember one occasion very well. The Hoffmans were holding a party and all of us were there. A lot of money had been spent to make it a success. The most lavish foods and wines, the house immaculate, oozing with that overblown baroque taste, which was such a perfect backdrop for

Ninette. And there she was, in a dress from Paris, dancing into the early hours. All of her husband's friends were there — but none of his family. We all commented on it, said how strange it was. But it must have been just around the time that Ninette blotted her copybook.'

'With her affair with Julian Gades?'

Frida nodded. 'They all shunned her when it came out. Hated the scandal.' Slowly she glanced over to her granddaughter. 'There's something else I remembered tonight. Ninette confided in me once about a young cousin of her husband's. A girl who visited her after the scandal became public. Of course this was a great secret, and the girl only came to see Ninette a few times, but it mattered so much. That she would risk the family's disapproval just because she liked her and felt sorry for her. Ninette talked about the girl often, said she would never forget her kindness.'

'Who was she?' Becky asked, intrigued.

'Oh, I don't know. I never met any of Ninette's husband's family. Apparently they were old money, and there were dozens of them all over the north-west. But I *do* remember that girl's first name. She was called Mary.'

★ ★ ★

'Col, calm down — '

'Don't tell me to calm down!' he shouted back at Adele, his face flushed.

'I was just making a point, Col. It's not good for you to get so worked up.'

310

'*You* work me up!'

'How do I work you up?' she asked, holding her ground and refusing to be cowed. Lately her husband had been capricious, almost spiteful at times. Nervously, Adele had soothed him and distracted him from his flare-ups and outbursts, but not this time.

'You don't want to be with me any more,' Col replied, running his hands through his hair. 'You spend more time with my bloody mother than with me.'

She laughed, walking over to him and putting her arms around him. 'That's not true. I want to spend all my time with you.'

'And what about Turner?'

'What about Turner?'

'He's been here too often lately, I think he likes you too much,' Col replied, shaking her off and pacing the bedroom floor. 'I want a proper wife. Someone who thinks the world of me. Someone who wants me . . . '

'No woman ever wanted a man as much as I want you,' Adele said, moving over to him again and taking his hands.

Adele was still young, inexperienced, learning as she went along — and afraid to somehow trip her husband into his old ways. God, she thought anxiously, if only her mother was still alive. If only Julia was nearby, she could have talked to *her*. Asked advice. As it was, she felt alone. And it seemed that every time Col became agitated, Mary pulled back. From her son, and her daughter-in-law.

'I'm bored!' Col said suddenly, snatching up

his jacket and moving to the door. 'You bore me!'

Stunned, Adele stared at him. 'Col, that's not fair!'

'I should never have married a kid!' he retorted, slamming the door as he left.

Later that night he came back, creeping into Oakham Lodge and the marital bed. Pretending she was asleep, Adele could smell brandy on his breath, and something altogether more disturbing: perfume . . . For an instant she was going to turn on him, demand an answer. But she didn't dare. Maybe he had just been to a club, or to see friends. It wouldn't do for her to overreact. He was doing enough of that for both of them.

Another few minutes passed, and then Col suddenly began to nuzzle her neck.

'Sorry, darling, sorry . . . I was a pig, I won't be so horrible again.'

She rolled over. 'You said you were bored with me.'

Kissing her neck, then her breasts, he mumbled, 'Not you, silly! Bored with work, that's all. I didn't say I was bored with you. Silly goose, you misheard me. Bored of my new wife? Never.'

★   ★   ★

Alone, Julia walked around the house on The Coppice. Her boyfriend, Henry, was still in cloth — but it had lost some of its sheen. Maybe that had something to do with the fact that he had reacted badly to discovering Julia was not keen

312

on getting free of her husband . . . But a divorce was the last thing she wanted. Unsettled, she paced the front room, then paused to straighten the cushions. Not that there was much point; people seldom came to the house any more. Adele visited now and again, but she was tied up with her own new life, and much of the time the house seemed quiet. Quiet and empty.

Of course Julia could have sold up, but instead she chose to take an allowance from Adele, an allowance which meant she could keep the house and revert to part-time work at the florist. Leaving her evenings free . . . Naturally Adele knew nothing about her sister's nocturnal forays. Married to Col and living at Oakham Lodge, she was no longer closely involved in her sister's life — and Julia welcomed the distance. Free to pursue her secret activities, she went out most evenings, taking the tram to Oldham, or Rochdale, or even Manchester. Eager for company, she visited dance halls and pubs, kidding herself that she was having fun, that she was still keeping the male sex on a string.

And yet there was never anyone who came close to replacing John Courtland. She tried to find a new love, but they were all substitutes. God only knew why, Julia thought to herself; he had hardly been a catch. Weak-minded, easily influenced, prone to pomposity — but she had loved him. And yet she dreaded any contact from him. After all, he wouldn't want a reconciliation, but a divorce. And her status as Mrs Courtland was — albeit a joke — her only achievement. So she kept wearing her wedding ring and kept egging the men on, until they started to become a little older and a little less attractive. After all, Julia had passed thirty, and there were many other, younger women to compete with.

Sometimes — when she allowed herself — Julia thought of the old days, living with Adele in The Coppice. But then she thought of Sam Ayres and what a fool she had been. By contrast, she had watched her sister's progression with incredulity. Her happy marriage to the attractive Col Vincent, her success with the Failsworth shop, her social confidence . . . *That woman had once been her little sister.* They had lain together, holding hands, the night their parents died. Adele had looked after her when John Courtland left, comforting her after the baby died. That successful, happy woman had once been her closest friend, her confidante.

But she wasn't any more. And whose fault had that been? Julia shook her head. She would go out, find someone successful and then parade him for everyone to see. Maybe even coax Henry back. She would show the world that she wasn't a failure. A woman with no aim in life, wearing a wedding ring that meant nothing.

44

'I'm just saying,' Adele went on, 'that we *could* get another shop.'

'What for?'

'Why not?' she countered, looking over to Ernest. He, as ever, took her part.

'I think it's a good idea.'

'You would,' Col replied, turning to his mother at the breakfast table. 'What do you think?'

'You don't need my opinion,' Mary retorted, her face as expressionless as the boiled egg she was about to crack.

Col looked over to Adele again. 'You've got enough on. I don't know why you have to be working all the time.'

'I enjoy it,' she answered, her words punctuated by the crack of Mary's spoon on the side of her egg. Smiling, Adele bit her lip, Col trying not to laugh.

'One thing's for certain, we don't need the money,' Ernest said evenly, rising from the table. 'Would you excuse me everyone, I want to get to the factory early.'

Hurriedly, Adele rose to follow him. 'Me too! I'm starting Kitty today.' She glanced over to her mother-in-law. 'Is there anything you want from the shops?'

'No, dear, thank you.' She smiled at her daughter-in-law warmly and Col felt a quick

315

pinch of envy. His mother had never been so openly affectionate with him.

Petulantly, he caught Adele's hand. 'Well *I* want something — a pound of affection, two bags of time and a leg joint of interest. What would that cost me?'

'More ... ' Adele replied, kissing him goodbye, 'than you could ever afford.'

Walking outside, Ernest paused by his car. 'You want a lift?'

Nodding, she slid into the passenger seat. It was a warm morning, the spring trees just coming into bud. Adele waved to the postman as they drove out into the road. Deep in thought, she was planning her next trip to an auction. This one was to be held in the Manchester auction rooms, in Deansgate. Leaning her head back, Adele sighed. It was good to be comfortable and she was grateful for her lot in life. She smiled at the pun. Her *lot* in life had turned out better than she could have hoped for. Her marriage was successful, her work absorbing, and slowly she was being accepted by the likes of French Kettering and Morris Devonshire. Dealers who wouldn't have given her the time of day before. Dealers she had once regarded with awe when she first came under the protection of Turner Gades.

She thought of her friend and smiled. The previous month Turner had married Clemmie Brooks. It had been a refined, quiet wedding, like the bride and groom ... And yet there was another side to Turner, Adele thought, amused, remembering an auction both of them had

316

attended. Both of them had been bidding for the same settle; Turner had won it. He wasn't *always* the perfect gentleman . . .

'Col is so happy with you,' Ernest said suddenly, breaking into Adele's thoughts. 'I'm glad it's all worked out so well.'

'So am I,' she replied, wondering if this was the time to mention Col's version of his past. One day she would have to ask Ernest about it, but then again, should she? Her first duty was to her husband, after all, not to her father-in-law.

'He's settled down at the paper factory too,' Ernest went on happily. 'Not that long ago I couldn't have hoped to let him run the Rochdale business. But now I don't give it a second's thought. *You've* done that, Adele. You've been a real blessing in all our lives.'

The compliment touched her. If she had been a blessing to them, what had they been to her? With the Vincents she had a ready-made home and family. A surrogate father in the kindly Ernest, while Mary, though aloof, was becoming closer every day. It was an ideal situation: Adele and Col had the upper floor as their quarters, with the older Vincents living below. Together, but not in each other's pockets. The perfect family.

If only Julia could be a part of it, Adele thought sadly . . .

'You're quiet,' Ernest said.

'I was just thinking.'

'About what?'

'About the auction,' Adele lied. 'About how I'm not going to let anyone get that Worcester bowl!'

Minutes later, Ernest dropped Adele outside the Failsworth shop. The place had changed dramatically. Now it had style, a dressed window with just a few good pieces of furniture. Nothing like it had been in old Saul Hill's day. As for the geese, they had been farmed out long ago, and the windows and doors were barred and covered by grilles at night. Nothing remained of the old man. Even the large building in the yard had been emptied and repainted. No shadows, no heaps of mouldering memories, no reminder of the day Saul Hill went mad. The day Adele could have lost her good name for ever.

'Morning,' a loud voice said suddenly. Kitty moved behind the counter to greet Adele. 'What can I do to help yer?'

'You look wonderful,' Adele replied, taking in the smart outfit and the obvious effort Kitty had made.

Kitty, dear oddball Kitty, who had been with Adele for a while now. And who stuck with her, defending her against the odds. Kitty who weighed little more than seven stone and yet could take on anyone. Fearless Kitty.

'I'm all ready,' she said, trying hard to keep her voice lower than usual. 'I said to Stan that I were going to make a go of it, and I bloody well will.'

'But I wouldn't swear at the customers,' Adele said wryly.

'No bloody chance.' Kitty answered, polishing the counter top with her cuff.

Smiling, Adele continued into the back room and took off her coat. She would get the accounts done, if she was lucky, and then leave early for the auction. Bid for the Worcester bowl . . .

The day passed without incident. Customers came and went; Kitty sold two plates and then had a scrap with a local lad who came in to lark about. Otherwise it was quiet. At six, Adele closed up shop, said goodnight to Kitty and left. She would hail a tram at the corner and be in Manchester in good time to meet up with Turner for the auction.

Her mind wandering, she jumped when she heard a car pull up at the kerb beside her. 'Col!' she said, delighted, getting into the passenger seat. 'Are you coming to the auction with me?'

'I just came to pick you up from work,' he said, smiling, and kissing her tenderly. 'I thought we could have a quiet night in.'

'But the auction . . . '

'You don't have to go.'

'Well, I don't *have* to, but I said I would. I'm meeting Turner.'

'I don't want you to go.'

Pausing, Adele studied her husband's profile as he pulled out into the street. He was obviously tense.

'What's up?'

'Nothing. I just don't want my wife out at all hours of the day and night.'

'Col,' she said, laughing, 'I'll be home by ten.'

'*I don't want you to go*,' Col said coldly, pulling over and stopping the car again. 'I hardly see you any more. Running that flaming shop and going from sale to sale. You're a married

319

woman, Adele, married to *me*. You should remember that.'

'I never forget that. Marrying you was the best thing that ever happened to me.' she replied, her tone careful.

She had spent the previous night going over and over what Ernest had told her about Col's breakdown. About his past moods, his boredom, his loss of control. About how they would never have to worry about them again because she kept Col stable . . . But she was failing, wasn't she? And unless she found a way to soothe her husband and make him happy again, her failure would become public. She thought of the trust Ernest had placed in her. To look after his son. How could she let him down? Hadn't she wanted the enormous responsibility laid on her shoulders? Hadn't she grown to love her complicated husband deeply? So how could she fail?

She wasn't going to.

'Col, darling, what's got into you?'

'*You* got into me!' he hurled back, his tone poison.

Startled, she jumped in her seat, reaching for the door handle. 'I'll see you later, when you've cooled down.'

Leaning over, he grabbed her arm, his grip tight. 'I don't want you going out tonight. I want to talk.'

'So talk to me,' Adele replied, trying to shake off his grasp. 'Col, let go of my arm. You can talk with your mouth, not your hand.'

But he didn't release her, just pulled her

further towards him. 'I've had a hell of a week, and you don't care. You don't even ask how I'm getting on at work.'

'That's a lie, and you know it!' she retorted hotly, suddenly short of patience. 'I'm always interested in the business. Anyway, you're doing well at the factory. You told me that only the other day.'

'That was the other day!' Col snapped, his fingers tightening on her arm. 'A lot's happened since then. An argument with my father, for one thing. And today another run-in with him. And what do I find when I get home? My wife out, at work, and worse, spending the evening at another bloody auction. You're not single any more, Adele, you should act more like a wife.'

Cautiously she took a breath. In the last few weeks she had seen Col repeatedly angry — but not like this. Tonight she was sitting next to her husband and realised with a shock that she didn't even know him.

'Col, I have to go,' she said evenly. 'I won't be long. I've put a bid in for a Worcester bowl and I said I'd meet Turner at the auction. I can't let him down, can I?'

'Turner is *our* friend. You are *my* wife. You answer to me first.'

Her tone froze. 'Actually, Col, I don't answer to anyone. I never have and I never will. Now let go of my arm and I'll see you at home later.'

Her husband's response was so unexpected that she barely had time to duck. Col's punch missed her face and hit her on the shoulder with such force that it knocked the breath out of her lungs. Shocked and frightened, she scrambled to open the car door, Col trying to stop her.

'Jesus, Adele!' he blundered. 'I'm sorry, Jesus, I'm so sorry. I didn't mean to hit you. I didn't mean it!'

A memory came back to her in that instant. A thump, a dull, waxen thud of fist on flesh ... She had been a child, hiding in the under-stairs cupboard. Her teeth had bitten down on her lip, drawing blood, as her father's heavy feet had echoed overhead. Terrified, she had huddled under the stairs, scrunching her six-year-old body into a tidy, hidden parcel of flesh.

'Adele?'

Her mind came back to the present, her panic complete as she wrenched open the car door and shook off her husband's grip.

'*Let go of me!*'

He jumped out of the car and began to follow her. 'Adele, wait!'

'Get away from me!' she snapped, backing off.

'I didn't mean it!'

'That's what they all say. All the men who hit women. *I didn't mean it.*' An image of her mother materialised before her on the street and she stopped in her tracks, Col catching up with her. He was pale, guilt making him almost incoherent.

'I wasn't thinking. I didn't mean it. God, Adele, please listen to me. Listen to me. I've never hit you before? Have I? Have I?'

Adele was still staring at the image of her mother, and then — just as suddenly as it had appeared — the image vanished.

'It will never happen again,' he went urgently. 'We're happy . . . '

'They were happy too.'

He frowned. 'Who were?'

'My parents, although my mother was always on the alert. Watching him.' She turned on her husband, her tone warning. 'I won't live like that. It was bad enough to watch it, I WON'T live it.'

Col caught hold of Adele again. This time the action was gentle as he pulled her towards him. She resisted, then gradually began to relax.

'Forgive me, please. I couldn't bear to hurt you. I was so upset, I just wanted you home with me,' he said tenderly. 'We're happy, you and I. So happy, you know that. It was an accident. I lost my temper.' She moved to go, but he clung to her. 'Adele, shout at me, hit me! Do what you like, but don't walk away. I couldn't live without you. You're my anchor, my rock.'

'And what are you?' Adele replied quietly. 'What are you for me, Col?'

'I love you,' he said simply, like a lost child. 'I love you with all my heart. God, Adele, don't ruin what we have. I'll make it up to you, I swear I will. I'll make you forget this ever happened.'

She could feel her shoulder aching. But it wasn't the pain that hurt her as much as the fact of the unexpected violence — from a source she had trusted so completely.

'Adele,' he said brokenly, his expression desperate. 'Please forgive me, please. It will never happen again. I swear it, on my life, it will never happen again.'

Slowly she nodded. But she didn't walk back to the car with her husband. Instead she continued down the road, catching the first tram that came along, destination Manchester.

★ ★ ★

It took twenty minutes for Col to rally himself enough to begin the drive home. He couldn't believe his loss of control, his stupidity. Hadn't those days been over a long time ago? Hadn't he thought that violence was a part of his past, not his present? Or, God forbid, his future. And to hit Adele, of all people. The woman he loved. The woman who had made him so balanced, so happy. *Happy* was such a simple, mundane word, but it meant so much to him. There had been many times in the past when Col Vincent had doubted he would ever know happiness.

Changing gears, he drove the car on slowly, turning for home. For the first time in a long while he thought of his ex-wife and the way she had cheated on him. Made a fool of him . . . He had hit *her* too. But she had driven him to it. Goading him, mentally and physically confusing him so much that his emotions became unbalanced. In striking her he had struck out at the world, at the madness she had inspired in him, at the way she had used him. She had been — no one would have disputed the fact — a vicious, manipulating bitch. A woman who could have made any man violent.

But Adele wasn't like that. He had no excuse this time. He had struck her without thinking, without hesitation. After so much loving, so much tenderness . . . Col shuddered. The look on her face had damned him. The loss of his wife's trust. And her expression — as though she didn't recognise him any more.

Which she didn't. That hadn't been him, that had been the old Col. The man from the past. Who had risen — so unexpectedly and so damningly — into his present.

★ ★ ★

Adele tried to keep her hands still, finally pushing them deep in her pockets. She had been shaking ever since she had boarded the tram, and now they were arriving in Manchester. In a few minutes she would have to get off, go to the auction, pretend that nothing had changed. When, in reality, everything had. Col had hit her. Suddenly, without warning, on such a flimsy pretext. *Col had hit her.*

Numb, Adele got off the tram and walked to the doors of the auction house. Her legs felt unsteady, her head throbbing. *Why had he hit her?* She thought then of his previous mood swings, his petulance. Was he sick? God, was he heading for another breakdown? Her first instinct was to help him, and yet — in that moment — she realised that she had to protect herself too.

Walking into the main reception room, Adele nodded to a couple of dealers she knew and then caught French Kettering watching her out of the corner of his eye. He smiled, that slow, amused smile of a competitor. But it was a genuine smile. He liked Adele, admired her skill. Even believed that, in time, she would prove herself a worthy opponent.

Taking a seat, Adele's mind wandered back to the incident with Col. *What had she said to provoke him? What had she done wrong?* Suddenly she felt vulnerable, her old unease stirring under the surface. Tentatively she touched her hair, although it wasn't out of place, and fiddled momentarily with her bag. Perhaps she should have worn the blue dress with the other shoes. Maybe she was overdressed. Wasn't that the way people could tell that someone hadn't come from money?

Her lack of confidence startled her, and the hubbub of voices around her was making her head swim, the questions circling endlessly around her brain.

What had she done to provoke Col? What had she been saying? It was her fault, it must have been . . .

And then she thought of her mother, the way Lulu had walked so tentatively around her husband, the way she had sat — always on the edge of her seat — as though ready to move, or run. Victor's violence had been hidden, covered up. But Adele had known, had sensed it. And now she was living with the same thing. *And yet her parents had been happy.* But was that the happiness she wanted for herself?

'Adele?'

She jumped, looking up to see Turner watching her anxiously. 'Are you all right?'

Nodding, she tried to smile. 'I'm fine.'

'You don't look fine. Are you ill?'

She laughed. God, she was laughing, covering up, pretending, just as her mother had always done.

'I'm fine, honestly, Turner.' Her gaze moved to the catalogue in her hands, her eyes unfocused, although her voice was steady. This was Turner, Col's best friend. The man who had been so protective of her. She couldn't let him know what had happened. 'I came to bid for the Worcester bowl.'

'Which you know I want,' he teased her. 'No mercy in business, Adele, you know that.'

She nodded, playing the game, as the auctioneer stepped on to the dais in front of them. Around her she could hear the fey voice of French Kettering, the bullish tones of Morris Devonshire, and the elegant bidding of the auctioneer. Watching the lots come up, she checked her catalogue and felt her attention drift. The ache in her shoulder increased, becoming almost as intense as the ache in her heart. *How could he? Why would he?* She would have to tell someone . . . But who? Her sister? No, those days were over. And certainly not Col's parents; they would be shocked. *Turner?* She glanced over to her companion. No, not Turner, he had been friends with Col long before Adele had come into their lives.

And then Adele realised that there was no one to tell. She would — like so many women before her; like her own mother — have to keep it a secret. Wasn't that the way it usually went?

Wasn't that the accepted way of behaving? Then again, Adele consoled herself, maybe it was different for her. Col was sorry. Hadn't he said so? Hadn't he looked bereft? He wouldn't do it again, he had told her that. Her hands clenched the catalogue tightly, the noise of the bidding increasing around her. She had come so far in life, *nothing* could be allowed to jeopardise her marriage, her career, her security. After all, it was something that had happened only once. And would never happen again.

'You lost.'

She blinked, glancing over to Turner. 'What?'

'You lost your lot, the Worcester bowl,' he said, looking concerned. 'You were miles away.'

A piece of china might have slipped through her fingers, Adele thought bitterly, but nothing else was going to.

45

Having always kept her feelings contained, Mary Vincent wasn't about to become emotional now. Carefully she looked down the breakfast table, noticing that Adele seemed more reserved than usual. Now what was that all about? she wondered. Was her daughter-in-law ill? Or angry about something? Her gaze moved over to her son. Col was eating a pork chop hungrily. The marriage had been successful, a happy union, with few ructions . . . She thought of Col's first marriage. The secret marriage. Had he told Adele about it? Surely he had confided in her? Or then again, maybe not. The incident hadn't been a glorious one; perhaps her son was still smarting. Not that she would have asked. Mary didn't want to know. Apparently Ernest had taken care of it, and in her mind it was all but forgotten.

The fact that she had grown so fond of her daughter-in-law had surprised Mary. What had surprised her even more was that she couldn't show it. Oh, there were the smiles, the squeezes to the arm, the odd exchanged glance of understanding. But the closeness she longed for wasn't there. The incident in her childhood — when she had pitied an outsider and been punished for it — had made her emotionally sterile. And now, even when Mary wanted to reach out, she found to her distress that she couldn't.

After all, she knew her son. She could see the signs in his erratic behaviour and wanted to tell Adele that she wasn't alone. That she had an ally in the house. But try as she might, she always missed her chance. The words escaped her, the timing eluded her, the moment always passed.

Her gaze travelled to her daughter-in-law again. 'Would you like some eggs, dear?'

'No thanks,' Adele replied, glancing up. 'I'm not hungry.'

'You work too hard,' Ernest said, down the other end of the table. 'You should have a holiday, you two. Get off for a few days together.'

Liking the idea, Col glanced over to his wife. 'Good plan, what about it?'

Her response was automatic. 'I have to be at the shop. Now that Kitty's on her honey-moon . . .'

'But she'll be back soon,' Col persisted. 'We could go then.'

There was a moment's pause before Adele answered.

'OK,' she said finally. 'We'll go.'

'You don't have to go if you don't want to!'

'I didn't say that, Col.'

'Then look more pleased about it, would you?'

Surprised, Ernest intervened. 'Don't lose your temper about it, Col.'

'I wasn't losing my temper!'

'You sound like you're losing it.'

'Just keep out of this, will you? It's between me and Adele.'

'Leave her alone,' Mary said quietly.

Adele shot her mother-in-law a grateful glance. The two women held the look, then Mary glanced away. But before she did so, Adele had noticed something in her eyes. *Pity*. Col's mother wasn't as detached as she seemed. Or as disinterested. She knew what was going on, but she couldn't get involved. Or didn't know how to.

Looking down, Adele's gaze fixed on the cutlery. It had been almost a month since Col had last hit her. He hadn't kept his initial promise, and had struck her a number of times. And she had pretended that nothing had happened. Confiding in no one, but always wondering if — or *when* — it would happen again. After all, her husband's affection — which had once come so easily to him — had become forced at times. Would a word or a look trigger off the violence again?

Adele was walking an emotional high wire and didn't like it. But it was too late to get out now. *Now she was pregnant* . . . The thought excited her and alarmed her at the same time. A baby would take her attention away from Col; how would he react to that? But then again, she would be giving him a child, which might be the making of him — and cement their marriage. They had been genuinely happy once; there was no reason to suppose that they couldn't be as happy again. When they were a family. When Col was a father, with the added responsibility to keep him steady.

It would be the making of him . . . *wouldn't it?*

'Sorry, Adele,' Col said suddenly, smiling at her. 'I'm an irritable bugger today.'

She smiled back at him eagerly. It was nearly a month since he had hit her. Nearly four weeks. Nearly thirty days — and counting.

★ ★ ★

Dumping an empty crate in the storage shed at the back of the Failsworth shop, Dave Lin looked round. Being on his own, without Kitty breathing down his neck, certainly made life easier. He was fond of Kitty, but she was so bossy. Not like Adele . . . Sitting down, Dave took out his Swiss Army knife and began to clean out his nails with the blade. He liked working in Failsworth, it was a decent place, not like the scummy streets of Hanky Park, only a few miles away. A man could breathe here. He sucked in the fresh air. If he had a bob or two he would buy a place in Failsworth. A little terraced house. Plant a few bulbs, get a bit of furniture off Tommyfields. Put a brass plate on the door.

Not that it would ever happen. Like every other day, Dave Lin would finish work and then go home. Down into the Hanky Park streets with their doss houses, abattoirs and mills. Down into the mess of smells, people and dog shit, the stench of the outside privies telling you when summer had come. He thought of the Hanky Park women, many worn down, others on the game. The respectable matrons wearing their worn old clothes and cleaning for the better-off. Like Kitty was cleaning for Adele.

But Adele wasn't a snob. Hadn't she promoted Kitty from skivvy to shop assistant? And hadn't she always treated Dave right? Letting him drive the van to collect and deliver goods. Not just muscle now; he was bloody respectable. Of course she didn't know what he felt for her. Nor would she. Dave smiled to himself drily. How could a big dumb crossbreed even dare to look at Adele Vincent? Even dare to day-dream? To fashion scenarios where he saved her from burning buildings and apocalyptic floods? It was all kids' stuff. But he *could* be useful, and stick around as long as Adele needed him.

That was enough for him, Dave told himself. After all, it *had* to be.

★ ★ ★

'It won't last.'

Stan turned to his new wife, Kitty, who was lying on the bed in the Morecambe hotel room. '*What* won't last?'

'All this lovey-dovey stuff. In about a month yer'll be shouting at me, wanting yer socks or yer dinner.' She rolled on to her side, poking him in the ribs. 'Yer better be good to me, mind. Or I'll bugger off and leave yer.'

His pale blue eyes rolled. 'Oh aye?'

'Oh aye,' she agreed, nodding. 'I'm not the kind of woman yer put upon.'

'I'd never have guessed if yer hadn't told me.'

'Anyway, I'm going up in the world, Stan, so yer better be ready to come with me.'

He mumbled something unintelligible and

reached for her, kissing her noisily on the mouth.

'Hey, yer big lump!' she teased him. 'I want to go to Blackpool this afternoon. On the Big Dipper.'

'I'll give yer the Big Dipper!' Stan replied, laughing. 'I've got a better ride fer yer here — and this one's free.'

★ ★ ★

Looking out of the window of his Rochdale shop, Turner motioned for Clemmie to come over. Smiling, he pointed diagonally down the street to where a plain, plump woman was taking down a FOR SALE sign. Evidentally wanting everyone to notice her, she made a great fuss of removing the sign from the shop doorway, then glanced round, nodding to passers-by. It was obvious from the look on her face that she was desperate to talk. Or was that to brag?

'Pauline Buckley!'

Clemmie glanced at her husband. 'You know her?'

'Do I know her . . . ' He smiled wryly. 'A long time ago I was supposed to be her suitor.'

Laughing, Clemmie raised her eyebrows. 'I have a rival? On my doorstep?'

He kissed the top of her immaculate blonde hair. 'No, darling, not exactly. I spent one of the worst evenings of my life with her and her parents. Poor Pauline was decked out like a May horse and I was so embarrassed I damn near ate the cutlery.'

Clemmie laughed again. 'So why has she

bought a shop in Rochdale?'

'To prove a point,' Turner replied. 'Not just to me either. She was always jealous of Adele — I've heard that more than a few times, from more than a few different sources. I reckon she's trying to compete in business, and snare a man at the same time.' He paused, his attention suddenly taken by a gawky, thin man in a bowler hat coming round the corner. 'My God, Donald Duckworth!'

'Who?'

Curious, Turner watched Donald pause outside the shop. 'He's very rich — and he's a widower.'

'With a huge Adam's apple and a stammer.'

'And weighing in at about half Pauline's size.'

'Look!' Clemmie said suddenly. Pauline was backing out of the shop with the board — straight into Donald. A moment of flustered agitation followed, then a handshake, then Pauline flushing crimson.

'*Bingo!*'

Clemmie turned to Turner, amused. 'What?'

'Miss Buckley has just seen her prey,' he went on, 'and now he's done for. I bet those two are married by the end of the year.'

'Strange couple. *Jack Spratt could eat no fat . . .*'

'*His wife could eat no lean,*' Turner finished. 'And before long there will be lots of little ones.'

'Little ducklings.'

They both laughed, Turner teasing his wife. 'Now Mrs G . . . G . . . Gades, how can you be s . . . s . . . s . . . so frivolous?'

Laughing, Clemmie shook her head, adding more seriously, 'I hope the shop works out for Pauline Buckley.'

'It won't matter for her when she's married to D . . . D . . . Donald. She won't need the m . . . m . . . money.'

'Oh, stop it! They'll make the perfect couple,' Clemmie agreed. 'But things *are* changing, Turner, especially in the north-west. All this unemployment is terrible. People aren't buying like they were.'

Sensing her anxiety, Turner put his arm around his wife's shoulders. 'Don't worry about the business,' he reassured her. 'We've got enough money to ride this out. You don't have to worry about anything.'

'Oh, darling,' she said, turning and smiling up at him. 'I don't worry about money. I just worry about *you* worrying about money.'

'In that case, relax,' he reassured her. 'We're secure.'

Slowly Clemmie turned back to the window. 'There are men walking the streets desperate for work, desperate to feed their families. Standing outside the factory gates at dawn to try and get a day's hiring. Dear God, can you imagine it, Turner? Living like that, wondering how you can feed yourself, your family? Wondering about paying the rent? If you'll have a roof over your head?'

He took her hand. Clemmie always worried about the underdog; was always the first to help. Always caring.

'The unemployment might not get worse.'

'You don't believe that any more than I do,' Clemmie replied quietly. 'We're so lucky, Turner. D'you realise that?'

'Only every minute,' he said, looking back into the street. 'Only every minute of my life.'

46

John Courtland stood with his hat in his hands outside his old house on The Coppice. His coat was pressed and brushed but worn; his hair already thinning, although he was only in his early thirties. He had learned a lot in the time he had been away. Like how stupid he had been to lose his wife, his home and his job. But then you only knew that when it was too late . . . John sighed. He recognised himself for what he was now, and knew his faults. Like being too easily taken in. It was dangerous to live your life on hopes and dreams. Especially those that were always going to be out of reach.

Not that John had learned all this overnight. Menial jobs, working for the corporation gardening all around the north-west, had slapped some sense into him. Living in one room, with no friends and no women interested, had underlined just how much he had fooled himself in the past. When he had been Julia's husband, he had had The Coppice to fall back on. A respectable job, with a nice home and even a little car. It was his possessions that had made him attractive, nothing else. On his own, with nothing to offer, he hadn't been good looking enough or confident enough to draw women. And his seduction skills had grown limp with lack of success. So finally — because God knows it had taken a while — he had seen reality.

Finally John Courtland was on terra firma. He might not like it, but he knew exactly where he was.

Taking a deep breath, he rang the doorbell. Over the fence he could see Mrs Redfern gawking through her front-room window. News of his visit would be all over the street in an hour.

Finally the door opened. Julia's jaw dropped when she saw her husband. Her heart pumping, she folded her arms. She was finding it hard to breathe normally. This was her husband, the man she hadn't seen for years. The man who had damn near driven her insane. And now he was back, looking pitiful.

'So?' she asked. She couldn't let him see that she was moved by him. After all, the bastard was probably just coming to ask for a divorce so he could marry some twenty-year-old tart. 'What d'you want?'

'Can I come in?'

She stepped back, watching him enter.

'Can I sit down?'

Surprised, Julia jerked her head towards the front room, watching John take a seat. Her mind went back to when they had been a married couple, living here, sitting in that same seat, curled up together. And the way she had cried, unable to sleep, night after night when he had left her.

'I want to talk to you.'

'Get on with it.'

Flinching, he unfastened his coat, laying his hat on the settee. Julia could see how much weight he had lost, how his collar hung loosely around his neck.

'Can you ever forgive me for what I did to you?'

'No,' she said simply. 'And if that was all you came to say, you can get out now.'

To Julia's complete astonishment, he began to cry. He cried silently, his tears falling, unstopped, and wetting his suit jacket. He cried from inside, his shoulders heaving, his head bowed. Julia watched him, not knowing what to do.

'I . . . I was so cruel to you . . . ' John stammered. 'I was so cruel . . . I wanted to come back . . . To explain . . . I couldn't . . . '

Julia's voice seemed to come from a long way off. 'So why are you back now?'

'I've been ill . . . '

'I was ill too,' she said mercilessly. 'I was ill for a long time when you left, John. I lost our child.'

His head jerked up. 'A baby? You lost our baby?' His whole body was shaking. 'Why didn't you tell me, Julia?'

'I did! But obviously you didn't believe me. It didn't stop you walking out that bloody door!' she snapped back. Drained, she flopped into the chair opposite him. 'You've been ill, so what? I could have died and you wouldn't have known.'

His eyes met hers and then he glanced away. 'I don't blame you for being bitter. I would feel the same in your shoes.'

'You've never *been* in my shoes, John! If you had, you wouldn't have acted the way you did. And kept quiet for so long . . . Do you think I don't realise why you're back now? You want a divorce, fine. I'll give you one with pleasure.'

'I don't want that!' he said, shaken. 'I don't want a divorce. I should never have left you. It was the worst thing I ever did, the most stupid mistake I ever made.'

'So she's left you then?'

He winced. 'It was over a long time ago with me and Susan Fleetwood . . . I've wanted to see you for a while, but I couldn't pluck up the courage after what I'd done to you. Julia, forgive me.'

She raised her eyebrows, refusing to weaken. No man was going to break her heart or keep her awake at night again. She was finally in control of herself and her life. And she was *staying* in control.

'Julia, take me back, please.'

The moment fizzed between them.

'Why should I?' she asked, almost sneering. 'You're not exactly a catch, are you?'

'Julia . . . '

'Where are you working?'

'I lost my job at the bank.'

'I heard about that.'

'I've been working as a gardener . . . '

'*Been?*' she parroted, her eyebrows raised.

'It's so hard out there, Julia. There are no jobs.'

'*I've* got a job. The same one I've had for years,' she said coldly. 'God Almighty, you are a prince, you know that? You have the nerve to come back to me, telling me some sob story about how you're no longer with your bloody girlfriend. About how you've been ill. And now you tell me you're unemployed — and you want me to take you back!'

Her voice shook him and he shrank into his seat as Julia towered over him. 'I should kick your arse out of this house, all the way down The Coppice and into the Irwell.'

'Julia, listen to me . . . '

'Listen to you!' she hollered. 'I've heard enough to last me a lifetime.'

'I love you.'

She paused, her hands on her hips, looking down at her husband. Dear God, she thought suddenly, how life changes. Time was when I would have eaten glass to make this man stay home with me. And now he's cowering. A thin, broken man with nothing to offer and nowhere to go. Slowly she sank into a chair, looking at her husband thoughtfully. She didn't go short. Not financially, anyway. But emotionally, she was starving. And seeing Adele's prosperity and happy marriage to a successful man had only intensified her hunger.

Every fibre of Julia's body was itching to hurl John Courtland out into the street. But she wasn't going to do anything of the sort. John was begging to come back, and now, finally, she had a way of regaining some status. If she did it on *her* terms. And her terms alone.

'Why should I even think of taking you back?' she asked, her tone imperious. 'I might have someone else in my life.'

John stared at her. 'Have you?'

'No one in particular, but I stopped crying for you a while back.' She walked over to the window. 'You have nothing to offer me, John.'

'I could look after you.'

'I can look after myself. I have done ever since Adele married.' Julia turned. 'Yes, my sister's married now, living in Rochdale.'

'You must be lonely. In this place, on your own.'

'Not that lonely!' Julia retorted. 'Not lonely enough to take in some sick deadbeat like you.'

'You've changed,' he said, stung.

'Yeah, I have. I changed when you left. What did you expect, John? That I would run into your arms, grateful that you'd come home?' she sneered. 'Look at yourself, you're pathetic.'

He nodded, resigned. 'Yes.'

'You used to have something about you,' she went on, circling him. 'Some charisma. Not any more.'

'If you say so.'

'Yes, I do say so! I say you're looking sickly, and you're going bald. I say you're a washout, a loser who hasn't got a job, a home or a woman.' Her spite burned her mouth. 'In fact, John Courtland, I would say that looking at you makes me want to laugh.'

Reaching for his hat, John stood up, facing his wife. 'I'll go then.'

'Yeah, you go!' she said viciously. 'Go back to wherever you came from. Sleep rough on the street, die there, I don't care. Do whatever you want, *but get out!*'

Almost staggering, he moved to the door, then turned. 'Do I have to beg?'

She nodded, smiling. 'Now you understand.

343

You *do* have to beg. Beg me to take you back. Beg me every day not to throw you out. Beg me to care about you. Beg me, beg me, beg me!'

Swallowing, John glanced at his wife. His voice almost a whisper, he said pleadingly, 'Please take me back. Please, Julia, I'll do whatever you say, whatever you want, just take me back. *I'm begging you.*'

And so he came back to his wife. And so Julia had her husband again. Repeatedly he told her he loved her. But she wasn't going to tell him she loved him. Not for a while, anyway.

47

She was breaking through ice, Mary thought, her skin flushed, her heart swelling. Suddenly all her reserve, her aching to show affection had been released. Not to her husband, her son or her daughter-in-law — but to her grandson, Paul. The birth of the child had delighted Adele and Col, but it had released Mary from emotional deadlock.

'My God,' she said, looking into the crib. 'Col looked just like him when he was born.' She turned to Adele, then touched the baby's hand tenderly. 'You're going to have the best of everything, my love. The best the world can offer.'

Having given her husband a son and heir, Adele tried her best to relax. As she had hoped, fatherhood changed Col. From the first he was excited, interested in the baby. Nothing was too much for this child. Nothing too expensive. Paul Vincent's pram, layette and nappies were not locally bought, but came from Kendal Milne, in Manchester. Turner and Clemmie arrived a day after his birth with an antique silver rattle. No baby was as welcomed. At Oakham Lodge the talk was of family, of Paul's future. At only a week old, Col was investigating the best schools, Ernest opening a trust fund, Mary redecorating the nursery because it wasn't good enough. The toys had to come from London; Manchester wasn't good enough.

After a difficult birth, Adele took a while to recover, relying on the support of her family and friends. It would take some time for her to regain her strength, Col was told, but she would be up and about before long. News came to her through a steady trickle of visitors. Kitty dropping by with a present for the baby, Becky visiting with a note from Frida Altman.

My dear girl
What wonderful news to hear of your son's birth. I wish Paul every marvellous joy in life and look forward to meeting him.
With affection from
Frida

'How is she?' Adele asked, looking at Becky.

'She's well. And so am I.'

Becky and Isaac had been married for over a year and had been more than contented. Isaac had a wife now. A family. Life was perfect, better than he could have imagined. And if his work at the library wasn't that interesting, or that well paid, so what? He was a happy man. And he knew it. As for Becky, she had a partner she loved to distraction. A kind man, who had kept his promise, forgotten the past and lived for the future. *Their future.*

'He's a handsome baby, like his father,' Becky said, looking at Paul again.

For a moment Adele wanted to confide, to say she hoped that her son wasn't like Col in temperament. She ached to tell Becky about her worries, share some of the responsibility which had been laid on her shoulders. Sometimes it was too much to bear ... But she knew she couldn't. The true state of her marriage had been a long-held secret and had to remain so. Besides, things might change now. Now that the baby was here.

Becky cleared her throat, her voice low. 'I'm pregnant.'

'That's wonderful!'

She nodded. 'I know. And Isaac said we mustn't worry about anything.'

'Isaac's right.'

'He says that he knows the baby will be all right.'

Adele smiled tenderly. 'Isaac's a scholar, a great reader, you must believe him.'

'I do,' Becky said, her voice quiet and proud. 'D'you realise our children will grow up together?'

Moved, Adele reached out and took her friend's hand. Becky smiled. 'We got what we wanted, didn't we? Both of us married good men and now we're both going to have families. God, Adele, when I remember how bad things were once, I can't believe our luck.'

That same afternoon, Julia called by. Although they had kept in contact, the two sisters hadn't seen each other for many weeks. Adele noticed at once that there was a change in her sister. Julia had a bloom about her, a confidence which had been missing for years.

'You look well,' Adele sat, sitting up in bed.

'I am well,' Julia replied, looking at Paul. 'Strong baby ... '

347

'I was thinking about you this morning,' Adele admitted. 'I was thinking that we should see each other more. We were so close once, Julia.'

Julia nodded, faintly smug. 'I was thinking the same.'

'You were?'

'Yes, I was,' Julia agreed. 'Besides, I have some news for you. John has come home.'

'*John?*'

'I knew you wouldn't be pleased!'

'I didn't say I wasn't pleased,' Adele replied shortly. 'I was just surprised.'

'He begged me. What could I do?'

Choosing her next words carefully, Adele asked, 'Are you happy?'

'I'm sure of him. So, yes, I am happy.'

I'm sure of him . . . Studying her sister, Adele felt uneasy. John Courtland had broken Julia's heart once; would he do so again? Or was she really sure of him? If so, she was the luckier sister. Because Adele wasn't sure of Col. From the outside her life seemed perfect — a good husband and lovely baby, financial security — but for one tingling instant Adele wanted to be able to say the words her sister had just spoken. *I'm sure of him.*

'I'll come by again soon,' Julia said suddenly.

'Do that,' Adele replied, catching her sister's hand. 'I want to see more of you.'

Touched, Julia stood up to go. Then she turned back and kissed Adele on the top of the head. 'I'm glad to see you again too.'

At once, time shifted backwards. They were suddenly very young again, Julia tucking her little sister into bed soon after their parents had died. She had leaned over Adele then, her hair falling over one shoulder as she kissed her goodnight.

'*Go to sleep, you're safe. I'm here, go to sleep.*'

And then Adele had heard her footsteps fade, Julia going downstairs in the house on The Coppice. A moment later she had heard the kettle humming and the sound of the evening paper falling on the mat.

And for one inexplicable instant — despite all she had — Adele wanted to go back there.

★ ★ ★

'I don't care what you say, Col! You have to be more careful!' Ernest was angry, his benign face flushed as he confronted his son. 'We have to take more care, save money at times like these.'

'We aren't hard up!'

'No, but we can't afford to throw money around!' Ernest retorted, sitting down. 'Col, let's not fight. We can talk this out between us. There is no reason to get excited.'

'You accused me of being careless.'

'I didn't. I said we had to be more careful.'

'Which is the same bloody thing!' Col replied heatedly. He was pacing his father's office, his impatience obvious.

Paul's birth had been the making of Col, but only for a while. Soon he was fretting, worrying about the baby's future, about how to secure his position in life. As Ernest had pointed out, Paul was only nine months old, there was no rush. But Col didn't see it that way. He pressed for another trust fund, put aside money of his own. Even bought some stocks and shares for Paul's future. For God's sake, Ernest had said, the family had money, but not that kind of money. And now here was his son, agitated, on edge — the way he used to be — all over a possible nursery school.

'Calm down, Col.'

'I have responsibilities now,' he retorted coolly. 'I'm only trying to do what is right for my son. I have to think of his future.'

'Which is commendable, but you should talk to Adele about this. She'll have her own opinion.'

'I make the decisions for the baby.'

'No, Col,' Ernest said quietly, '*both* parents make the decisions for their baby.'

★   ★   ★

Lying on her side on the bed, Adele tickled Paul's tummy, laughing as the baby curled up his legs. A bad dose of colic had meant a number of sleepless nights, but much as Col wanted to let the nanny attend to it, Adele refused. Paul was her baby, she wanted to look after him. The nanny was a great help, naturally. She could take Paul out on long walks in the pram and do the washing and mundane duties, but Adele wouldn't have minded doing any of that — if Col had let her.

'You don't need to do the boring things,' he

said, kissing her. But it wasn't a suggestion, it was an order.

'I might like to.'

'No, darling, let the nanny do the dirty work.'

The dirty work . . . Blowing on Paul's tummy, Adele giggled, the baby laughing. It was lucky that she had trained Kitty Gallager up as her assistant. Now she wasn't worried about the Failsworth shop — although she did miss being involved. Going to the auctions, and the fairs. But still, people weren't holding as many as they had done because of the Depression. She hated the word — and she was rich; God only knew what it meant to others. All Adele had to worry about was her baby — and the length of her hemline.

At least that was what Col told her. That he was in control of everything now, that she had nothing to worry about. She didn't have to work. She was a mother, and mothers stayed home. Lucky mothers did, Adele thought, but Hanky Park mothers didn't have it so good. Hadn't Clemmie told her only the other day about a family who had ended up at the Poor Hospital because they couldn't meet the rent? And then there was an Oldham carter who had killed himself, hanged himself on the factory gates of the Yates mill. The place he had visited every morning for the last six weeks without success.

Still lying beside her baby, Adele jumped as the door opened and Col walked in.

'Hello there, you're home early.'

Grunting, Col walked into his dressing room,

leaving the door open. He was bored to tears. It was all right being a father, but after all the excitement and congratulations, what was left? He was getting shut out now, his wife and mother lavishing attention on Paul whilst he was just working like a dog to keep everyone. What a life, what a bloody future! he thought, his temper getting the better of him.

He could feel the old sensation of irritation and boredom, and instead of trying to fight it, he let it fester. Obviously he shouldn't hit his wife, but he was finding it harder and harder *not* to criticise Adele. God knows, he had reason. Hadn't his own mother been reserved all his life? And now his young, pretty wife was going the same way. Turning her attention on to their son and moving away from him.

Slowly, he walked back into the bedroom. He could see Adele playing with their son on the bed, and instead of delighting him, it inflamed him. 'Paul should be in bed by now. He'll get tired.'

Automatically, Adele held the child to her. 'I know what's right for him; he needs time with his mother.'

'You spoil him,' Col replied critically.

'I don't. He's just a baby.'

'I was never spoiled.'

She bit her lip, fighting the impulse to say, *Yes, and how happy did you turn out to be?* But as usual she didn't retaliate. Their sick marriage was her fault, and she was determined to rescue it from total breakdown. Whatever it took.

'Col, come over here and play with me and the baby.'

He shook his head. 'Aren't you going to get ready?'

'For what?'

'We're going out for dinner tonight, with the Clarks.'

'Oh yes,' Adele said awkwardly. 'I forgot.'

'Christ! You don't have *that* much to do.'

'I look after Paul.'

'We have a nanny for that.'

'I didn't ask for a nanny.'

He ignored her and walked back into his dressing room, calling out through the door, 'What are you wearing tonight?'

'Clothes,' Adele mumbled, taking the baby to the nursery and laying him in his cot. 'I'd rather stay with you, sweetheart. We would have more fun than going to a lousy dinner.'

The dinner was in honour of Mr and Mrs Gregory Clark, who had been married for twenty years. Younger than most people present, Adele was relieved to see Turner arrive with Clemmie for pre-dinner drinks. She was about to make a beeline for them when she felt a hand on her arm.

'Adele, where are you going?'

'To say hello to Turner and Clemmie,' she replied, looking at Col, surprised. 'What's the matter?'

'You look odd,' he said. 'Messy. Can't you do something with your hair?'

Self-consciously, Adele touched her head. 'It looked all right when I left.'

'You've put on weight too.'

'Only a few pounds,' Adele replied, mortified. 'I'll lose it.'

'You said that a month ago.'

Stung, Adele glanced at her husband. 'Why are you being so nasty to me?'

'Oh, don't act like a child! We already have a baby in the family.'

Only Turner's approach prevented Adele from walking off. Smiling, he greeted her, while Clemmie kissed her on the cheek.

'You're glowing.'

'If a little plump,' Col added.

'Not at all,' Turner replied, tapping Col's stomach with the back of his hand. 'Anyway, you can talk.'

It should have been a light-hearted gesture, but Adele sensed at once that Col was mortified. His face paling, he sipped his drink, Turner immune, Clemmie raising her eyebrows at Adele. Her look said clearer than words: *Are we going to have trouble tonight?*

'So, Col,' Turner went on, 'how's your son?'

'Spoilt,' he replied, sipping his drink again.

'He's a baby, I believe that's what you're supposed to do with them.'

'Only if you're a poor parent.'

Turner gave Col a slow look. 'You're in a bad mood tonight.'

'I wouldn't be if other people knew how to behave,' Col replied.

Turner laughed. 'Oh, for God's sake, relax!' he joked. 'We're going to have a good evening.'

They all knew *that* wasn't going to happen.

★ ★ ★

Deep in thought, Ernest turned to his wife. He was about to say something and then checked himself. He couldn't talk to Mary about their son, not really. After all, she didn't know the full story of Col's breakdown. No one did. Oh, Ernest had partially confided in Adele, but that was different. He had felt *obliged* to tell her, to explain his son's temperament. And he had made her promise to keep their conversation a secret . . . Ernest suddenly wondered if his son had confided everything to his wife. The thought made him unusually nervous. Then he relaxed. Col wasn't the confiding type, and besides, even if he had made a clean breast of it, Adele would keep quiet. She was good at secrets.

Thoughtfully, Ernest studied his wife. She had been a revelation to him, adoring their grandson, spending time with him, and even becoming quite loquacious on the subject of good schools. Her reserve with her husband, with Col and with Adele never extended to Paul. Ernest considered his grandson with pleasure and then thought of Adele. He was delighted that their arrangement had worked out, but was astute enough to suspect that the marriage was shaky.

'Mary?'

She looked up, composed. 'Yes?'

'Are you happy about our life? Our grandson.' Ernest found that he was blathering. 'Having a family around us?'

'What do you want me to say, Ernest?'

'What you think.'

355

'No,' she replied, 'I don't believe you do. I'm not stupid, Ernest. I may say little, but I see everything that goes on. And I know you. You want me to say I'm happy and that everything is fine — when we both know it clearly isn't. We can both see where our son's marriage is heading.'

'Col and Adele are happy!'

'Oh, for God's sake,' Mary replied, sighing. 'You got what you wanted, Ernest. You don't have to pretend with me.'

'Pretend what?'

Shrugging, she rose to her feet.

'My sister isn't too well. I thought I would go and look after her for a week or so. But not for long, I would miss my wonderful grandson far too much.'

'But you can't want to leave now!' Ernest blustered, incredulous.

'There's nothing I can do,' she replied, fixing him with an unflinching look. '*You* built the castle — you don't need an audience to watch it collapse.'

48

Two months passed. August slid into September, September into a dry, unusually warm October. On the 15th and 16th there was unbroken sunshine, 'The Little Summer of St Luke', as common folklore had it. Those last bright days before the autumn stumbled in. Over the previous few weeks the news had all been about the Mersey Tunnel. What an achievement, the papers said. The same papers later recorded that the police in Bristol had clashed with the jobless. Which wasn't quite such an achievement. Then followed the hunger marches, starting in Lancashire, the unemployed walking all the way to London. In the East End, even royalty took the brunt of people's anger, Prince George being greeted with the chant: 'Down with the means test, we want bread.' In Trafalgar Square, fifty protesters were injured and forty arrested.

Faced daily with too many men and too few jobs on offer at the paper mills, Ernest put Col in charge of the Rochdale works and the main office. But the extra responsibility weighed heavily on his son, and together with his increasing mood swings, Col's outbursts were becoming more frequent as each week passed. Confronted with a situation she could see was getting out of hand, Adele tried to reason with her husband, but he wouldn't listen and had even taken to showing her up in public.

One particular occasion stuck in Adele's mind and made her almost hate him. There had been a small retirement celebration at the Rochdale factory for one of the workers, who had been with the business for forty-five years. Asked by Ernest to make a presentation, Adele had dressed herself up and gone with Col. Listening to Ernest's introductory speech, she had suddenly realised that her husband had wandered off. Alarmed, she looked around, but he was nowhere to be seen when she gave the factory worker his presentation clock and thanked him sweetly. As people clapped, Adele then noticed Col swaggering back into the room, a young woman smirking behind him. She noticed it — and so did everyone there, people nudging each other and whispering.

But she didn't challenge him. She didn't dare. In fact, as time wore on, Adele found herself scared to say anything to her husband. The gentlest rebuke was met with fury, and, later, repentance. But gradually the pleading for forgiveness became intermittent. At times Col would apologise; at other times he would go on the defensive.

'You have no idea what it's like out there, in the real world,' he would say shortly. 'You don't know how easy you've got it here.'

'I didn't always have it easy,' Adele would reply cautiously. 'And I know I'm lucky.'

Who was she kidding? Adele thought. In some ways, her life was harder than ever. Her husband was developing into a vicious stranger; a shadow of her parents' marriage echoing eerily in her own. But what could she do? She was trapped. A woman didn't leave her husband — if she did, she had better have good reason. And Adele had given her oath that she would never expose Col's past. God, she thought angrily, she should have questioned him, found out more while he was still in love with her — while she still could. But she had missed her chance. Her husband's past was unclear, and would remain so. As for thinking she could still save him, that was impossible. You could only save someone who *wanted* to be saved. And besides, Adele had another, more pressing concern than her husband's mental health: her son. So finally she came to a decision. Even if it was difficult, she would stick with her marriage, in order to give Paul a good home and security. It was too late now to ask questions or walk away. It wasn't just about her any more. She had another life to think of.

'You don't even work now.'

She winced, turning to her husband. '*You* told me not to work any more!'

'I didn't expect you to turn into some drudge.'

'You said you wanted me to stay at home and look after Paul! I *wanted* to work.'

'Oh yes, of course you did,' he replied sarcastically. 'Come off it, Adele, you couldn't exist in the real world any longer. You've lost your drive, your edge. You're not fit to run anything.'

Stung, she turned on him. 'I didn't want to give up managing the shop!'

'*You want, you want,*' Col snapped. 'That's all I ever hear — what *you* want.'

She was stunned by the unfairness of the accusation and was about to retaliate, then stopped herself. Let it go, she thought, let it go. He'll leave soon. If you say anything, it will only escalate into an argument . . . Turning away, she busied herself with Paul. But the baby could sense the atmosphere and began to whimper.

'Look at that!' Col snapped. 'He doesn't cry when the nanny takes care of him. Honestly, Adele, you can't do anything right any more.'

Her hands balled into fists. She wanted to turn round and hit him. But she didn't dare. There was too much to lose — and besides, she was still prepared to give her husband the benefit of the doubt. The conversation with Ernest came back to her, as it had done so many times over the past few months. Perhaps, if she was understanding and unobtrusive, Col would get over this rough patch. All she had to do was stay calm and not provoke her husband in any way.

And so it had gone on, with Adele suppressing her own character more and more every day. Gradually her outgoing, feisty nature started to dissolve as she became timorous, on edge. Nothing she said could please her husband, the father of their baby; nothing she could do, was right. He flirted with other women and belittled her in public, and as for lovemaking — it was always at his instigation, short and unfeeling. And then Adele realised something: she loved her child with a passion, but she didn't love Col any more.

She leaned over Paul's crib. The child was

whining, crying as she picked him up. 'Come on, baby, it's all right.'

'You shouldn't pick him up all the time,' Col said, walking over to them. 'If he cries, he shouldn't be rewarded. Otherwise he'll do it all the more.'

'I can't just leave him upset in his cot,' Adele countered diffidently. 'He's a baby.'

'Yes, and I'm his father.'

'And I'm his *mother*, Col.'

He paused, looking at his wife. 'Put him down.'

Hesitating, Adele could feel her heart speed up. 'No.'

'I said put him down.'

'And I said no,' Adele replied, her tone calm but determined.

Oh God, there would be another quarrel now, another awkward evening, Ernest looking at her pityingly down the dinner table, and no Mary around. No small — but comforting — gesture of support from her mother-in-law.

'Adele, I won't say it again,' Col warned, leaning forwards to take hold of Paul. 'If you won't put him back in his cot, I will.'

Without thinking, she resisted. Paul was now crying openly clinging to his mother.

'Leave him alone!' Adele snapped, turning away. 'He's upset and he wants me.'

The blow struck her from behind, Col's fist landing on her left kidney. Gasping, Adele dropped to her knees, still holding the baby. Struggling for breath — Paul screaming in her arms — she tried to get up again, but Col

361

snatched the child away.

Holding Paul, he looked down at his wife with distaste. 'You're not fit to be a mother! This child will grow up soft, spoiled. He needs a strong father — not a weakling like you.'

Gasping with pain, Adele watched her husband holding their child. Jesus, she thought, why had he hit her? Why so violently? Gasping for air, she reached for a nearby chair and pulled herself up. God, what if she had let go of the baby? *What if she had dropped her son?* She could hear Col talking to Paul as he laid his son back in his cot. There was no anger in his tone any more. It was as though nothing had happened. And he hadn't even turned to look at her. Or say sorry. He wasn't going to apologise this time. Or ever again.

Fighting a wave of nausea, Adele leaned back in the chair. The pain roared through her body, shock making her cold. Did Col know how hard he had hit her? Did he care? Her gaze rested on him warily as he stood over their son's cot. He hadn't even glanced at her to see what damage he had done. In his eyes, Adele had disobeyed him. It didn't matter that in hitting the mother of his child he could have injured his own son. If Adele had relaxed her grip when she was struck, Paul would have fallen . . .

Finally Col turned. 'It's your own fault.'

She said nothing.

'Paul's not crying any more, is he?' Col went on, his tone smug. 'You see, I know what's best for my son and I won't have you telling me what to do.'

Again she said nothing.

Col walked over to his wife, looking down at her. Intimidated, Adele could hear the blood rushing in her ears and tensed for another blow.

'You have no idea how to care for a child. They have to know who's boss from the start.' He paused, looking into his wife's eyes, willing her to show resistance. 'Oh dear, Adele, you're not like you used to be, are you? Time was when you'd have stood up to me, but now you're like every other woman, weak and cowed.'

Still she said nothing.

'You'll have to buck up your ideas, Adele. I'm bored to death with you, and unless you're very careful I might find someone else who understands me better. A better wife — and mother.'

'Don't threaten me!' Adele hissed between clenched teeth.

He bent down towards her, menacing. 'You want to take me on? I wouldn't bother, Adele. You're nothing without me and my family. D'you think any court in this land would give you custody of Paul?' He saw her wince and pressed on. 'I could take my son away from you any time I liked. I'm the one with the money and the power — remember that.'

'I've never forgotten it.'

'Of course, if it all gets too much for you, Adele, you can go whenever you want — but you leave Paul behind.'

'Like hell!' she shouted, beside herself at the thought of losing her child. 'He's my son!'

Horrified, she watched Col walk back to the

cot and look at Paul. Leave him with his father? Never. Leave him to grow up with Col? To grow up *like* Col? Unstable, violent — or worse, abused. She could imagine Col's reaction to a child's fretful crying, or a toddler's demands, and the thought made her wince. Jesus, she thought, Col would have to *kill* her before she left Paul alone with him.

'You don't have to stay if you hate me so much. You can leave any time you like. *But alone.*' He turned at the bedroom door. 'Paul is my child, and don't you ever — ever — forget it. He is my flesh and blood. But you, I could get rid of you any time I liked.'

Only after she heard her husband leave the house did Adele rise painfully to her feet. Her back ached as she walked over to Paul's cot, and looked down at her baby. Her son, Paul — not yet a year old. Gently she touched his hand. Her husband was right. She *was* weak and cowed. He had done that to her. But when he had hit her, with their child in her arms, then threatened to take Paul away from her, something had shifted inside her.

She might have changed, might let herself be bullied, but no one — *no one* — was going to hurt her child. Holding Paul's hand, she leaned against the cot. Perhaps if she went to Ernest she could get help? Or appeal to Mary? But what would it mean if they told her they would take care of Paul? That she could escape? What escape would there be without her son? Oh, she wanted to get out, but not if it meant losing her child. Shaking, Adele fought panic. She knew how unbalanced Col was, and realised that his threat hadn't been an idle one. *What if he took Paul away? Went abroad with him?* He was capable of it. It would be typical of his increasing whims . . . Adele stroked her son's forehead, desperately trying to think. She had grown used to Col's beatings, but she wasn't going to stand by and see Paul victimised. What kind of mother would do that? Her back ached, the pain making her queasy. At Oakham Lodge Paul had his grandparents, and their money. He would have a good life, a secure life. Could she deny him that?

But how secure would he really be? Financially safe, but emotionally bereft. Adele shook her head, bewildered. Could she risk leaving with her son? Exposing him to hardship and struggle? But could she risk staying, making him vulnerable to fear and injury? After all, Col had hit her whilst she was holding Paul — how long before he struck out directly at the child? Maybe he never would — *but did she want to take that chance? Did she want to gamble with her son's safety?*

And then Adele asked herself the most important question of all. If she stayed at Oakham Lodge, how long would it take for Col to ruin his son's life?

PART FOUR

Beware of pity.
Trad. proverb

I remember watching Col eating dinner later. He was so composed, so eerily unconcerned as he cut into some fish. I don't remember what type, only that the juice spread into the white sauce and snaked around the vegetables, a little clinging to the corner of his mouth. He ate slowly, saying little. Ernest was preoccupied with business. I watched my husband finish his meal and lean back, turning to me. But I was already looking down. Cowed, I suppose he thought.

He had always been a heavy sleeper, and that night was no different. Beside him I waited, my back throbbing with pain. I waited patiently, hating him and thinking of the bag I had already packed, and put on the tray under Paul's pram. I didn't know exactly where we were going, only that we were no longer safe at Oakham Lodge.

I knew only too well what I was leaving behind: respectability, security, status. And it had meant a lot to me, once. But not now. What was money compared with the safety of my child?

As if he knew, Paul was quiet when I laid him in his folding pram, packed with as many possessions and clothes as it could carry. Even when I walked out of the back door and clicked the latch, he never murmured. That early morning was bitter, a mist coming over from the moors, but I never hesitated. Tensely I waited for the tap on my shoulder, the sound of Col shouting after me. But it never came. I pushed that pram down the drive, round the corner and away.

We were making for the coast, putting distance between my husband and my child. I knew that, off season, I could get accommodation cheaply and find work. With a baby in a pram, there was no question of a normal job, so I was going back to what I knew. The antique trade. Only this time there were to be no dinner-jacketed auctioneers, no French Kettering, no Morris Devonshire. No tales from Turner about the Lydgate Widow. I was going to work the hard end of the business, as a knocker, going from door to door asking if people had anything they wanted to sell. Anything I could trade in at the markets later.

I knew what kind of person usually did the job. And I knew that with so much unemployment there would be many extra men out working the streets, looking for the same bargains I was. But I had no choice. To stay with my husband was unthinkable. Col wasn't fit to be a spouse, let alone a father. And if it came to a fight over custody of Paul, I knew who would win. Did I think Col would come after us? Oh yes. I worried about that all that long night, and then realised what I had to do to keep him off our trail. It meant damning myself in everyone's eyes, ruining my own reputation. But it would keep Col away from us. And it would keep my son safe.

And so the next part of my story began, on that early October morning. St Luke's Little Summer was over, and a chill had come into the air . . .

49

Dear Turner,

This is so difficult to write. That I should let you down. You, of all people, when you have always been kind and encouraging. But I want to explain why I have left Col. Your oldest friend, the man you introduced me to.

I have met someone else — and I have left Col to be with him and our son. Yes, Turner, *our son*. Paul is not Col's child.
Forgive me, if you can, for letting you down. For not being the person you thought I was, and for throwing away the opportunity you so readily gave to me.

If you and Clemmie cannot think kindly of me, I will only ever think kindly of you.

With regret,
Adele

Slowly she read the letter again, then she put it in an envelope and sealed it. It was the biggest lie of her life, but the only way to explain her departure. Telling the truth was impossible. Honesty would only injure Turner, who had been fond of Col for years and unendingly kind to her. Adele also realised that if Turner knew the truth he would never forgive himself for endangering her by bringing her into contact with Col. He would consider it his fault. Would agonise over her being hurt, and her child's safety being threatened.

Besides, Adele had made a promise to Ernest Vincent — and she was going to keep it. She might be marking out her son in everyone's eyes, but she had no choice. In time she would explain. In time they would be so far away that the lie wouldn't matter. All that *did* matter was the present. What she had to do to keep Col away and her son safe.

Pulling another piece of paper towards her, Adele began to write again:

Col,

You know why I've gone. But no one else will. I have told Turner that I've left you for another man, who is Paul's real father. You can tell everyone the same — think of the sympathy you'll get. But I'm not doing this to save your face, Col, just to keep you away.

If you come after us, or tell anyone the truth — not that you'll risk your reputation — I'll expose your past. Remember, Col, I have a secret. Or should I say *secrets* now? Threaten me and I'll ruin you. Come after us and I'll tell the world what you did to me.

If I were you, I would stick to my version of events.

Adele

She put this letter in its envelope and reached for a third piece of paper.

Dear Ernest,

I'm so sorry to cause such upset, but you'll know by now that I've left Col. He was violent and I was afraid for our child. As I promised, I'll keep your confidence. You can say I ran off with another man. Believe me, it's a small price to pay to get away from Col — and *keep* him away. I'm sorry, I know he's your son, but he's ill. Or just cruel. I don't know, he would never explain.

Thank you for all you did — and tried to do — for me. I'm sorry I had to take your grandson away — I know how much you and Mary love him. But Paul will be safer with me. Perhaps, one day, we might see each other again. I hope so.

I will tell Paul all about his grandfather — and how he was a good man.

Adele

The final letter was to her mother-in-law.

Dear Mary,

Forgive me for taking Paul away. I know how much you love him, and how much you will miss him. Believe me when I say that I would *never* have done this if I had had any other choice. But I had to get us both away from your son.

Thank you for your kindness. I know you were always on my side — even when you couldn't show it. I will take good care of your grandson and please God, one day, bring him back to you.

Adele

She picked up the other two letters beside her.

One was to her sister, simply saying she had left Col; the other to Becky, asking her not to believe what she heard and promising that she would be in touch soon. As with the rest, there was no return address. Then, carrying Paul in her arms, she headed for the nearest postbox. The letters made a soft thud as they hit the bottom of the box.

By the following morning, the news would be all over Rochdale — and beyond.

50

The seafront was deserted, a bitter wind blowing in from the Irish Sea as Adele retraced her steps back to the Morecambe boarding house. As she had guessed, accommodation was cheap, as it was fast approaching the hard time of the year for seaside landlords. The hard time of the year for everyone. Especially a young woman with a baby in tow.

Pausing on the seafront, Adele looked out to the chilled grey sea, choppy with waves. She thought suddenly of the still clear water of the lake outside her honeymoon window, and the way she and Col had made love. The memory ached inside her as her hands pulled the shawl warmly around Paul's face, the baby sleeping. Not that he had slept last night. It had been her son's first time away from Oakham Lodge — the only home he had ever known. Whether he was unhappy, Adele wasn't sure. Certainly he was picking up on her anxiety as she tried repeatedly to soothe him.

'Sssh, baby,' she had whispered in the early hours, dry-eyed with lack of sleep. 'You have to be quiet and good, or they'll tell us to go.' She stroked her baby's head, trying to comfort him. 'Things will get better, Paul, I promise. Soon everything will be fine again. We'll get a nice little place, just you and me, and we'll have some good times. We will,' she told him, wondering if she was trying to convince her child or herself. 'We're going to make a new life, baby. A good life.'

Finally he dozed off, Adele sitting on the bed beside him. Her heart felt as though it had been squeezed dry. But she had done the right thing. She had made sure they were safe. *But would they be safe here?* she wondered, looking round. The place itself was clean and functional, but the difficulties of managing a baby in one room were only just beginning to hit home. Fighting loneliness and panic, Adele sat staring into space.

Her landlord, Mr Finchley, hadn't wanted a child around, but had relented when Adele told him she wanted to take a month's rental of the room. In Morecambe, in early October, when there were no trippers, a month's rent was not to be sniffed at.

'My son is very quiet,' Adele had gone on to reassure him. 'He won't be a nuisance.'

'If he is, you're out. Month's rent or no month's rent. I have my other residents to think of.'

His other residents consisted of a down-at-heel couple in their forties — pretending gentility — and an elderly woman who had been widowed five years earlier. Straitened circumstances had left Mrs Reynolds in the boarding house, eking out her savings and bitter to the bone.

'She has the room opposite yours and she won't take kindly to a baby keeping her awake,' Mr Finchley had continued, his greasy hair combed over the top of his balding head, his feet in tartan slippers. Not seedy, just getting by. 'And I don't want mess either. How are you going to cope with feeding the baby and cleaning up after it?'

'You said there was a cooking ring in the room,' Adele had replied. 'I can manage. I can make his food that way.' She had looked at the man, insistent and yet imploring. 'It will all work out fine, I promise. We'll be no trouble.'

Sighing, Adele leaned back on the bed, putting her arm around Paul, who was well wrapped up in a blanket. She had had enough money to pay for the month's rental of the room, plus another thirty pounds — taken from Col's wallet — and her engagement ring, which she would pawn if she had to, along with a pair of pearl earrings her parents-in-law had given to her. But that was all she had in the world . . . Her heart speeded up. It was OK, she told herself hurriedly, she would start work tomorrow. A gust of wind struck the window suddenly, and Adele imagined the depth and force of the sea outside. She had never been to Morecambe or any of the seaside towns in winter. Never seen them in the cold northern light, when the trippers had gone, the amusement arcades were closed and in every boarding house window was the sign VACANCIES.

The seaside was like another place off season. All the summer music and laughter had gone. All the outside tables, the rock stalls, the donkeys on the beach — all gone. Now only the cold waves skittered over the empty sands while the likes of Mrs Reynolds looked out over a future as bleak as the wind coming off the Irish Sea. Kissing the top of Paul's head, Adele tried to push away her anxiety. It might be hard at first, but they would survive. And most important of all, her baby was safe.

But although Paul slept that night, Adele did not. She heard every changing hour, the unfamiliar toilet cistern flushing in the night, the tired footsteps padding up to lonely rooms. She heard Mrs Reynolds coughing, and — as an eerie and unending backdrop — the cold call of the sea beyond.

★ ★ ★

'I don't believe it,' Turner said, pushing the letter aside. 'Dear God, Clemmie, it can't be true.'

'But if Adele told us — '

'She's not that type of woman!' Turner replied emphatically. 'I've known Adele since she was a kid, and she's not the type to cheat on her husband — or pass off another man's child as his. She was always so responsible. So interested in life.' He paused again. 'She'd changed, since last year. I could tell there was something wrong. She wasn't interested in the shop.'

'She was a new mother.'

'No,' Turner replied, 'it wasn't just that. I know she was married and had a baby, but the old Adele would never have given up so easily on her passion. And it *was* a passion, Clemmie. I remember her going to the pub auctions. Only a kid, all the confidence in the world. And then working for that venal Saul Hill — not many

379

people could have put up with him. But she did; even rode out that accusation and all the gossip.'

'What are you saying, Turner?'

'I'm saying that she was a sticker, a fighter. She wasn't someone who gave up on things. The old Adele would have kept up with the shop — she used to talk about having her own place, for God's sake! She was full of ambition — and she could have done pretty much anything she set her mind to. But she changed, she became quieter around Col. Especially this last year . . . I should have talked to her, Clemmie, asked her if she was all right.'

'She knew you were there for her, Turner.'

'I introduced her to Col,' he went on, preoccupied. 'I keep wondering if I should have done that.'

'It wasn't your fault,' Clemmie said firmly, getting to her feet and walking over to him. 'You're weren't responsible for Adele.'

He didn't seem to hear her. 'There was something wrong with that marriage . . . '

Always tactful, Clemmie chose her next words with care. 'Turner, sometimes people aren't how you imagine them.'

'Adele was not an adulteress!'

'You just don't want it to be true.'

'Do you?' Turner countered, turning to his wife. 'You were very fond of Adele; do you really think she would be capable of this?'

'I think,' Clemmie said quietly, 'that we never know what goes in other people's lives.'

Sighing, Turner slumped back in his seat. 'I saw Col this morning. He was badly shaken.

Walking around stupefied. Asked me if I'd heard from Adele — well, what could I say?' He turned to Clemmie.

'What *did* you say?'

'That I'd had a letter.'

She raised her eyebrows. 'How did he react to that?'

'He started blathering,' Turner replied, his tone wary. 'Said Adele was no good. That she'd fooled him. Cheated him, lied about Paul. He said that he had had nothing but trouble from her from the start. That she pretended to be one thing whilst in fact she was something else entirely.'

'Really?' Clemmie responded. 'Are you sure he was talking about Adele, and not himself?'

★ ★ ★

John Courtland looked at his wife, dumb-founded. Her expression incredulous, Julia read Adele's letter for the third time. Adele had left her husband, gone away with her child. No explanation at all. And yet — even if she had chosen not to confide in her sister — the gossips had supplied Julia with further information. *Apparently Adele had left her husband for another man . . .*

'She's not — '

Julia spun round on her husband. '*What?*'

'She's not coming back to live with us, is she?'

Poor John, Julia thought with pity; now that *would* be like old times.

'No, she's not coming back here,' she said

thoughtfully. 'You know, I heard something else this morning about this whole affair. Or rather I *overheard* it in the butcher's queue.'

'What?'

'That Paul isn't Col Vincent's child.'

Goodness, John thought to himself, Adele *had* been a dark horse. But then again, he had never taken her for a tart. Feisty, outspoken, opinionated, yes — but a scrubber? No, not Adele.

'What did you say?'

Julia shrugged. 'I said that Adele's private life wasn't anyone's business.'

'That was nice of you.'

'She stood up for me,' Julia replied, holding her husband's gaze, 'when you walked out. Adele and I might not be very close, but she's my sister and I reckon that if she left Col Vincent, her nice home and all that money, it was for a damn good reason.'

★ ★ ★

Deeply asleep, Frida Altman stirred on the daybed. She was dreaming of a dance she had attended many years before, while she still lived with her family in Vienna. She had been very young, very appealing, and that night she had danced nonstop. The belle of the ball — but one of *two* belles that night. The other beauty had been Ninette Gayor, long before she became Ninette Hoffman, long before she became the Lydgate Widow. They had both been in high spirits, lit up with all the fizzy excitement of

382

being very young and very much admired. Ninette, tall and dark, had been wearing a dress the colour of cognac, whilst Frida had worn silk the colour of new cream.

Sighing in her sleep, Frida's thoughts shifted, then suddenly moved on. Gone was the party; now there was war and a hurried leaving. A dark journey across water, after a snatched goodbye on the dockside, her family holding on to her desperately. And then the pull away, the hurry up the gangplank, the leaving behind of all the beauty and the dances and the lights, to go towards an unknown land, impoverished and alone.

Disturbed, Frida stirred again. Now she was married. Now widowed. Now living with Rebecca. Now sorting out her money and finding it had all but gone . . . In her sleep her fingers moved fretfully over the covers, trying to hold on to imaginary coins. She jumped suddenly, imagining the hated sound of the hooter coming from the Ash mill. Then she was watching her granddaughter walk off into the foggy morning: her beautiful girl, disappearing into the cold and the echo of the mill girls' clogs.

'Oomi . . . '

She jerked awake to find Becky bending over her. 'Are you all right?'

'I was having a dream,' Frida replied, looking round urgently and then remembering where she was. '*You're married.*'

'Yes,' Becky replied, laughing. 'I'm married.'

'Of course . . . ' Frida said, stupidly relieved, her mind clearing. 'Of course! You're Mrs

383

Rebecca Jacobs now.'

'Yes, Oomi,' Becky reassured her. 'That's right. Everything's fine.' She knew instinctively how to soothe her grandmother. 'All the bad times are over. No more worries, no more struggling. We've got a nice little house now. All paid for and cosy. Good food, a wage coming in regularly. A man to look out for us. A good man . . . We made it, Oomi, we escaped.'

'And you're happy?'

'Oh yes,' Becky said with feeling.

'And are you safe, Rebecca?'

'We're *all* safe. This is a new life, Oomi, a new life for all of us. There's nothing to be afraid of any more. You looked after me and now we're all together, looking after each other.'

Sighing, Frida relaxed back against the pillows. 'It's all good.'

'Yes,' Becky said gently. 'It's good. Everything's good now.'

At one thirty that morning Frida Altman died.

51

Looking after a baby in a rented room was harder than Adele had imagined. Aside from trying to make up his powdered feeds — and her own food — on one cooking ring, there was the problem of the nappies. She could scrub them in the bathroom, but drying them was another matter. Mrs Reynolds had soon complained about them being hung out in the bathroom, so Adele was then forced to dry them on the kettle in her room. Or the stone hot-water bottle. Both methods took hours, and Adele was terrified of putting a damp nappy on her baby.

And then there was the problem of Paul's colic. He had been good for the first few nights, but then became fretful, Adele spending most of the long hours walking him up and down to soothe him. Finally, he would sleep, Adele exhausted beside him. There was no nanny to help out, no Ernest to baby-sit; not even Col . . . Then Adele would remember *why* she had left and push the old days out of her mind. Paul was safe with her, and her child's safety was all that mattered.

It took Paul nearly a week to get over his bout of colic — and then Adele knew the time had come. She had to start to make a living. The first day she wrapped her son up warmly and tucked him in the pram, pulling up the hood to protect him from the cold. It wasn't raining, but there was a stiff breeze blowing as she left the boarding house on the seafront and headed towards the residential area of Morecambe.

Enthusiastically she talked to her son as they walked along, even though she knew he was too young to understand. She told him about Turner and how he had saved her from buying the old clock, and laughed when she remembered tipping over Samuel Ayres' stall.

'He was no good,' she told Paul, 'no good at all. We don't need men, do we? We can cope on our own.'

Heading into a middle-class area, Adele quickly checked her reflection in her handbag, winked at Paul, and then rang the bell of a well-kept house set slightly back from the road.

A moment later the door was opened by a middle-aged woman. 'Trade round the back.'

Adele hesitated, then tried to explain. 'I've come to see if you've anything you would like to sell. I can offer a good price — '

'We don't want hawkers!'

'I'm not a hawker, I deal in antiques.'

The woman looked her up and down, then glanced at the pram. 'What kind of dealer walks around with a child? You should be ashamed of yourself, dragging your baby about the streets.'

Flushing, Adele turned to go. But the brake on the pram jammed, and as she struggled, the woman continued to harangue her. '*Dealer!* You're one of about five we've had calling this week. Dealer! *Knocker*, more like!'

Humiliated, Adele struggled with the brake.

'I suppose you think you can get sympathy, do

386

you? Dragging a baby with you. Probably not even yours — '

'*How dare you!*' Adele snapped, flushing.

But the woman was in full flow. 'Oh, don't act the innocent! People are doing it all over the place, borrowing kids to make themselves better beggars.'

'I'm not a beggar!'

'Not yet,' the woman retorted. 'But you soon will be. Now clear off with you — and that child. And don't count on people's good feeling round here. I think you'll find sympathy's hard to come by. There's many an unemployed man working the streets now. If you take my advice, you'll go home to your husband — if he'll have you.'

'And if you take my advice,' Adele hurled back, 'you'll thank God you're not in my situation!'

The door slammed closed in her face.

Stunned, Adele walked back to the road. A passing van threw up water from a puddle which sprayed the pram wheels and her legs. Adele bent down to rub off the mud. It was just the first house, she told herself; other people would be different.

But they weren't. House after house closed their doors on her. No, they had nothing to sell. No, they didn't do business on the doorstep. Get away, some said. You should be ashamed of yourself, others told her. What kind of an existence was it for a baby to be trailed around?

By two thirty that afternoon Adele realised just how difficult her new life was going to be. She also realised that if she was going to survive

— and provide for her son — she was going to have to toughen up. The middle-class homes weren't the right stamping ground. In the Depression everyone was struggling; there was little money to be made in these roads, where people were holding on frantically to what they had. She was almost offensive in respectable Morecambe, a reminder of what the residents might be reduced to one day.

The answer was obvious — she would have to head for the poorer areas. The thought unsettled her. She was a woman on her own, with a baby in tow. Her competition was going to be the hard men who had worked the streets for years. The wide boys and the desperate family men who wouldn't want a woman on their patch, stealing trade. Adele paused, then made her decision. She hailed a tram and paid her fare to Blackpool. The seashore went past the window slowly as they left the Morecambe promenade, passing the affluent Midland Hotel. A place Adele had gone to once, with Col, for dinner. A smart dinner with the Clarks and the Butterworths, the well-to-do people she had socialised with because of her marriage to Col. Another memory followed, of the auction at the Midland she had attended with Turner, in the glossy times . . .

For forty minutes the tram moved slowly along the coast. At last the Blackpool Tower came into view, the sharp metal spike knifing the winter sky. Getting off at Sparrow Street, near the station, Adele hesitated. She was hungry and so was Paul. And he needed changing. Glancing round, she spotted a shabby — but clean

— corner café and went in.

A sullen waitress took her order for tea and a bun. Adele looked at her hopefully. 'Is there somewhere I can feed the baby?'

The waitress was unsympathetic. 'It's not a nursery.'

'Hey, yer!' an older woman said quickly, walking over. 'There's no need to be bloody rude!' She peered into the pram. 'Nice baby. What's his name?'

'Paul,' Adele replied, touched by the first kindness she had been shown that day. 'He's nearly one.'

'And good?'

'Not really,' Adele explained. 'He's had colic for the last five days, but he's settled down now.'

The woman was well into her fifties, very thin, her hair dyed red, her face powdered. Underneath her apron she was wearing a dark woollen dress and black stockings, darned at the heels.

'Having a hard time, luv?'

Adele felt the tears prick behind her eyes and didn't trust herself to speak.

'Oi, yer!' the woman called to the waitress. 'Get that tea over here, and a bun. And be sharp about it.' She turned back to Adele. 'My name's Florrie, Florrie Sullivan. I own this place.'

'Adele . . . ' She hesitated, then used her mother's maiden name, as she had done for the landlord. 'Adele Schofield.'

Florrie noticed the hesitation, but said nothing. She had had enough hard times of her own. 'You could change your baby and feed him in the back.'

'Oh, could I?' Adele said, relieved beyond measure. 'I would be so grateful.'

'Well, it's not much to speak of,' Florrie went on, 'but it's warm and clean. Yer go back there with yer baby — and don't worry, take yer time.'

Half an hour later Florrie was sitting with Adele in the back room of the café. The place was shabby, but warm, with a good fire in the grate. Apparently Florrie was in the mood to talk, and unwilling to let Adele go.

'He looks peaceful now,' she said, glancing at Paul. 'Where are yer living?'

'Boarding house in Morecambe.'

Florrie blew out her cheeks. 'How yer managing?'

'The nappies are the hardest. You can't dry them easily.'

Florrie nodded. 'I know, I've had kids of my own, and two I raised myself when my husband died. No fire in your room?'

'Only in the evenings,' Adele answered, getting to her feet. 'You've been very kind. But I have to go now.'

'Yer going knocking round 'ere?'

She nodded. 'Yeah. No luck in Morecambe.'

'Well that's no surprise,' Florrie responded. 'Yer might do all right here. But I'd steer clear of Hale Street and Dunstance Road, luv. Bit rough, if yer follow my drift.' She studied Adele carefully. 'D'yer know what yer've let yerself in fer?'

'I'm not sure,' Adele replied truthfully. 'But I have to make it work.'

'Tell yer what,' Florrie said suddenly, 'if yer

390

come here every day — except Sunday — to buy yer dinner, yer can feed the baby and change him in the back. In fact, yer can wash yer nappies and leave them to dry here, collect them the next day.'

'You don't want to be bothered with all that,' Adele replied incredulously.

'Course I do! I get money fer yer dinners — and yer get a helping hand.' Florrie smiled. 'Times are hard, luv. We do what we can to help each other. It's no skin off my nose to have a few nappies drying on the rack. I've me old dad upstairs, I'm looking after him now. What's a few more bit and pieces drying in amongst all the rest?'

'I can't thank you enough,' Adele replied, moved.

'Everyone needs a mum around sometimes. And as yer haven't got yers — I've guessed that much, luv — *I'll* have to do,' Florrie said phlegmatically. 'I know what's it like to be struggling. I couldn't live with myself if I didn't lend yer a hand.'

A few minutes later Florrie Sullivan watched Adele walk off, pushing the shiny pram down Sparrow Street. She looked full of hope, the baby dry and fed. My God, Florrie thought to herself. She had seen all sorts come and go over the years, but she felt really sorry for Adele Schofield. A decent young woman, trying to do her best. But had she any idea what it was going to cost her? Florrie thought of some of the men she knew who worked as knockers, and cringed.

'Yer mind yerself,' she whispered under her

breath, as Adele rounded the corner and disappeared out of view. 'And keep yer wits about yer.'

★ ★ ★

Collar turned up, Nicky Gosforth was leaning against a door jamb on Gordon Street, chatting up a blowsy woman of about forty. Putting his dimp behind his ear, he smiled leerily, winking at her. Good God, Nicky thought, what a bloke would do to make a living.

'Yer said to come back to see yer.'

'Did I now?' the woman simpered. 'And why would that be?'

'I'm a knocker . . . '

She tittered.

' . . . and I've a mind to ask you if you've got anything yer'd like knocked up.'

'Oh, Mr Gosforth,' the woman teased, 'yer cheeky devil!' Disappearing into the back of her terraced house, she returned a moment later with a pair of fire irons.

'Well now,' Nicky said, weighing them in his hands. 'Nothing too special about them, is there?'

'I've a bracelet too,' the woman replied, pulling a cheap bangle out of her apron pocket. 'It's Austrian.'

Austrian, my arse, Nicky thought. 'Tell yer what — 'cos I like yer, I'll give yer three shillings fer both.'

'Never!' she replied. 'I can get more down the market.'

'Yer could have done a while back, but not these days,' Nicky said, his tone regretful. 'How long have yer and I been dealing? Yer know I wouldn't gyp yer. Times have changed . . . Four bob's highest I can go.'

She hesitated, tempted. 'I've had that bracelet since I was a kiddie . . . '

So that made it a hundred years old right away, Nicky thought drily.

'All right, luv, 'cos it's yer,' she said. 'But I wouldn't let it go that low fer anyone else.'

★ ★ ★

On the street running parallel, Bellows Street, Adele was just knocking on the door of a terraced house. A net curtain twitched, then finally a woman answered.

'Yeah?'

'I was wondering if you had anything to sell. Bric-a-brac, jewellery . . . '

'Do I look like I've got bloody jewellery?'

'China, ornaments.'

The woman blinked, wrapping her cardigan tightly around her. 'What we had went long enough since.' She jerked her head down to the pub on the corner. 'Try Lily Armstrong, she's always got something.'

Before Adele could thank the woman, the door was closed in her face. Taking in a deep breath, she walked towards the pub, hesitating outside. Nothing was going to make her leave Paul on the street, and yet she knew for certain she couldn't take a pram into a public house. So she wrapped the baby up in his blanket, then walked in and made for the bar.

A wary-looking man eyed her up at once. 'What d'yer want?'

'I wondered if you had anything to sell?'

'LILY!' he shouted. 'LILY!' Almost immediately a corseted woman wearing a bad wig came running into the bar.

'What now? I was just putting my feet up.'

'This woman wants to know if yer've got anything to sell.'

Wearily Lily Armstrong glanced over to Adele. She studied the good-looking face, and the baby in her arms. God, not another hard-luck story.

'I've nothing today, luv.'

'Are you sure?' Adele pressed her. 'I mean, I'm willing to look at anything. Anything at all.'

'I bet yer are, luv, but I've nowt today. Try me next week, yer might be lucky then.' She paused. 'Mind yer, this patch is well covered; yer won't get too many rich pickings that haven't been spoken fer already.'

'No one minds my asking, surely?' Adele replied.

Pausing, Lily looked her up and down. Respectable, good clothes, nice blanket wrapped round the baby, and a wedding band that didn't look like it would turn your finger green. This girl wasn't slum material.

'Yer new to this, aren't yer?'

'Yes. But I know my stuff. I can give good prices, I know what a thing's worth.'

'I daresay yer do, luv,' Lily replied, 'but nothing's worth nothing. And nothing is what I've got.'

Resigned, Adele walked out, then stopped dead on the pub doorstep. *The pram had gone* . . . Stunned, she looked round, but it was nowhere to be seen. Someone had taken her child's pram. Whilst she had been inside the pub, trying to get business, some opportunist had done his own business. Overcome, she stared up and down the street, almost willing the pram to reappear. Stealing a child's pram, what kind of person would do that? she thought miserably, then gripped her son tightly and began to walk. Paul *needed* that pram, he slept in it at night. And *she* needed it; needed it to carry anything heavy she bought. Bloody hell, Adele cursed, it was her own fault. She should have known better. Didn't it just go to show how hopeless she was? How ill equipped to cope? Maybe Col had been right; maybe she *was* cowed, useless. Maybe she had been ungrateful, selfish. Maybe she should have stayed at Oakham Lodge, at least made sure that Paul had a proper home. And a flaming pram.

Walking quickly, Adele could feel her self-pity begin to lift. Who was she kidding? Col wasn't fit to be a husband or a father. She had done the right thing — and she would stand by it. So someone had stolen Paul's pram — she would have to buy another one. Not a Marmet, she couldn't afford that, but it had been too clumsy anyway. A smaller pram would be cheaper and easier for her to manage. Easier to get on and off the trams, to push around. Adele could feel the salt air drying the threat of tears. She would pawn the earrings, that would raise enough for a pram. You'll manage, she told herself. Remember how you were before, when you were only a kid . . . Memories strengthened her. The times she had stood in for Mrs Hodges at Tommyfields. The sales at the covered markets, and the pub auctions. Had she got so soft that she couldn't look after herself any more?

Oh no, Adele told herself, forcing her confidence to rise with every step. She could do this. She was more than capable. She would knock on every door, in every street, until someone sold her something — and then she would sell it on for a profit. Go back to the market stalls, to the people she had known when she had been that feisty kid, longing to be like her father.

'Don't you worry,' she told her son, kissing his forehead. 'Let them take the bloody pram; we'll get another. No one can stop us, Paul. Nothing and no one.'

52

Desperate, Dave Lin had walked around Failsworth without success. Then he had moved on to Rochdale, searching everywhere for Adele.

'No one knows where she is,' Kitty said, sighing. 'Honestly, Dave, you could spend the rest of your life looking.'

'I could ask yer father.'

'In jail?' Kitty said dismissively. 'Pa's no idea what's going on at the moment. Won't for a while — about three years.' She glanced over to the huge Chinaman. 'Yer'll lose yer job if yer keep taking time off. Mr Gades won't have it. He needs yer around.'

'He can get someone else . . . I like Mr Gades, but I can't hang around here, not when Mrs Vincent's gone.'

'Maybe she doesn't want to be found,' Kitty suggested. 'She did run off, after all.'

'I never liked her husband. Not the way he talked to her, looked at her sometimes.'

Kitty shrugged. 'Yer in love with her, Dave.'

'I know! I know!' he snapped, uncharacteristically rattled. 'And I know it's stupid, but I can't stop how I feel.'

Dear God, Kitty thought, he had got it bad. Hadn't he heard the story — that Adele had run off with another man, the real father of her baby? Hadn't he heard the vitriol, the gossip, the slaughter of Adele's good name? And did it make a damn bit of difference? No, of course not. After all, Kitty had heard the version Adele had left behind, but she hadn't believed it for an instant. Having grown up as part of the notorious Gallager family, she knew the whores in Hanky Park, the women who would sleep around and palm off a kid on any sucker. But not Adele. She was respectable. She had left for another reason entirely.

Which might have something to do with the bruises Kitty had seen on her arms and legs. The bruises she had explained away as a fall in the stock room. Or a tumble down the stairs. *Those* sorts of bruises.

'Where d'yer think she is?' Dave asked again.

Kitty shrugged. 'I dunno. But I know one thing. Times are hard. If a woman's got the guts to leave, she's got the guts to survive.'

★ ★ ★

Taking a deep breath, Adele pushed the second-hand pram along the Blackpool streets. Paul was asleep again, thank God, after another long night. A night which had ended with Mrs Reynolds moaning and banging on her door, and Mr Finchley telling Adele that she would have to go. He wasn't running a bloody nursery, he said angrily.

'And I'm sick of the crying too,' he added, although Adele had heard her landlord's snoring every night and knew Paul hadn't disturbed his sleep. 'I can't have you here. Sorry an' all, but that's final.'

'I paid for a month!'

'I'll give yer back the last week's money,' Mr Finchley replied.

'But I've nowhere to go!' Adele pleaded. 'Just give me time to get a new place.'

'Yer've had time. And two warnings. Sorry, get yerself out today. I want yer gone.'

Incredulous, she stared at him. 'It's November, it's freezing. You can't throw us out . . .'

'I can, and I will. There are other places yer can stay,' he replied emphatically. 'People are glad of rental in the winter.'

'You were glad of it.'

'I were,' he agreed. 'But I'm not going to lose the only long-term guests I've got just to let yer stay here another week. Sorry, but yer out.'

Sorry, but you're out . . . Packing her case, Adele left minutes later, Mrs Reynolds' acid face watching her go. Catching the tram to Blackpool, her first stop was Florrie Sullivan's. Surprised to see Adele so early in the day, Florrie was outraged to hear what had happened.

'Well, the mean sod,' she said flatly.

'Yeah,' Adele agreed. 'I was thinking of renting a place in Blackpool. I'm working around here after all.'

'If I didn't have my father with me, luv, I'd let yer stay here.'

'You do enough for me already,' Adele said hurriedly. 'I'll find somewhere. It'll probably be better in the long run.' She paused. Long nights and worry had taken pounds off her, but the look in her eyes was steady, determined. 'I just want to find somewhere to stay put for a while.

For a few months. Until I get on my feet properly.'
She looked at Paul, stroking his forehead. 'And I
need somewhere clean and warm for him.'

'You could try Lily Armstrong at the Piper's
Arms.'

Adele grimaced. 'I went there the first day I
started knocking. She didn't have anything for
me to buy.'

'No, but she might have a room to rent.'

'In a pub?'

Florrie shrugged. 'It would be warm, safe as
houses. Noisy, I grant yer, but then Paul's been
making enough noise of his own. And I happen
to know,' she went on, her tone confiding, 'that
Lily's missing her daughter.'

'So?'

'She wants some company. And I daresay a
nice young woman like yer would give a little
tone to the place.' She watched Adele's face and
then tapped the back of her hand. 'I don't ask
and I don't want to know. Yer business is yer
own, Adele, and I guess that living over a
pub's not what yer used to. But yer could do
worse. It'll be safe there. Rough, yes. But safe
for a woman on her own with a baby to fend
for.'

★ ★ ★

Like Nicky Cosforth, Lennie Bolton was working
the streets, but there the similarity ended. Lennie
was no charmer. He had worked as a factory
hand for many years, until he had been laid off,
with a wife and four kids to feed. His tongue ran

400

over his bottom lip thoughtfully. All he had to do was keep his head above water. And he wasn't going to do that with this new girl around. He glanced down the street, to the corner. Lennie had never been a villain in the way of Pa Gallager. Never been violent. But he was desperate — and desperate men did things that were out of character. Fixedly he watched the street, waiting for Adele. Of course, a pretty young woman with a baby in tow could pull at the heartstrings a lot quicker than a solitary man could dream of doing. And hadn't she worked at it? he thought bitterly. At first he had thought — like the other knockers — that Adele would get short shrift. And at first he had been right. But after a few more persistent weeks she had managed to buy a dressing table set, a pair of scales and a landscape drawing. All of which she had sold on at the Blackpool market for a profit. Not much, but a profit that Lennie had decided was money taken out of *his* pocket.

She was, he told himself, stealing from him. His family was going short — and all because of this bitch — He kept his dark eyes fixed on the corner, knowing she would come round it at any time. Only a year earlier Lennie wouldn't have recognised himself as this furtive figure, shifting his feet, suspicious and street cunning. Only a year earlier he had had a job and some decent furniture. First the job had gone, then the furniture. He had tried to get work, Christ knows. Like all the other men, he had stood outside the factory gates waiting to be hired. But it was never him. And he wasn't qualified for skilled work. Soon there were only two options left — knocking, or thieving.

Morality wasn't the only reason Lennie had chosen the former. If he was caught stealing he would be jailed, and then where would his family end up? So he had begun working the streets. And when he didn't make enough to buy fags, he picked up the cigarette butts that had been discarded, half smoked. The rest of the time he grubbed around, trying to charm people, trying to make a profit from the slurry of old possessions he had bought. And he had just — *just* — managed to keep himself and his family afloat.

Until some fucking woman with a kid in tow had come along . . . Taking a deep breath, Lennie watched a figure come round the corner, but it wasn't her . . . He was just going to warn her off, Lennie told himself. Just going to put the frighteners on her. Get her to clear off, go home to her bloody husband. Because there had to be one somewhere. And if there wasn't a husband, she was good looking and could find a man soon enough. It would be easier than working the streets as a knocker.

Tensing, Lennie finally saw Adele come round the corner and under the streetlamp. It was only five in the evening, but already dark. Just as he wanted it to be. Dark enough to catch her off guard and give him some cover. He was sorry she had the kid with her, but what could you do? It was her or him.

'Hey, yer!'

Adele stopped, turning and looking into the

darkness. Her tone was cautious. 'Hello? Who's there?'

'I'm warning yer, keep off my patch.'

'Who's there?' she repeated, her voice still calm. 'Who is it?'

'This is a warning,' Lennie said, coming up behind her, looping his arm around her neck and pulling her head back. He could feel her body freeze with terror. 'Keep away from here. Yer got that? *Yer keep away from here.*'

Sure that he had frightened her, Lennie finally let go and ran back into the shadows.

Turning, Adele caught only a brief sight of him before the darkness swallowed him up — then she started shaking, her hands trembling so much she had to grip the pram rail for support, her legs barely able to move. Then slowly, step by step, she began to walk, pausing to look around repeatedly. Finally she reached the Piper's Arms, the sound of welcome music coming out into the street as she made for the back stairs. Step by step she climbed, with Paul in her arms, pulling the old pram up behind her. At last she made it to their room, hurriedly locking the door behind her.

From below came the noise of the old piano, the yard dogs barking and the raucous laughter of Lily Armstrong. Never had anything sounded more comforting, Adele thought, her breathing finally beginning to slow down. Sitting on the edge of the bed, she laid Paul on the coverlet beside her. He was sleepy, hardly moving. Slowly she traced the outline of his cheek with one shaking hand, her attacker's words repeating themselves over and over again in her head: *Yer keep away from here . . .*

She felt leaden; the eviction, the attack welling up and overwhelming her exhausted senses. She had been working as a knocker for over two months now, rapping on doors in all weathers, being told to bugger off, having door after door slammed in her face. But sometimes — now and again — a woman had asked to look at Paul, or offered to make Adele a drink. Once she had even been invited into an elderly lady's house and given a sandwich. And an old-fashioned coat — because the woman thought she was poor. Or a beggar. God only knew which . . . Sighing, Adele hung her head. Her perseverance on the streets *had* paid off. She had bought some china, a few books, a very good engraving and other sundry items, selling them on at the markets. But the profit she had made went on rent and food, with nothing left over.

Necessity forced her out day after day, walking the streets with her son in his pram. After she had worked the Blackpool streets for a while, she had been forced further afield, into the affluent Lytham St Annes. But she had had no luck there. One week her takings were so low she had ended up working part time as a barker at the Blackpool market. It had been demeaning work, but the pay wasn't bad — the only problem was that it was temporary. So it was back to the streets. By the middle of November she had walked so far that her feet were blistered, and the engagement ring had been pawned. But she hadn't given up. Hadn't even considered it. Her faith in herself was relentless. She was going to make this work, she was going to be successful. Like the Lydgate Widow she would — one day — have a big stone house with a wall around it. To keep the people she loved in, and the rest of the world out . . .

From below the piano pounded on, dud notes sounding, the laughter rising. And Lily's dogs barking in the back yard. It was a hell of a place to end up, Adele thought, unexpectedly depressed. She might dream of the Lydgate Widow and her house, but reality was *this*. This room over a pub. This was her home. Her son's home . . . Jesus, Adele thought, shivering, what had she done? *What had she done?* She might be getting by — but at what cost? The work had always been hard, but now she knew *how* hard. It was one thing to be worn out, another to be threatened and afraid. And when she was threatened, so was her son.

'Adele?'

Jolted by the sound of her name, Adele opened the door an inch. Lily was looking in anxiously at her. 'What's up?'

'Someone came at me from behind, tried to warn me off,' Adele replied, trying to keep her voice even.

'Yer look bloody,' Lily said, walking in and handing Adele a tot of brandy. 'I saw yer — face white as a week-old corpse. Who were it gave yer the gypsy's warning?'

'Some man,' Adele said, drinking the brandy gratefully. 'I didn't see him clearly.'

'I told yer, don't go out when it's dark.'

'I've got to make some more money!' Adele replied shortly, her tension showing. 'I have to do more.'

'I reckon yer'd do better on yer own. Why don't yer leave yer little lad here? I can keep an eye on him.'

'No!' Adele snapped. 'I can't leave Paul.'

Lily threw up her hands. 'OK, OK, that were just *one* suggestion.' She smoothed down her wigged hair. 'The other is Capone. One of the dogs. Take him around with yer and the little lad. No bugger will come close then. He's an Alsatian.'

'But wouldn't he put people off? I mean, customers?'

'Yer sit him by the pram, tell him STAY, and he won't move an inch until yer do,' Lily replied sitting down, her stays creaking. 'Yer never know, he might convince a few people to give yer something — just to get him off their bloody doorstep!' She patted the bed beside her and Adele sat down. So close, she could smell camphor balls and cheap rose perfume off the market. It was oddly comforting. 'Yer know, luv, knocking's a hard trade, and yer can do one of two things — give up, or get some protection. Capone's the best dog in the neighbourhood, there's no one will mess with him. Or touch that baby of yers when he's around.'

Adele smiled gratefully. 'Thanks.'

'No trouble,' Lily said, relieved. 'Just don't pet him, yer hear me? Capone's never been petted and I don't want that changing. He's a guard and that's what he's been trained to be. I'll feed him, like always; don't give him any treats or anything, got it?'

'Got it.'

'So yer going to go out there and give it another crack?'

Adele nodded. 'Christmas is coming. I want to pay my bills and have a bit over to spend on Paul. I mean, he's only a baby and he won't even know . . . '

'Oh, they know, luv, believe me, they know.' Lily paused, moving her position, her corset squeaking momentarily. 'Yer've no family to go home to?'

Adele shook her head.

'Good thing yer ended up in a pub then. Always people in pubs on the holidays.' She studied her tenant for a long moment. 'Yer know, when I were young I had lovely hair like yers. I mean,' she touched her wig, 'mine's not what it used to be.'

Adele picked up the hint. 'Your hair looks lovely.'

Flushing, Lily smiled. 'Well, thank you, luv. People always said it was my best feature. But to be honest,' she dropped her voice, 'this is a wig.'

'*No!*'

Lily nodded. 'Yes, it is. I spent the best part of a week's takings on this, God knows how many years ago. But it pays to keep yerself looking nice. *Yer* must do that, luv. Even if yer had man trouble before, keep yerself pretty fer the right one. They aren't all buggers.'

'I'm not interested in men,' Adele said firmly.

Wow, Lily thought, that had struck a nerve.

'Well, luv, whatever. Yer just look after yerself and yer kid — and the rest will come when the time's right.'

53

Combing his hair, Col studied his reflection in the mirror and then looked away impatiently. He was tired of all the problems, the bloody questions. Adele had been gone for a couple of months now, and yet people were *still* prying. He smouldered with fury. She had left him! And taken his son. His trump card . . . It never occurred to Col to take responsibility for his wife's departure. In his eyes, Adele was a poor wife and mother, and he was better off without her. It soothed his conscience to make her into the villain. Made it easier for him to lie to everyone — particularly Turner, who was still astonished by Adele's departure.

After a number of repetitions, Col found that he could pass on Adele's lie without pause. After a little while longer he actually believed it. Wasn't it so much easier to let people think he had been duped, the boy Paul another man's bastard? He had been very fond of the child, but to be honest he had tired of marriage, fatherhood *and* Adele. She had failed. She should have been his rescuer, but she hadn't been up to the task. Instead of keeping him interested and steady, she had let him browbeat her — and then turned into a typical mother. Putting their son first. Always Paul at number one, always Paul at the forefront. Not Col any more. Her husband . . . For one instant the truth filtered through Col's webbing of self-deception. *He had been a poor husband, he had hit his wife and driven her away . . .* As always, he shrugged off the thought. *She* had changed, not him. If Adele had stayed the way she had been when they first married, they would still be together.

Still thinking of his absent wife, Col walked down the stairs to find Turner talking to Ernest in the hallway.

'Turner,' he said simply. 'Good to see you.'

'And you,' Turner replied. 'I just popped by to say I had a piece of Worcester you might be interested in. A good compote.'

Col's expression was distant, and Turner noticed it at once. 'Is everything all right?'

'Apart from my wife having left me for another man, you mean?'

Ernest shot a startled look at his son. 'Col, what — '

'I don't see why we should pussyfoot around,' Col went on, propelled by his own bitterness. 'Adele let us all down badly.'

Embarrassed, Turner coughed, then tried to change the subject. 'Clemmie was saying — '

'You can't trust women!' Col went on, growing hotter by the instant, his erratic mood nose-diving. 'There's not one of them you can trust.'

'I'll call back later . . . '

'It was all your fault anyway!' Col snapped. Turner looked taken aback. 'You introduced me to Adele. You said she was so talented, so amusing, so spirited . . . '

'But *you* fell in love with her,' Turner replied,

his tone unreadable. 'I only wanted the best for both of you.'

'*The best!*' Col hissed, laughing mirthlessly. 'How noble of you, Turner.'

Unnerved, Ernest stepped between the two men. 'Col, where are your manners? Turner is a guest in our house.'

'Like Adele was?' he parried, turning from his father back to his friend. 'Makes me wonder, Turner. You were always so fond of my wife — perhaps you had more than antiques in common?'

Snatching up his coat, Turner moved to the door and then turned back.

'How dare you even imply something so despicable! I'm leaving now, Col. And from this moment on, you and I are no longer friends.'

'Turner,' Ernest said imploringly, 'Col didn't mean it. My son has been under a lot of pressure lately.'

'Everyone knows that. Everyone has made allowances,' Turner replied, unimpressed. 'But I've seen something in his behaviour tonight I'd never have believed possible. And frankly, it makes me wonder about the *real* reason Adele left.'

'She was cheating on me!'

'Why?' Turner asked coldly.

'She was a whore! She passed that bastard off as my son.'

'I don't believe it.'

'*You didn't know her!*' Col snapped, spittle appearing at the sides of his mouth, his anger out of control. 'You think you knew her — but you didn't. You landed me with Adele when she wasn't worth even a second glance. She was just a nobody. It was you, *you*, that fobbed a scrubber off on me — '

'Col!' Ernest said, enraged. '*Stop it!*'

As if suddenly coming back to reality, Col turned away, wiping his mouth with his handkerchief. He would have to get away, he realised, away from bloody Rochdale, away from people and questions — and the look in Turner Gades' eyes.

'What the hell are you staring at?'

'At someone I used to like,' Turner replied coldly, 'and now loathe.'

* * *

Although she hadn't seen Adele in over three years, Mrs Hodges spotted her the moment she entered the covered market in Blackpool. She was still good looking, but worn down, pale skinned, not the cheeky kid she had been once. My God, Mrs Hodges thought, whatever Adele had done, she looked like she had more than paid for it . . . Smiling, the older woman waved, her arm raised high above the shoppers' heads.

Surprised, Adele saw her, and hesitated. Perhaps she should ignore her and move on? But that would only make the woman gossip more. So instead Adele walked over to her.

'Hello there,' she said tentatively. 'You're a long way from Oldham.'

'I am that,' Mrs Hodges replied. 'And I've been hearing more than a bit about yer, luv.'

'I dare say.'

'Such gossip . . . '

'I never expected to see you in Blackpool,' Adele said anxiously.

Mrs Hodges was no slouch. 'Enough said. I haven't seen yer, all right?'

'Thanks.' Relieved, Adele dropped the hood of the pram. 'This is my son, Paul.'

'Fine boy,' Mrs Hodges replied, questions burning her tongue. 'So, yer buying or selling here? I heard yer were out knocking. I heard plenty who said it weren't respectable too.'

'And some who said that *I* wasn't?'

'Oh aye, more than one said that.'

Reaching under the pram, Adele took a parcel off the carrying tray. Serious, she handed it over to Mrs Hodges. 'You buying?'

'Always on the lookout, yer know me.'

Adele nodded to the parcel. 'It's Wedgwood.'

'Yer never!'

She watched as the older woman studied the piece avidly, her head cocked over to one side, her eyes piercing.

'I heard yer left yer husband fer another man . . . ' Mrs Hodges glanced up and then looked around her like a pantomime dame. 'Can't see no knight in shining armour . . . '

'How much will you give me?'

'Yer two split up as well, did yer?'

'How much for the piece?' Adele persisted.

'Mind you, a real man wouldn't want yer out and about earning a living like this, now would he?'

'It's not marked or scratched. You won't find a

better trinket box in the north-west.'

'Giving up on Col Vincent. My, that other man must have something going fer him.' Mrs Hodges glanced up at Adele, then realised she wasn't going to get anything out of her. Smiling, she nodded. 'OK, I'll give yer ten bob.'

'Two pounds.'

'Get away with yer!'

'It's worth it,' Adele replied. 'You know it is.'

'One pound and ten shilling.'

'One pound fifteen,' Adele pushed her. 'You know you can sell it on. Come on, buy it — or I go over to Solly Geldman.'

'All right, all right! Yer always were a pushy little sod,' Mrs Hodges replied, fishing into her pocket for the money. 'I don't mind yer robbing me. Seeing as how it's Christmas.'

Smiling, Adele put the money into an inside pocket of her coat, a trick she had learned watching the other knockers. Suddenly she had the feeling that she was being watched, and quickly turned round. But no one was looking at her, everyone preoccupied, going about their own business.

'Yer jumpy.'

'Yeah,' Adele agreed. 'It's a hard business.'

'Getting harder too,' Mrs Hodges went on. 'Yer husband's gone off, yer know.'

Shaken, Adele flinched. '*What?*'

'Col Vincent's gone abroad. He and his father had a right falling-out and he buggered off.'

'He left the business?' Adele said incredulously. 'And Oakham Lodge?'

Mrs Hodges nodded. 'Yep, upped and gone.

414

Been gone over a week now. And rumour has it he won't be coming back.'

Adele laughed bitterly. '*Rumour!* How reliable is that?'

'I know for a fact he's away now,' Mrs Hodges went on. 'How long he's away, who knows?' She kissed Adele's cheek, smiling. 'Happy Christmas, luv. To yer *and* yer kid. I hope things get better. And if anyone asks — no, I haven't seen yer. I haven't set eyes on yer fer years.'

★　★　★

It *was* her! Delighted, Dave Lin ducked back into the market, behind a stall full of old military uniforms. He had found Adele at last, after all this time. And she was looking so tired . . . He paused, stepping back again, the top of his head striking an old German helmet.

'Aye! Yer break anything, and yer pay fer it!' the stall-holder said sharply. Then he looked Dave up and down slowly, amazed by the huge Chinaman with the long black hair. 'Bleeding 'ell, what are yer?'

'Sorry about the helmet,' Dave replied. 'I haven't broken it.'

'Yer Japanese?'

'Nah, I'm Chinese.'

'They don't make Chinese yer size!'

'They don't make Japanese my size either.'

'So how did yer *get* that size?' the man asked, transfixed.

'Luck,' Dave replied, looking back to Adele.

She was turning over some lace with one

hand, the other hand firmly gripping the pram handle. Beside her the dog stood patiently, the other market shoppers giving the Alsatian a wide berth.

'Is it exercise?'

'Yer what?' Dave asked, turning back to the stall-holder.

'Yer size — did yer get that way with exercise? 'Cos I have to tell yer, there's a bloody Chinaman down our way and yer'd make ten of 'im.'

Seeing Adele move off, Dave followed, keeping his distance. Even in the hard days of the Depression — as the papers were relentlessly calling it — there were people around, looking for a bargain, or trying to sell. Christmas was coming fast and everyone wanted to pretend life was still good. If only for one day of the year.

It wasn't just the poor either. Ernest Vincent was trying to make something of the holidays too . . . Dave thought of his part-time employer and the way he had talked about Adele and his grandson. And about Col Vincent too. Col had apparently left the country for a while. On business, Ernest said, but Dave hadn't been convinced. One thing *was* certain, however — Ernest Vincent wanted to find Adele. Maybe now that Col was out of the way, he thought there could be a reconciliation with his daughter-in-law.

Dave liked Ernest Vincent. And he would like to get Adele back to Oakham Lodge, back to her old home, where she and Paul would be safe.

And when she was back, she could return to the shop, couldn't she? Where Dave could look out for her — just like old times.

★ ★ ★

Everyone had always expected that it would be Daphne who would die first. But they were wrong. It wasn't the sickly sister, but the sturdy, unemotional Mary. Whilst looking after Daphne, she had had a stroke. No previous history had intimated any problem. She died as she had lived, aloof. When the news reached Ernest he refused to believe it. Told them they were mistaken; it was Daphne, always Daphne, who had been the invalid.

After the first shock of grief, he was angry. How could his wife go off and die like that? How could she keep an illness to herself? How could she slip away from him without his even knowing she was planning an escape? Mary, remote, self-contained Mary, the woman he had presumed would be around for decades. The woman he had never really known. Had he loved her? Yes, as much as she would allow him to . . . Ernest winced. He had never been sure if that had been enough, but it was all that had come his way and he had never been a man on the hunt for sexual adventures. Had never had the confidence to seek out a mistress. He had taken on the role of the kind man instead. The benign, fatherly figure everyone trusted.

When he had first heard that his wife was dead, Ernest had walked the floor. Paced endlessly, marking out an emotional marathon with no finishing post. He felt turned inside out by her death, emptied like a pocket, limp like a pulled weed. Then the lack of love in his life — *in all his life* — suddenly became obvious, and painful. It barked at him constantly, like a fretful dog.

And he was bearing it all alone. He had told Col about his mother's death, of course, but after the funeral Col had returned to Italy. Although he could never say it to anyone, Ernest was relieved. He was exhausted by his son's moods and bullying. Glad to be rid of the canker in the house. But lonely, terribly lonely. Only a few months earlier, Oakham Lodge had been full. But now it was suddenly empty of people — and of promise.

Which was why Ernest Vincent found himself calling for Dave Lin. Turner had told him about the Chinaman's obsession with Adele, and Ernest was more than willing to put that devotion to some proper use. He had been abandoned, but it was only going to be temporary. The solution was within his grasp.

It was time for Ernest Vincent to recover what he had lost.

★ ★ ★

'Mrs Vincent?'

Adele whipped round as though she had been stung. Then, seeing Dave, she shook her head in amazement. '*Dave?*'

'I've been looking fer yer. Yer father-in-law, Mr

Vincent, asked me to find yer.' He was watching her face, the way her eyes widened. 'He wants to see yer and the baby.'

Automatically Adele glanced at Paul and then looked back to Dave. 'I won't go back.'

'Mr Col's gone abroad.'

'So it's true then?' Adele said, leaning back against a nearby stall. 'I heard that he had gone away, but I didn't believe it.'

'It's true all right,' Dave went on, 'and his father's desperate to see yer. To help.'

Adele looked at her son. Paul was flushed, probably too hot, but she was always keen to keep him warm. And she couldn't be too careful. After all, the baby went everywhere with her. In cold winds, rain, whatever the weather, she, Paul and the dog worked the streets. Over the past months she had organised some places where they could stop and shelter. The Blackpool library was always warm and let her stay for a while, pretending to read books. They had a decent lavatory too, where she could change Paul. Of course she continued to have her dinners with Florrie Sullivan, and Lily pressed leftovers from the pub on to her — but the sudden memory of Oakham Lodge tugged at Adele like a longing.

At first fretful, Paul had gradually become a very docile baby. It was as though he knew he had to be good. That after getting them evicted in Morecambe he had to make amends. His goodness somehow made it harder for Adele. Paul would lie next to her at night, looking into his mother's face, and she would tell him all about the past. About her father . . . Lately she had found herself thinking about Victor often; forgetting about the dark side of her parents' marriage and remembering his caring nature. He hadn't *really* been like Col. Oh yes, they had both been violent men, but Col had relished his temperament, while her father had tried to fight his. And Adele admired that.

'Mrs Vincent?'

Adele's thoughts snapped back to the present. 'Don't call me that, Dave.'

'Sorry . . . ' He hesitated, noticing her discomfort, her hands roughened by the weather, her coat too thin for the winter cold. Obviously every penny Adele had made had gone on looking after her son. 'Mr Ernest wants to see yer, he wants to help. If yer don't mind me saying, yer look like yer could do with it.'

'I can cope.'

'Sure,' Dave agreed. 'But it's nearly Christmas. Yer'd have a nice place to stay and somewhere for the lad. And Mr Ernest would look after yer.'

Adele could feel the tears pricking behind her eyes. Her exhaustion caught her unawares. The chance of a respite, even temporary, was irresistible. She would be able to rest up at Oakham Lodge, get some sleep, let someone help to take care of Paul for a while. And if Mary was there, she would love to see her grandson . . . It wasn't a long-term solution — Adele didn't trust Col to stay away indefinitely — and she wasn't going to give up her hard-earned freedom. But she trusted Ernest. He had never shown her anything but kindness. How like him to come looking for her when Col had gone. How like him to forgive and extend his hand to her. And how fortuitous that he had found her now, just before Christmas. Because Adele had been dreading the holidays. Had been dreading trying to make a decent Christmas for her son, with so little to offer him. And now here was a chance to make it a wonderful time for him. No point thinking about afterwards. About the year which would follow. No point worrying about what was to come. They could just enjoy a few days of comfort, off the streets, safe — without Adele constantly looking over her shoulder.

They were going to have Christmas at Oakham Lodge. Paul would be reunited with his grandparents. There would be a tree and decorations and presents. Lots of presents for her son. New objects to replace the worn-out toy lamb he had clung on to for months.

Tearfully Adele picked up her child, and whispered in his ear: 'We're going home, baby. We're going home.'

54

A fine misting of ice had settled on the front pathway up to Oakham Lodge, and the late afternoon sky was bloated with snow. In the bay window there was a large decorated Christmas tree, and a wreath of holly was fastened to the front door. Pushing the pram towards the house, Adele could feel her spirits rise. When she rang the bell, she could hear the sound echoing throughout the house and tensed. Relax, she told herself, Col isn't here. You're safe . . . A moment later she could hear the bolt being drawn back, and Ernest was holding his arms out in greeting. Without hesitation she went to him, hugging him — then stepping back and gesturing to her son.

'My God,' Ernest said, picking Paul out of the pram. 'He's grown so much. He looks well, Adele. But it must have been hard for you managing on your own.'

'I was so sorry I had to run off like that, Ernest.'

'That was the past!' he said simply, walking into the house. Adele fell into step with him as they moved into the drawing room.

Everything was so familiar to her, so achingly well known. She could see the same paintings, photographs, the same fire burning in the grate. On a side table by the window was the same lamp, a half-drunk glass of whisky beside it.

Typically Ernest. Col had never liked whisky
. . . Adele watched Ernest playing with his
grandson, Paul laughing. *He knows he's home,*
she thought happily. *My God, he's only a baby
but he remembers . . .*

'Are you hungry?'

She nodded. 'A bit . . . Ernest, we should talk
about the way I left.'

He brushed it aside. 'You don't have to explain
anything.'

'But — '

'No, I don't want to hear it,' he said, his
beatific face turned to her. 'I don't judge you, or
my son. I don't judge anyone. Life is too
precious. I have you and my grandson home.
That's all I've been dreaming of. All I've
wanted . . . ' He trailed off, his voice falling. 'Did
you hear about Mary?'

She tensed. 'What about her?'

'Mary died a month ago . . . '

Shaken, Adele stared at him. *Mary dead . . .* It
was unbelievable. She had dreamed of bringing
Paul home and handing him back to his
grandmother. Of watching Mary play with
her grandson, smiling, her coolness melting
. . . Sitting down heavily on the sofa, Adele
thought of the woman she had liked and would
miss. Of the woman she had wanted to get to
know better. There had always been some
reserve about Mary Vincent, but sensitivity,
humour and kindness underneath. Qualities
Adele had glimpsed now and again, when Mary
let down her guard. As if to say: *I am not what
you think. Or what my husband and son believe*

I am. I am someone else entirely and one day you'll know who that is.

But now Adele never would.

'I'm so sorry . . . ' she said, close to tears. 'So sorry. I didn't know she was ill.'

'Neither did I. It was a terrible shock . . . ' Ernest replied, changing the subject hurriedly. 'I'm so glad to see you, Adele. And my grandson.' He studied the baby's face. 'That's why we have to think of the future and forget the past. We have to make a new life now.'

Hesitating, Adele held her tongue. She didn't want to spoil the moment, especially after hearing of Mary's death. But she was anxious to know when — or if — Col would be coming home. She had to be gone long before her husband returned.

'Come on, sit over here with us,' Ernest said.

Smiling, Adele sat down beside them, Paul rocking on his grandfather's knee, the fire crackling in the hearth. A wave of tiredness overtook her, or was it relief? After another moment she could feel her eyelids closing. Let go, she told herself, you're safe here. Let go . . . Down, down, down into sleep she went. Down past the Blackpool back streets, and the gas lamps on the market stalls. Down beyond the sound of the barkers and the hum from the pub trade. Down, down, into safety and comfort and the quiet heartbeat of trust.

She woke suddenly, aware that something was wrong. The fire had burned down and Paul was nowhere to be seen. Jerking upright, Adele felt a hand on her shoulder and, alarmed, swivelled round.

'You were dozing,' Ernest said kindly. 'I've put Paul back in his pram, he's fast asleep.'

'Oh, thank you,' Adele replied, flustered. 'That was rude of me, sorry. I've not been getting enough rest.'

Smiling, Ernest sat down beside her on the sofa. His expression was paternal, caring. 'You can't go back to what you were doing, my dear.'

'I can't stay here.'

'Why not?'

'You know why not . . . *Col*.'

'He's abroad.'

'For how long?'

'A long time,' Ernest replied, reassuring her. 'My son isn't going to come home.'

'How can you be sure of that?'

'Have I ever lied to you before?'

She shook her head. 'No, never. I've always been able to trust you.'

'You don't know how much it pleases me to hear you say that,' Ernest told her. 'It's been so lonely here without you and Paul. Then Col left, and Mary died, and the house was suddenly empty. My son and I weren't seeing eye to eye, I have to tell you that. Col and I argued.'

'Is that why he went off?'

'One of the reasons . . . ' Ernest replied, his tone grave. 'I don't want to live here on my own any more. It would be stupid to have such a big house, a family house, just for one person. Not when times are so hard for so many others.' He held her gaze. 'They've been hard for you too, Adele, I can see that. But you don't have to struggle any more. Stay here, with me. This is your home.'

She hesitated. 'I want to, but . . . '

'But what?'

'I can't help thinking about Col. Remembering . . . '

'You want to put Col out of your mind!' Ernest said, his tone hardening. 'He wasn't good enough for you.'

'Ernest!' she said, surprised. 'You don't mean that!'

'Maybe I do,' he replied, his face setting. 'Col should have valued you more. But he was a fool. Acted stupidly.'

'He wasn't a steady kind of man,' Adele said, her tone wary. 'You know that, you told me that. Col had had a breakdown, he was always temperamental. We knew we had to make allowances and be careful around him.'

'He was a fool.'

Alarmed, Adele stared at her father-in-law. It was so unlike him, so harsh.

'I loved your son once,' she said evenly. 'I don't regret marrying him, I just regret the way it ended up. Anyway, I knew what I was taking on from the start.'

'I should have warned you off, not encouraged you. That was my fault, asking a young woman to take on someone like Col — it wasn't fair of me.' He paused, unsettled. 'But I thought you would be good for him. He loved you very much . . . And besides, I wanted you around.'

She frowned, baffled. 'Why did *you* want me around?'

'Adele, don't you understand?' He paused, then suddenly took her hand. 'I can't pretend any more. I've loved you for years . . . '

Stunned, Adele stared at him, words failing her.

'I only realised how *much* I loved you after Mary died. It was my fault you never knew. That I never showed my feelings. I never have. Not really, not to anyone. I've never been loved, Adele. Not properly. Oh, everyone likes me, good old Ernest, kindly Ernest, but no one loved me. Not like a man. Not like a man should be loved.'

Horrified, Adele tried to draw her hand back. 'Ernest, don't — '

'I could look after you so well. You could have this house, do what you want. I've loved you for years, watched you.'

She felt suddenly repulsed. All the times she had sat at the table with this man, the times they had talked, confided in one another. And he had been looking at her not as a father, but as a man. Her heart slowed with revulsion. He had been watching her whilst she been living under his roof. Watching her intimate moments with his son, his grandson. Watching her laughing and arguing, watching her pass him in the corridor in her dressing gown . . . Suddenly Oakham Lodge no longer seemed welcoming. It seemed malignant. She snatched her hand out of his grip.

'I could give you the world,' Ernest went on. 'I

promise you that. It wouldn't be like Col, you wouldn't have to answer to me at all.' He slid to his knees in front of her, his face stupidly pleading. 'Adele, no one has to know about us if you don't want them to. I would be content if you just loved me. I could look after Paul — '

'Who is your grandson!' Adele snapped, jumping to her feet. 'Are you mad?'

'I *was* mad. But I would have done anything, said anything to get you into this house.'

She stared at him, her pulse speeding up. 'What are you talking about? What are you talking about!'

'Forgive me . . . '

'*For what?*' she snapped, her voice rising with panic. 'What have you done? What have you done?'

'I had to lie, I had to . . . '

Beside herself, Adele screamed at him: '*What have you done!*'

'I lied about Col.'

'About Col?' Adele repeated numbly. 'What about Col? About his breakdown?'

Ernest nodded.

'I know,' Adele said, almost triumphantly. 'He told me the truth. He'd never had a breakdown, he'd had a car accident. Abroad . . . ' She could see Ernest's expression change and was suddenly very afraid. 'What *was* the truth? *Did* Col have an accident?'

Ernest nodded. 'Yes.'

'But no nervous breakdown?'

'No,' he croaked.

Something was wrong, terribly wrong. Adele

428

knew it, but she didn't know how bad it was. For a moment she didn't *want* to know, then she pushed him.

'*What is the truth?* What happened to Col? Was he sick? Was he injured in a crash? *Was* he even married?'

'Yes,' Ernest replied, his voice almost a moan.

'Did he have a car accident?'

'Yes . . . '

'Was he . . . ' she struggled to say the next words, 'was he driving? Was Col driving?'

Numbly, Ernest nodded. Adele's voice was barely more than a whisper. 'Was his wife killed in the crash?'

Lifting his head, Ernest looked up at her imploringly. He was unrecognisable. 'I love you! I had to get you into the house, near to me . . . '

'Was his wife killed in the crash!'

'She was very badly injured . . . Col knew it was all his fault. She told him that, over and over again. She said he *wanted* to kill her. That he had done it deliberately.'

Adele stepped back. 'When did she die? *When!*'

'She's still alive.'

A dull humming sound started in Adele's head. It hummed and hummed like a wasp caught in a bottle.

'My husband is still married to her? As well as me? *He's married to two women?*'

Ernest was stammering, falling over his words. 'Adele, I know it was wrong not to tell you — '

'**WRONG!**'

'But no one knew, or could find out about her.

No one could ever know. I never thought your marriage would break up. I never thought Col would go back to her. That she would ever want him back. I thought it was all in the past. I *had* to lie to you, Adele, I had to get you here — '

'How could you!' she hissed. '*How could you!*'

'I love you, Adele!' he wailed, ridiculous and sordid in the same moment. On his knees he came towards her as she stepped back again. 'I've always loved you. I have a right to be loved. *I have a right!*'

'You have a right to burn in hell!' she snapped, running into the hall and looking round anxiously. 'Where is my son? *Where is my son!*'

Ernest had crumpled on his knees and was sobbing. Taking the stairs two at a time, Adele ran up to the first floor, but there was no sign of Paul. Running downstairs again she made for the dining room. Pushing back the doors, she stopped, seeing the pram and her sleeping son inside. Her hands shaking, she grabbed the handlebar, then reached for her coat and bag off the hall table. Finally she flipped the brake off the pram, then made for the front door. She could see Ernest on the floor in the drawing room, crying like a child, and the huge flamboyant Christmas tree lit up behind him. It was grotesque, she thought, looking around her. Her life had been a sham; every moment in Oakham Lodge had been pretence. All the time she had been with Col he had been married to someone else. All the time she had lived under this roof Ernest Vincent had watched her, tricked her, longed for her.

Everything she had lived and believed was false. The illusion of safety was a joke. She wasn't safe in Oakham Lodge. Money didn't make her secure. Benevolent father figures didn't protect her. She was no safer in this rich house than on a Blackpool back street. Wrenching open the front door, she stepped out into the cold December night. The snow had stopped falling, a brilliant moon lighting her way like a torch. She was leaving Oakham Lodge for the second time. She was going out into the world again. Just her, and her child. Only this time Adele knew she could — and *would* — survive.

It was two days to Christmas. And the world was wicked that night.

It is always the small things that stick in your mind. I can remember the way the front door jammed when I tried to close it, and how the air seemed to smell of apples. Which was stupid, of course, at that time of year. Slowly I pushed the pram down the road. I could see the lights of the town in the distance and wondered about all the rows of houses. About what the people in those houses were doing. Eating, sleeping, making love. All those simple activities seemed so poignant then. Because it was nearly Christmas and even the word seemed to mock me. Christmas was for families and children . . . I walked on blindly. Col had already had a wife when he had married me. Our bond was illegal, our marriage void. Worse, our child was illegitimate.

Numbly, I walked on, pushing the pram through the town. Everything was so normal on that most abnormal of nights. Eventually — I don't remember how — I found myself standing outside the Piper's Arms. The old piano was taking a beating, Lily's voice churning out a carol so loudly you could hear it in the street.

It was Christmas. And I remembered how my sister had bought that goose when we were so poor; how Col and I had got tipsy with a bottle of port our first Christmas together; how my father had returned with an oversized pot

cupboard in the back of the old car, so long ago
. . . Standing there, it seemed that I remembered every Christmas of my life. I was traumatised, revolted, lonely — and hungry. And that was what saved me — I was hungry. However shocked my brain might be, my body was still alive, still functioning. I realised then that if only a part of you still feels, you can go on. Whilst you feel, you live.

So I opened the doors of the pub and walked in, pushing the pram. Lily was still singing, tipsy, her crazy wig sliding over to one side. Suddenly she saw me, frowned, then put out her arms.

And I picked up my baby and went to her.

55

Standing under the awning outside the Blackpool covered market, Lennie Bolton and Nicky Gosforth stared out disconsolately. The wind had given way to rain, and now the July streets were mottled with grim puddles, the drains overflowing. Some summer ... Behind them the market bustled with trade, but it was everyday business. Food, vegetables, clothing. Nothing special, nothing from which to make much of a profit. Taking the dimp from behind his ear, Nicky Gosforth lit up. Lennie looked at him enviously.

'I haven't even got the money for a fucking smoke.'

Nicky ignored him. He wasn't about to share the little bit of baccy he had. Not with the spiteful Lennie Bolton. Besides, he didn't hold with men hitting women, and although Lennie had never admitted it, Nicky was sure it was he who had attacked Adele. Not that his warning had done him any good in the long run. When the news came out, people were more sympathetic to Adele. Which, thought Nicky, served bloody Lennie Bolton right.

'I'm going to a house clearance this afternoon.'

Lennie looked at him slyly. 'Why tell me? Yer normally keep things like that to yerself.'

'I might need a bit of muscle,' Nicky said,

glancing over to the venal Lennie. 'Not that yer've got much.'

'I'm strong enough!

Nicky nodded. Lennie was desperate to do anything for money, and Nicky suspected he had already slipped into thieving. Along with some other men, honest men who had tried to get work and failed. Men Nicky would have liked once, even admired. Not like Lennie — Lennie was a bastard.

'Bring a cart with yer. And mind yer don't go getting light-fingered.'

'I'm no fucking thief!'

'I'll believe yer, Lennie,' Nicky replied, stubbing out his cigarette. 'But if yer do feel the urge, don't try it. Not on my bloody territory. I'm going to look at a wardrobe and a bed. If I get them, I'll give yer something for helping me move them.'

'Where's the house clearance?'

Nicky smiled. 'Ah, now I don't think I'm going to tell yer that, Lennie. Let's just meet up at three, on the corner of Buck's Yard.'

★   ★   ★

At five minutes to the hour, Adele crossed Buck's Yard. For once, neither Paul nor the dog was with her. Her son was being looked after by Lily at the pub, Adele calling in a favour. Not that Lily minded; she would have babysat Paul any time. I can't take him to a house clearance, Adele had told Lily, he'd get crushed. Walking on, Adele turned into Benning Street and then

435

stopped. She didn't have to bother checking the door numbers. It was obvious from the half-dozen or so knockers outside number 130 that word had got round. God, she thought, this was going to be a bun fight.

Spotting her approach, a couple of men nodded brusquely, Nicky Gosforth tipping his cap. As for Lennie, he just stood there, watching her.

'No one opened up yet?'

Nicky shrugged. 'The legal bloke's not been round.'

'No relatives?'

'Mr Carter had no family,' another man said, pushing towards Adele, his toothless face close to hers. 'Died alone in his bed. Choked to death on his own blood, they say. Could be he had something catching.'

It was an old ploy and one Adele was used to. Put around a rumour that the deceased had something infectious and the bed would go cheap. Or might even be thrown out — into the arms of some likely lad in the ginnel behind.

She looked at the hollow-cheeked man coolly. 'I heard Mr Carter died of old age.'

'Well . . . if yer want to take the risk.'

The door of number 130 suddenly opened, the press of knockers moving forward as one, Adele struggling to keep on her feet. Into the narrow hallway of the terraced house they scurried, separating out into the front and back rooms. Adele made for the upstairs. Life had toughened her, deceit and poverty had made her resilient — and yet there was still something of

436

the old, tender Adele left. Moving into Mr Carter's bedroom, she paused in the doorway, her glance taking in the unmade bed, the dead man's outline still visible on the sheets. And a used potty underneath. Sordid, but sad. Brushing aside her feelings, Adele moved into the room, noticing a number of dead flies on the window ledge and a dusty glass of water by the bed. Tentatively she opened the wardrobe door. A few clothes were hanging there, including a shabby, old-fashioned suit. Mr Carter had been a town hall clerk, respectable, refined. Adele turned to inspect his threadbare underwear, his used hairbrush and his bedside bible — and shuddered. It was like picking over a corpse, she thought. She studied the bed professionally. The cover was good and would fetch a nice price at the covered market in Blackpool.

'Hey! I want that wardrobe!' Nicky said, hurrying into the bedroom, Lennie behind him. 'I've had my eye on that fer days.'

'Well I don't want it,' Adele replied, folding the counterpane, her hand lingering on the sheets for an instant.

All at once the squalor of her situation hit her. That she had been reduced to this: taking the clothes off the bed of a corpse . . . Her eyes closed for an instant. Thank God Paul wasn't with her. She would never bring him to the house clearances. Never.

'I want the bed too.'

'You can have it,' Adele told Nicky. Lennie Bolton ignored her and jerked his head towards the door.

'Oi, Nicky, yer'll have to give me a hand getting this downstairs.' He gave the wardrobe a sudden push, jolting Adele.

'Watch it!' she snapped, stepping back.

'Then mind where yer standing!' Lennie replied viciously, watching her as she walked out.

At the top of the stairs Adele paused, looking at a jug and pitcher on the window ledge. Momentarily she wondered how much it would be and if she could sell it on. Nicky Gosforth broke into her thoughts.

'Yer know something?'

She gave him a level stare. 'What?'

'I've been thinking. Me and yer are in the same trade; perhaps we could join forces.' He winked. 'In more ways than one.'

'I don't think so.'

'No need to get all uppity!' he snapped, flushing. 'Yer not such a bloody catch yerself. No bloody money and a kid in tow — yer lucky I'd give yer the time of day.'

'Sure I'm lucky,' Adele replied, stung. 'I'm a lucky, lucky girl.'

Downstairs she paid for the worn coverlet and began to push her way out of the house. She couldn't stay there a moment longer. The place smelt of damp. It reeked of sadness. A decent man's privacy raided by a bunch of jackals. And she was one of them. She, Adele Ford, the woman who had believed she would make it big. Where were her ambitions now? She was grubbing with the lowest to make ends meet. Clawing a greasy living from dead objects and discarded tat.

Reaching the street, Adele breathed in the fresh air. Shame winded her. At least no one from her past could see her now. She had cut off all contact. Obviously she had severed any connection with Ernest Vincent, but the scribbled notes she used to send to Julia and Kitty had stopped too. One letter, though, Adele *had* made sure she sent — to Becky, hoping that her new baby was well and that her family was in good health.

Since Ernest's confession Adele had closed down emotionally. She couldn't understand how she had been duped by Col and his father so easily. How she had believed them both, even trusted Ernest, turned to him when Col had let her down. And it had all been a charade ... Embarrassed, she thought of her mentor, Turner Gades. How he would cringe, seeing her now ... Another thought snapped at her heels. *Was this life the best she could do for her son?* Paul was growing up; before much longer he would need to go to school. And what kind of school would that be? Some council school? His future as a carter or a miner worked out for him from the start? Paul was the son of Col Vincent ... Adele stopped walking, wondering where her husband was now. If he was with his first wife. *His first wife* ... So what did that make *her*? Adele knew the answer only too well. She had been to the library, studied the legal books, and knew the truth of her position. Her marriage to Col was invalid. Which made Paul illegitimate. The irony mocked her. For very considered reasons,

Adele had let it be believed that Paul wasn't Col's son. That he was effectively a bastard. It had, of course, been untrue. But now she had discovered that her lie, although inaccurate, *was* actually a fact. Paul was illegitimate. The bastard son of an illegal marriage.

Taking a deep breath, Adele shook herself out of her uncharacteristic melancholy. She would survive and so would her son. She had been a knocker for many months — hadn't she made a living? Paid the rent? Fed and clothed herself and Paul? Hadn't she bought and sold on her goods, albeit with small profits? Hadn't she kept them out of debt? Oh yes, she had done all that. And she would continue.

Clutching the bedspread to her, Adele walked on. She had her son, and they were safe. What else really mattered? Optimism lifted her spirits. Who knew what was about to happen? Good or bad, she could deal with it . . . Turning her face up to catch a little unexpected sun, Adele glanced into the clouds. She knew there was only a limited time before Paul was old enough to understand what his mother did for a living. That their home was just a rented room over a pub. But suddenly Adele didn't feel depressed or overwhelmed. She felt fired up. So *what* if they had to struggle? She would have her shop in the end. She would make a future for her son, and herself.

Suddenly something her father had once said came back to her: *Do something with your life, Adele . . . Don't be like me. Make the most of your abilities . . . Be someone. Be someone you can admire . . .*

Uplifted by the words, she suddenly realised what he had meant, and knew that — on one level — she had already succeeded. Because she *did* admire herself.

As for tomorrow, whatever came, she would survive.

56

Bernard Hoggard reckoned that he was probably the only man on earth who wanted to go bald. That way, he reasoned, he could finally control his gaudy frizz of red hair. In fact, he *liked* the idea of having a shiny bald pate. It would be cool in summer, and it would save him a fortune in pomade. Sniffing, he pulled a file towards him and began to read. Then he paused and looked up. Then he read the words again.

Good God, he thought, astounded. Good God ... He checked the letterhead on the piece of paper. Yes, quite legal and above board. He even knew the company of solicitors. Very respectable. But the news was extraordinary ... Amazed, Bernard ran his hands through his hair and then winced, impatiently rubbing the grease off with his handkerchief. What an incredible thing to happen. No one had had any idea. No one had even suspected a connection.

My, my, my, Bernard Hoggard thought. This was going to set the county alight.

★   ★   ★

Pensive, Julia looked at her post. That was the thing with solicitors, they never told you the whole story. Warily she glanced over to her husband. Poor, tame John, so pleased to have his home back, and his food made for him. Julia

442

considered her husband thoughtfully. What a timid little soul he had turned out to be, she thought. Life had proved to be too much for John Courtland. It was sad, but his forays into adultery and ambition had completely floored him, rocked him to his core. Curious, Julia watched her husband bite into his toast. Evenly spread, a little more marmalade than butter, his tea poured in his cup beside him. Two sugars.

And she had once cried over this man, longed for him, even gone a little mad . . . Honestly, Julia thought, how the roles had been reversed. He was in love with her now. Watchful of her. As for his banking ambitions, they had hit the buffers. He had fouled up his chances at his old place of employment and even Mr Lockhart looked the other way when he saw his neighbour coming. So the banking career had been replaced by a new profession — as a chiropodist. There was something delightful about the idea, Julia thought mischievously, remembering how John had trained, his books laid out on the table, a selection of corns and bunions colourfully illustrated amongst the text.

You couldn't believe how life turned out sometimes . . . Glancing back at the letter from Bernard Hoggard, Julia decided she wouldn't write back, but would call in on her way to the florist's.

'Anything interesting?' John asked, gesturing to the letter in his wife's hand.

She glanced over to him, catching the adoration in his eyes. 'No, darling.'

Taking her hand, he squeezed it — and

unexpectedly she felt warmed by the touch.

'I have to go to town, John.'

He nodded, gulping down his tea. 'I'll walk you there,' he said anxiously. 'After all, I don't want anything happening to my girl, do I?'

★   ★   ★

Life went on, Turner thought dully. Of course it did. Bills and auctions and meals and every other action humans undertook went on. Nothing had stopped since his Clemmie died: a bout of influenza unexpectedly exacerbating a mild heart problem. Within a week she had gone from health to death, and he couldn't bear it. Turner knew how happy they had been, but there was more to it than that. Clemmie had been his friend. His lover, yes, his wife, yes, his companion, yes. But more than anything, his greatest friend.

Cruelly there had been no time to prepare for her leaving. He had nursed her, teased her, and lain beside her when she slept. But he had never — never — anticipated that she would leave her bed for her grave. Afterwards he had stripped the room of her things: her clothes, her hairbrush, her books. He didn't need them. They were just memories. He needed images of her life, not her death. It was — in fact — the only way he could survive.

'Dave! Dave!'

The Chinaman leapt to his feet in the storeroom and walked out into the yard of the Failsworth shop.

'I want a word with you, please,' Turner said, his tone serious.

Dave stared at his employer. Clemmie's death was showing badly on Turner. He was, as always, courteous and well mannered, but he was patently reduced by her loss.

'I don't want you to betray anyone's trust,' Turner went on, 'but I heard you'd found Adele Vincent just before Christmas.'

Dave flushed. He had hoped that his endeavours would result in her return to Oakham Lodge and the shop. But instead Adele had left again. Ernest had given little explanation. Just mentioned something about his daughter-in-law wanting to keep away from her old matrimonial home.

'You *did* find Adele, didn't you?'

Dave nodded. 'Mr Vincent asked me to bring her back with the baby.'

So the rumour *had* been right. Any other time Turner would have followed the matter up with Ernest. But he had been so involved with Clemmie back then . . .

'Do you know where Adele is now?'

Dave hesitated before answering. 'I'm . . . I'm not sure. I mean, she asked me never . . . not to tell . . . '

'I understand,' Turner replied, nodding. 'But this is very important, Dave, or I wouldn't ask you to break your word. I need to know where Adele is. *I have to find her.*'

'But — '

'I wouldn't do anything to harm her, you know that,' Turner said simply. 'I understand your feelings for her, Dave, but you have to trust me. I need to contact her. For her own good. Please tell me where she is.'

Dave Lin would have died rather than give up the information to anyone else. But this was Turner Gades. And *he* was above suspicion.

'She was working in Blackpool.'

'*Was?*'

'I heard she moved for a while. Went Manchester way, then Cheadle.' Dave paused. 'She were back on the Blackpool covered market a fortnight ago. But not since . . . '

He flushed, and Turner nodded. 'You were keeping an eye on her?'

'When I can . . . It's not spying!' Dave said hurriedly. 'I'm not spying on her.'

'It's all right, it's fine,' Turner replied, reassuring him. 'Do you know where she *lives?*'

Dave shook his head. 'Nah . . . But the last two weeks I've seen her at an outside market in Salford. On a Saturday. It's a rum place, but she's there in the afternoons. Got a stall.'

Got a stall . . . Turner could picture it. A rundown market, with rundown stalls, paraffin lamps going on in the winter. And in the late summer — like it was now — steamy evenings when the louts came round and hassled the female stallholders.

'Yer won't tell her I told yer?'

'No,' Turner said sadly, 'I won't tell her, Dave.'

'And yer'll not worry her 'bout anything?'

Turner frowned. 'Why would I?'

''Cos she's had a bad time of it, yer see. Looking after that baby on her own. And working, struggling, with no one to protect her . . . well, I just don't want anything else bad to happen to her.'

'I would never do anything to harm Adele,' Turner said, suddenly anxious. 'Is she all right?'

'She's OK. But she's changed . . . Yer'll know what I mean when yer see her.'

★　★　★

Bending over the pram, Adele offered Paul a dummy. She didn't like to, but it was the quickest way to send him off to sleep. He hadn't been sleeping a lot lately, what with cutting his teeth and getting more active. It was only to be expected. He was beginning to walk now, pottering and crawling about their cramped room, Lily taking him downstairs to show the punters. And then bringing him back a few minutes later, smelling of tobacco and beer. Like a little tippler, Adele thought, smiling ruefully. Her baby should have smelt of talcum powder and fresh soap, but what could you do? Lily loved Paul. Her husband, Wal, might not have a way with babies, but Lily was a natural. How could Adele deny her time with her son when she had been so kind to them?

Putting her hands in the small of her back, Adele stretched. God, she ached. The pub bed wasn't that comfortable, but at least it wasn't damp like the first one had been, back in Morecambe . . . Glad of the warm afternoon, Adele glanced back at the stall. People had quick, greedy little fingers and she had found out

— to her cost — that there were thieves around. Sighing, she rearranged a few things, but her offerings were meagre, and trade was poor. Who could blame people? There was so little money around, what with all the unemployment. People wanted to sell, not buy.

Smiling hopefully as a woman approached the stall, Adele asked, 'Anything you're interested in?'

'That tea cosy, how much?'

'A shilling.'

The woman picked it up and turned it over in her hand. It was knitted, clean, but the colours had faded.

'OK,' she said sullenly, passing Adele the money. 'And what about that soap?'

'A ha'penny.'

'What!'

'You'll get no cheaper at the chemist,' Adele said reasonably. 'It's fine. Monkey brand. I use it.'

In fact it was poor soap, but Adele wasn't lying when she said she used it. Good soap for the baby. Cheap soap for her.

'All right,' the woman agreed. 'I want a paper bag, though.'

Only three stalls away, a distinguished, greying man was watching. He had spotted Adele almost twenty minutes earlier and had been studying her ever since. Pity had made Turner glance away at first, but then he looked back at the young woman he had so admired. She was changed, he thought sadly. Still good looking, but mature — and poor. That much was painfully obvious, from her dress to the battered pram in which Col Vincent's son lay sleeping. Everything was clean, but mortally worn. And as for the stall . . . Turner looked at the pitiful items on offer. Old prints, a battered car horn, tea cosies, *soap*. Dear God, he thought, only the poorest sold soap. It was the last thing people resorted to . . .

And then he remembered the Adele he used to know. The glowing, feisty young woman who had dreamed of the Lydgate Widow and some marvellous future — which had been well within her reach. The kid who had nearly bought the ugly old clock at auction, the girl who had captured Col Vincent's heart. The woman she had become. Sleek, confident, enthusiastic. With an obsession with beauty, an eye for style. A woman who dealt in Royal Worcester and Sèvres — not soap.

Deeply moved, Turner found himself pitying and admiring Adele in the same instant. God knew how, but she had kept her head above water. And her son provided for. He was impressed by that. Impressed by her courage, her bravery. Her willingness to do anything for her child. And then Turner realised something — a woman like that would never be an adulteress. Would never stoop to passing her son off as another man's child. Adele's explanation had never convinced him. If she *had* been so hard-faced, she wouldn't have been struggling now. There would have been a man supporting her. And there was no man around . . . Oh no, Turner thought, Col might insist that Adele had cheated on him. She might say the same. But he didn't believe it for one instant.

'Adele?'

She turned at the sound of her name, sunlight striking her face and making her momentarily porcelain.

'*Turner?*' She flushed, looked away. 'I didn't want you to know . . . I'm sorry. I didn't — '

'Can I buy an old friend a cup of tea?' he asked, as though nothing had changed. 'You stay there, Adele, I'll bring us some over.'

She thought for a moment that her heart would break. Humiliation, relief, gratitude all mingled together. Suddenly Turner Gades was back in her life. She didn't know why. Didn't even care. Just knew that from now on, things would improve. This was the only person who had never let her down. She had lied to him, cut him out of her life, and yet he wasn't angry. Wasn't judgemental. The world could sneer at her, gossip about her, grind her into nothing — but not this man.

Standing behind her impoverished market stall, Adele watched her old friend return. He was holding cups of tea. But he came to her smiling, as though he was bringing champagne.

57

Much to her annoyance, Mr Hoggard wasn't telling Julia anything. In fact he was pressing *her* for information.

'So you don't know where your sister is?'

'No,' she said for the second time. 'Why, what do you want to contact Adele for?'

'I'm afraid that's privileged information.'

'But I'm her *sister*, Mr Hoggard,' Julia went on firmly. 'How long have you known me? I raised Adele, I can't think why you won't trust me. I only have her interests at heart.'

'I don't doubt that,' Bernard ploughed on. 'But this is a private matter. Is there no way you can contact Adele?'

'She stopped writing to me a while back,' Julia replied sheepishly, then rallied. 'After what happened, I suppose she was ashamed. You know, her leaving her husband and taking the baby. I mean, I don't judge her, but, well . . .'

'Quite,' Mr Hoggard replied, rising to his feet. 'If you do hear from your sister, please ask her to contact me.'

'Perhaps I could give her a message?'

'Just to contact me.'

'A hint?' Julia went on manfully.

'I have information that would be of interest to her.'

Julia's face set like putty. She was up against

an immovable ginger-haired object that wasn't going to budge.

'Very well, Mr Hoggard, I'll get Adele to contact you — if she contacts me.' She turned, then turned back, going for a last-ditch attempt. 'She won't miss out on anything if we can't get in touch with her, will she? I mean, that would be terrible. And as her nearest relative . . . '

'She has a husband.'

'But he's abroad!' Julia snapped, thwarted.

'Just get Adele to contact me, if you would,' Bernard Hoggard concluded deftly. 'And thank you for your help.'

★ ★ ★

Taking another sip of his tea, Turner leaned against the side of the stall, looking at Paul. The baby had woken and was now sitting up, rocking himself in the pram. Strong child, Turner thought. It was a pity he had never had a family of his own, but Clemmie had been older than him when they married and a child had never come into the equation. He pulled a face at the baby suddenly, Paul clapping his hands with delight.

'It's good to see you,' Adele said quietly.

She was surprised at the change in Turner. His hair was now very grey, but his face hadn't aged and he seemed younger than before. It was strange, Adele thought. Previously he had seemed so much her senior, but now — in the sunlight — Turner Gades looked like a relatively young man.

452

'I lost Clemmie, you know. She died . . . '

Adele winced. 'Oh God.'

'She had a heart condition no one knew about . . . ' He trailed off.

So that was why he seemed quieter, sadder, Adele thought, remembering the elegant Clemmie. Kind hearted, supportive, warm, always making people feel comfortable. God, she thought bleakly, what a loss. What a stupid, terrible loss.

'I'm so sorry. I can't imagine how much you must miss her,' Adele said sincerely, 'But I'm glad to see you.'

'I'm pleased to see you too,' he replied. 'I've been looking for you — to give you some news.'

'News?' Adele said warily. News meant trouble, and trouble she had plenty of.

'It's all right,' he reassured her hurriedly. 'Your solicitor, Bernard Hoggard, wants to see you. Said it was nothing unpleasant. Implied it was beneficial, in fact. He's my solicitor too, you know. And he hoped we were still in touch.'

Adele flushed. 'How did you find me?'

He wasn't going to break a confidence. 'Luck.'

'I didn't want to go off like that.'

'You must have had your reasons.'

'Oh, I did,' she said sincerely. 'Otherwise I would never have acted so drastically.'

'Or lied.'

She looked up at him. 'What?'

'It *was* all a lie, wasn't it?' Turner asked, his face unreadable. 'I never believed that you ran off with another man, Adele. Or that Col wasn't Paul's father.'

Mortified, she looked down. At that moment she wanted, above all, to confess, to tell him everything. To blow apart his belief in his friend, and in the duplicitous Ernest. But how could she? Turner had been her mentor, but they had never been emotionally close. How could she admit to this respectable, successful man — the one person she admired above all others — that her marriage was illegal and her son was a bastard?

'The marriage . . . ' she struggled to find a plausible explanation, ' . . . didn't work.'

'You can say that about a car, or a clock,' Turner replied wryly, 'but not about a love match. For a few days now I've been thinking about what Clemmie said. When I told her that Col had accused you of being something you weren't, she said, 'Are you sure he's talking about Adele and not himself?''

'Clemmie was a very perceptive woman,' Adele replied, moved.

Turner nodded. 'Yes, and she was seldom wrong about people . . . What did Col do to you?'

She couldn't tell him. Wanted to, but did not dare. Was, quite simply, terrified that she would alienate him. That he would walk away — just as she had done.

'I can't tell you,' she said at last.

He paused, surprised and yet pleased that she hadn't lied to him. In time Adele would tell him the reason why she had left, would explain about Col — but obviously now wasn't the time. And Turner wasn't a man to push anyone.

'You should go and see Bernard Hoggard as soon as you can.'

'I will,' Adele said hurriedly, then paused. 'Would you come with me?'

Her voice faltered, her embarrassment obvious. How *could* she ask if Turner Gades would accompany her? How could she expect that he would even want to be seen with her? In her old clothes, with Paul's battered pram? The disgraced Adele Vincent coming back to Rochdale, after all that she had done. After all the gossip . . . Was she mad to ask?

'That was a stupid thing to say. I'm sorry, forget it.'

He put up his hands to stop her continuing. 'If you can get someone to tend your stall, we could go now.'

★　★　★

Pauline Buckley was sure that she was having a brainstorm. Openmouthed, she gawked through her shop window at the approaching couple. *It couldn't be Turner Gades with Adele Vincent.* Her gaze fixed on them, then she felt an arm sliding around her waist and relaxed. She had no reason to be jealous of Adele any more; she was Mrs Donald Duckworth. Oh, her husband might not look like Turner Gades or Col Vincent, but she was safely married. And deliciously, delightfully smug.

'Oh, that poor girl,' she said. Donald followed her gaze to the street.

'Who, d . . . d . . . arling?'

'There,' she replied, pointing to Adele. 'She used to be so pretty. But then there was a terrible disgrace. Awful. Shame really, but then she was very rude to me once.'

Donald swallowed, his Adam's apple bobbing up and down. 'She was w . . . w . . . w . . . what?' he said, on the defensive.

'Rude to me.'

'R . . . r . . . r . . . '

'Rude, yes!' Pauline snapped, so intent on watching the couple's progress that she leaned too far forward and lurched through the half curtain at the back of the window. Cursing, she scrambled to her feet, Donald helping her, his thin frame bent double as he tried to lift her hefty carcass. Finally Pauline was back on her feet — just in time to see Turner Gades and Adele Vincent as they passed her shop.

'You know,' she said lightly, 'Turner Gades was very fond of me once.'

Impressed, Donald stared at his wife. 'He w . . . w . . . w . . . was?'

'But I didn't love him,' she went on, turning and kissing her unfortunate-looking but wealthy husband passionately. 'No one will ever match you in my eyes.'

★ ★ ★

As they walked along, the sun shone on Adele's clothes and showed them up for what they were. The faded patterned dress, the scuffed shoes, her stockings darned at the heel. And the pram seemed even shabbier on that well-to-do street,

Paul banging his rattle on the side, a woman staring.

Chastened, Adele walked alongside Turner Gades. She wanted to stop and shout, *My husband hit me, he could have hurt our child. I left to protect us*, but she knew she couldn't. She had left her family. She was a disgrace. And she had done nothing to help herself, sending out a false story. The decent people of Rochdale were seeing Adele Ford for what she really was — a nobody. A woman on her uppers. With a bastard kid in tow.

A few moments later they entered the cool offices of Herbert, Herbert and Hoggard. The wait was short; Adele was soon shown into Bernard Hoggard's room, while Turner remained seated outside.

She paused in the doorway. 'You can come in if you want.'

'You sure?' Turner replied.

'Oh yes, I'm sure.'

Putting the brake on Paul's pram, Adele sat down and looked over the desk at Bernard Hoggard. His hair, she thought, suppressing a near-hysterical laugh, was as fiery and upright as it had always been.

'Well now, Mrs Vincent,' Bernard said, smiling. 'So pleased to see you at last.'

She nodded. 'I've been — '

'Quite,' he replied, the word covering everything. 'Well, I have some news for you. Important news. You have inherited a property.'

'Pardon?' Adele said blankly. 'A *property*? I don't think so — what property?'

'The late Mrs Mary Vincent owned a property. Her estate was very complicated and it has taken a while for us to sort everything out, but she has left a house to you, Adele.'

Shaking her head, she stared at the solicitor. 'I don't understand. My mother-in-law would have left it to Col.'

'On the contrary, Mrs Vincent stipulated — entirely legally — that you were to be the sole beneficiary of Lydgate House.'

The floor moved underneath Adele's feet, her head swimming. Slumping forward, she fainted, banging her head on the side of the desk as she fell. A few black, hazy moments followed, Adele only coming round when she heard her name being called.

'Adele, Adele!' Bernard Hoggard repeated, his red hair coming into focus. Hurriedly Turner passed her a glass of water and helped her back into her seat.

'That's a real bump you've got there,' he said, concerned. 'Are you fit to go on?'

She looked at him, then nodded. 'I thought Mr Hoggard said I'd inherited Lydgate House.'

'You have,' the solicitor said. 'Mary Vincent left it to you.'

'But I never even knew it was hers!'

'No, no one knew. But apparently it was left to Mrs Vincent — I have all the notes here, it's all perfectly legal — by her cousin. Or rather, I should say, by the *wife* of Mrs Vincent's cousin,' Mr Hoggard went on, glancing back to his notes as Adele touched the bump on her head gingerly. 'A Mrs Ninette Hoffman . . . '

This time it was Turner who took in a breath. His father's mistress, Adele's long-term heroine . . . It was incredible. It was unbelievable. It was meant to be.

'. . . who used to own Lydgate House.'

'The Lydgate Widow.'

'Pardon, Adele? Oh yes, I see what you mean, she *was* a widow for a time,' Mr Hoggard went on hurriedly. 'Well, Mrs Hoffman had no children and she left the house to her husband's cousin, Mary Vincent. Apparently it was Mrs Vincent who arranged for it to be maintained — secretly — for over thirty years.'

'But why didn't she use it?'

'She said . . . ' Bernard paused, then read from his notes:

Many years ago, when I was very young, I showed kindness to Ninette Hoffman, my cousin's wife, a woman my family ostracised. I should have done more, but I allowed myself to be bullied into their way of thinking. However, my limited kindness was apparently much appreciated — and not forgotten — by Ninette Hoffman. When she died she left me Lydgate House.

Perhaps Adele will understand this, but I told no one. Secrets are sometimes our only consolation. I maintained the house in the belief that one day I would seek refuge there. But it wasn't to be me.

In time my daughter-in-law, Adele, may well need a place of safety, and one that is wholly her own. Because of this, I leave

*Lydgate House to her, to use as she sees fit
and to provide herself and her son — my
much-loved grandson Paul — with a substan-
tial property.*

*I believe that Adele will understand why I
have taken this course of action — and accept
my apology for not intervening more. Or
sooner. I cannot make amends for my laxity,
but hopefully this action may assist her greatly
and go some way to absolving my own
guilt . . .*

With the letter was a photograph, which
Bernard handed over to Adele. She had thought
it would be of Mary, but it was of a woman she
didn't know. A striking, dark-haired woman, with
the name *Ninette* written on the photograph
underneath her feet.

Surprised, Turner glanced over to Adele.
'What was Mary Vincent talking about? That you
may need 'a place of safety' and 'absolving my
own guilt'?'

Both men were looking at Adele, waiting for
her reply. 'I'm not sure,' she said, skirting the
issue. 'But I can't believe it — *I own Lydgate
House.*'

'Yes, you do,' Bernard Hoggard agreed. 'It's all
yours. Why? Do you know the place?'

58

One day I will have a big house, with a stone wall around it. To keep the people I love in and the rest of the world out . . . Adele's own words came back to her as she turned the key in the lock of Lydgate House and walked in. Lily was looking after Paul for the afternoon, Adele taking the chance to absorb her astonishing good fortune alone. Slowly she looked around. The house seemed vast, or perhaps she had been cooped up for too long in the rented room over the pub. Arched windows, partially unboarded, let in some of the late August sunlight. Adele's footsteps echoing as she moved around. This was the dream of her childhood . . .

At once, her mind went back, her father's voice coming clearly: *Don't you remember the story? She's locked to the house for ever. There, look, can't you see her? She's there, outlined against the horizon. She's alone. Always alone . . .*

And now Adele was going to be the owner of the place she had admired for so long. She was going to be the mistress of this property. A woman of power, standing. The thought fizzed inside her as she moved further into the house, pulling back shutters and throwing dust sheets off opulent, eclectic pieces of furniture. It was dusty, smelling of age and time, but to Adele it was a sanctuary. And it was hers. Hers and

461

Paul's . . . Giddily she ran up the stairs, stopping at the top and glancing out of the landing window. The garden was thick with flowers and leaves, and for an instant she thought she saw a movement by the pond . . .

'Adele!'

Spinning round, she saw Turner walk into the hall and ran down to him. 'Isn't it wonderful!' she said, her face radiant. 'Isn't it incredible! I've always loved this place, since I was a little girl. But I never thought I would end up here. Never believed it would be possible . . . ' Moving past him, she made for the library, tossing back the doors and walking over to the bookcases. Her fingers ran longingly over the dust jackets and the gilded spines, her euphoria heady. 'Thank God this place has been maintained all these years. Look at these books for Paul to read when he gets older. And a garden. And . . . ' She stopped, flushed. 'Is it real?'

'Is *what* real?'

'All this? Or will they read the papers again and find out it was just a joke? That I don't own it, that they were wrong.'

His heart turned. 'No, Adele, it's not a joke. It's your house now.'

'Of course I'll have to maintain it,' she went on hurriedly, 'but I've been thinking about that. I can run the business from here. Sell antiques from the house. That way I could have them on display with no overheads . . . ' She paused, looking round. 'I'll make us a drink. If I can just work out where the kitchen is.'

'Through those doors, first on the left.'

She nodded — then looked back to Turner, surprised. 'You know this house?'

He paused before replying. 'I used to come here when I was a child. With my father.'

'Why?'

'To see Ninette Hoffman,' he said, reluctantly, almost embarrassed. 'She was my father's mistress.'

Adele stared at him in amazement. 'The Lydgate Widow was your father's mistress?'

'Yes.'

'You never mentioned it before.'

'It's hardly the kind of thing you tell people, is it?' he replied, raising his eyebrows. 'And anyway, you've not explained your inheritance to me, Adele. Not a word about why Col's mother left you this house. Or about what she wrote . . . ' He watched her face colour. 'All right, it's none of my business.'

Adele took a deep breath. 'Col was violent. And he threatened to take Paul away from me. That's why I left. We weren't safe with him. I had to get out. I put the story around that I had gone off with another man.'

'Why would you do that?'

'It was a bargain,' she said evenly. 'So Col wouldn't come looking for me, or for his son.' Adele was uncomfortable, determined to say nothing more. She couldn't tell Turner about her illegal marriage; she was too ashamed, and too protective of her son.

'Where's Col now?'

'Abroad. And I believe he'll be staying there.'

Turner was clearly angry. 'Where abroad?'

'I don't know,' she lied, hurrying on. 'Forget it. It's in the past now. To all intents and purposes Col is dead to me. I'm the new Lydgate Widow.'

'Don't ever say that!' Turner snapped, unexpectedly sharp. 'You don't want to be her, Adele. She wasn't a happy woman. She married a man who fell out of love with her — and that made her turn to my father. Ninette believed that her husband would be jealous, but he wasn't. He didn't care. But my father did. He cared more and more for Ninette, whilst she longed more and more for her husband's affection. It was an impossible situation. So don't ever say you want to be like her, Adele.'

'But she had this place,' Adele replied, sticking to her guns. 'I've always dreamed of a house like this, Turner. To actually get here is incredible. Don't you understand? I can give my son status here. No more being pushed around the streets in an old pram, tucked behind a market stall. No more living over a pub. Paul will be somebody. If I work and save money, he can go to a good school, make something of his life. Hopefully he'll never even remember the way things were for us.'

'That would be a pity.'

'A *pity!*' Adele replied, horrified. 'No, Turner, it wouldn't be a pity. What glory is there in having a mother who worked as a knocker? A woman with a doubtful reputation, who ended up selling soap off a market stall?'

His face was stern. 'I liked that woman. She was brave, courageous. She ruined her own name for the sake of her child. I liked her.'

464

She was suddenly annoyed with him. 'Well I didn't! I want to forget what I was. What I had to do to survive. And I don't want Paul to even know about it.' Her voice rose. 'I'm going to be the successful woman I always said I would be. I'm going to give Paul the best chance in life. This house was made for me, Turner. That's why I used to dream about it so much, why I felt so drawn to it. I understand Ninette Hoffman.'

'You aren't a widow.'

'As good as!' Adele countered. 'I've told you, my husband is dead to me.'

'But Col *isn't* dead, is he? And one day you might want to marry someone else.'

'I don't want to marry again!' she snapped, averting her face. 'Sorry to shock you, Turner, but I'm not a very good judge of character. And I don't want to make any more mistakes . . . Now I've got this place, I don't need to rely on a man. On anyone. I can fend for myself, and my son.'

He was staring at her curiously, listening to the words and wondering what she was covering up. The vehemence was unlike her, but then again, perhaps Col had changed her.

'I'm sorry.'

She frowned. 'For what?'

'I introduced you to Col.'

'It wasn't your fault,' Adele reassured him. 'You didn't know what he was like.'

'Neither did you.'

'No, I didn't.'

And there it was, the intimation of what Adele was hiding. It was obvious that she didn't trust

Turner enough to confide yet. Or perhaps it wasn't his business . . . But Turner had always been protective of Adele and felt responsible for what she had suffered. He also knew that if he ever saw Col Vincent again he would make him pay for what he had done.

'Don't change, Adele,' he said quietly. 'Don't shut the world out and imagine you're safe that way. Living is letting people in.'

'I'll let *you* in any time you call. You're my closest friend, my rock,' she replied. 'But I don't like what I've seen of the world, Turner. I don't like what it did to me, and what it could have done to my son. I want to be safe.'

He nodded, walking to the door. Then he paused and turned back to her.

'When I was very young I came here with my father. I used to wait in the kitchen with the staff whilst he was visiting Ninette. He was so in love with her, it used to hurt to see him that way . . . ' He paused for a long moment, thinking back. 'The last time we came it was a boiling hot day. There were dragonflies in the garden, and some lemonade getting warm in the sun on an outside table . . . '

Silent, Adele listened.

'Andreas Hoffman was standing on the terrace, smoking. He looked over to me and said nothing, as though he was looking through me. As though I was a ghost and didn't exist for him. Or maybe *he* was the ghost . . . A week later he was dead.'

Adele's voice was barely more than a whisper. 'What happened?'

'He had a riding accident. A gelding threw him, broke his neck. But I think back to that day and remember his face. He knew it was all over for him.' Turner glanced at Adele. 'He was already dead. There were four of us that day. Two of us died within twelve months. My father and Andreas Hoffman. Later Ninette . . . Now there's only me left to remember this house. And the way we all were then.'

Surprised by his eloquence, Adele suddenly saw Turner Gades in a completely different light. The honourable gentleman, admired and respected by everyone, was far more complex than he seemed.

'Why are you telling me this, Turner?'

'Because love injures people, Adele,' he said gently. 'But a lack of love kills.'

59

'So *she* was the Mary!' Becky said suddenly.

They were in Lydgate House, Adele having invited her oldest friend round to look at the place which had played such a part in their childhood.

'*What Mary?*'

Becky turned to Adele, the memory vivid. 'Frida remembered something just before she died. About Ninette and the young girl who visited her. A girl called Mary. It was Mary Vincent all along.' She smiled, looking into the pram beside her. Her little daughter was asleep, just as Paul was in the bedroom upstairs. 'Well, that's one old mystery solved. And to think how you loved this place when you were a kid.'

'I know, it's incredible,' Adele replied, sitting down next to Becky. 'I used to talk about it all the time. Even when I married Col, I used to sometimes refer to it . . . I've been wondering if Mary heard me.'

'She must have done,' Becky said, frowning. 'But — I keep wondering about this — why would she leave it to you and not Col? After all, he was her son.'

And that was the moment when the truth came out. Slowly and carefully Adele told her friend everything about her marriage. About the sham happiness, the violence, the terror she felt at losing Paul. About why she had lied when she left. Silent, Becky listened, then shook her head.

'Why didn't you tell me sooner?'

'I couldn't.'

'I would have helped you. You know that, Adele. I wouldn't have let you down.'

'You'd had enough, Becky. Your life was finally looking up, you were happy with Isaac. How could I dump all my problems on you? I had to get away. From everyone.' Adele paused, thinking back. 'I had to do it alone. To prove something to myself. To prove that Col was wrong — that I *hadn't* been broken by him. Or by life.'

★ ★ ★

'Yer joking!' Kitty Gallager said, grinning. 'Yer want me to come and work fer yer in yer big house?'

Adele nodded, gasping as Kitty turned round. From the back she had looked as she always had — thin arms, thin legs — but when she turned round it was obvious that she was about eight months gone.

'God!'

'No, a baby!' Kitty replied, laughing. 'Stan says he wants twins. I want a very, very small baby.' She put her head on one side. 'I'm glad to see yer. Wondered when I'd see yer again, and now all this gossip. People are going mad to hear yer got that big house.' She screeched with laughter. 'Did me bloody good, I can tell yer, to see so many noses out of joint. All of them had been saying yer were washed up, finished — and now this!'

'Kitty — '

'Of course, I knew yer'd make good.'

'Kitty!'

She blinked. 'What?'

'I wanted to offer you a job. But you're pregnant.'

'So?'

Adele raised her eyebrows. 'So you couldn't cope.'

'Like hell!' Kitty replied. 'Yer said it were a live-in job? Looking after the shop, cleaning, filling in?'

Adele nodded. 'Yes, and there's plenty of room for you. A flat in the outbuildings.'

'*A flat!*' Kitty said, delighted. 'Yer know Stan were laid off?'

'I didn't, no.'

'Yeah, like so many others. We were wondering about how to make the rent, and now this. Stan could do anything fer yer. He's good with his hands.' She winked. 'And other parts.'

Adele shook her head, laughing. 'I need a handyman and a gardener, so Stan can do that. But can you manage with a new baby?'

'Like yer don't know about looking after a baby?' Kitty replied. 'I can cope. So yer going to run a shop from the house? Keep it in the family, so to speak. Almost like old times. Will it be just you, Paul and us?'

Pausing, Adele shook her head. 'No, there's someone else coming.'

'Dave, of course.'

Adele frowned. 'Dave Lin?'

'Yeah, yer can't run a house and shop without Dave.'

'I don't think I've got enough cash to pay him.'

'He'd work fer nowt if yer gave him bed and board. Yer know he's crazy about yer. And think how safe yer'd feel with him around.'

Adele liked the idea. Keep the few people she trusted with her, in a tight, safe little enclave. The place was huge, more than big enough to house her old comrades. Adele hadn't forgotten anything that had happened. Or anyone. Just as she wanted to cut Col out of her life, so she wanted to repay the few who had given assistance. And who needed some help themselves.

Which was why she found herself later that afternoon back on Sparrow Street, Blackpool. The CLOSED sign was on the door of the café; the nets were drawn. That wasn't like Florrie Sullivan, Adele thought, walking around to the back entrance. The door was half open, a smell of bleach coming strongly into the yard. It was obvious that there was no cooking going on.

Florrie's sparse little form was humped over a dolly tub. She jumped as she heard Adele's footsteps, flushing to her dyed hair roots.

'Oh, luv, how nice to see yer! I weren't expecting yer.'

'Didn't you get my letter?' Adele asked, noticing the untidiness of the kitchen and the pile of laundry on a chair.

'I got no letter, luv. In fact I were just wondering about yer. Why I hadn't seen yer in over a week.' She was hassled, overwrought. 'I thought maybe yer'd come and seen the café closed and then not come back.'

'Of course I'd come back, Florrie,' Adele replied, searching her face. 'Are you all right?'

'My father's bad. And I can't seem to run the café any more and there's bills up to here . . . ' She trailed off, close to tears. 'It hard fer everyone. Look how yer've struggled . . . '

'That's the point. I'm not struggling any more,' Adele replied, taking the posser out of Florrie's hands. 'I've had a lucky break and I want you to share it with me.'

'Why me?'

'Because you were kind to me when I needed help. Because you let me feed and change Paul here. And dry his nappies.'

'What's a few nappies?'

'*What's a few nappies?*' Adele repeated gently. 'More than you could ever know.'

'Luv, I'd like to help yer, sure I would,' Florrie said, at a loss. 'But I've my dad to think of.'

'You can bring him with you.'

'Bring him with me!'

'Of course,' Adele replied, her tone firm. 'I want you to be my housekeeper, Florrie. You can both live in. God knows, there's enough room. I've inherited a big house — and I aim to run a business from it. So I need you to look after the place for me.' She paused. Florrie was staring at her, transfixed. 'You'll have plenty of help with the heavy work — I just need someone who can cook and take care of me and Paul . . . ' Her voice fell. 'Don't you want to come?'

472

Florrie had sat down heavily at the kitchen table, staring ahead. 'All this, just fer drying a few nappies?'

'No,' Adele replied, 'for being family. When I had no one else.'

★ ★ ★

Stiff-necked, Julia walked up the drive to the big house. She couldn't face telling John about her sister's good fortune and felt ashamed of her own envy. But honestly, she thought rancorously, how lucky was Adele? Conveniently forgetting the hardship her sister had endured — and her own betrayal — Julia stopped on the driveway and stared at the extraordinary house. It was far too big for one woman and a child. She noted the plethora of windows, the unusual carving over the front door, the glint of the copper roof over the conservatory . . . She would have loved to be mistress of a house like this. As a wife and mother . . . But that was never going to happen. John was limited, to say the least, and motherhood seemed to be off the cards for Julia. After she had lost her baby when John walked out, there had been no others.

But, she comforted herself, at least she had a husband around. And, for all his faults, Julia loved John Courtland. Almost as much as he now loved her. It might not be much, but she was Mrs Courtland, while Adele's marriage had failed. Her bitterness embarrassed Julia. She had loved her little sister once; they had gone through so much together. But later jealousy had set in. Competition — on her side, not Adele's. Julia had sympathised with her sister when she ran off. Had been anxious for her, worried about her, thought often of her — but in the end Adele had come back not with her tail between her legs, but as a woman of standing.

The gossips would still talk. People would still judge Adele and make spiteful remarks, but Julia knew only too well how the world worked. Adele was the mistress of the big house now; her sins would be lessened by her status, remarks once made within her hearing now muted, hidden. Bricks and mortar had carried her up on to the moral high ground. Dear God, Julia thought cynically, her sister could probably commit murder now and get away with it.

Slowly Julia's hand reached for the bell. Then she paused. She ached to see Adele again, to talk about the past, when they were young and struggling and yet full of possibilities. She wanted to hold hands with her sister, as they had done after their parents had died. She wanted to remember how Adele had bought her that ugly little pot pig when she was so hard up. How she had comforted her in those dreadful days after John walked out . . .

A million words and memories swamped Julia in that moment. But instead of driving her towards her sister, they pushed her away. After all, she thought, they had nothing in common any more. Adele didn't need her, and she certainly didn't want to be patronised. Not that her sister was like that. But what could Adele offer but charity? *Only love* . . . Julia thought, ashamed.

Her hand hovered over the door bell. She couldn't face remembering what she had done. What she had lost. And she couldn't face playing second fiddle. So she turned away and headed back down the drive. She had almost reached the gate when she heard her name called.

'*Julia!*'

Turning, she saw Adele shouting for her, then running towards her. Immediately Julia dropped her handbag and put out her arms.

60

May 1934

Nearly eight months had gone by since Adele had moved into Lydgate House. Months which had passed slowly, locked in a cold winter, the building drying out thoroughly, fires lit in many rooms. The constant maintenance had made sure the roof and all the plumbing and piping were sound, but the mechanics of the house were old, the boiler rattling as it lighted, the water pipes banging on the upper floor.

In the back of the house, in a separate area, lived Kitty and Stan, in their rooms, and Florrie and her father 'Sniper' in theirs. Apparently he had got the sobriquet after managing to shoot down dozens of Germans, but Florrie wasn't convinced.

'More like bloody pigeons,' she said curtly.

Although Sniper was approaching eighty and confined to a wheelchair, he was not a man who liked to be idle. Adept with his hands, he had offered to restore some furniture for Adele, and although she was reluctant at first, he had proved to be very able. Dave Lin — now living in the old stables — would take the piece up to Sniper's rooms and lay it on a trestle table, the old man wheeling himself over to it and nodding authoritatively. Life at the café in Blackpool had bored him, but now he was working again, a magnifying glass strapped over the left lens of his glasses, his old-fashioned smoking cap perched on the back of his head. Meanwhile, Florrie was keeping house and cooking, while Kitty was running the shop at the front of the house. Her son Terry was only a couple of months old.

'You don't have to work such long hours,' Adele had told her. 'Take some time off.'

'Oh, I don't want time off!' Kitty had replied, horror-struck. 'I like being busy, and I can't hang around a baby all day.'

Her husband however, didn't like being busy. In fact, Stan was achingly slow. His virtue lay in doing the garden. For a man born and bred in the Hanky Park slums, he was surprisingly good with plants. The heavy work Stan loathed; the mowing, the rolling of the lawns was met with a sullen look and muttered curses. But the planting out was another matter.

'Look at these,' he said, calling Adele over to the greenhouse. 'I reckon yer'll have more dahlias than yer'll know what to do with next year.'

Gently she touched the head of a flower. 'What about vegetables?'

'They'd look a bugger in a vase.'

She pulled a face. 'But we could all *eat* them.'

'Yer don't want veggies in this garden!' he told her. 'Rows of bloody spuds! Who wants that? Yer want roses and azaleas.'

'And carrots,' Adele said practically. 'Don't forget the carrots.'

It was a struggle to maintain the house, but nothing compared to what she had endured before. It had taken her a while to organise the two large front rooms into showplaces for her furniture and goods. She reasoned that if people could see the antiques in a home environment they might be able to picture them more easily in their own houses. The trouble was getting the word out. She couldn't advertise, and she certainly wasn't putting up any signs on the house or the drive. Instead she was relying on word of mouth, which was proving slow.

Preoccupied, she moved back into the house. The coolness welcomed her as the day was stuffy, the doorbell breaking into her thoughts.

'Turner!' she said with delight. 'Come in. I haven't seen you for days.'

Taking off his hat, he moved into the shop portion of the house, looking round admiringly. All the ambitions Adele had had since a child were beginning to come to fulfilment. Her clever eye for furnishings and paintings had transformed two superb entertaining rooms into salons. A very new approach, very original for the times . . . Slowly he looked around. People were talking about Adele yet again. Staying how it was a disgrace, how she must have something on the Vincent family to have inherited the house from Mary. No one believed for an instant that she had come by it honestly. They already believed her to be an adulteress, a woman who would pass off a bastard child — so how could someone like that be lucky by chance?

But how could anyone *not* see how honourable she was? Turner thought incredulously. How could anyone, looking into Adele's face, *not* realise she was a good person?

478

'Very stylish.'

'But a bit quiet,' she replied, smiling and handing Turner some lemonade.

'That's welcome,' he said, draining the glass and holding it out to be refilled. 'I've been to the auction in Leeds.'

'Was it good? Was it busy? How many there? Was there any china?'

He smiled. The old Adele was back. All her enthusiasm had returned, her eagerness for the business.

'They had a nice supper table. Georgian.'

'You bought it, Turner!' she said, laughing, 'How many supper tables have you got now?'

'I sold one last month.'

'Which leaves about ten,' she teased him. 'Honestly, you're like my father — only he had an obsession with washstands.'

'I bought a military chest too,' Turner continued, looking round. 'Which would look good in here.'

'How much?'

'Make me an offer when you see it,' he replied. 'I'll send Dave round with it tomorrow.'

Without making it obvious, Turner watched Adele as she poured herself some lemonade. Her rise in status had had the strangest effect. There was no arrogance about her, no gloating — she just seemed at home. The strange old house didn't faze her; she belonged there. It was, Turner realised, quite simply her home.

'You look pensive.'

'I was thinking,' he said, smiling. 'I saw French Kettering. He said he'd popped by.'

'Oh yes, he 'popped by' all right,' Adele replied. 'He came in here, rooting around like he was trying to find a gas leak. He offered me so many congratulations on my good fortune — all the while looking like he wanted to knife me.'

Turner laughed. 'Morris Devonshire took the news well too.' They both laughed. 'Did you never suspect?'

'What?' Adele asked, wrong-footed.

'About Mary Vincent. Did you *never* suspect she was on your side?'

'I knew she *wanted* to be on my side. She was so isolated in a way. Her husband and son didn't understand her at all. I think they were in awe of her, but it was so sad, because there was no connection between them. I used to wonder what Mary's childhood had been like, and when I read her letter about Ninette Hoffman, it all clicked into place.'

Turner frowned. 'How?'

'Mary was punished for showing compassion. Afterwards she felt it, but she didn't dare to show it. Not with adults. With children, yes. She adored Paul, worshipped him. But with adults there was this crushing reserve.' Adele paused, thinking back. 'Funnily enough, I miss her.'

'People didn't get close to Mary,' Turner replied. 'Ernest was always the kind one.'

Adele flinched at the mention of her father-in-law's name. Turner noted the reaction with interest. He had waited for Adele to confide in him more. To explain how life had been with Col at Oakham Lodge. But she never had. Instead it was as though — having escaped

480

— she wanted to put more and more distance between her past and her present. Neither her husband nor her in-laws were mentioned. In fact, Turner had thought often, it was as though Adele had never really lived that portion of time. But *why* she had so ruthlessly dismissed it, he didn't know. And he wanted to. In fact, to his growing amazement, Turner realised that he wanted to know all about her.

'What's the matter?'

'About what?' Adele replied lightly.

'About Ernest Vincent.'

'He wasn't what he seemed,' she said at last, fidgeting and getting to her feet again. 'I love this place so much, Turner. And it's coming together well. Not overnight, but in time I'll have a real reputation in the business. As for Paul, he'll really have something to inherit one day. When I'm gone.'

'That's a long way off!' Turner replied, surprised. 'I never thought you were the morbid type.'

'I'm not morbid, I'm realistic.'

'You're only in your twenties — '

'I've heard *you* talk of death before,' Adele remonstrated. 'And you're what? Fifty? You don't even look it.'

'I'm grey.'

'That's your *hair*,' she said, laughing. 'Your face is still young.'

But he suddenly felt very old.

'Talking about death is different for me, Adele. I was in the war. I saw death all around me. We lived with it then — the thought that it might happen to any of us, at any time. It was so close, it was familiar ... But you don't have that excuse. And you should be thinking about life.'

'I am,' she replied firmly. 'I have my son, my business, and this marvellous place.'

'Which is a house. Not a life.'

She paused, then walked to the window. 'For a man who is understanding about many things, why is it so hard for you to realise what this place means to me? I feel safe here, Turner. I feel complete. I have friends around me, help. Familiar faces — and most importantly, my son. What else could I possibly want?'

Turner struggled with the next words. 'Most people would say that their lives were nothing without a partner, without someone to share things with.'

She turned back to him, her tone gentle. 'You had Clemmie, you loved her and she loved you. You had a happy marriage, Turner, good times to remember ... You think about love and you think about contentment, security, happiness. I think about love and I feel only confusion. Even fear.'

His voice hardened. 'If I ever meet Col again — '

'I don't think you will,' Adele replied hurriedly. 'From what I've gathered, he won't come back to this country.'

'But why would he go abroad anyway?' Turner persisted.

His usual patience was dissolving fast. He wanted to understand and he couldn't, because he didn't know the whole story. And he was also confused by how much he *wanted* to know. It wasn't his business. He would never normally interfere in a friend's life. But somehow he couldn't stop himself.

'Why *did* Col leave England, Adele?'

'I don't know.'

'I think you do,' Turner replied, pushing her.

'He used to live in Italy.'

'That must have been before we became friends,' Turner replied, musing. 'But why go back there?'

Unnerved, Adele became restless. Why was he asking her all these questions? This was Turner, the one person who was too well mannered to pressurise anyone. So why wouldn't he back off? She couldn't tell him about Col, about his first wife. About the fake marriage — or his illegitimate son.

'I don't know any more, Turner.'

'Of course you do.'

'I *don't!*' she snapped, then moved over to a small chest, changing the subject. 'Look at this, isn't it perfect? I think I might have a buyer . . . '

'Why did Col go abroad? And why did you react so badly when I mentioned Ernest?'

'I've got a beautiful card table coming too,' Adele went on hurriedly. 'Quite the best.'

'I don't want to talk about card tables!' Turner retorted hotly.

'Well I don't want to talk about anything else!'

'So you're just going to ignore that part of your life, are you?' he went on. 'Just going to pretend nothing happened? No husband? No past? For God's sake, Adele — '

'No, for my sake!' she snapped. 'For my sake, and my son's. Back off, Turner.'

Angry, he stood up and walked over to her. 'Adele, I have never pressed you before, but I want to understand. I never believed what you told me in that letter. Or what people said about you. I have always known you were a good and honest person. But I can't seem to get you to trust me.'

'It's not that!'

'So what is it? I introduced you to Col. You must know that I feel some responsibility for that. Just as I regret all you suffered afterwards.'

'*You* did nothing to hurt me.'

'Well, *you're* hurting me.'

Stunned, she glanced at him. '*How?* How am I hurting you?'

'By not trusting me,' he replied, shaking his head. 'I know there was a reason for everything you did. For running off, for all those lies, for ruining your own reputation. You say it was to stop Col coming after you, but that's not the whole story, is it?'

'Forgive me, Turner, but I want you to go now,' Adele said, turning away. 'I'm sorry, I really am. But I want you to go . . . I'm happy and safe again. I want to stay that way. I've got my son and my house — '

'It's bricks and mortar, Adele!' he shouted, startling her as she spun round. 'Bricks and mortar! No one loves a building unless they're dead inside. You talk about the Lydgate Widow, you think Ninette was a heroine. She was empty. Aching inside. She was the most beautiful woman I ever saw, and the most unhappy. She was dead long before she stopped breathing. Dead from disappointment and loss. *I don't want you to turn into her.* Admire someone, by all means, but not *her.* Not her life. You think she was safe — that she had the big stone wall to keep the people she loved in and the rest of the world out. She did. And now you have it . . . But be careful, Adele, don't make a friend of a ghost and a lover of a dead house.'

Turning, he left, the front door echoing as he slammed it closed behind him.

61

Frowning, Kitty glanced over to Adele. 'What's up?'

'Nothing.'

'Must be summat. Yer've got a face like a twisted plimsoll.'

Kitty was busy locking the front doors and windows and making the rooms safe for the night. There were too many valuables around to risk a burglary. Walking into the hall, she could hear Adele following her, the net curtain over the landing window fluttering in the evening breeze.

'Stan's still outside,' Kitty said with relief. 'Thank God, gives me more time for myself before Terry wakes up.' She glanced over her shoulder towards Adele, still standing silently in the hall. 'I were going to take Terry over to the fair on Saturday. D'you want me to take Paul too? Yer look like yer need some time on yer own.'

Frowning, Adele glanced up to her. 'Do you like it here, Kitty?'

'Sure do!' She hurried on. 'Why, yer not happy with us? Yer don't like — '

'I love everything you and Stan do,' Adele replied, interrupting her. 'No complaints at all. Florrie's the perfect housekeeper. Even Sniper's earning his keep.'

'So?' Kitty asked, folding her arms. 'When people count what they have, it's usually 'cos they want to convince themselves they're not missing out.'

Adele nodded her head. 'Very smart, Kitty.'

'Yer missing out on summat?'

'I didn't think so,' she admitted, confused. 'Until today I thought I had everything I ever wanted.'

'Yer going to let someone change yer mind fer yer?'

'Not without putting up a fight,' Adele replied, her tone firm. 'Not without putting up a damn good fight.'

★ ★ ★

Becky had to admit that Lydgate House was a long way from The Coppice or Hawkshead Pike. Now a regular visitor to the house, her friendship with Adele had deepened over the previous months. There was no jealousy on Becky's part. She was more than content with her husband and her daughter and celebrated Adele's good fortune.

'I think,' Becky said, watching her baby daughter in the garden with Paul and Kitty, 'that your son is going to turn out to be a gentleman.'

'Which is more than his father ever was,' Adele replied, uncharacteristically tart.

'Ouch! What brought that on?'

'It's Turner . . . ' Adele replied, irritated. 'We had an argument about Col.'

'Oh.'

'He was asking so many questions, prying. Asking about Col and the past. Can you believe it? *Turner*, of all people!'

'Unbelievable,' Becky replied, her exotic face impassive as ever. 'After all, if he hadn't found out where you were, you wouldn't have this place. Without him you wouldn't have learned so much about antiques. Wouldn't ever have had a mentor . . .'

Slowly Adele turned. 'You're right, I should trust him.'

'You've told *me* everything that happened to you. Why not tell Turner?'

'I *can't* tell him,' Adele replied. 'Look, you and I go back a long way. We know everything about each other. God, Becky, we were kids together.'

'And how long have you known Turner? Almost as long as you've known me.' Becky paused, leaning back into her chair. 'He deserves to be told the truth.'

'Why? He was angry enough about Col when I told him he was violent. What good would it do to confide the rest?'

'What good does it do *not* to confide?'

Adele shrugged. The question was an awkward one. 'I don't want Turner to know that my life was a sham. That Paul is really illegitimate. That I was never married . . . God, what if it came out, Becky? I could never hold my head up again.'

'You let people think you were an adulteress.'

'There was a reason for that!'

'To keep Col away,' Becky said, nodding. 'I know. But Col isn't going to come back, Adele. You've told me that. Turner knows that. So why are you holding on to a man you say you hate?'

488

'I'm not holding on to Col Vincent!'

'You are,' Becky replied, her tone impassive. 'You want it both ways. You say that you've taken over from the Lydgate Widow, because your husband is dead to you. But you let everyone else think you're still married to him. So yes, Adele, I think you are still holding on to him.'

'Paul is safe this way . . . '

Becky leaned forward in her seat. 'But what if you want to marry someone else?'

'I don't!'

'You might, one day.'

'No, Becky. I don't want a man near me again,' Adele replied, turning back to the window. 'God, you sound like Turner.'

'Poor Turner.'

'Why *poor Turner?*' Adele questioned. 'A friend should understand. You do.'

'Yes, but I'm not in love with you.'

'What are you talking about?' Adele asked, moving over to Becky, her face set. 'Turner isn't in love with me. He's my friend. He's my mentor. Turner taught me . . . ' She threw up her hands impatiently. 'Turner is . . . *Turner.*'

'For a clever woman, Adele, you're stupid about men,' Becky said gently. 'Now, if my grandmother had still been alive, she would have told you the same. Frida knew all about love, and men.'

'You're talking about *Turner!*'

'And what's Turner, if not a man? A successful, attractive, honourable man at that.' Becky paused, then took a different tack. 'Adele, look at me and tell me that you've never once thought of him romantically.'

Adele paused, confused. Until recently she *had* never thought of Turner as anything other than a friend. But their conversation weeks earlier — compounded by their recent argument — had made her think. To her surprise, it seemed that Turner Gades was a rather intense man. Not showy, not temperamentally capricious like Col. But a man with very strong feelings underneath a veneer of composure.

'I . . . I did wonder about some of the things he said,' she admitted at last. 'He was talking about love, about companionship being so important. I thought he was talking indirectly about Clemmie, but . . . '

'*But?*'

'He was telling me about the Lydgate Widow. Warning me, if you like. Insisting that there was more to life than this place and wanting to be safe.' Adele flushed, unexpectedly discomforted. 'Of course I wondered about what he said! But I pushed it to the back of my mind. Then he was angry that I wouldn't trust him. Said I had *hurt* him . . . I did wonder afterwards why it mattered so much to him.' She glanced at Becky and then glanced away again. 'Oh, forget it! I can't get it right with men. I pick the wrong ones, I don't know why. But Turner isn't for me . . . I can't make another mistake, Becky. I can't trust my choices.'

'*You* didn't make the choice,' Becky replied evenly. 'Turner did. I think he's loved you for a long time, and didn't realise it until now.'

'When I saw him the other day, when he was

so angry . . . ' Adele paused, reluctantly admitting her feelings. 'I *did* see him differently. He was suddenly so fiery, so full of life. And I wanted him to stay. When he walked out, I wanted to run after him . . . ' She shook her head as though trying to shake off the feelings. 'I wanted to touch him . . . '

'And you're telling me that you're not in love with him?'

'Oh, I don't know!' Adele exploded, exasperated. 'I don't know what love means. I loved Sam Ayres, I loved Col . . . '

'Do you miss either of them?'

'No.'

'But what if Turner was to walk out of your life and never come back? What if you never saw *him* again?'

'I would be lost . . . ' Adele said softly, stunned by the admission.

Smiling sympathetically, Becky asked: 'So what are you going to do about it?'

'Nothing. What can I do? Anyway, if Turner cares about me, why has he never said anything?'

'Perhaps he thought he was too old.'

'Too old!' Adele laughed. 'He's not old.'

'Be sure to tell him that,' Becky retorted. 'Because I'd think the age difference is worrying him a lot.'

Incredulous, Adele stared at her friend. 'How d'you know what I feel? What he feels?'

'Come on, Adele!' Becky retorted. 'Forget what *I've* been saying, think about what *you've* been saying — and what *Turner's* been saying. A man doesn't talk about love to a woman he thinks of as a friend. He's not Samuel Ayres, or Col, or Ernest Vincent for that matter. Turner Gades is not what you've been used to — but that's no reason to mistrust him and turn your back on him. I know what Frida would have said if she was here now: *Don't reject gold because you've only ever had brass before.*'

'But what if you're wrong?' Adele said desperately. 'I can't risk it, Becky. I just can't! I'm safe now, I don't want any more traumas, any more heartbreak.'

'It's your choice now,' Becky replied. 'But if you have to lose someone, let it be through war, or sickness — but not through lack of courage. Cowardice has never been your way.'

62

Still in his dressing gown at two in the afternoon, Ernest Vincent ignored the phone ringing in the hallway. Let them call and keep calling, he thought bitterly, what did he care? Blundering forward, he moved into the drawing room of Oakham Lodge, looking round. Nothing meant a damn thing any more. His life had been a waste, a complete mess. He had put in an amateur performance, and he *hated* amateurs. Catching his reflection in the mirror over the fireplace, Ernest regarded the balding, puffy-faced man who looked back at him so unattractively. No wonder Adele had run a mile; no wonder Mary had been barely able to tolerate him — he was a joke, a seedy caricature. In the end his mock kindness had done him no favours. His efforts had been for nothing. All his machinations — so carefully plotted — had been sterile. He was never going to be loved — and anyway, what the bugger did it matter any more?

Unaccustomed to being drunk, Ernest weaved around the room, limp with self-pity. He had only one clear thought — that he wanted revenge. Of course revenge on Mary was out of the question. She was well beyond his reach. But he could still get his own back on his son. On Col, and on Adele. It would serve them both right for rejecting him. Col for using his father

493

and then leaving him, Adele for being repelled by his offer of love ... Ernest belched, his mouth momentarily full of bile. Of course no one would expect it of him. Not Ernest Vincent. Hadn't he always been a kind man? The benign figure everyone trusted? Stupid bastards! Ernest railed, bumping into the side of a Georgian table. He would show people what he was really like, flash his true colours before it was too late.

Stumbling into his chair by the desk, Ernest grabbed some paper and began to write.

Dear Col,

I am writing to tell you that I am ill and not expected to live more than a year. As we are not close, I doubt this news will cause you much distress, but one thing which will interest you is that I am going to sell the business. You have no objection, I trust? Especially as you will profit nicely from the arrangement. Which will make up for your mother's decision to give Lydgate House to Adele and your son.

He smiled to himself, greedy with spite.

Adele is not some poor victim any more. And she has an admirer, Col. The very person who introduced you. Turner Gades has been calling at the house in Lydgate and playing with your son. I'm afraid the clever girl has you over a barrel. I mean, you can hardly object, can you? Not with so much to lose. So many secrets you made me keep, Col, and for what in the end?

494

Probably better that Adele knows everything now.

Ernest paused, thinking back, remembering how he had manipulated Adele into marrying his son. All the careful enticement, playing on her youth, her inexperience, her compassion — and on Col's nervous breakdown. Never mentioning that he was already married. But then how *could* Ernest have let Adele know that? If she had known, she would never have married Col, or come to Oakham Lodge. Would never have been under Ernest's roof so he could watch her, enjoy her, for years.

Trying to focus, Ernest continued to write.

Incidentally, I got your letter and I'm sorry that your Italian marriage is over.

He was smirking as he wrote. Poor Col, now his first wife didn't want him. For all his looks and appeal, his son was as useless with women as he was. Slowly, Ernest formed the next words, the black ink joining up the syllables which would cause such exquisite — and intended — pain.

Seems like you have very little luck with your wives! Mind you, like father, like son.

I will be in touch again soon.

Regards,

Your father

★ ★ ★

Missing his bid at the auction, Turner glanced over to a triumphant French Kettering with his young male lover in tow. The dealer was grinning, nodding at Turner with glee as the hammer came down. *I got the ormolu mirror,* his look said. *I won.*

Turner had a momentary impulse to tell Kettering where he could put the mirror, but instead he turned away, pretending to read the auction catalogue. Row after row of Sèvres plates, indifferent portraits and English furniture met his eye. His *jaded* eye, because for once, Turner wasn't interested in antiques. He was interested in why he was feeling so nettled, so out of sorts. And all since he had fought with Adele.

Of course he had no right to tell her what to do. A friend didn't order another friend around. Or pry. Or preach to them about love . . . He flushed suddenly, staring at the catalogue in a welter of confusion. What *was* the matter with him? He was acting so oddly, so childishly. He had never behaved this way before. Shooting a quick glance over to French Kettering, Turner noticed the look which was being exchanged between Kettering and his lover.

The expression went straight to Turner's heart and lodged. It was unmistakable. He wasn't a stupid man, he knew love when he saw it. *And when he felt it* . . . He kept his gaze fixed on the catalogue, apparently mesmerised by the photograph of a Dutch vase. Did he love Adele? God, *did* he love her? He couldn't, he told himself, he hadn't felt like this when he was married to

496

Clemmie. But Clemmie had been older than him, an elegant, kind-hearted woman, not a feisty female in her twenties. *In her twenties* . . . The thought pounded into him. He couldn't expect Adele to be interested in him. He was too old for her. Any relationship between them was impossible.

In that instant Turner finally accepted that he had been thinking the exact same thoughts for weeks. It was no good lying to himself. Pretending he hadn't considered the age gap or the love he felt for Adele. The passion aroused just by hearing her name. He was in love. If he wasn't, he wouldn't have remembered the way she had pinned up her hair the other day. Or the way she always pushed up her cuffs when she was busy. If he wasn't in love he wouldn't have noticed the mole on the back of her neck, or the way she could whistle, piercing a man's eardrums at ten paces.

If he wasn't in love he wouldn't want to march over to the house in Lydgate and kick the door open . . . Oh God, Turner thought, mortified, what was he thinking? He wasn't a Neanderthal, he was a civilised man. He had to control himself. But why? he asked himself, impatiently. What for?

Standing up, Turner tossed his catalogue on to his seat and made for the door. His life had changed in the instant he had admitted to himself that he loved Adele. Now everything had altered. The auction was boring. His fellow dealers were tiresome. The world was achingly, screamingly dull.

Because she wasn't with him.

63

Docking at Liverpool, Col Vincent made his way to Rochdale by car, arriving in the early hours of 12 August. The roads were quiet, only a few other vehicles travelling, the moon full bellied, the planets high-riding. His plan had been to stay in Italy, and he would have done just that had it not been for his father's letter. A letter which had arrived out of the blue, shimmering with bitter news. A letter which was poisonous with hate.

Driving fast, Col put his foot on the brake to slow down. The roads were familiar to him, and unwelcome. He had not wanted to come back to the north of England, to the place which had such uneasy memories for him. It was true that he had run away, but why not? What possible reason was there for him to stay? His father didn't really need him. In fact, to Col's surprise, after Adele left, Ernest seemed to lose all interest in his son. So Col had returned to his first wife in Italy — and now she had left him too. What a mess, he thought, bewildered. What a bloody mess.

But why had his father sent him that letter? What was the point? The old man was dying, but why should Col care? They had never had an open relationship. Both of them were capricious, manipulative people — although Ernest had taken care never to show that side of his nature.

People accepted that Col was highly strung, moody, but never Ernest . . . So was it because Ernest was near death? Or because he had nothing to lose? His son had left home, his daughter-in-law had gone, taking his grandson — so what did he have left?

Spite, Col thought with amazement. Pure bile was all that remained of his father. Why else would he write to tell his son about Turner Gades? Col already knew about his mother leaving the house to Adele. But as Ernest said, he could hardly object. Adele was keeping his secrets — it was bound to cost him something in the end. But to torment him with the news of Turner Gades, to know that his old friend was sniffing around his wife and child — it was too much on top of everything that had happened. And his father knew it. Realised that in telling Col, he was torturing him with the fact that he had lost. And Adele knew everything.

Pulling up at the kerb, Col turned off the car engine. Dawn was breaking on the horizon and he was only an hour away from his home. Only sixty minutes. Overcome, he laid his head on the steering wheel and clenched his teeth. What was he doing? What had he come back for? He couldn't get revenge on Adele. If he tried to damage her, she could destroy him. Bigamy meant years in an English jail. And shame; Col Vincent relegated to being an outcast.

Turn back, a voice said inside his head. Turn back while you still can . . .

But Col had been headstrong too long. He

had been wilful all his life, reckless, acting on impulse without thinking more than twenty-four hours ahead. He didn't know what he was going to do; only that he was angry. That he felt belittled, betrayed. At no point did he admit to *why* Adele had left him, why she had run off and taken their child. At no point did he take any blame for the way his life had turned out. He just sat in his expensive car, his head on the steering wheel, and brooded.

One thing only was certain in his mind — he was back. And no one was going to forget it.

★　★　★

Sleeping uneasily, Adele opened her eyes and then looked at her son, nestling in the crook of her arm. Usually she didn't allow Paul to sleep with her, but that night he had been unusually restless and only became quiet when he lay with his mother. In the back of the house Adele could hear a toilet cistern flushing, and thought suddenly of the terrible days in the Morecambe boarding house. When Paul had been a baby, crying incessantly with colic, the sea wind blowing relentlessly against the salt-ingrained windows.

Shuddering, Adele got up, putting pillows around Paul to stop him from rolling out of bed. The room was stuffy, smelling of lilies, as she padded into the bathroom and turned on the light. What was troubling her? she wondered, splashing her face with cold water. Maybe it was just too hot to sleep . . . Moving back into the bedroom, she checked on Paul and then decided to go downstairs.

The moon light flooded in as she moved down the staircase, automatically checking that the doors which led to the shop rooms were locked. They were. Relieved, Adele then checked the front door, which was also locked. Of course it was, she thought, Kitty or Stan locked up every night, checked everywhere was safe.

Still unsettled, she moved into the kitchen, smelling the aroma of apple pie as she pushed the door open. That was just what she needed, something to eat, then she would go back to sleep. Walking to the fridge, Adele could see the vast shadow of the horse chestnut tree outside, huge in the moonlight, and heard a fox barking in the distance. Taking out the pie, she cut herself a piece and ate it hungrily. But her mood still didn't lift.

After another few minutes she decided to go back to bed and made for the kitchen door, turning off the light. The hall seemed very dark and she paused to get her bearings, then moved towards the staircase. Moonlight from the landing window pooled down the stairs as she walked up the first few steps.

And then she saw him. Standing in the moonlight.

'Col!' She stepped back, her heart hammering. 'What are you doing here? How did you get in?'

He didn't say anything. Just stared at her as he used to, as intimidating as ever.

Adele could feel her hands sweating, her grip

slipping on the banister rail — and then she turned and ran, as fast as she could, down the stairs. At the bottom she snapped on the light, her hand shaking as she struggled with the door lock. Frantically she tried to open it, but couldn't. Panicked, she turned to look behind her.

There was no one there.

64

'I tell you, it was him!' Adele repeated vehemently, shaking as she paced the floor. 'I saw him, standing up there on the landing. It was Col.'

Baffled, Turner walked back out into the hall and then moved up the staircase. He had been amazed when Adele had called him, asking him to come over. Unusually panicked, she had been almost incoherent, only calming down long enough to tell him that her husband had returned to England. To her house. In the early hours.

That had been enough for Turner. He had driven over as fast as he could to find Adele restless, Paul asleep in a chair in the room with her.

'He was here . . . '

'Are you sure you weren't dreaming?'

'Do I look hysterical to you?' she asked, then calmed her tone. 'I saw him, Turner. I swear it. *Col was in this house.*'

'Did anyone else see him?'

She shook her head. 'No, no one else knows he was here. I don't want them to know. I just called you.'

He paused. *Adele had called on him.* When she could have turned to the others, she had called on him. That meant something, surely?

'How could he have got in, Adele?'

'His mother owned this house once. Maybe he had a key.'

Turner nodded. 'What did he say to you?'

'Nothing,' Adele replied, dropping her voice. 'I just saw him . . . ' She shuddered. 'Then I turned on the light and he wasn't there any more.'

'Are you sure it was him?'

'God, Turner, I'm not hallucinating!' Adele replied frantically. 'He was there one minute and gone the next . . . I was so scared, I ran upstairs to check on Paul. Don't look at me like that, Turner! *Col was here.* My husband's back.'

'But why would he come back?' Turner asked her. 'Why now, Adele?'

'I don't know!'

'You must do,' he replied firmly. 'You're terrified of him. Understandably; he was violent. But he's been out of the country for a while now — and you believed he wasn't coming back. So what changed? He's left it a long time to contest the will.'

'He can't contest the will,' Adele said, shaking.

She was beside herself. And no amount of checking on Turner's part had allayed her fears. He might have gone around the house and searched the outbuildings, but it was no consolation. Col had been in the house. She knew it. And it terrified her.

'*Why* can't he contest the will?'

She had no energy left, no will to hide any more. 'Because he has too much to lose.'

'Like what, Adele?'

She turned to him slowly, her voice low so that

no one in the house could possibly overhear.

'Col already had a wife when he married me.'

'*What?*'

'His wife was Italian. Well, she still is. I didn't know anything about it, of course, or I wouldn't have married him. And Ernest was very clever . . . '

Turner didn't understand. 'Where does Ernest come into all of this?'

'He convinced me to marry Col. He told me that Col had had a nervous breakdown and that I was the one special person who could make him happy. He made me feel like it was my duty. He flattered me, kept telling me how much Col loved me.' She paused, glancing over to Paul, who was still sleeping on the sofa. 'He begged me never to talk about Col's past to anyone — even his son. Of course I believed everything he told me. It was only much later that I realised he had been lying all along.'

Turner's face was ashen, his voice incredulous. 'But why?'

'When I left Col, I made for the coast. After a long while, Ernest tracked me down. It was Christmas, and I was so glad to think that I could give Paul a holiday at Oakham Lodge.' She glanced away, the memory sour. 'Ernest told me that Col was abroad and was never coming back, and then . . . and then he said he loved me and that he always had.'

'Jesus,' Turner said softly.

'I got out of that place as fast as I could. But how could I say anything? If I did expose him and his son, everyone would find out that my marriage was a sham.' She paused, fighting tears. 'From the day I left Oakham Lodge, I'd been prepared to do *anything* to stop that coming out. And to keep Paul safe. So what if people thought I was an adulteress, that I had run off with another man? I'd escaped from my husband, that was all that mattered. And I'd got Paul out of danger. Col knew I would never expose him. Just as Ernest did.'

'So why would Col come back now?' Turner asked, moving over to Adele and touching her arm. 'You should have told me about this!'

'How could I?' she replied. 'We were friends, but not *that* close. You were married to Clemmie, I worked for you at the Failsworth shop — God, Turner, *how could I tell you?* Especially when you were so friendly with Col and his father.'

Turner's voice was eerily calm. 'I'll pay them back for what they did to you.'

'I just don't want Col anywhere near me, or my child!' She paused, unnerved. 'Why has he come back now, Turner? What for?'

Overcome, he caught hold of her, expecting her to resist. For a long, scintillating moment he caught his breath, and sensed that Adele had too. Then the house seemed to exhale for them, both of them caught in a momentous instant of realisation. *They loved each other.*

Sighing, Adele allowed herself to be held, Turner kissing the top of her head, his feelings almost overwhelming him.

'I won't let anything happen to you. Or to Paul.'

'You don't know Col!' Adele said desperately. 'The marriage was happy at first, but it deteriorated until it was impossible. You have no idea what it's like living with someone like that. Loving them when they're kind — hoping, praying the bad times are over. But they never are. A week later, or a month, and he would be violent again. You spend your life wondering what mood they'll be in. If you'll please them. Anger them. If something you say, or the way you look, will trigger them off. I thought being a father might settle Col down, but it didn't, he got worse.' She shook her head. 'I won't go back to that! And I won't let my child go back there. Col would have ruined Paul's life.'

Distressed, Turner caught hold of her hands. 'God, Adele, this isn't the time or place. Or the way I wanted it to be. But you have to know how much I care about you. There's nothing I wouldn't do for you. Nothing I wouldn't give — '

She was shaking uncontrollably. 'It's no good! Col's back and he'll spoil it.'

'Oh no,' Turner said firmly. 'You're wrong. I love you, and if you love me, you'll trust me when I tell you we can sort this out.' He gripped her hands even tighter. 'Do you love me?'

'What about Col?'

'*Forget him*! Do you love me?' he persisted. 'That's all I need to know. *Do you love me?*'

'Why do you love *me*?' she replied, confused. 'Don't. For your own sake, don't love me. I'm not lucky in love. Never have been. I've told you, Turner, I've tried to warn you off so many times.

I'm still married. Col is still threatening my life.'
She looked into his face tenderly. 'Don't you see,
I can't risk you. I can't risk hurting the one man
who never hurt me. Who believed in me when no
one else did. Who forgave me, stood by me.
Never made me feel stupid or small. You ask me
if I love you — how could I not? How could I
not love you?'

'That's all I needed to know,' Turner replied,
letting go of her hands and moving to the door.
'Lock this after I've gone, Adele, and don't open
it for anyone except me. You understand?'

She ran after him. 'Where are you going?'

'I have to see someone.'

'Don't, Turner. Don't go after Col.'

'I'm not afraid of him,' he said shortly. 'But he
has good reason to be afraid of me.'

65

It was just coming into morning when Turner drove up to Oakham Lodge, Rochdale. Parking his car, he looked around for signs of activity, but saw none. Moving to the back of the property, he glanced round. There was one lamp burning in what he knew was Ernest's study. Angrily he moved to the French doors and rapped. There was no response. He tried the handle. It was open, so he walked in.

Ernest was sitting at his desk, still in his dressing gown, dried food and spittle smearing the front of it. Hearing Turner's entry he looked up, but couldn't focus properly.

'Turner . . . '

'Yes, Turner,' he replied, looking down at Ernest Vincent with disgust. The benign, good-natured businessman whom everyone had liked had dissolved into a crumpled, soiled wreck, his thin hair dirty against his sweating scalp. It was obvious from the overwhelming odour of alcohol that Ernest was drunk, and it looked as though he had been living in his study for days. Around him were burnt-out cigar butts, old sandwich crusts, even a half-bottle of sour milk. Ernest had drunk himself into a stupor. He no longer knew — or cared — what was going on around him.

'Where's your son?'

Ernest's head rocked back as Turner gripped

the sides of his chair and shook it. 'Where's your bloody son!'

'My son . . . ' Ernest mumbled incoherently. 'My son's abroad . . . '

'Col is back in England. Where is he?'

But there was nothing to be got from Ernest Vincent. His eyes closing, he let his head flop forward on to his chest, his breathing laboured. From the number of bottles around him, he had been drinking for weeks, not days. All the antiques he had enjoyed and collected still surrounded him, but they were covered in ring marks from glasses, or greasy fingerprints. Under his bare feet an Aubusson carpet stank of spilt booze and stale urine.

Incredulous, Turner looked about the room. Whatever Ernest had done, it had caught up with him. He was finished. But Col wasn't . . . As he walked into the hall, Turner had no doubt that his old friend was back. A large battered suitcase lay on the floor, an overcoat alongside it. Taking the stairs two at a time, Turner made for Col's rooms, throwing back the doors and walking in. But they were empty. Frustrated, he moved back on to the landing, stopping as he saw Col enter the hall. He was composed, uncannily so, his attractive face tanned from the Mediterranean sun, his eyes betraying nothing.

'Turner, what a surprise.'

Holding Col's gaze, Turner looked him up and down. 'I told you once that if you ever hurt Adele I would make you wish you had never been born.'

'Enter the conquering hero,' Col replied, smirking. 'My father — that old soak — wrote to me while he still could. Told me all about you and Adele. How you'd moved on to my patch, seeing my son . . .'

'The son you didn't give a damn about!' Turner barked. 'As for Adele — how could you?'

'How could I *what*?'

'Marry her when you were married to someone else?'

'She told you!' Col replied. 'Broke my confidence. What was it, Turner, pillow talk?'

'Why don't you come here and say that to my face?'

'The honourable Mr Gades, stealing another man's wife . . .'

'Don't try to make yourself look innocent in any of this,' Turner replied, moving to the head of the stairs. 'You're a wife-beater, Col. You're on a par with the worst Hanky Park lout. You've been spoiled and indulged all your life and where did it get you? The gutter. Adele was so afraid of you she ran off with her son. Fending for herself. Struggling to make a living on her own. Something you never had to do. Did you care? Did you hell as like! You ran off, went back to your first wife. And you knew Adele would keep quiet. You even let her take the blame . . . I can see you now, Col, railing on about how she had cheated on you.' Turner paused, loathing in his voice. 'You knew Adele would keep your secret for Paul's sake.'

Col's tone was one of wounded indignation.

'Well, she hasn't now, has she?'

'Only because you came back,' Turner replied, walking down the stairs. 'That was the worst mistake you've ever made in your life. Apart from crossing me, Col. Apart from betraying me. I thought you were a decent man. Otherwise I would never have introduced you to Adele.'

Col was getting nervous, seeing Turner's approach. Glancing to his right, he looked to see if the front door was open, then nervously glanced back.

'You didn't want her!' he snapped. 'You told me that.'

'You don't understand, do you?' Turner replied, walking over to Col and standing in front of him. 'You just don't understand. You're a liar, a cheat. Not that it's all your fault, your father taught you well, Col. That bastard in the other room has a lot to answer for.'

Thinking he saw some chink in Turner's armour, Col gabbled, 'My father's dying. He's not got long to live.'

'Good,' Turner said simply. 'I've seen a lot of things, but what your father did was despicable.'

Col blinked slowly. He had been so stupid to come back to England. His father was past reasoning with — and now he had to square the whole sordid scenario with Turner. But then again, Turner was a genuinely good man. If he was clever, Col thought slyly, he could still wriggle his way out of this. After all, they had been friends once.

'Look, there's no need for us to fall out . . . '

'Do you know why your father encouraged your marriage to Adele?'

He shrugged sullenly. 'No.'

'He was in love with her himself.'

Turner had the satisfaction of seeing his old friend pale. He thought for an instant Col would pass out, such was his shock. He had been so arrogant, so selfish, so adept at using people himself that he had never considered that *he* had been manipulated too.

'I don't believe you!'

'Of course you don't,' Turner replied coolly. 'Your father was a funny little man. Not attractive to women; they saw him as the fatherly kind. But he fell in love with Adele, and in order to get her, he was utterly ruthless. He surprised me, I have to say,' Turner went on, Col still stunned with disbelief. 'And I know that people aren't always what they seem. But Adele was very young, she would have trusted both of you. She wouldn't have known that you two were bastards until it was too late. And I hate you for that.'

Without another word, Turner struck out. The blow hit Col squarely on the face, his top lip splitting, blood running down his chin and on to the glaring whiteness of his shirt.

Backing away, he put up his hands. 'Jesus! Stop it!'

'Unpleasant, being hit, isn't it? It hurts. But then you didn't know that before — not when *you* were doing all the hitting.'

'Turner, listen to me . . .'

'I want you out of Adele's life,' Turner said,

grasping Col's lapel and jerking him to his feet. 'I want to know that you're gone. Once and for all.'

'She's my wife, you can't have her!' Col snapped, enraged. Desperate to hold on to what he saw as his property. 'And Paul's my son, not yours.'

'You didn't care about them before, why pretend now?'

Mewling with self-pity, Col cringed. He had underestimated Turner and knew it.

'I'll stay away from her.'

'Get out of the country.'

'I've nowhere to go!' Col said pitifully. 'There's nothing left for me in Italy, my wife threw me out.'

'I don't give a shit!' Turner snapped. 'You can wander around like a nomad for a while. Like Adele did. You can see what it feels like to have no one to turn to. No home . . . '

'I've got a home! *This* is my home.'

Turner's grip tightened. 'If you stay here, I'll call the police. You'll be charged with bigamy. And that means a long jail sentence.'

'If you exposed me, you'd expose Adele!' Col blustered. 'And everyone would know that Paul is a bastard.'

Pulling Col even closer, Turner stared at him menacingly. '*I don't care, Col.* You do your worst and I'll do mine. And we both know who'll come out the best. You think you can threaten exposure? Go ahead. What the world thinks about Adele and Paul doesn't matter to me. I know what *I* think; the rest is less than nothing.' He smiled coldly. 'You're finished, Col. You've no family, no home. You've got exactly what you deserve . . . Now, make a run for it, like the bloody coward you are. Because I'm warning you, if I ever see you again, your life will be over.'

66

The following morning Adele woke very early, turning over in bed and thinking about what Turner had told her. Col had gone. He was out of her life for ever. He wouldn't dare to harm her, or expose her. She was free. And more than that, she knew how much Turner loved her. As much as she loved him . . . Rolling over on to her back, Adele stared upwards, for the first time allowing herself to picture a future with Turner in her life. She thought then of Paul, her beloved son. How much he liked Turner, and how easy they were together. Could it be possible that they might one day be a family? It would be complicated because of the circumstances, but it might well be possible . . . Smiling, Adele pulled the covers over her head. She was being fanciful, giddy. But it felt good. Felt wonderful to have a man she could rely on. A man she admired, rather than feared.

It was so different from her relationship with Col. Then she had always been on edge, trying to pacify or soothe him. She had put him first until she became ephemeral; someone he could bully and intimidate, with no other use in life. But now she felt whole, comfortable with Turner, and — now she admitted it — attracted to him. Of course she must have seen it before, but suppressed it. Maybe they had loved each other for years without acknowledging it. And now, finally, it was out in the open. She was in love with Turner Gades, and he loved her.

Restless, Adele slid out of bed, surprised that for once Paul hadn't joined her as he usually did in the early hours. Silently she pushed the adjoining door to his nursery fully open and tiptoeing over to his bed, smiled at the unmoving little figure under the blankets. He was fast asleep. Gently she pulled back the covers to kiss him — and then flinched. *Paul wasn't there.* Panicked, she tore off the sheet and blanket, looking under the bed, calling out for him.

'Paul! Paul, where are you?' she shouted, running out into the corridor and looking down the stairs.

Had he woken and gone wandering about by himself? That wasn't like him. Hurriedly she ran downstairs looking into the hall below. But there was no sign of him. Dawn had broken and the first light was turning the morning from dark into a misty autumn day. Terrified, Adele ran into the drawing room, calling for her son. Then into the study, calling Paul's name repeatedly. Maybe he had gone into the other part of the house to find Kitty, she thought, moving quickly towards the stairs at the back of the house.

The misty pale morning light fell into the kitchen suddenly and mottled the black and white floor tiles. Adele stopped in her tracks as she saw the back door open. Rigid, she moved towards it, the garden beckoning. Her bare feet were chilled on the tiles as she stepped from the kitchen into the garden, the soft sound of creaking coming eerily through the haze. Blindly she stepped forward, the huge horse chestnut tree looming out of the mist, the creaking louder. She looked up, shaking.

Above her head hung Col, his face distorted, his tongue protruding from his mouth. And beneath him, playing with his toys, was Paul, his father's body swinging only feet above his head.

67

It was Kitty who told Turner what had happened. How she had woken to hear Adele screaming, then seen her run inside, holding Paul and soothing him. Her face had been drained, her hands white as she held her child to her, rocking him. Hearing the disturbance, Dave Lin had come round from the back, meeting Kitty just as she walked out of the kitchen. Together they had seen the old tree and the body of Col Vincent.

'Christ!' Stan had said, emerging beside his wife, the mist swirling around the three of them. 'What did he go and do that fer?'

Without saying a word, Dave Lin cut the body down, Col flopping over the Chinaman's shoulder.

'We'd best get the police,' Stan said. Kitty was staring into Col's bloated face.

'The bastard . . . Paul were out here with him.'

'*What?*'

'He took Paul from his room and brought him out here. To watch . . . Dump the bastard in the outbuildings,' she said to Dave, walking back into the house and calling Turner.

Like all of them, he was shaken. 'Stay with Adele. I'll be over as soon as possible.'

'Good.'

'You said . . . ' Turner struggled with the image, ' . . . Paul saw his father hang?'

'Yeah,' Kitty said, repulsed. 'Beats all, doesn't it? I come from the slums and I never seen anything like it.'

Adele was still nursing Paul when Turner arrived. He walked in, sat beside her and put his arms around them both. Paul was mute, staring ahead, Adele little more than a ghost, still barefoot, cold to the touch.

'I've called the doctor,' Turner said gently, kissing the top of Adele's head.

Had *he* done this? he thought desperately. Had he, indirectly, caused Col's suicide? No, he told himself, Col Vincent had killed himself in an act of revenge . . . But to take his child to witness his end — that was beyond belief.

'Paul?' Adele said softly, looking into her son's face. 'Are you all right, baby?'

He nodded, leaning against her, his eyes closing. Over the top of her son's head, Adele looked at Turner. Her expression was one of such suffering he thought his heart might stop. In her eyes was grief, anger, incredulity. She said nothing, but she didn't have to. He could read it in her face as easily as if she had written it up on a blackboard: *I could have lost my son.*

'We'll get through this,' Turner said gently, getting to his feet as the doctor was shown in. 'Adele, remember, we'll get through this.'

★   ★   ★

She was very cold, colder than she had ever been. Dully, Adele could hear people talking around her: Kitty's voice, Stan's, and then the

520

doctor's. And Turner's, concerned, strong. She heard them all, saw them moving about. But louder than anything else was the sound of the rope creaking as it swung on the branch. And clearer than anything else was the sight of her son, sitting underneath his father's body. Christ, she thought desperately, of all the despicable things Col had ever done, this was the worst. Outwardly still, Adele glanced at her son. Would he remember? Was he old enough to remember? For the image to haunt him?

Interrupting her thoughts, the doctor leaned down to her suddenly. 'I'll just take a look at Paul.'

'No!' she snapped. 'Don't take him from me.'

'I just need to check him over,' the doctor replied, sensing Adele's terror. 'You hold him, I can check him whilst he's on your knee.'

Rocking Paul, Adele watched the doctor examine him.

'Your son isn't injured.'

'Not where it shows.'

'What about you?'

'I'm fine,' Adele replied, her tone dull. 'I just want to be alone with Paul.'

Nodding, the doctor turned to Turner and whispered something she couldn't hear. But she didn't care anyway. She didn't want to hear anything else. She had heard enough for a lifetime. All she wanted now was silence. Safety and silence, with her son.

'Adele,' Turner said, touching her shoulder, 'I'm going to sort everything out. You just rest with Paul.'

She looked up at him without expression, a stupid, irrational thought striking her. This was her punishment. Col had maimed her with his death. Had managed to mark her, and possibly their son, with an image so dreadful it could never be wiped out. And she had believed she could be happy. That she had found a good man, a surrogate father for her son. How *could* she have believed such nonsense? Adele thought helplessly. Life didn't have happy endings.

Another thought struck her, making the hair stand up on the back of her neck. *The Lydgate Widow*, Ninette Hoffman. Only now Adele really was the Lydgate Widow. She had achieved her childhood ambition, the big house with the high stone wall. Only the wall hadn't been high enough, and the house hadn't been strong enough.

And now it had one more ghost.

68

'I can't believe it,' Becky said, shaking her head. 'How could anyone do something like that? In front of a child ... Thank God Paul didn't seem to know what was going on. Maybe he won't remember it ... God, how *could* Col Vincent do it?'

'He was mad.'

'No,' Becky corrected her husband. 'Col Vincent was never mad. He was vicious, but not insane. I'm going to call by this afternoon.'

'You've been up to Lydgate four times,' Isaac said patiently. 'Adele's not seeing anyone, you know that. Kitty tells you that every time. It's early days. She'll come round in her own good time.'

Unusually irritated, Becky turned to him. 'And what if she doesn't? What if she shuts herself up in that place with Paul? And she could, Isaac, she is capable of that. You know she'd do anything to keep that child safe, especially after what he's been through.'

'She's got help ... '

'That isn't the same,' Becky replied. 'You know that. Adele has people around her, but she's not letting anyone close. As for Turner — she's shut him out completely.'

'Does she blame him?'

'No,' Becky replied. 'But Kitty told me that

she doesn't want any man in her life. Doesn't want to risk it.'

'Risk what?'

'I know what she means,' Becky said evenly. 'She doesn't think she deserves a good man, a happy marriage. In her mind Adele believes that love brings pain — even horror now. She'll think she's protecting Turner, herself *and* Paul by cutting him out of her life.'

'What does *he* think?'

'I don't know,' Becky admitted truthfully. 'But I wouldn't want to be him. To be rejected when you most want to help. To be turned away when you want to protect the person you love. I know Adele wouldn't think it, but he probably believes he's failed her. And Turner Gades hasn't had an easy life in some ways. Perhaps Adele forgets that. He lost Clemmie, and now he's lost her . . . ' Becky was momentarily hopeless. 'It's as if Col has won. As if he was prepared to kill himself rather than let them be happy. Dear God, can you imagine the malice that drives a person to do that?'

★ ★ ★

Staring into the burnt-out fire, Turner heard the bell ring on the shop door. He ignored it. Despair had capsized him. Perhaps it was all his fault; perhaps he had driven Col to suicide. He had certainly driven Adele away from him. She hadn't returned his calls, replied to his letters. For how many days had he longed — *prayed* — that she would get in touch with him? But he knew now that it wasn't going to happen. It had been three weeks since Col Vincent had killed himself. Three weeks in which every phone call, every visit, every note had been ignored.

Adele's housekeeper, Florrie, had been maternal, offering advice.

'She'll be all right in time. Yer just keep in touch, Mr Gades. It's been a right shock to her.'

But for all the kind words, Turner didn't believe it. He knew that some change had come over Adele, some belief that she could not be safe *and* loved. Some idiotic thought that she was now exactly what she should be — the Lydgate Widow, made flesh . . . Turner kicked at the fire ashes with the toe of his boot. He hated the house in Lydgate. Hadn't he seen love turn sour there before? Hadn't he — as a child — watched his father's anguish over Ninette Hoffman? But to arrive — decades later — back at that same house, watching the woman *he* loved turn into the woman he remembered . . . it was too much.

If only there was a way he could get through to Adele. Some way he could reach her. But she wouldn't let him in. His future, which had seemed so brilliant before, now curdled inside him. He ached with longing for her, with a need to help her, reach out to her. He burned with the thought of losing her, and Paul.

A memory of his father came back to Turner and he winced. Was that to be *his* end? A lonely life, spent watching, forever watching the Lydgate Widow, high up on the hill?

★　★　★

Impassive, Adele watched her sister walk back down the drive. A moment later Florrie came in with a note.

'She left this,' Florrie explained. 'Yer sister said she understood you didn't feel up to it, but she wanted to talk to yer. That she were right sorry 'bout what happened, and that she'd call again later.' Florrie glanced down at Paul, crayoning on the table. 'That's nice, luv, yer a clever boy.'

'I'll read it later,' Adele said, taking the note from Florrie and putting it on the sofa next to her.

'Might be important.'

'Nothing's important,' Adele replied, touching the top of Paul's head. She had spoken to the doctor again and he had told her it was unlikely that her son would remember what had happened. Paul was very young, the doctor said, he had been playing. He might not even have sensed that something bad was happening. Children were very resilient, he told her. Pity adults weren't the same.

'I think yer should read it,' Florrie persisted.

Preoccupied, Adele glanced up. 'Sorry, what did you say?'

'The letter. Read it, luv,' she said, taking Paul's hand. 'I'm just going to give the little one his tea. We'll be back soon.'

Nodding, Adele watched them leave. It had taken her three weeks to let her son out of her sight. Absurd, she knew only too well. Col was dead, and she was safe. But old habits died hard . . . Weighing the letter in her hand, Adele was tempted to put it in the drawer with all the others. She would reply to everyone eventually. Even Turner . . . But instead of pushing the letter to one side, she found herself opening it.

Dear Adele,
    Just a quick note.
    John and I have been redecorating and clearing out the attic. We found a load of bits and pieces, and this letter, addressed to you. Thought you might like it.
    Your loving sister,
    Julia

Surprised, Adele looked at the envelope, recognising her father's handwriting. Her heart speeded up, memories coming back of hiding in the under-stairs cupboard, her father shouting. And other memories, good memories, of him bringing home the washstands, well dressed, handsome in his way. Always trying to do better, to be someone. Memory piled upon memory. His encouragement, his pride in his family, the stories of his kindness that Adele had heard long after his death.

Now, yet again, Victor Ford was talking to her.

My dear daughter,
    I am writing this on a very cold Monday morning. Your mother is downstairs and I am off to an auction soon. You are going to school with your sister, and I'm wondering how your life will turn out. I know Julia will be all right, she's got a steel core. But you? I worry

527

sometimes. You're a fighter, I know that, but fighters don't always know when to stop throwing punches. Yes, I know what you're thinking, Adele, you could always see through me. And I understand you.

Don't hate me too much for my worst faults. I love your mother more than life, although you might wonder about that. I'm not proud of some of the things I've done, but I'm proud of my family. Do well in life. You can fulfil all my ambitions. And more. And be happy.

You can't understand how it is with your mother and me — no child can — but believe me when I tell you that I love her. That I would die for her. That my life would be nothing without her.

You'll do well, I know that. And you'll see life for what it is. Not fantasise, like I do. I make things up to make life more interesting. Like the story of the Lydgate Widow.

Adele winced, then read on.

I never could see her, you know. I just thought it made a bit of a story. She isn't a ghost, up in that old house. It wasn't even a good tale really. I mean, what's clever about someone cutting themselves off from life?

The only ghosts are those a person makes for themselves.

Stunned, Adele reread the words, then continued.

Find a reason to live. And someone to live for. That's the secret of life, Adele. It's not much of an inheritance, I grant you, but it's the best I can do.

Your loving father,
Victor

69

Tired from another broken night's sleep, Turner opened his shop and then returned to the back room. He had cut himself shaving, and was irritated, wondering if he should call by at Lydgate House later, or if it would be another wasted trip. Over a month had passed; maybe he should give up. But the thought was abhorrent to him, and he knew he would never relent.

Hearing the door bell ring, Turner ignored it. Then he remembered that his assistant wasn't coming in that morning and pulled on his jacket. Hurriedly he moved into the shop just as a young woman entered. A young woman he knew. A young woman he loved.

'Good morning,' Adele said, smiling tentatively.

He felt his heart pumping, his head swimming with excitement. 'Good morning.'

'I believe you have something very special in your shop,' Adele went on, teasing him, her eyes full of affection. Just like the old Adele, the girl he had first met. Who had enchanted him, amused him. *That Adele.*

'We have a lot of special things here,' he replied, playing along.

'But you're the only place that has this particular thing.'

'Really?' He smiled. 'What is it?'

'It's very rare. You can hardly find one

anywhere ... ' Her voice suddenly became serious. 'I'm looking for the heart of a good man.'

He paused, his eyes filling. 'There's one here, yes.'

'Can I have it?' she asked, her voice hardly audible.

'On one condition,' Turner replied, holding her gaze. 'On one condition, and one condition only.'

'Which is?'

'That you keep it for a lifetime.'

How easy a promise was that to make? Years later I would look at Turner and wonder how I could possibly have considered losing him. How near I had come to being estranged from my own heart.

My rescue was due to my father. When he wrote that there were no ghosts, suddenly it all made sense. That it's fear that hobbles us, makes us close up, blocks our emotions until we are little more than spirits, watching, not living in, the world.

So Turner and I married and lived at Lydgate House. Kitty and Stan continued to live and work with us; Florrie stayed on when Sniper died, because she had nowhere else to go. And besides, she was like a grandmother to Paul. Lily came by often, always in the same bad wig, always with the dog in tow. Only Dave Lin moved on when I married Turner. Later we heard that he had run off with a woman from Hanky Park.

Over in Rochdale, Ernest Vincent stayed bottled up in Oakham Lodge and drank himself to death. It took him three years.

As for Becky, her daughter survived and became successful — but she lost Isaac in the Second World War, and never married again. Perhaps surprisingly, my sister stayed married to John Courtland. Stayed when he lost his hair and his job as a chiropodist, and even nursed him through a serious illness. Were she and I ever close again? Yes. We argued and made up. We criticised each other and defended each other. We didn't understand each other, and knew each other inside out. Even when we were old, we scrapped like kids. But we never forgot who we were — we were sisters. And that was for life.

As the doctor had predicted, my son did not remember his father's death. He never spoke of it, and when I gave birth to Turner's daughter, Paul had a childhood companion and, later, a trusted confidante. He was not harmed by what Col had done, not marked, nor disturbed by it. He never remembered that day . . . But for years I never forgot it. When the mist came down in the early mornings I sometimes imagined I could hear the rope creaking in the horse chestnut tree, and a dark shape swinging from the branches above.

And then one autumn night there was a storm. It was the most violent in living memory and it brought down the old tree. When we walked into the garden the following morning, the horse chestnut was felled, toppled on its side like a huge dead animal. That November we burned it on Guy Fawkes Night, the children watching the flames, Turner by my side.

And every ghost that had ever lived in or around me — good or bad — perished, the smoke curling upwards to heaven and taking them home.

We do hope that you have enjoyed reading
this large print book.

Did you know that all of our titles
are available for purchase?

We publish a wide range of high quality
large print books including:
Romances, Mysteries, Classics
General Fiction
Non Fiction and Westerns

Special interest titles available in
large print are:
The Little Oxford Dictionary
Music Book
Song Book
Hymn Book
Service Book

Also available from us courtesy of Oxford
University Press:
Young Readers' Dictionary
(large print edition)
Young Readers' Thesaurus
(large print edition)

For further information or a free
brochure, please contact us at:
Ulverscroft Large Print Books Ltd.,
The Green, Bradgate Road, Anstey,
Leicester, LE7 7FU, England.
Tel: **(00 44) 0116 236 4325**
Fax: **(00 44) 0116 234 0205**